THE BRIDLES OF ARMAGEDDON
©) COPYRIGHT
Keith Madsen
2004
Cover design by Ron Shepherd

A New Sea Publishing, LLC
PO. Box 6024
Portland, Oregon, 97228-6024
anewsea.com

ISBN 1-932903-00-3
Library of Congress #2004095041

This is a work of fiction. All the characters and events
portrayed in this book are either fictitious or are used
fictitiously.

This book is dedicated to my wife, Cathy
for her support for all my creative ventures.

The Bridles of Armageddon
By Keith Madsen

Chapter One

George Marshal knelt down. He reverently cupped into his hand the rich, black dirt and passed it slowly under his nostrils. He felt he could smell in it the aroma of centuries, even though he knew that he personally had over a mere twenty years worked into this patch of ground the peat moss, the manure, the decayed living material, that had given it its richness. As he held it now, he was filled with awe for its life-giving power. Gently he returned it to its home, blending it into the furrow he had prepared for seed.

"How come you smell the dirt, Grandpa?"

The question had come from Jeremy, his five-year old grandson. He had come out from the house and approached quietly from behind the gardener.

"Smelling the dirt is part of the fun of gardening, Squirt. You might just as well skip eating the vegetables at the end of the process as omitting smelling the dirt at the beginning. It's all part of enjoying the earth that God has given."

"Oh...can I help put in the seed?"

"I was relying on you to volunteer for that. Here, I have the package open and waiting for you."

George guided the smaller hand along the furrow he had prepared, showing him how to tap the package to release just the right amount of seed.

"You want them close, but not too close. Seeds are like people. They like each other, but they also need their room to grow. Otherwise they have to fight each other for the nutrients. Of course, we'll have to thin them out a little later anyway. But we want them to have their best chance at a good start."

"Do seeds fight with each other like people do, Grandpa?"

The question jolted George Marshal. But he tried not to show that to his little grandson.

"Oh, I suppose we're kind of alike in that way, too. No one likes to feel like he or she is being crowded out, not made room for in this world. The funny thing is that sometimes people feel that way whether it is truly happening or not."

"You mean like Uncle Brian?"

The older man breathed deeply. "Yeah, I suppose like your Uncle Brian."

Both remained silent as they emptied that seed package and then one more. They were the last two packages George Marshal had to plant.

"There. Now we pat the dirt over the top. Right, Grandpa?"

"Right."

"I have some tomato plants to transplant from indoors," said George. "Do you want to help with that too?"

No sooner had the question come out of his mouth than the doorbell rang.

"That's probably my mother," Jeremy said, with no effort to hide his dejection.

"Well, there will be other days."

Marshal pulled himself up to his feet, trudged to the gate of the security fence that surrounded his generous backyard, punched the electronic release button, opened the gate part way and stuck his head out the opening.

"We're back here!"

A petite blonde rounded the corner of the house and trotted down the stone walkway toward the gate. She was thirty years old, but her freckles, upturned nose and childlike smile made George feel she was still that little one who once upon a time rode upon his shoulders. The childlike demeanor, however, quickly turned into something much more displeasingly adultish, as a censorious scowl crossed her face.

"Dad! You came to the gate awfully quickly. Did you check the monitor we set up for you?"

"Uh...we knew it was you, so..."

"You knew nothing of the kind! Dad, you just don't take this whole thing seriously enough."

"People have been fighting about these things for a long time, Dear..."

"Not like now, Dad! Not like now!" Shawna Forester just closed her eyes and shook her head. "Dad, you..." Instead of finishing her sentence, she let out a deep breath and tried again, this time looking into her father's eyes.

"Please, Dad, just do it for me. Okay?"

"Okay, I'll try. But it's against my nature."

Shawna smiled and reached up and kissed her father on the cheek.

"Grandpa and I planted all the seeds, Mom. We're going to do the tomato plants tomorrow."

"Well, sounds like I better get you home or I'm not going to have any time with you at all this weekend."

Shawna took the hand of her son, but before she turned and headed with him back to the car, she glanced up at her father one more time.

"Remember what you promised, okay?"

"I remember, I remember."

George watched as his daughter led Jeremy back to an older model Honda Accord, belted him into the backseat, and then slipped into the driver's seat. She waved at him one more time, and then put the car in gear, guiding it almost silently around the large circle drive and out onto the boulevard.

Why did that idiot Ron Forester ever let her go? He couldn't figure it out. But then again maybe that was because she was his daughter. George shook his head and turned and walked back through the gate, carefully shutting it behind him.

George took a moment now to admire the yard he had so carefully manicured over the past twenty years. The stone walkway that started in the front of the house wound its way through this side yard, past lush plantings of mountain laurel, sword fern, rhododendron and lilac bush. Lining the walk were wildflowers of every color and hue, and rising above these were a corkscrew willow and a Douglas fir. Towards the back of the

9

property he could see and hear the small creek that cut diagonally across his land, as it sought to find its way to the Columbia River. To the right was an old log bench where he loved to go to meditate. He had spent much time there two years ago when Helen had died.

Now he also used this area for his video projects. It was a second hobby that he had taken up after his wife's death. Like other grandparents he had videotaped his grandkids, but what brought him a unique pleasure was videotaping the drama that was played out daily in those tiny communities formed around his plants: spiders spinning their webs and lying in wait; ants in their seemingly endless projects; ladybugs fastidiously cleaning up his plants of unwanted pests. These dramas hardly ever gain a human stage, but there was something about how they played out that fascinated Marshal and brought him back for encore after encore. His actors were hardly ever camera-shy, and they seemed to say to him, "Watch and learn."

George strolled around the corner of the house. There to his left was where he always planted the vegetable garden. The blackness of the dirt contrasted with the many shades of green all around. Next to the blackened area was an atypical patch of red and blue. George walked a little closer. It was Jeremy's jacket. Well, he would be back tomorrow. He probably wouldn't need it before then.

There was a tapping at the gate. *I guess I was wrong. They saw it was missing and came back for it.*

George picked up the red and blue jacket and retraced his steps along the stone walk to the gate. He hadn't opened it one inch when he felt the surging pressure from the other side, pressure that knocked him to the ground. When he looked up he was looking into a face that would have been much more familiar had it not been for the glazed-over appearance of his eyes.

"Brian!"

His youngest son pushed through the gate. He was wearing army camouflage, as were three other unfamiliar faces that followed him in. They were all holding guns with silencers.

"What the...?"

"You brought this on yourself! You should have listened to me!" Brian's voice vibrated with emotion. His face seemed to pull back before his now-protruding eyes. His chest heaved as if he had just run a marathon.

It was then that George Marshal felt the burrowing streams of heat entering his abdomen.

"Jesus said it, Dad! 'Brother will betray brother to death, and a father his child. Children will...will...'"

A bullet now jolted George's chest, and blood shot up like a geyser into his face. He felt his life energy draining like a suddenly unstopped sink. He had to talk fast.

"Father...forgive them...for..."

No more words could escape his mouth, and those which entered his mind now, were from a different area of his life.

Fade to black. Fade to black.

■■■

"I'm not saying I agree with their tactics!" Drew Covington had spoken with an irritation born of intense emotional struggle. He hurried into his office at *The Oregonian*, with editor-in-chief Harold Carmichael close on his heels. Carmichael quickly shut the door.

Covington continued, "The man was well-respected in the community – a much-loved college professor who wanted to put what he had learned academically into practice, and so became a legislator. That shows character. Personally, I even liked him. All I am saying is that this group has some legitimate points. Conservatives have had a growing frustration with this country for a long time. That's why I have such a big readership. The election of Albert Packard to the Presidency was the last straw for a lot of these people. He's already dismantling everything we have worked for. He's reinstating everything we had thought we were putting behind us with the Clinton era. Funding of abortion, arrogant refusal to recognize and support a parent's right to home school or choose a decent private school, kissing up to environmental radicals while business people trying to make a profit are treated like criminals, stripping honest gun-owners of their rights – we thought we had made some progress with these things! The conservative Supreme Court will probably be history in a matter of months...."

"All right, Drew, all right!" Carmichael interrupted. "I know your position on these things, and I respect it. But I also know you're not one to condone violence and murder."

"I know, I know. I'm blowing off steam, okay?! I've got to be honest and say, I never thought they would stoop to killing a man like George Marshal. It shocked me. It's got me spinning in circles, not knowing what to say, not knowing whose side I really ought to be on."

Harold Carmichael's previous look of consternation was suddenly transformed into a chuckle.

"Drew Covington not knowing what to say. Who would have ever thought it to be possible?!"

"Yeah, well, just hope that it's a temporary phenomenon, okay. My having a lot to say is what puts meat on your table."

"Oh, that's right, I forgot. We at *The Oregonian* don't have any other writers."

"None that actually say anything, anyway."

Carmichael now laughed outright. "You're one arrogant SOB! But I guess I am glad that you're our arrogant SOB."

Drew Covington just quietly nodded and descended into his chair like a king claiming his throne. He began tapping a pencil on his desk while staring out his window at the Portland skyline.

After a minute or so, Drew broke the silence. "How do we know this isn't the Arabs?"

"The note spray-painted on the fence – 'The hour has come. Death to baby-killers! Death to all enemies of God!' Also, a couple of witnesses saw some white men in army camouflage in the area. One thought that he recognized the face of E.J. Conrad as one of them."

"Doesn't sound like he's doing a very good job of hiding what he's doing."

Harold just shook his head. "The FBI has had a hard time pinning anything definite on him so far."

Carmichael paused to give his next words some thought.

"This isn't just a little radical militia group anymore. In the past few months E.J. Conrad has done one hell of a job of recruiting. U.S. Senators are numbered among his advisors. The FBI estimates that their membership has increased ten-fold in the past year, and they see no signs of that slowing down. Drew, as you know, some of your fellow conservative commentators are writing articles supporting these guys."

Drew Covington nodded, and then he leaned on his desk and gazed into his editor's eyes.

"Why George Marshal? I mean, I didn't agree with the guy, but he was by no means the most left-wing guy they could have chosen. He was not really pro-choice on abortion. Yeah, he basically defended Roe vs. Wade, but he was at least seeking ways to limit abortion while getting unwed fathers to do better at paying child support. He was a man of religious faith and principle, and I know that on a number of occasions he stood up to the ACLU. So, why him?"

Harold Carmichael smiled, pleased that he could offer information to one who many considered to be one of the most intelligent conservatives in America.

"I've seen their web site. I believe a quote that was at the bottom of it gives you your answer: 'He who is not for me is against me.' It's a quote from Jesus, as I understand it. Conrad was making a statement. In this battle, there will be no moderates."

Drew turned and stared out the window again. In the distance he could see the shadowy form of Mount Saint Helens. He had been only five years old when it blew. What he was looking at now could shake the world even harder – and longer.

"How is the family doing?"

"Funny you should ask that," responded the editor. "I want you to pay them a visit."

Drew's head jerked around and he stared at Carmichael in disbelief.

"Excuse me?"

"As part of an article that I want you to write, an article against E.J. Conrad and his Armageddon Brigade..."

"Whoa!!"

"By visiting the family you can help those who might be wavering on the edge...you can help them see the human side of this, the pain that violent attempts at a solution can cause."

"I'm not a grief counselor, Harold."

"I'm not asking you to be a grief counselor. I'm asking you to interview some grieving people as part of a writing project."

"I don't know, Harold. This is not what my readership expects from me. I don't think I'm the right guy for what you are asking."

"You are exactly the right guy! You are a voice that is respected by the very group we are needing most to reach. And, since when are you concerned about what people expect of you?"

Drew Covington threw his head back and looked up at the ceiling. He was trapped.

"Okay, if I did this, what family members would I need to be interviewing?"

"The main one would be his daughter, Shawna Forester. She is a thirty-year old public school teacher who lives in the Beaverton area. She has a five-year-old son named Jeremy. She was hit pretty hard by this. When you talk to her, try to be at least a little tactful with your political rhetoric. From what I hear, she is more liberal than her father."

Drew Covington shot up out of his seat. "That does it! I'm not pussy-footing around with some bleeding-heart liberal public school teacher!"

"Sit down! Sit down!"

The writer skeptically complied with his editor's request.

"I'm not saying you can't speak your mind to her. I'm just saying that it wouldn't hurt in this situation to be a little tactful. And it's not like I'm asking you to spend the next year holding her hand. An interview or two. You can stand being tactful for that long, can't you?"

Covington let out a groan. "Perhaps if I took a sedative. Who else would I need to talk to?"

"Well, the other one may actually be a little tougher..."

"Great!"

"It's his son, Brian Marshal. He hasn't gotten along with his parents since his teenage years. He's wandered around from job to job since his high school graduation. Then Conrad recruited him. Drew, even though the evidence is pretty thin right now, speculation is that he was in on the murder."

"His own father?"

"That's the way it looks. And that's why your article has to be written. That's how dangerous this situation has become. Drew, there may already be as many as a half million people, many of them young men like Brian Marshal, officially aligned with The Armageddon Brigade. Estimates are that within a year that figure could double or even quadruple. That may include only part of the sympathizers on the sidelines, many of whom send them financial support. They have quite a few former military people, and they are heavily armed."

"How do I talk to this Brian Marshal, then?"

"That's the tough part. Use your contacts. Find out."

Drew Covington picked up a copy of the front page of that morning's *Oregonian*, which his secretary had brought in earlier. On it was a picture of George Marshal. After studying it a few seconds, he tossed it back down on his desk.

"Okay, I'll do the interviews. But I'm not committing to doing this article yet. I want to see what I find out first."

"Fair enough. I guess I believe that if you open your mind to this, you'll do it. I trust your integrity."

"Don't you suck up to me, Harold!"

Harold Carmichael laughed as he stood up and headed for the door. "I know better than that, Drew. Let me know what you find out."

As his editor left, Drew pushed the intercom button.

"Carol, is Ashley Cambridge available?"

"Do you want her to be?" came the voice on the other end.

"Of course!"

"Then my guess is that she is available."

"Send her in here ASAP."

It wasn't thirty seconds later that the intercom spoke again.

"Ashley Cambridge here to see you, Mr. Covington. Should I send her in?"

"I asked for her, didn't I?"

"Certainly, sir."

Drew was studying the picture of George Marshal again when Ashley Cambridge entered the room, but he could see her long slender legs above the top edge of the paper and that would have been all he needed to recognize her, even if he weren't expecting her. No woman he knew had legs like Ashley Cambridge. And she was not a woman who cared for conservative professional business dress.

"You sent for me, Mr. Covington?"

Ashley's whisper-smooth voice lured the writer's eyes up from the newspaper – and her legs – to her emerald-green eyes, perfectly set between the waves of dark brown hair that flowed down below her shoulders. Ashley flashed a coy smile that told Drew Covington that she had noticed —and appreciated his gaze. But he was determined to return quickly to professionalism.

"I have a job I want you to help me with. You've heard of Edward James Conrad and his Armageddon Brigade?"

"Of course. I'm a reporter."

"I want you to research everything you can find on them, and send what you find to me as an e-mail attachment."

"When do you need it?"

"By Friday noon."

"Sounds pretty urgent."

Ashley swayed over to a leather chair across from Drew's desk, deliberately crossed her legs and smiled into his eyes.

"Of course, for you, I could do this. But...it might help to know why you need the information."

"I figured you would want to know that. But remember that I am telling you this on a need-to-know basis and that this should be treated as confidential information."

Ashley nodded her assent.

"Harold wants to me to write an article appealing to conservatives to condemn this group and their tactics."

Ashley's smile now contorted into a look of confusion.

"Excuse me, but...why? Why would you consider such an idea? I mean I can see why Harold would want it – a lot of people want to read about that stuff and it would be good for his paper. But why would you want to go along with him and write it? I mean, Drew, you write for a lot of people – people like me. We're tired of all the diversity and help-the-poor-minorities crap. We're tired of the gay and lesbian crap. We're tired of the 'Everything is gray and there are no absolutes' crap. And as a woman I have to say, we're tired of the 'PC' talk of men needing to be more like women and women needing to be more like men. I..."

Ashley threw her hands up and shut her eyes as she sought to regain the control she had so uncharacteristically lost. She looked back at Drew.

"I like men who are men. And I like men who stand strong for what is important. Men like you."

Ashley smiled that smile again.

"Drew, you write for us, not them. Okay, so a group like The Armageddon Brigade has gone off the deep end a little bit. Let the liberals write about them. They created the Brigade by disrespecting conservative concerns. At least the Brigade is making this county take conservative dissatisfaction seriously. Get rid of the Brigade, and it will be back to the liberals ignoring us while they do whatever they like."

Ashley had a point. It was the very point that Drew had considered when he first resisted Harold Carmichael's proposal, and Ashley had voiced it passionately. Still, there was something that Drew Covington couldn't get out of his mind. It was that picture of George Marshal. Something in his eyes didn't fit in with theories and the clashes of political and religious ideology. Something was there that he really did need to find out about.

"I hear what you are saying, Ashley, but I do need to check this out. If you don't want to do this for me, I can find someone else."

"Oh, no. It's okay. I'll do it. You know that I would do anything for you."

Ashley's last phrase caused Drew to immediately flash back in his mind to nearly a year ago. His divorce had just been finalized.

Carrie, his wife of eight years had finally tired of his workaholic tendencies and turned her back on him. Drew had needed comfort, and Ashley was there. She would do anything for him. Drew could use that kind of comfort again. But he had pushed her away, mostly for professional reasons he had told himself.

"Yes, Ashley, I know." He avoided looking into her eyes as he sought to sort through all the turmoil inside of him. "Is there...uh...anything else you need to know to get this job done?"

"No, I'll get right on it."

Ashley Cambridge couldn't hide the disappointment in her voice, but Drew couldn't tell whether the disappointment was political or personal. As she exited through his door, Ashley glanced back one more time in his direction. She was checking out where his eyes were focused. Drew had seen that trick many times before, and this time he met her eyes with a professional smile. He just wasn't ready right now for anything – or anyone – who sought to divert his attention the slightest from the job that was his identity.

Drew glanced out his window once again at the distant mountain across the Columbia River. It was an uncharacteristically clear day for Spring in Portland. A small, wispy cloud draped itself across the mountain, and Drew wondered if it were a cloud or an emission of steam from the mountain's crater. It had been some time since the mountain had unleashed its fury, but Drew knew the fiery turmoil was always there not far beneath the surface.

Chapter Two

It was just an old barn. But as the old professor stood near the door he could hear the murmur of more than a hundred new students he knew were packed inside. No, it wasn't like the large, clean well-equipped classrooms that he had become used to when he had taught at UCLA, but that didn't matter. The students were there because they wanted to be there, and when he spoke they listened. That was what mattered.

As he entered, a hush fell over those gathered. That also was different than UCLA. There he had always encountered some who would totally ignore his entry and would have to be quieted down. At that university too there were always those whose minds remained elsewhere. But here every face showed attentiveness. Every ear seemed tuned to hear what his first word might be. Every body, rather than being slumped into a comfortably padded chair, sat erect and poised for action. They sat on the ground. They sat on bales of hay. They sat in the loft, with the same attitude as if in prime seats at a posh concert hall. This was his domain.

"Good morning, students. You will open your Bibles to Revelation."

E.J. Conrad opened his own Bible to the book in question, and he glanced around at the crowd of mostly young, mostly male faces.

"I have taught the world's greatest literature at one of the world's greatest institutions of learning, and let me tell you something. There is no greater literature than this. The Bible. God's Holy Word. The King James Version is the only version we use. It has the true inspiration. It has the poetry. Not that I'm here to teach you poetry. No, this literature is great not because of a clever choice of words, but because of the God it reveals. A God of majesty. A God of power. A God who is far bigger than the God our society politely invokes into its polite little gatherings. This is the God who can create and destroy with a single word. This is the God of Revelation."

Conrad's body now became more animated as he began strutting across the hay-strewn floor that was his stage.

"And the really exciting thing about reading about this God is that as we read about him, we learn what history really means, and where this world is going. We learn that God has placed us in history's most exciting time, a time when what he has planned since the beginning will come to full fruition. My friends, this world is on the verge of passing away, and a better world is coming, a world governed directly by our Lord and Savior Jesus Christ, a world where all that is ugly and evil will be no more. Let's read about it! Turn to Revelation 21:1-8.

There was a shuffling throughout the room, as his students turned to the passage.

Conrad read: "'And I saw a new heaven and a new earth: for the first heaven and the first earth were passed away; and there was no more sea. And I John saw the holy city, new Jerusalem, coming down from God out of heaven, prepared as a bride adorned for her husband. And I heard a loud voice out of heaven saying, Behold, the tabernacle of God is with men, and he will dwell with them, and they shall be his people...'"

Conrad paused as he looked out at his audience with enraptured eyes. "And this is the part that I really love. I've got to tell you that I am unashamed to admit that it brings tears to my eyes every time I read it.

"'...and God himself shall be with them, and be their God. And God shall wipe away all tears from their eyes; and there shall be no more death, neither sorrow, nor crying, neither shall there be any more pain: for the former things are passed away.'"

Sure enough the professor's eyes glistened.

"'And he that sat upon the throne said, Behold, I make all things new. And he said unto me, Write: for these words are true and faithful.'"

"'And he said unto me, It is done. I am Alpha and Omega, the beginning and the end. I will give unto him that is athirst of the fountain of the water of life freely. He that overcometh shall inherit all things; and I will be his God, and he shall be my son...'"

Conrad looked up at his audience and shouted, "Did you hear that? You will be God's sons!" Those gathered shouted and broke out into applause. They slapped each other on the back and stomped the floor. Conrad noticed only one, an armed guard toward the back, an early recruit there to help keep order, who did not show the same enthusiasm. The word "son" seemed to have hit him more like a blow from above. The professor made a mental note to deal with him later.

Conrad now projected a most somber appearance. "But," he continued, "there is a warning. 'But the fearful...and unbelieving...and the abominable...and murderers...and whoremongers...and sorcerers...and idolaters...and all liars...shall have their part in the lake which burneth with fire and brimstone: which is the second death.'"

E.J. Conrad put his hand down reverently on the Bible, closed his eyes for a moment, and then looked out at his audience.

"You know, there are people who will say that I am a dangerous, violent man. There are people who will say that I turn the God of love preached by Jesus into a God of anger and wrath. But the people who say that must never read their Bibles! They must never have read about the God who destroyed the whole world with a flood because of the iniquity of mankind. They must never have read about Moses and what God did through him to the Egyptians. I'm not just talking about those whom he drowned in the Red Sea. He turned the Nile River to blood. He sent a plague of locusts that devoured everything so that the people went hungry. And he killed all their firstborn. And Revelation tells us that many of these same plagues will come at the end of time. Do people think that I wrote these things in the Bible? Do they think I am making all of this up?"

Conrad now glared out at his students, as if daring one of them to answer.

21

"Or maybe they haven't read about what Moses did when the people of Israel made the Golden Calf. While he was on Mount Sinai, receiving the very *Word of God*, written with God's own *finger*, the people rebelled and made a Golden Calf, and worshipped it as if it were God. Now, we might say, 'Well, what's so bad about that? They had an *election!* They had an election and decided they wanted a Golden Calf to be their god instead of the Creator of the Universe. Who are we to question a fair election?'"

Throughout the building Conrad's young audience laughed and sneered.

"But you know what God had Moses do? He selected some to be his servants and he armed them with swords and he sent them in amongst the people and ordered them, 'Thus saith the Lord God of Israel, Put every man his sword by his side, and go in and out from gate to gate throughout the camp, and slay every man his brother, and every man his companion, and every man his neighbor.' And that day they killed three thousand men!"

"Or maybe they haven't read about what God did through Elijah the prophet. The King and Queen and seemingly the whole country wanted Baal to be their god. They had an *election!* What could Elijah do? Well, I'll tell you what he did! After showing up the so-called prophets of Baal and their so-called god, he selected some to be his servants, and he had them slaughter those prophets like so many hogs for bacon!"

Young voices throughout the old barn whooped and hollered.

"Now, I understand," Conrad continued, "that in this country we had an *election...*"

The whoops turned to boos.

"And the people elected someone who wants to pay for aborting babies, someone who wants to keep prayer out of the schools, someone who wants to take away our constitutional right to bear arms, someone who wants to coddle the fags and give them positions in his government. We may not like these things, but what can we do? They had an *election!*

"But let me tell you something, dear friends. The election is not over until the last vote is counted, and the vote of the Lord God Almighty has—yet—to—be—counted!!"

Those gathered now stomped and roared and shook the rafters so that in his more pragmatic moments E.J. Conrad would have wondered if the old barn would stand. But now these actions just enflamed his rhetoric all the more.

"Now I want you to know that I am here as God's servant and witness to announce his vote – and let me tell you also that there are no 'hanging chads' here – and here is his vote: 'Woe, woe, woe to the inhabitants of the earth!' God is selecting 144,000 servants – and you young men will be part of that force! – to lead an eventual army of 200 million to wreak the vengeance of God on those who have defied him for so long. And hear what the Word of God says for our time from Revelation 14: 'And another angel came out from the altar, which had power over fire; and cried with a loud cry to him that had the sharp sickle, saying, Thrust in thy sharp sickle, and gather the clusters of the vine of the earth; for her grapes are fully ripe. And the angel thrust in his sickle into the earth, and gathered the vine of the earth, and cast it unto the great winepress of the wrath of God. And the winepress was trodden without the city, and blood came out of the winepress, even unto the horse bridles, by the space of a thousand and six hundred furlongs.'"

E.J. Conrad looked up and gazed solemnly out at this new class of followers. "Gentlemen, that is a one-hundred and eighty mile river of blood. We have our work cut out for us."

■■■

The professor watched as his students filed out of the old barn. A second class would be that afternoon, and the evening would see him host a third. He was finding the process exhausting, but it had to be this way.

"Hi, Grandpa!"

Conrad turned around just as six-year-old Emily broke past a guard and started running in his direction. He gave her a big smile, knelt down and held out his arms to her. She obliged him by jumping into them.

"How is my little angel?"

"Fine, Grandpa. Mom and I were picking wildflowers this morning!"

"Sounds like a great morning!"

Conrad turned toward his daughter-in-law Amber. "I thought I told you not to bring her here when we're having classes."

"Well, I knew the class was done. I didn't think..."

"Even if the class is done, I don't want her over here around these men. From now on, please just do what I ask, and don't try to adjust my orders according to what you perceive my intent to be."

"Oh...okay."

Conrad quickly returned his attention to his granddaughter.

"Oh, and you have such a pretty spring dress on today! I like the way the blue in it matches your eyes. I just hope your daddy is going to be up to beating off all the young men who come around after you when you grow up."

"Oh, Grandpa, I don't like boys. Just you...and Daddy."

"Well, then you will surely break a lot of hearts, little girl."

Emily blushed and rolled her eyes.

"Oh, Grandpa...!"

The attention of the six-year-old was quickly diverted to the remaining men exiting the building.

"Grandpa, why do all these men come here to hear you talk?"

Conrad gave an irritated glance over at his daughter-in-law. "Oh, I guess they think I have a lot of interesting things to tell them."

"What do you tell them?"

"I tell them how to get rid of some bad things in this world, so that God can make the world better...better for children like you."

E.J. Conrad picked up his granddaughter and held her close in his arms.

"You know, Emily, God wants all children like you to be able to live in a beautiful world, a safe world. But evil people have brought in a lot of ugly things to this life, and we just can't let them stay here any more. God created the world to be a garden. You've heard about the Garden of Eden in your Sunday School, haven't you?"

Emily nodded.

"It was a beautiful garden," Conrad continued, "where everything was perfect. Adam was the perfect man and Eve was the perfect woman. They would have been the beginning of a perfect world, if they hadn't sinned. But they did. And now we have mean men who hurt children, and a justice system that lets them get away with it. We have a lot of ...weeds...in the garden. We have to get rid of them so that God can help us have a perfect world again – here on earth, a new Garden of Eden."

Envisioning the world of which he spoke had brought E.J. Conrad into a kind of trance, and his granddaughter had to tap her little hand on the side of his face to regain his attention.

"Is God helping you, Grandpa? How do you know what it is that he wants you to do?"

"His Spirit speaks to me – through the Bible, and sometimes just like you have been speaking to me right now. Other times I hear his word in my mind, but still I know what it is that he wants me to do next."

"Do other people hear God's voice like that?"

"No. Not like I do. A lot of people have some sense of what God wants, but they don't hear his voice like I do. Mine is a special gift."

"I want to hear God's voice like you do. Can you teach me?"

"It's a gift from God, honey. Giving it is his choice. And I'm not sure I would want to wish this gift on you." The intensity of what Conrad now felt caused him to lower his own powerful voice to a near whisper. "Hearing God's voice is sometimes a painful burden."

Emily seemed to sense her grandfather's feeling, and held him even more tightly. "I bet God is very proud of you, Grandpa."

"I hope so, honey. I hope so."

■■■

Brian Marshal studied the faces of those leaving the old barn. He didn't know what he was looking for in them. Perhaps for reassurance of the rightness of their mission. If that could be seen in cocksure faces, there were certainly plenty of them. Smiles flashed like cameras at the arrival of a movie star. Eyes were lifted up, as if in the belief that nothing would dare cross their path that might cause them to stumble. If Brian were looking to recover how he used to be when he too went through this training, he could have seen it in these faces also. But somehow looking at these faces left him empty.

There were other faces too. Some stared straight ahead, deep in reflection. A few glanced around nervously, as if wondering who might see them there. Still others glanced back and forth at the different faces around them, perhaps seeking one to be like.

The faces that Brian studied the longest were the reflective ones. They were more like he was right now. They were looking to put the puzzle together.

One of the smiling faces stopped right in front of him, like one of those tourists who get in front of your camera just when you've lined up your shot. Brian returned his now steely gaze.

"So," the other young man proceeded, "when do you think he'll let us start popping some heads?"

Brian winced. "Excuse me?"

The other young man tapped the barrel of Brian's automatic rifle, then he tapped his own head and made the sound of an explosion, with his eyes nearly popping out.

"Popping heads! It's what we're here for, isn't it? Or is that gun you're carrying just a toy you use on your girlfriend instead of your dick?"

Brian quickly flicked the barrel of the rifle into the man's face, shoving it part way into the man's left nostril.

He spoke more deliberately than he had acted. "Well...why don't you try screwing around with me, and we'll find out if this is a toy or not?"

The other man sneered. "You're bluffing, asshole. I can see it in your eyes. I don't think you've killed a man in your life!"

Brian could feel his flesh turn almost instantly cold and clammy. Even so he wasn't about to back down from this guy.

"I wouldn't bet on that right now, if I were you. I might just have to prove that I can squeeze this trigger."

The antagonist coldly stared into Brian's eyes for a few seconds, and then he flashed a smile.

"Hey! I was just shittin' ya'! No harm meant. The name's Cody. Cody Wiley."

Cody held out his right hand. Brian ignored it.

"That big metal building over to your left. That's where you're supposed to be heading now."

Cody's face turned hard again.

"You haven't answered my question. The old man. He has a way with words and he got my juices flowin'. I'm ready to act! What is he, like some cock-teasing cheerleader who gets you horny and then slams the door in your face? When do we get to pop some heads?!"

Brian felt his stomach tighten and turn.

"Plenty soon. Plenty soon. But first you have to learn to use the weapons you are given. That is why you have to go to the next building for training. And as I said before, the building where that happens is over to your left."

"I already know how to use every weapon in the book," Cody spit out, "but I suppose I don't mind showing them I know it."

Cody turned and headed towards the metal building Brian had indicated.

Brian quickly searched for more inviting eyes than the ones he had just encountered. There were none. Those few left who hadn't gone into weapons training now just seemed like variants of Cody Wiley.

Brian wondered why he hadn't warned Cody about his language. It wasn't so much that such language offended him. He had certainly heard it all. There were plenty of times he had used it himself. But he was beginning to learn all the idiosyncrasies of E.J. Conrad, and he knew the religious fervor that drove him – religious fervor that detested foul or sexually obsessed language. If Conrad had heard Wiley speak the way he had to Brian, Conrad would have thrown him in detention – or worse. Perhaps that's why

Brian hadn't warned him. Detention was just the place for Cody Wiley.

But now another thought came to Brian's mind. *Was language the only difference between Cody Wiley and E.J. Conrad?* The thought was disturbing. A few weeks before he would never had had it. Conrad had become not only his professor and general, but his personal mentor. He was the epitome of personal righteousness. He was the Old Testament prophet come to life. But he was also the one who had ordered an act that, even now, Brian wasn't sure was a hellacious memory or just an eerie nightmare.

A hand reached from behind and touched Brian's left shoulder. Brian looked back and jumped away. It was E. J. Conrad.

"If I had been the enemy, you would have been dead, Son."

"Yes, Sir. I...uh...guess I had let down my guard. It won't happen again."

"Make sure you don't. It won't be long before they will really be coming after us. We can't let God down."

"Yes, Sir. I understand, Sir."

E. J. Conrad looked carefully, but not uncaringly, into Brian's eyes.

"I was watching you during my presentation back there, Brian. You looked...distracted."

"Yes, Sir. I...probably was."

"We gave him plenty of warning, you know."

Brian could feel the tears welling up in his eyes. "Yes, Sir."

"We gave him more warning than we will to most. But his ears were closed. He was one like Isaiah spoke of, 'Hear ye indeed, but understand not; and see ye indeed, but perceive not....'"

To Brian, Conrad's eyes now seemed to glaze over, as he quoted Scripture without hesitation, as if he were reading it.

"'Make the heart of this people fat, and make their ears heavy, and shut their eyes; lest they see with their eyes, and hear with their ears, and understand with their heart, and convert, and be healed.'

"'Then said I, Lord, how long? And he answered, Until the cities be wasted without inhabitants, and the houses without man, and the land be utterly desolate....'"

"Yes, Sir," responded Brian when it was clear that his professor had stopped reciting, "but...I mean, even though we didn't get along, there was so much that he did seem to understand. There was a lot of...good...in him."

"I'm sure there was, son. But that's not enough. There's got to be devotion to God and God's will. That's what your father was missing. We tried to talk to him – many times. He wouldn't listen. He gave aid and comfort to abortionists. He took the side of the gays and lesbians who are undermining our families. He encouraged the secularization of our schools and voted against measures to post the Ten Commandments. He was a state legislator and he could have fought for the things for which we stand. Brian, either the positions he took are against God's will and we should fight them with all our being, or they're not and we should let them slide. That's the decision you have to make. Jesus said, 'He that is not with me is against me.' So, which is it, are you for him or against him?"

"I'm for him, sir. I am."

"I believe you are, Son. I understand the pain you feel, believe me, I do. And God understands. You've got to remember that such is part of what this is all about. 'And God shall wipe away all tears from their eyes; and there shall be no more death, neither sorrow, nor crying, neither shall there be any more pain' – remember that? When God is victorious, that is what the world will be like. But before that can happen, we've got to clean this place up a bit. We've got to clean it out of those who stand in the way of it happening – those who want to run this world their own way, and not God's way."

Brian felt his head swirling. "Yes, sir."

"That's what it is all about, Brian. *Winning for God.* Some people call us 'terrorists.' They lump us in with those Arabs who blow up buildings to get Americans worried, and to pressure us to get out of the Middle East. But we aren't about stupid little pressure tactics. And we aren't about terrorizing people. We're on this earth to *win for God.* Yes, there will be violence at first, but our end isn't to terrorize people, but to set them free. To set this whole corrupt earth free! That's a worthy goal, Brian. The worthiest goal of them all."

Brian found himself slowly and quietly nodding his head at what Conrad was saying. He wasn't sure if it was true agreement, or if he just didn't know what else to do. He gazed off in the direction of the woods. He found himself suddenly drawn towards the shadows there. But Conrad's presence was too immediate and too demanding for Brian to lose himself there for long. He looked back at the professor.

"I guess that's just what he didn't understand, sir. All he understood was that I was his son..."

"Exactly! The morality of our nation was nothing to him. Unfortunately, that's the way it is with too many in our country. We have chosen the narrow way, and 'few there be that find it.' You know there was a time there, after the attack on the World Trade Center, when I almost thought things could be different here. People were praying. People were singing, 'God Bless America.' More people were going to church. For a short while I was fooled by all that. I thought I may have misunderstood God's will – that God was bringing people back to him without the kind of war that I was even then preparing for, the kind of war Revelation talks about. But time has shown that I was temporarily deceived, and that what God has said from the beginning was right. People flee to God in a crisis. But there is no depth in what they do. There is no true love, no true devotion. It's like what God said of Israel through Isaiah the prophet, 'Forasmuch as this people draw near me with their mouth, and with their lips do honour me, but have removed their heart far from me, and their fear toward me is taught by the precept of men: Therefore, behold, I will proceed to do a marvelous work among this people, even a marvelous work and a wonder: for the wisdom of their wise men shall perish, and the understanding of their prudent men shall be hid.'"

"I want to honor God and to bring about the world you talk about, sir. I'm just...It's just all the killing...especially..."

"I understand perfectly, Son. I don't like the killing myself. And I don't fully trust those young men I've seen around here who do. You, I respect. But you've got to trust me, Son. You've got to bear with this for a while. There will come a time --'no more death, neither sorrow, nor crying, neither shall there be any more pain' – you just have to keep going back to that."

"Yes, sir."

"Well, I've distracted you long enough. You get back to keeping an eye out for enemies of God's Work here. I know it's not exciting work, right now, but there are some operations coming up real soon that are going to get things moving around here, and I want you to be part of them."

"Yes, sir."

E.J. Conrad slapped him on the shoulder and set off with a determined stride toward the weapons training shed.

"Sir?..."

Conrad stopped and looked back at Brian.

"Can you tell me something, sir? It probably isn't important. But did I...did I actually fire my weapon at him. Or was I just like...there?"

Conrad just stared at Brian for a few seconds. Then he turned on his heels and continued his trek, but with his answer echoing back from the woods.

"You're right, Son. It's not important."

■■■

Ashley Cambridge bent over her computer keyboard. Her search for information on E.J. Conrad and the Armageddon Brigade had yielded far more articles and abstracts than she had anticipated. Most were sympathetic to him. Only a few, mostly written in liberal publications, raised words of warning.

Conrad had been a highly-respected Professor of English Literature at UCLA. He developed what almost could be described as a cult following of students who crowded his classrooms and attended every public lecture. He was a master of English prose himself, and had written a book on Alfred Lord Tennyson that was considered a classic in the field. His class on the Bible as Literature was so popular that only seniors, persons with influence in the office of the Registrar or those who had the permission of Conrad could get in. It was this class, however, that seemed to get Conrad in the most trouble. In spite of Conrad's control over the class, there would always be some who would get in who didn't appreciate his style. There would be complaints about how Conrad would leave behind the issue of the Bible as literature and get into what could only be described as a sermon about what was wrong with the country, and how attending to biblical principles could make it all right. Students who questioned Conrad's interpretations were sometimes made fun of in class. Conrad's supporters were sometimes accused of harassing such students after the class session was over. No formal complaints were filed, however.

In his personal life, Conrad had married a woman named Emily Blair, who had been his high school sweetheart back in North Carolina. He claimed to have won her through love poems he had written just for her, but which he later shared with some of the young men he mentored. He claimed a near 100% success rate for his poems in winning the hearts of young women.

Conrad had often referred fondly to his wife in his lectures at UCLA. Their relationship had become almost legendary. When she died of cancer four years ago, it had crushed Conrad. There were rumors that he wanted to resign and withdraw to a cabin somewhere in Idaho. When he bounced back, he came back with even more zeal for his biblical expositions. The book of Revelation became his passion. The students in his classes were even more divided over the political and religious messages he preached. But those who were for him were really for him. They wrote home to their parents in glowing praise. Some of those parents were conservative, influential leaders in business and the military. They began visiting with him when they came to see their sons and daughters on campus. That was the beginning of the Armageddon Brigade.

Frustrated with increasing pressure from the Dean's office and some of the liberal student groups on campus, Conrad finally did resign and moved to that cabin in Idaho. But by now a lot of students and family members of students were ready to come with him. That cabin quickly evolved into a complex of buildings.

Rumors of a cache of weapons that was being built up on his property were flowing. Neither Conrad nor any of his advisors had any kind of criminal record at that time, and no one could point to any threats or acts of violence, so there was very little any one could do. Popular conservative commentators were having him on their shows, and he was becoming a household name.

The election of Albert Packard to the Presidency, along with the election of some other liberal Senators and Congressional Representatives, fanned the anger of conservatives, and Conrad's recruiting of young to middle-aged conservatives seemed to take off. Still, there were no acts of violence that could be attributed to him. That is, until the death of George Marshal.

Ashley pushed back from her computer screen and stared out her window at the city of Portland below. What did she think of this E.J. Conrad? Her own conservatism had not come from religious roots. Oh, she had attended a Catholic school, and her parents had taken her to mass, but she was never really into it. She felt her own conservatism was based on more intellectual roots. Traditions became traditions because they worked. Making changes that disrupt the society, trying to fix that which isn't really broken, only serves to send everything into chaos. That is what had happened to the United States back in the 60s. The country had been thrown into a turmoil from which it still hadn't recovered. She considered herself enough of a student of history to understand that. Now, there were those who seemed to want to go back to those times. Did people never learn? E.J. Conrad was at the very least a smart man who didn't want the country to go backwards.

Sure, there was the evidence that he was at least moving in the direction of violent action, if he had not already crossed over the barrier with George Marshal. But was it any different from what the patriots of the American Revolution had done nearly two and a half centuries earlier when they also had turned against their own people to make the country free?

Ashley had to admit that what was crossing her mind were surprising and frightening thoughts. She had never considered herself to be a supporter of violence. Maybe she was feeling

33

particularly frustrated right now. It didn't help that Drew had taken this assignment. He had been her standard-bearer. He had been her Mel Gibson leading the patriot charge. But why was she worried? He probably would be again. Conrad probably had overstepped. Drew would write an article to reign him in, and then Drew would once again take on the enemy, thrusting them through with his rapier wit and intellect. And when he did he would owe her big. She smiled thinking of the many ways she might collect.

Chapter Three

Drew Covington pulled his pearl white Lexus up in front of a row of duplexes. In an expensive housing market, this was about what a single mother could afford. All of them looked the same, with only subtle variations from the beige color of the one in front of him. A thin strip of grass out front, with a couple of small bushes, were what passed for a front yard, and Drew could see that the back yard was virtually non-existent.

A couple of police officers were making their way toward his car, while a young boy who had been waiting on the small porch slipped into the house through the front door.

"Good afternoon sir. May I ask your name and your business here?"

In spite of the officer's cordiality, Drew quickly showed his irritation. "They didn't tell you I was coming?"

"Well, sir, that depends on who you are."

"Drew Covington! My picture's in the newspaper every day. Can I assume that you at least occasionally read a newspaper?"

The officer ignored the attempt at an insult, and held out his hand. "Can I see some identification please?"

Drew pulled out both his driver's license and his press identification. "Will these do, or do I need to go back to New York to get a note from my mother?"

"Those will do. Ms. Forester is expecting you."

Drew eased past the first officer, then stopped in front of the second, who seemed to be eyeing the Lexus' interior. Drew lifted his car remote to this man's eye-level and firmly pushed the "lock" button. The officer just scowled and turned away.

By the time Drew reached the front door, the young boy he had earlier seen withdrawing into the house had returned and was

35

holding the door open for him. Drew knew this to be five-year-old Jeremy Forester. He thought the young eyes looked tired and the face expressionless.

"Thank you," he ventured, "that's very polite of you. Not all children are that polite these days."

Jeremy just shrugged.

"His grandfather taught him politeness," said a female voice inside the house.

The shakiness of the voice had conveyed great pain, and yet it had also carried with it a less easily described tone in which Drew sensed strength and resolution. He turned in the direction of the voice, and saw a young woman who even with eyes wearied by grief, remained stunningly beautiful. Her short blonde hair was of a style that did not suffer from her neglect of it, and any make-up that could have been added to the softly-sculpted lines of her face would only have marred its artistic merit. She sat on the living room sofa, deliberately erect, still staring wistfully out her front window. Drew suddenly wished again that he had pursued his college interest in art. This woman would make the kind of portrait that could establish an artist's career.

"Shawna Forester?"

The young woman pulled her eyes from the window and looked in his direction.

"Yes. You must be Drew Covington. I was told that you would be coming."

"Yes. I...uh...I'm not sure if I'm the right person to be doing this. I never know what to say in situations like this. I'm sorry for what happened to your father..."

Jeremy came over and cuddled up to his mother's side.

"That will do fine, Mr. Covington. But I have to admit that I'm not sure you're the right person either. I've read your columns, but I can never get through one of them without getting angry. I can't say that I really trust you to write things that would reflect well on my father and what he stood for."

Drew Covington could feel his stomach starting to twist and turn, and the rest of his body wanted to emulate that action.

"Yes, well, of course you have to know Ms. Forester that, while I am sorry to hear of what happened to your father, I am not really here to write a eulogy for him. The assignment you are being asked to help with..."

"I know what I'm being asked to help with, Mr. Covington! Your editor wants to personalize what is happening in the hope that it will stop the violence. Well and good. But the problem is that it won't stop until writers like you stop stirring people up over the supposed oppression of gun-toting rednecks."

"Hey! I didn't ask for this assignment! And I certainly didn't ask to be lectured to by a bleeding-heart school teacher! My only offense is sticking up for the rights of those who don't hide behind some kind of 'minority' label!"

"You guys talk about the 'rights' of rich white Americans, and the 'rights' of the so-called Christian majority and the 'rights' of people to carry hand-guns and assault weapons and...whatever! What about the rights of people to think differently from you? What about the right to work in your garden and not have to worry about who might come to the gate of your yard and shoot you down?"

Shawna's last statement started Jeremy crying, and she began to stroke his head. Still, her own eyes did no more than become moist, as she continued to stare at the one she considered to be a predator against all she held to be sacred.

Drew shut his eyes and looked away, seeking to regain his composure. What was he doing causing a grieving mother and son to cry? Still he could not let emotion keep him from doing his job. He looked back over at Shawna.

"I'm sorry, Ms. Forester. I really didn't come here to debate these things. I am a good writer. I really am. That's why our editor Harold Carmichael sent me on this assignment. I can write an article that might make it less likely that what happened to your father would happen again. I'm sure you want that or you wouldn't have consented to my coming in the first place. So, can we start over and work together on this?"

Shawna Forester's face remained steeled for several more seconds and then it began to soften.

"Okay, okay. I'm sorry. I guess right now I have a tendency to believe the worst about people. Let's give it a shot. Please sit down."

Drew pulled up a chair opposite the sofa on which Shawna and Jeremy were sitting. He motioned toward the boy.

"Should he be here while we talk about this? Maybe he would rather play..."

"No, he needs to be part of this, too. His grandpa was very important to him. Besides, he may know some things that I don't – and he's part of the 'human situation' your editor said he wanted people to hear about."

"As you wish."

Drew pulled a note pad and a small recorder out of his coat pocket.

"Do you mind if I record our talk? It will help me in my writing."

"No, of course not."

"Ms. Forester..."

"You can call me 'Shawna.' If we're going to do this, we should be less formal."

"Okay...Shawna, what can you tell my readers about what your father was like?"

The young woman shut her eyes and sighed, as if sorting through memories in her mind. When she opened her eyes again, she looked down at Jeremy who was sitting quietly beside her.

"My father was a man who had learned how to live life, especially since my mother died. I don't know, it seemed to me that he always had a lot of wisdom. But after Mom died, he just seemed to slow down and...kind of absorb life. I mean, sure, he mourned her for a long time. But I think he also learned from losing her just how precious life is. Earlier in his life he was kind of driven. Driven to succeed. Driven to make a name for himself. Driven to make some kind of vaguely-conceived contribution to this planet. But one day a few months after her death, he came over to our house, and he was so quiet, so reflective. He spent the whole day with us, and then before leaving he said, 'Shawna, life isn't where you are going, it's where you are right now. Never forget that.'"

Shawna looked up at her interviewer. "And I haven't forgotten it. It was what he was teaching to Jeremy as well."

Jeremy's face abruptly took on a stern appearance as he looked up at his mother. "Grandpa was teaching me gardening!"

"I know, honey – that too."

"Shawna, tell me – I don't want this to be taken wrong – some people say things like that, but it's like they are trying to convince themselves..."

"No, no. He didn't just say it. He lived it. Oh, sure, there were times when he seemed to have a relapse, but for the most part these past two years I think he lived life more completely, and with more of a sense of peace, than any other period of his life."

"Two years of living life, knowing what it's all about – it doesn't sound like a lot, but I don't think most people get that much."

As Drew said these words he looked into Shawna's eyes, and he noticed that those eyes were suddenly softer, more understanding than they had been only minutes before. They were now safe eyes, eyes that drew you in like the sight of a fireplace through a frosty window.

"Okay, I guess I should say I don't think I've lived that much real life," Drew continued. "It makes me wish that I would have been able to meet him."

The corners of Shawna's mouth turned up in a smile that was subtle and genuine. "I really think that most people who took the time to know him were glad that they did."

Drew wanted to just quietly look at the gentleness of the smile before him, and he feared that if he spoke it might vanish, like a doe that has appeared unexpectedly out of a forest. He did gaze at it longer than he would normally think advisable, long enough to feel embarrassed when he was jarred back to awareness. Now he could only do what he was trained to do – the questions, he had to get back to the questions.

"But the people who killed him – they hadn't taken the time to know him. What was there about your father that they hated, that they were trying to get rid of?"

Shawna's smile fell instantly, and Drew had to stifle a moan.

"Well, I'm sure that most of those involved didn't know him at all. And I can't say that I understand what it was that they thought they were striking out against. Not to start our little fight back up, but you probably know that better than I. Maybe it was that some people like to see the world in black and white, and those who see shades of gray are the ones who anger them the most. Maybe some people need a world where they can place everyone into some neat little category, and since he didn't fit into any of their categories, they killed him."

Drew could feel his stomach tightening up. "Perhaps. But conservatives aren't the only ones who try to fit people into neat little categories, you know. Once a liberal hears one conservative opinion from you, right away they think they know the totality of who you are: 'He doesn't care about the poor': 'He's only interested in money and business'; 'He's a judgmental bigot'..."

"Okay, maybe so!" Shawna's eyes were now flashing fire. "But those liberals weren't the ones who killed my father! That's the subject we're talking about, isn't it?"

Drew shut his eyes and sighed, seeking to regain his composure. He ripped a white sheet of paper from his note pad and waved it in the air.

"Sorry. You rubbed against a sensitive old combat wound. I'll try to hold my fire from now on."

"Do you really think you can do this, Mr. Covington? I mean, I can see you're trying, but I think we're both loaded with ideological land mines for each other to trip on. We may end up killing each other while working on an article to make peace!"

Drew laughed. "Hey, that was a good image. Maybe you should be the writer."

Drew had successfully drawn out that smile from Shawna again.

"I had thought of being a writer once. I guess I just decided I would rather work with kids than grumpy adult editors."

"Good decision."

Drew looked down at what he had written on his note pad. The last words were "they didn't know him." He looked back over at Shawna with all the compassion on his face that his hardened features could muster.

"Shawna, you were talking about how the men who killed your father didn't really know him. That was no doubt true for most of them. But there are reports, as I'm sure you have heard, that at least one of the men there did know your father – your brother Brian. What can you tell me about his relationship to your father, and how much credibility would you give to the reports?"

Shawna looked down at the young face now resting in her lap. Right away Jeremy got up and ran back into his bedroom.

"I'm afraid that has been the part that has been hardest on him. There wasn't anyone Jeremy loved more than his grandpa, but his Uncle Brian, well, they had a special relationship too. Brian was always at his best around my son. I'm sure Jeremy never really sensed the dark forces at war in my brother's heart. He was just a guy who played with him and teased him, and did all the vigorous rough-housing with him that his grandpa had gotten a little too old to do."

Shawna had now turned back to look into her interviewer's eyes, and Drew could feel his heart melt.

"I'm not convinced that Brian was involved in the killing. But if you were to ask me, am I one hundred percent convinced that Brian wasn't part of it, I would have to say – no. Their relationship for many years has been, well...excruciatingly painful. Every time I thought they had taken steps toward each other, something would happen, and there would be this cold wall."

"What was behind it, do you know?"

"Only in part. I'm not sure anyone knows all that it was about, even Brian himself. Its roots were when Brian was in high school. Brian was pretty rebellious. When I think of how he was then, and how conservative he is now in so many of his opinions, there is just this huge disconnect. I don't understand it. Brian was always so defiant of Dad's authority. Now he apparently follows this Conrad guy who thinks he's God, and he is falling right in step.

Brian always seemed angry at Dad, and without any apparent reason. He got angry when he thought Dad was being too strict, and he got angry and disrespectful when he thought Dad was being soft on him. Whenever anyone would talk of Dad's accomplishments, the students he had influenced, the teaching awards he had won, or the legislation he had gotten passed when he was in the legislature, Brian would seem especially angry and disrespectful. A lot of guys would be proud of a father like that, but it just seemed to make Brian madder."

"Raging male hormones, maybe. They can make a guy pretty competitive."

"Maybe. But every teenage guy has that. Well...at least every teenage guy I ever knew."

Shawna's last comment had made her blush, and she turned her face away briefly. Drew wondered if she sensed how much his own hormones were raging in her presence.

"Anyway," she continued, "I think there is more to it than that. It all seemed to come to a head when Brian got this girl pregnant. Suddenly, he thought he was ready to be responsible and all, and he wanted to marry this girl, and for her to have the baby. But she didn't want that. She had an abortion. Then she went her own way. Brian was devastated. He didn't see how she could do such a thing, and him not even able to have any say in the matter. Dad was supportive of Brian in many ways, but he said that he thought it was the mother's choice. He thought Brian should put it behind him and commit to a girl before having a child with her. Brian felt Dad didn't understand, and that Dad was somehow part of a conspiracy to deprive him of...of whatever it was that he wanted. Brian moved away soon after that."

Drew just shook his head. "Okay, you've got to know that I agree with Brian about the abortion thing. Not to debate it or anything. Just to say what you already know. But still, I can't think that would be something that would make a young man be part of killing his father."

Shawna buried her head in her hands. "Well, I don't either. But it's all I could think of. I've been racking my brain for other things, but none of it makes sense of...of what the law enforcement people say Brian did."

"Well, the police and the FBI haven't been certain enough to put out any warrants yet. And even if they were, they've been wrong before."

"Yes, I suppose. I hope you're right. I pray you're right. But still, something in my heart is afraid that they may be right – that somehow Brian has been caught up in some evil that I don't understand, an evil that is beyond any kind of rational understanding."

"Conrad sure doesn't see his group as evil. He thinks his Armageddon Brigade is part of the work of God in bringing about the Millenium and the kingdom of God on earth."

Shawna's body seemed to stiffen again. "And you? What do you think?"

"Relax. Just because I agree with some of his political opinions doesn't mean that I agree with his methods – or even of his way of looking at the end of the world. I'm not sure what I think about that. But I don't think killing a good man like your father is a way to accomplish anything."

"Wonderful. We agree on something."

The two sat quietly for what must have been a minute or two, sometimes looking each other in the face, sometimes diverting their eyes to the floor or some other part of the room. For Drew it was a peaceful quietness, but he knew that for Shawna it was full of tumult. Neither of them heard the phone ring until Jeremy came into the room.

"Mom! Aren't you going to get the phone?!"

"Oh. Yes, Dear, of course. Thank you."

Shawna bolted for the kitchen, where she picked up the receiver that had been left lying on the counter.

"Hello."

"Uh...yes, he's here. Who is this?"

Shawna looked over at Drew and held the receiver out to him. "It's for you. It's your editor."

Drew took it. "Hey, you're not my father, so why are you checking up on me?"

Harold Carmichael was in no mood to play. "Drew, I thought you should know there is an interview coming on which you should listen to. You know Charlie Hanks?"

"Of course. He's had me on his show."

"Well, he's broadcasting today from an 'undisclosed location,' and I'll give you one guess as to who he is interviewing."

"Conrad?"

"E.J. Conrad himself. I don't know if Ms. Forester would like to listen with you. That could add to the story. But if she doesn't, you better get out to the car and listen yourself."

Drew shouldered the receiver and looked over at Shawna. "Charlie Hanks is interviewing E.J. Conrad on his radio talk show, *Patriot Nation*. Are you up to listening?"

"Oh, God, what if we start throwing things at each other?"

"No need to worry about that."

"You can keep your opinions to yourself?"

"No -- but I'm a lousy shot. Ask my ex-wife."

Shawna gave a little laugh, and then nodded affirmatively. "I guess it's like when you go by the scene of an accident, you've got to look, even if you're afraid what you'll see."

Drew looked into her eyes a moment longer, to check for any hesitation that would call for a delay in relaying her answer to his editor. Seeing nothing definitive, he returned the speaker to his mouth.

"It looks like we'll be listening together. I'll compare notes with you when I get back."

As Drew hung up. Shawna was already turning on her stereo. "What station?"

"AM 750. It's one of those all-talk stations."

The interview was already in progress.

"Mr. Conrad, they used to talk about 'the lesson of Vietnam,' and liberals and conservatives would debate back and forth what 'the true lesson of Vietnam' was. But today, in regard to your movement, people are talking more about 'the lesson of Osama Bin Laden.' Some would say that the lesson is that acts of violence and terrorism will not work against the United States, but that they will only bond the country closer together. What do you say to that?"

Conrad's answer was immediate. "Actually, Charlie, I tend to agree. The American people are a loyal, patriotic people, and will not be terrorized. But there are several things that some people don't seem to understand. I know that you understand these things, Charlie, because you are a true Christian and a true patriot, but I want to explain them for members of your audience who may not. One is that we are not terrorists. Terrorists try to frighten people into submission to their power and control. Terrorists attack the innocent. Terrorists play off of people's weakness and cowardice. None of that is in any way what we are trying to do.

"We are warriors for God. A war has been going on in this country, and indeed in this world, for a long time. It is a war between good and evil. In recent times it has been fought mostly with political weapons, weapons of popular votes and political maneuvering. When those are the weapons, the forces of evil win most of the time. That is because, as our Lord said, 'wide is the gate, and broad is the way, that leadeth to destruction, and many there be which go in thereat.' If you give people a vote between good and evil, they will choose evil nearly every time. And as long as we proceed in deciding things in that manner, this world will continue on the broad way to hell. In Bible times, God didn't give them that kind of choice. He called the godly people to arms and sent them to defeat the forces of evil, and it didn't matter if the people who wanted to choose evil were in the majority. The Bible also says in the end times, the fate of this world will not be put to a vote, but that the forces of God will rally militarily in a great battle to defeat the forces of Satan and evil. That is what the Armageddon Brigade is about.

"We are patriots, too, Charlie. We aren't at all trying to destroy this country. We are trying to save it. Save it from itself. Save it from the liberals and secular humanists who have infected it with hedonism and self-focus. Save it, and the rest of this world, for the God who made us all and deserves the loyalty of us all."

There came a round of cheers in the background.

"And might I say," interrupted Charlie Hanes, "It's about time!"

More cheers.

"But, Professor Conrad, if I might play devil's advocate here, Christians generally agree that God will defeat the forces of evil in the battle of Armageddon at the end of time. But most of us have been taught that such a battle will not be led by a human leader such as yourself, but by Jesus Christ himself. It will not be a battle between human fighters, but a battle between God and the demonic world."

"Again, I agree. This is not a normal war like people have had since the beginning of time. It is nothing less than a battle between God and Satan. But what people don't understand is that there is a difference between what is happening in the spiritual realm and what we see played out before us in human history. I am not Jesus Christ, and I don't pretend to be. That would be blasphemous. But as I lead the forces that God has chosen to eventual victory, it will not really be me at all who is doing it: it will be the Christ riding with me, who will be defeating Satan. God has always acted through people, and even in this last of all battles, he will do so again."

"And, who is it you are really fighting against, in human terms?" asked Charlie. "I know it is Satan in spiritual terms, but who are the actual, physical targets here? You said you are not like terrorists who attack the innocent. Who are the innocent and who are the ones you target?"

"We are targeting those in power in this country who use that power to maintain the present liberal, valueless system. That means the government, businesses that profit from human vice, and leaders that want to keep the old way of doing things. If they stand in the way of change, they have made their choice, and their blood will be on their own hands. Others who are tired of all the crime, pornography, and sin, we call to come along and support us. Some will just want to go about their own business and try to stay out of the way. They may be believers in Christ and innocent of the evil that has come into our country, and we will not target them. But we cannot assure people that there won't be 'collateral damage' in this war. We will not target innocent people, but some who are innocent will die, because that is the nature of war. Better for them to come and join with us, because God blesses those who take a stand for him."

"Professor Conrad, let me get specific here. Some have linked your group to the killing of George Marshal, a former college professor and educator. Was he your target, and if so what was your purpose in attacking him?"

"I'm sorry, Charlie, but we can't comment on specific actions. To do so would be to provide those who want to destroy us with the ammunition to do so. I will say, however, that George Marshal stood for many of the things we oppose: so-called abortion rights, keeping Christian values out of our school system, calling pornography 'freedom of speech' and the like..."

"Asshole!" Shawna Forester could restrain herself no longer. "That man has no concept of what my father stood for! My father spoke up for freedom of speech, but that doesn't mean he supported those who abuse it! And if he wants to complain about the abuse of freedom of speech, how about himself? He's calling for insurrection in this country! If he's consistent, how can he not say we should arrest him just on the basis of his words? I tell you, I'm not feeling much like being consistent. I have always spoken for freedom of speech, but I sure wouldn't mind if someone..."

"Shawna!..."

The angry woman stopped talking long enough to shoot an angry glance in Drew's direction.

"Shawna, you have a right to be angry, but I really need to hear the rest of this. Could you hold off for a little while longer?"

Shawna's body seemed to shudder.

"Okay, okay. But if it goes on much longer, I'm going for a sledge hammer to smash the damn radio!"

Charlie Hanes had gone on to another question.

"Professor Conrad, you have truly taken on Goliath here. You're going up against the most powerful country in the world, and in the end you want to go beyond that to change the whole world for God. Do you really think you can win this thing?"

"The image you started with was just the right one, Charlie. We have taken on Goliath. But what happened when David took on Goliath, Charlie? He won, didn't he? And why did he win, Charlie? Because God was on his side! God knew the nation had to be changed, and David was the one to do it. But I won't win this thing. God will. God is the true Goliath – the Goliath of all Goliaths. 'It is a fearful thing to fall into the hands of the living God.' There are a lot of people in this world who are about to learn that."

Charlie Hanes announced that they were out of time, and as he began thanking his guest, Drew turned off the stereo and looked over at Shawna, who was once again sitting on the living room sofa. She buried her head in her hands.

"Don't talk! Don't talk! I don't want to fight with you right now!"

"Okay, no talking."

Drew slowly walked over and sat beside her on the sofa. Neither looked at the other for well over a minute. Then Shawna spoke just barely above a whisper.

"I just want the world to feel safe again."

Drew offered her his shoulder. Shawna hesitated only a second and then she gently rested her head on his shoulder. Drew curled his arm around her and softly stroked her arm.

"A safe world – yeah," he agreed. "That would be nice."

Chapter Four

The only thing Brian Marshal was really sure of at the moment was that he was feeling light-headed. Whether it was because of his racing heartbeat, the fact that he hadn't eaten much that day, or just the torrent of thoughts and feelings swirling in his brain, he wasn't sure. He grabbed a nearby railing to steady himself, and hoped that the young man standing to his right didn't notice.

Brian looked over at that young man. If there were similar stress in him, one would never know it. His cold, steely glare was focused on the eighteenth floor of the building opposite them. But then again, from what Brian had seen of Cody Wiley to this point, nothing ever fazed him. He was slowly chewing on a toothpick as if he were hanging around a sleepy little town waiting for the day's mail. Cody now glanced over at him.

"Do you know what the lesson of September 11th was, pussy breath?"

Brian shook his head.

"Never trust a fuckin' Arab."

Just then a young man, walking briskly out of the front door of the building they were watching, looked over in their direction and nodded. Cody Wiley reached in his coat pocket for a small rectangular device whose outline was barely visible to Brian, even though he knew it was there. Brian shifted his attention to the building just in time to see the bright flashes that were followed quickly by thunderous explosions.

He quickly shifted his attention to Cody, who was grinning like child looking at a fireworks display.

"All right! I guess that put a damper on their day. Let's roll!"

After those words Cody turned quickly on his heals and disappeared into a suddenly panicked crowd. Brian knew that he needed to follow him, to keep his face turned from the building erupting in flames, but he could not. Shards of glass and falling debris crashed to the pavement, as the people in the street ran in all directions. Brian's mind seemed disconnected from his body. In what seemed like a dream sequence he saw flaming figures appear at blown-out windows and fall, as in slow motion, to the pavement below. Crying, screaming people now streamed out of the doors of the first floor. Some fell, only to be fallen over by others. The honking horns of traffic penetrated through to Brian's mind and he was suddenly aware that he had drifted out into the middle of the street. *What was he supposed to be doing right now?* The answer to his question was blocked from his memory. All that he could think of was that he needed to run – run anywhere, run not to avoid danger or avoid being caught, but run to get away from what he was seeing, run from what he was partly responsible for, run from the darkness in himself.

Slowly his rubbery legs began to respond, and Brian found himself moving. He wasn't sure where. But faces and lampposts and doorways streamed to either side of the eyes that were now his somewhat foggy window to the world. The beating of his heart was amplified as if his arteries had suddenly become a stethoscope with ear pieces attached to his brain. The sound was at once frightening and reassuring – frightening because the beating seemed to be pursuing him, but reassuring because it drowned out the noises of the panicky crowd.

Brian now felt his foot hitting something and his face floated downward to the sidewalk, bouncing slightly on the pavement. He lifted his hand to his forehead. When he brought it back in front of his eyes, it was covered with blood.

Someone had grabbed Brian under his arm and was lifting him to his feet. Brian turned to see a burly, middle-aged man with a hardhat on.

"Young man, are you okay? Were you in the building?"

"The building?"

"Yeah, the building!"

The burly man turned to a younger man beside him. "Help me with this guy. I think he was in the building."

"I didn't...I wasn't..."

"Don't talk now," the burly man said. "You're going to be okay. We'll take care of you. We'll get help for you."

Brian wanted to tell them it was a mistake, but something in the gentleness with which they handled him, soothed and calmed him. And his head really was throbbing.

The two men now lifted him into the back end of a station wagon, and laid him next to an old man whose left shoulder was bleeding profusely from a large embedded shard of glass. The man was staring wide-eyed at the ceiling of the vehicle.

"Oh God...oh God...oh God..." The man was mumbling the words over and over.

Brian reached over and touched his trembling arm.

"It's okay. They're taking you for help."

"Why do they do this? Why?"

The old man's question hit Brian like a kick in the gut. He wanted to run again, but the vehicle door was closed and they were speeding off down the road. Brian became aware of a conversation now in the front seat.

"The damned Arabs! Don't they ever give up? How many times do we have to kick their butts?!"

"It may not be Arabs."

"What do you mean, 'It may not be Arabs'? Of course, it's Arabs!"

"The radio was saying that they hit the eighteenth floor. That's the national headquarters of the American Civil Liberties Union. Arab terrorists don't have anything against the American Civil Liberties Union."

"Arabs have something against everything with the word 'American' in it."

Brian impulsively tried to sit up, but as he did the world started to swim around him. He had to get out. He had to go. He reached for the door handle.

"Hey, Buddy, you can't do that. You try to get out at this speed, and you'll kill yourself for sure!"

Brian heard the words, but the meaning escaped him. Someone grabbed him, and he tried to turn and pull the hand away from his shoulder, but then things really started to spin and he lost all sense of orientation. The last memory he had was a voice trying to reassure him.

"It's okay! It's okay!"

Then all faded to black.

■■■ı

Brian woke to a glaring light in his face. There were voices whispering in the room, but Brian couldn't tell the identity of the speakers or what they were saying. Then one person came near, appearing at first only as a shadow in the light.

"I think he's beginning to come to."

Gradually Brian made out the face of what appeared to be a young doctor.

"What happened? Where am I?"

"We're not entirely sure, but you took a blow to the head. You have a concussion. What do you remember?"

Brian squirmed.

"I remember...someone picking me up and putting me in a station wagon. I had blood on my head. They lay me next to an old guy with a bloody shoulder."

"But what about before that? Who are you? How did you get your injury?"

Brian just lay there staring at the ceiling for a moment.

"I...I don't remember."

"You don't remember how you got your injury, or who you are?"

Brian shook his head, and then he winced because of the pain the motion caused.

"Just answer yes or no. You'll be more comfortable."

A nurse came up beside the young doctor. "He had no ID, doctor. No wallet. Not a thing in his possession."

"Do you remember anything about where you live?"

"No."

"Do you think you might be living on the street?"

"I don't know."

The nurse began gently checking his head bandage. "He needs his rest, doctor."

"Of course. You get your rest. It might help you start remembering."

The doctor turned and moved out of Brian's still limited range of focus. But to Brian's relief the nurse stayed there, checking his vital signs and periodically giving him a reassuring smile. Brian estimated that she was in her early 20s. She had short auburn hair and green eyes. But more impressive than that to Brian was her gentle touch. He wondered if she would have been so gentle if she knew what had broken through his memory far more than he cared to admit.

The doctor had now moved back into Brian's field of vision.

"Well, as they say, I've got good news and bad news for you. The good news is that we have discovered your name. You're Brian Marshal. The bad news is that we learned it from the FBI, and they need to talk to you now."

Brian looked over at the young nurse, whose face suddenly turned white. She quickly looked away. Without further word she and the doctor left the room, and in came two men in conservative business suits. One of them, a younger more slender man, casually surveyed the room. The other, a man with gray in his mustache and temples, strolled over to Brian's bed.

"Busy day for you guys, yesterday, huh? Oh, I'm sorry. I forgot. The doctor said you don't remember. Let me refresh your memory. You bombed the national headquarters of the American Civil Liberties Union, creating fairly significant collateral damage, I might add; you attacked the offices of the National Organization of Women with assault weapons – I'm sure only your *bravest* warriors were sent on that mission! – you bombed Universal Studios in Hollywood; and you turned a protest by Greenpeace into a blood bath. Bloodiest day of terrorism since September 11th. And, oh yes, you somehow also managed to get a bomb into the Supreme Court Chambers. But I'm afraid all you managed to blow apart there were two janitors. A pity – and with such a big decision coming up on what cleansers to use on the Court toilets. Have *I* forgotten anything?"

Brian opened his mouth, but he shut it again quickly to hold back the contents of his churning stomach. It was just as well. He could think of nothing that he could say. The younger man came up beside the bed.

"No response, huh? Maybe he wants his lawyer. Oh, Alex, you forgot to read this poor victim his rights!"

"Oh, yeah. Let's see...how does that go again? You have the right to remain a complete asshole, while taking away the rights of others. You have the right to find a lawyer who will lie for you and find loopholes in the constitution so that you don't have to be held responsible for your actions. You have the right to a cushy jail cell so you don't bruise your little tush while waiting for trial. You have the right to make millions publishing your memoirs and accounts of the people you killed. Those are the rights you were talking about, aren't they Jack?"

"Yeah, something like that."

The agent referred to as Alex now leaned over Brian, staring directly into his eyes, and almost hissing his words.

"Except that we all forgot one thing: This is post-September 11th, you're a fuckin' terrorist, and so you ain't got no rights!"

Alex drove home these last words by pounding on Brian's forehead, and the room started to swirl around him. When he was able to re-focus again, he saw the face of the older FBI agent still leering at him.

"Oh, maybe you could call the American Civil Liberties Union. I heard they help people like you. No wait – THEY'RE ALL DEAD!"

Brian turned his head as far as he could from the accusatory glare, but with his injury it wasn't far enough to suit him.

"It's what happens in war."

Brian had heard that answer many times from other lips than his own. He wasn't sure if they fit on his own lips, but those words were all he had.

"War, huh? I don't remember war being declared. That is customary, you know."

"You haven't been listening, then. A civil war. We had one before, you know. The only difference is this one isn't about slavery or a North-South power struggle. This one is about the forces of God against the forces of Satan, and it will spread to a worldwide confrontation. This is just the beginning."

"Yeah, well, another thing that is customary about wars is that you don't attack innocent civilians! You have the balls to fight armed soldiers!"

"Really? Is that what we did in Vietnam? I recall a place called My Lai. I also seem to recall us dropping some bombs on civilians in Afghanistan and Iraq..."

"Not intentionally, asshole! You want me to bring in here some of the kids who lost parents in your little 'war' yesterday? You want me to drag you around to some beds in this very hospital where women younger than you are going to have to learn to live without a leg or two? Or how about showing you pictures of a sweet old grandma who was visiting her daughter in the ACLU office yesterday? I would have to show you a picture because we can't find enough of her to piece back together."

Brian could hold back no longer. His stomach rolled over and Brian jettisoned the contents into a nearby basin. Alex jumped back as some of the overflow splattered onto his arm.

"Holy shit!" The agent quickly followed his expletive by grabbing a nearby towel.

Brian collapsed back onto his pillow.

"All right! All right! No more. No more. That wasn't what I wanted. But you aren't going to get what you want by badgering me."

"Sorry! I flunked 'Nursemaid 101.'"

"I'm not asking you to be a nursemaid. I just need to get my head together. I just need to talk to someone."

"What, a shrink?"

"No."

"Yeah, just what I figured," interjected the other agent who had been quietly observing the process, "now he wants to talk to a lawyer. He's looking to wiggle out of this. He's..."

"No, not a lawyer either."

"Who, then?"

Who then? That was the question. But no sooner had he turned that question over once in his mind than the picture of the person made its way into Brian's consciousness. He wasn't sure why. He wasn't sure what he wanted to say. But he knew who the person needed to be.

"I want to talk to my sister."

■■■

Brian heard the sound of the footsteps coming down the hallway and then stopping at his doorway. There was whispering. Brian figured that whoever it was, was talking to the officer placed there to watch him. After about a minute, his sister entered, followed by a man he didn't recognize.

Shawna glanced at him very briefly, and then walked around to the far side of the bed. She looked out the window.

"You wanted to see me?"

Even with her looking away, Brian could see the tears streaming down her cheeks, and he could hear those tears in her voice.

"Yeah, I did. Uh...thanks for coming. I know you...well, I would suppose were reluctant to...to come."

Shawna slowly nodded her head.

Brian glanced over at the man who came with Shawna. "I was really hoping you would come alone, though."

Shawna snapped back, "Yeah, well, Brian, all I can say is that if half of what they are accusing you of is true, you're going to feel a lot more comfortable talking to that stranger than you are to me!"

Brian quickly turned away from the icy stare that his sister now sent his way. He found himself looking down at the bland repetitive pattern in the blanket on his bed. Out of the corner of his eye he saw the stranger edge nearer and hold out his hand.

"Uh, Brian, I'm Drew Covington."

"Oh...yeah. I've heard of you. I've read your column before. You write some good stuff."

Brian took his hand, but he was more acutely aware of the face now turned away from him than he was of any of the features of the journalist.

"Brian, there's just one thing I need to know," his sister said, now more quietly than before. "Your answer will determine if there's anything else I'm willing to talk to you about. Did you kill our father?"

Brian instantly shut his eyes, as if trying to protect them from a punch, but the question that held so much pain for him had gotten through nonetheless.

"I...I don't know. I think maybe I did."

Shawna stared at him for a moment with wide, glassy eyes.

"You *think* maybe you did? You don't know?"

Brian pushed himself up as far as he could in his bed. It caused his head to throb even more, but he didn't care. Somehow he thought that if he could be even that much closer to the sister who once knew him, he could get through to her, and in the process get through to himself.

"Shawna, this is why I called you! You've got to understand that I don't know who I am any more! One minute the things I was doing seemed like fighting for what I believed, and the next minute they seemed like the acts of a crazed maniac who was no longer me. I loved our father...and...I hated him. I hated him because...because he never seemed to be heading in the direction I was going – and I wanted him to – I wanted him to see why I felt so strongly about things. And I wanted us to fight side by side for the same causes. But it was almost like he always insisted on being on the other side..."

"*He* insisted? He was your father! He tried to guide you, to teach you! You were the one who seemed to deliberately take up every cause he hated."

"I didn't take them up because he hated them!..."

Drew eased up beside Shawna and put his hand on her shoulder.

"You know, if I might say here..."

Shawna swung around and held a firm fist in front of Drew's nose. "You! One word out of you and I'm going to hurt you!" He stepped back.

Shawna quickly returned her attention to her brother.

"You had a good father, Brian. You had a father who wanted to love you, even though he didn't know how. You were fortunate. You have no excuse for this. And now...now you've killed others...people you didn't even know, people who were just living their lives..."

"Shawna, I didn't ask you here to try to justify what I did! I can't. Even to myself anymore. I haven't slept hardly at all since Dad died...except in the sense that what life I have had has seemed like sleepwalking...like I'm walking through a nightmare where I'm playing a role. I've killed people. And the government, they're probably going to kill me for it. I know that. I can even accept that. But you've got to know that even though I knew how angry I was at Dad, the one thing I didn't understand until he died was how much I loved him..."

Tears were streaming down Brian's face. The words he spoke next came through a trembling jaw that wanted to stay shut, but which was forced open by Brian's resolve.

"I'm not asking you to forgive me. I'm not asking you to help me get out of this. I just want one thing. You're my sister, Shawna. You knew me once. Have mercy on me in this one way. Help me to know myself before I die."

Shawna's whole body started trembling. The moisture from here eyes was quickly dissolving her modest amount of make-up and brown streams were making their way down her cheeks.

"Die!...Oh my God, you probably are going to die too, aren't you? You took my father and you're taking my brother, too! How could you do this to me?"

Shawna collapsed onto Brian, throwing her arms around him and sobbing.

"How could you do this to me? How could you do this to Jeremy?"

Brian lightly stroked his sister's blonde hair.

"I don't know. You've got to believe me. I honestly don't know."

Drew Covington came up beside the bed and put his hand lightly on Shawna's shoulder.

"Shawna. What your brother is asking. If you want me to, I could help with that. It's part of a journalist's profession to unravel mysteries, and get the story behind the story, so to speak."

Shawna nodded her head, which was still buried in her brother's chest.

"But, Brian," continued Drew, "there is one thing you have to understand. I think I probably agree with you on many points, but I can't support what you have done. You've done a lot of damage to a lot of people. If you want my help in any way, you're going to have to cooperate with the FBI."

Shawna sat up. "That's right, Brian. If your tears are real, that is how you have to show it."

Brian stared up at the ceiling for a moment, and then he slowly nodded his head.

"But we have to act fast. Do you know what Conrad sees as the real lesson of September 11th?"

Drew and Shawna glanced at each other and then shook their heads.

"When you hit your enemy hard in the gut, be ready immediately to swing for the head...." Brian's gaze remained on the ceiling, as if he were trying to look at something beyond it. "If you're not ready," he continued, "don't bother to swing at all."

■■■

"You know that I can't promise this will save your butt, don't you?"

Brian looked up from his hospital bed at Agent Alex Branson. "I never asked that it would."

"I see. Just wanting to be a good guy now, huh?"

"Whatever."

Agent Branson looked down at him with derision. Brian wondered how many cases like his this agent had worked on – and what kind of people he was being lumped in with. The agent put a small portable tape recorder down on the stand next to Brian's bed.

"I want you to listen to this tape with me. It's a recording of a message from Conrad broadcast by a lot of conservative talk shows earlier in the day. Conrad apparently sent the message to them and they played it. I want you to tell me what you think it means. You got any problem with that?"

Brian shook his head, and the agent pushed the play button.

"This is what the Word of the Lord says to the people of America today: 'Come out of her, my people, that ye be not partakers of her sins, and that ye receive not her plagues. For her sins have reached unto heaven, and God hath remembered her iniquities.'

"The time for judgment has come, America. The blood that has already started to flow in our cities will become a torrent that will wash through our streets. If you have thought that you could stand next to the sin, and not be burned by its judgment, then be warned. We don't want to see any innocent blood shed! But you must choose this day whom you will serve. Jesus himself calls us forth: 'Then let them which be in Judae flee into the mountains: Let him which is on the housetop not come down to take any thing out of his house: Nether let him which is in the field return back to take his clothes. And woe unto them that are with child, and to them that give suck in those days! But pray that your flight not be in winter, neither on the sabbath day: For then shall be great tribulation, such as was not since the beginning of the world to this time, no, nor ever shall be.'

"Do not be deceived! This is not a little insurrection by a few dissidents. This is nothing less than the judgment of God. 'Come out of her, my people, that ye be not partakers of her sins, and that ye receive not her plagues.'"

Alex pushed the stop button, and looked questioningly down at Brian.

"You shouldn't need me to interpret that. He's got something really big lined up, and it's not going to be pretty. I don't know what it is, specifically, and it may be too late to stop some of what is going to happen. But you have to let me rejoin them. Only then will I be able to help."

"To help?" The agent folded his arms tightly and scowled down at his injured adversary. "Right. But to help *who*, that is the question."

Brian folded his arms in the same manner as the agent standing before him.

"It seems to me you don't have much of a choice. If I help them, I'm just one more person in their force. If I help you, I might be the only one who can get the information you need to stop this thing. You've got to trust me."

"Trust you?" The agent walked to the door of Brian's room, and turned to look back. "Is that what this world has come to?"

■■

"Can you blame him, really?"

Drew turned and looked at Brian. Brian squirmed in the leather-upholstered chair that was across from Drew's desk.

"No, I guess not. Still, it kind of pissed me off. You know what I'm having to do here, don't you? I'm having to turn against someone who does trust me to help a person who doesn't trust me."

"You're doing this to help out an FBI agent?"

More squirming. "No, you're right again, I guess."

"This is what you have to do, Brian. You don't just act and decide later why you did it. Act deliberately. Know why you are doing what you are doing."

"Yeah, well, that is what I need you to help me see, thank you very much. I don't understand why I do what I do sometimes."

"Okay, okay. Let's talk about why you decided to turn against Conrad. It wasn't to please some FBI agent you hardly know. Why then are you doing it?"

"I'm not sure."

"Is it so your sister won't be mad at you any longer?"

Brian sat quietly for a moment, staring into his own consciousness. "I don't think so."

"To save your own life?"

"No. My life doesn't mean that much to me any more."

"To make up for your role in the death of your father?"

"Yeah...I guess that's a big part of it." Brian held his head and shut his eyes as tightly as he could. "But you see, that just begs the question. The real question is why did I take part in killing my father?"

Drew pulled a chair up next to Brian's and put his hand on the younger man's shoulder. Brian opened his eyes and looked at him.

"Brian, your sister mentioned something about a girl you got pregnant and an abortion."

Drew could feel Brian flinch. Then Brian looked down at the floor.

"Yes?"

"Do you think that had anything to do with your action?"

"I don't know."

"What is your best guess, then?"

Brian started slowly shaking his head. "I was pretty mad at him then. He was supposed to be the moral one. I mean, in the midst of all the stuff I did that...uh...that wasn't too good, he was always the moral one. He got after me when I started to smoke. He jumped on my case when he learned that...well...my girlfriend and I were doing it. But then the moment I actually rely on him being a moral voice, to be the one to say, 'Be responsible and take care of this new life you created,' he didn't do it! He said it was her choice! He said, 'Don't bring an unwanted life into the world'! Can you imagine? It was like I switched over to be on his side, and automatically he switched to the other side! I didn't get it. All I knew was that I finally was ready to be responsible with someone, and he let her pull the rug out from under me."

"You believe life is sacred?"

"Yes...I do."

"So do I. That's why I've always opposed abortion."

"Right!"

"So, then, why did you take part in killing your dad? And in the killing of others as well?"

Brian froze in place, staring at a wall. Drew waited for what seemed like several minutes before Brian made any response at all, and then it was a slight sideways quiver of the head, which Drew took for Brian's now standard, "I don't know."

"You did all of this killing because you were angry at your dad for being inconsistent?"

"No, no!" Brian put his hands to his head again, as if trying to keep it from exploding. "That's not it. It can't be it. I still loved my father, even when I was mad at him. It's just Conrad made it seem like it was all the right thing to do, and...and... I just don't know!"

"You don't know, or you don't want to know?"

Brian jumped up and pulled back toward a corner of Drew's office, like an animal seeking an escape route. "Why are you doing this to me, why?"

"Take it easy, Brian! You said you wanted to know yourself. I'm not a psychiatrist, and I'm doing the best I can at that."

Drew stood up and took a few tentative steps in Brian's direction. "I mean, do you want to get to the bottom of this or not? I'm a reporter, and to get to the bottom of things I've learned to ask tough questions."

"But your questions hurt! They hurt me!" Tears again streamed down from Brian's eyes and mixed with mucous from his nose, but in his distress he paid no attention to it, and the mixture dripped off the end of his chin.

"Yes, they hurt. But they will get the answers for us, if we're patient."

Brian's breathing had become noticeably rapid, but now in the silence that followed, Drew noticed that it began to slow down again, to return to normal. He slowly walked back to the chair he had been sitting in, and sat down again. Then he motioned for Brian to do the same. Brian hesitated only a second or two, but then complied. Drew gave him some Kleenex, which the younger man used to wipe his face.

It was Brian who broke the silence. "You believe in most of the things Conrad taught me to fight for. I know you do."

Drew nodded his head. "Yes, I do."

"So what the hell do you have in common with my sister?"

Drew let out a little chuckle, in spite of himself. "I think both of us have been asking that question since we met."

"Yeah, well, she is pretty. I mean, even a brother can notice that."

"Yes, she is."

Brian picked up a pen from Drew's desk and started repeatedly clicking it. Drew could tell that he was searching for something in his mind. After a few moments more of silence, he seemed to find it.

"Drew, do you believe in demons?"

"In what?"

"Demons. Evil spiritual beings that possess you."

"I don't know. I don't think so. Why? Do you think you're possessed by demons?"

"Maybe. Some of the people I knew when I was with Conrad spoke of demons all of the time. They thought the demons were in people on the other side, of course. It always scared me because...I mean, they're in the Bible and all, and they can just take hold of you. They can make you hurt others and hurt yourself."

"Brian, that's the oldest excuse in the book – the Devil made me do it."

"But, listen to me! I'm serious about this. Haven't you ever done things, mean things, hateful things, and then wondered later how you could have ever done such a thing? Haven't you ever felt a darkness inside of you, and wondered how it ever got there? I mean, maybe it's just me. But when I think that maybe I killed my own father..."

Brian put his hand up to his mouth in an ineffectual effort to stop the emotion that poured forth. Drew thought for a moment that the young man might even choke on the intensity of his own emotion. He handed him some more Kleenex, but Brian just waved him off. His chest heaved, as he seemed to be regurgitating old tears, tears which erupted rather than flowed, and which spattered on Brian's arms, legs and even the floor beneath him. Drew said nothing until this eruption subsided several minutes later.

"I guess I have come across some people in my profession who claimed to have been possessed, but to tell the truth, Brian, I've never taken it seriously before. Maybe I need to rethink that."

"Yeah, well, it seems I'm pretty much rethinking everything right now, so I would welcome the company."

"Brian?"

"Yeah?"

"If there really is such a thing as demons and they've been involved in what you have done..."

"Yeah?"

"...then how can you be sure it won't happen again? How can you be sure what you will do when you're there with Conrad? To put it in another way, you were irritated when the agent had a hard time trusting you. But the real question now is... can you trust yourself?"

Brian sat back in his chair, and stared out the window of Drew's office. He wrinkled his brow several times as if thinking of something painful or getting ready to say something hard to say. Finally, he spoke again.

"I guess it always hurts when someone else says something bad about you that you're afraid of yourself. It's like I'm getting ready to walk into a dark and frightening forest, having no idea what's in there, but knowing that the only things still worth something in my life are on the other side. What else can I do but enter it?"

Drew nodded his head. "Yeah, well just so you know, there'll be a whole world of people waiting to see if you come out on the other side."

Chapter Five

E.J. Conrad strolled out the cave entrance and looked out at the valley below and the mountainous horizon beyond it. His eyes fixed on one particular mountain. Its once proud cone now leveled, Mount Saint Helen's still had a majesty about it. It spoke of the power that created it over the centuries. It spoke of the trauma to which even the earth is heir. It spoke of contrast and change. Snow on its upper slopes concealed its inner turmoil, and a wisp of steam arose from its crater.

Conrad, turned and retreated back into the recesses of the cave again, where waited the inner core of his military leadership.

"Armageddon. The real war to end all wars. That's what we're talking about here. The army of Jesus Christ pitted against the forces of the world, forces directed from behind the scenes by Satan himself. Only such a war has meaning. Little wars to determine who controls this piece of land or that piece of land, or who controls the oil, or access to shipping lanes – what do these ultimately mean, really? It's all only for a while. God owns all ultimately – we only rent it for a while. Twenty-five hundred years ago the big war was the Peloponessian War. Athens and Sparta. What was it about? Who cares anymore? Greece is just a place to look at ruins and get a sun tan. Nearly a century ago there was a war they called 'the Great War' and the 'War to end all wars.' What did it solve? Many thousands died because of the assassination of one archduke and the inability of European countries to cooperate economically. Far from ending war, it laid the groundwork for the next one. Am I starting to sound like some hippie peacenik? Well, as much as I hate to admit it, they aren't entirely wrong.

"What Armageddon is about is a war that truly matters. That is why we have to be firmly resolved here. That's why we can't 'put our hands to the plow and look back.' Yesterday was just the beginning. And yes, there was some collateral damage. We all hate to see that. I know I do. People on adjacent floors to the ACLU. Janitors just doing their job, and ignorant of the politics involved. Maybe even some Christians who were in the wrong place at the wrong time. But God has called us to do what we are doing, and he'll take care of those people. He's taken them to himself, and what will it matter since his kingdom on earth is coming soon? Those who died in Christ will rejoice with us and understand."

Men throughout the cave were nodding their heads and several said a quiet "Amen."

"Now, men, we have a lot more to do, and those under our charge have got to know that. You all know of the operations that will soon be under way. Go out and encourage your men."

The men around Conrad shot up from their seats as if an alarm bell had been sounded and dispersed toward three different exits from the cave. When all but his personal attendant had left, Conrad strolled back to the main cave entrance and looked up again at Mount Saint Helens. His attendant came up beside him.

"Uh...excuse me, Sir. General Dawson has asked me to remind you that he recommends against you doing this. You need to stay in the recesses of the cave where you aren't as visible or as vulnerable as you are here...with all due respect, Sir."

"Your warning is duly noted and appreciated, Lieutenant Mason. I respect the military insights that the General brings to our team. How could I not? -- a fighter with experience in Vietnam, the Persian Gulf and Afghanistan. God has truly blessed us with his presence. But the General does not always understand the spiritual, and looking at that mountain is part of my own spiritual preparation for battle."

"Sir?"

Conrad glanced over at the young man and smiled, before returning his gaze to the mountain.

"Do you know the meaning of the word, 'Armageddon,' Lieutenant?"

The young man straightened up proudly and beamed. "Yes, as a matter of fact, I do, Sir! Our pastor taught us all about that in my Southern Baptist Sunday School class down in Laredo. It means 'Mount Megiddo,' the place where the final battle will be between God and Satan."

The young man's face now twisted into a look of confusion. "Uh...will we be going down to Mount Megiddo soon, Sir?"

Conrad chuckled. "Yes, yes, that is what many believe. But they look at the word without creativity or true spiritual insight. The word *har* does mean 'mountain' and *mageddon* is derived from *Megiddo*, that is true. But what is the meaning of *Megiddo*? -- that is what they fail to ask."

The old professor looked up at the mountain rising before him.

"It means 'marauding mountain,' Son. The final battle will be fought not on the plains near Mount Meggido, but at the site of a great marauding mountain. A marauding mountain with such great power that it speaks of the power of God himself. A marauding mountain that for anyone who has seen it in action, humbles the puny powers of mankind. This is that mountain, Son, I know it. It reminds me of the power of the one who fights alongside me."

The Lieutenant's gaze turned in the same direction as his commander-in-chief. Together they surveyed the swiftly-rising slopes and the majesty of the outcroppings of solid rock.

"I see what you mean, Sir."

"We must feel sorry for those who will be coming after us today and in the weeks to come," Conrad continued. "They will be humbled by this mountain and the power of its Creator."

"Professor Conrad!"

E. J. Conrad turned to see the scowling face of General George Dawson.

"Sir, I thought I was clear that you shouldn't be showing yourself so near the entrance of this cave. It compromises security and endangers our entire operation. Lieutenant, didn't I make this clear to you as well?"

"The Lieutenant was indeed faithful in reminding me of your warning, General Dawson. I could repeat to you the justification for my being here that I gave to him, but I don't really want to take the time right now. Instead, I will follow you back inside, and we will discuss today's operation."

"That would be a relief to me on both counts, Sir."

Conrad dismissed the Lieutenant and followed Dawson into an inner chamber far back into the cave.

General Dawson wasted little time.

"Sir, all of the anti-aircraft guns that we have procured are in place. However, I still feel we must proceed immediately with Operation Baywatch in order to delay the possibility that we will have to defend our position here right away. There are confusions about procedure that we must clear up. In addition, a show of power will help instill more confidence in the men for our leadership."

"I agree, General. Corporal Cody Wiley is moving into position as we speak, and his execution of our orders will be within the hour."

"Wiley? Wiley volunteered for this operation? I have to say, I'm surprised. I've been meaning to talk to you about him, Sir. A real loose cannon in my estimation. And, if I might say so, not at all the kind of young man of character we should be having as part of our forces. Yes, I know he talks the talk around you, but my men inform me..."

"I know how he talks when he is not around me, General. He is a foul-mouthed, sociopathic blight on society."

"You know that?"

"Certainly. You may think of me as an ivory tower professor, General Dawson, but I know what is going on. Wiley probably joined our forces out of some perverse pleasure he gets from blowing things up and killing people. When I discovered that, I knew he would be perfect for this particular operation."

"Really? How is that?"

As Conrad turned and faced General Dawson, he gave him a knowing smile.

"Wiley thinks he's in San Francisco to blow up another building."

Cody Wiley checked his watch: 2:37 p.m. Precisely. He thought that was pretty cool. They had set his watch according to Greenwich time, to the second. He knew his role was really vital to them, since they wanted to time it that precisely.

That it was now 2:37 p.m. meant that his waiting was almost over. It was the waiting that he hated the most. Action is what he craved. It was like food to him. When something blew up he could feel his heart come alive. His senses filled with the deafening roar, and the bright flashes, and the varied smells of smoke from wood, plastics and flesh. People who walked around like shadows suddenly were fighting and clawing for life, as if it all really mattered; and when he saw people for whom life seemed to matter, it almost made it matter for him as well.

Cody looked around at his room. What a hole it was. The blankets on the bed were moth-eaten. Crusts of bread from a previous guest were piled in one corner of the floor. The picture over the bed was a faded print covered over by broken glass. Cockroaches scurried along the floor as if they were all late for important meetings. Cody gave several of them the only meeting that really mattered – death by the heel of his shoe. He didn't know what he would have done if he had been told that he had to actually sleep here.

Cody turned on the old nineteen-inch television set. The news was on. He turned up the volume.

"The city is buzzing today over the imminent visit of President Albert Packard. He is here for a conference of mayors where he will address inner city concerns across the nation. Several of the President's closest advisors wanted him to cancel this trip in light of the acts of domestic terrorism that occurred yesterday, but Packard would not relent. He told reporters this morning that if we let these terrorists disrupt the normal functioning of our nation, they will get what they want, and that will ultimately encourage more acts of terror. We go to the downtown Marriott for a report from Sally Chan."

The picture on the screen switched to an attractive young Asian woman.

"Thank you, Burt! The President's motorcade is just now pulling up in front of the Marriott. Security is heavy down here, let me tell you. Just about thirty minutes ago I reached in my purse for a portable tape recorder, and I had two men in suits on me like teenagers on a rock star. But you know, it's reassuring in a way, because I know these people are looking out for my security as well as for that of our President.

"As you can see, the President is stepping out of the limo now, and the large crowd around him is responding enthusiastically."

Cody Wiley scowled. "Arrogant bastard! If Conrad had the balls to send me after you, you would be down right now."

Wiley mimed aiming a high-power rifle at the screen.

"Pop! Pop! The President is down! The President is down! Whine, whine, whimper."

The news anchor broke into the remote broadcast. "Sally, are there any signs of protestors down there?"

"Yes, Burt, there are maybe a hundred people with signs about a block away. They are trying to shout over the crowd, but I can't hear them very well from here."

"Great," interjected Wiley again, "Wimpy protestors! That's why the world needs us."

The picture on the screen switched back to the anchor.

"Thank you, Sally. The reason more protestors are not down there might be that many of them have packed up and left town."

The broadcast cut to a video of a stream of cars backed up on an interstate highway. The camera zoomed in on a pick-up truck, overflowing with household belongings and with a banner on its side: "Come out of her, my people, that ye be not partakers of her sins, and that ye receive not her plagues."

"Thousands of San Francisco residents have responded to E.J. Conrad's broadcast yesterday to 'flee to the hills and mountains.' Conrad, by the way, is still on the loose, but Federal officials speaking on the condition of anonymity are saying that they have received a number of leads and expect to close in on him soon."

Wiley switched the television off.

"Assholes! All of you deserve to die. Every one of you. Well, all in good time. I'm ready to do my part."

Wiley looked at his watch. It was 2:50 p.m. Time to move. He picked up the unusually heavy suitcase he had been given and slid it up against the north wall of the room, as he had been instructed. Then after checking his pocket for the remote, he headed out the door.

On the stairway down he passed a muscular young man wearing nothing but cut-off shorts. His chest and arms glistened with oils that had been massaged into them like linseed oil into expensive hardwoods. Both ears were studded with earrings, and tattoos of snakes made their way up rippling forearms. As he spotted Cody, he flexed his biceps, making those snakes dance. Then he winked.

Cody felt himself starting to gag. He tried to get past the man without touching him, but the young man swerved deliberately and brushed Cody's butt with the side of his own. Cody hurried down a few more steps and then looked back.

"Yeah, you wish, fairy boy!"

The man just looked back, smiled and gave him the finger.

"Yeah, 'Have a nice day' to you, too, asshole!" Cody headed further down the stairs, and then added under his breath, "...since it's your last."

He was hurriedly descending the last flight of stairs when a little white fluffy dog darted around the corner and under his feet. Cody sidestepped it, but then his foot slipped off the stair, and he found himself tumbling down a half flight of stairs. As he came to rest he looked up into the heavily made-up face of an aging transvestite.

"Oh, my! Goodness, goodness, goodness! I'm so sorry, dear. Let me help you up. I'm afraid my little Snowball gets easily spooked. She doesn't mean to cause trouble or hurt anyone. Are you okay?"

Cody just nodded and checked his pocket for the remote.

"I don't know what gets into her sometimes. Sometimes it seems like she is possessed! Anyway, I was going to take her outside to do her business, and she got away from me. Are you sure you're okay? Are you sure you're not injured? I would hate to have been responsible for anyone's pain."

Cody looked up at the sagging face that seemed genuinely on the verge of tears. He quickly looked away.

"I'm okay. I'm okay. I just need to go. I need...to do things."

"Well, listen, if you find later that you really are hurt, I want you to feel free to come to me and let me know. I'll even pay if you need to see a doctor. Now, I'm not rich, but I do have some resources, so I won't take no for an answer, you hear? They call me Staci – with an 'I'. I live in apartment 102."

"Fine...uh, thank you."

Cody avoided Staci's caring eyes and looked down at Snowball, whose eyes were still darting around. Snowball yipped at him a couple of times. Cody offered her his hand to sniff and she started licking it.

"You want me to take your dog out?"

"Why, God bless you, Son. That is such a nice thing to offer. An old fairy like me, most men, especially straight men, wouldn't think of helping me. I really do appreciate it. To tell you the truth, I have a bad leg, and I often can't catch up with her if she tries to run away. It's so nice of you to offer!"

"Sure."

Cody took the dog in his arms and she continued to lick Cody's hand.

"Doesn't seem too shy around strangers, like most little dogs."

"No, she is the most trusting little thing. She doesn't know how the world really is sometimes. Anyway, again I want to say, God bless you. You know it is the people who help strangers who are truly God's children."

Cody nodded, turned and walked out the door without looking back.

"Remember, room 102! When you come back I'll give you some cookies to take with you!"

Cody ambled somewhat deliberately across the street, where there was a little park. He looked at the little white dog in his arms, and then back at the building from which he had come. Next to that building was the California headquarters of the Rainbow Coalition. It was his main target. But Conrad thought it would be a bonus to take down apartments known to be infected with gays as well.

Snowball was pawing at his arm, trying to break free. Cody stooped down and put her in the grass, giving her a gentle shove in the direction of some bushes about ten feet away.

"Go on. You're on your own, little critter."

He looked down at his watch: 2:59 p.m. Then he stood, looked back at the building, and felt in his pocket for the remote. His index finger lightly felt the surface of the button. He wondered what Staci was doing at that moment. Still baking cookies? Straightening his apartment because someone was dropping by? Cody's grandmother would have been straightening the apartment. His grandmother would have had all the cookies out on a cookie sheet with their aroma filling the room. She would have been singing old Baptist gospel hymns while she was doing her work. He looked at his watch again: 2:59:50. Why was it so important that it be at 3:00 p.m. exactly? What would change if he waited? He looked again at the apartment building, Staci's apartment building. Then his finger once more found the button. *He was probably just after my cock.* Then he squeezed the button.

The last thing Cody was aware of was that the flash that came was much brighter than he had expected.

∎∎

Drew Covington felt his office shake slightly. He glanced out the window at Mount Saint Helens. Its top was shrouded in clouds, but there was no evidence of activity.

"I'd say a 5.0, maybe as much as a 5.2."

Ashley Cambridge smiled coyly from her chair on the other side of Drew's desk.

"Oh, I'm sure the two of us could rock the earth more than that."

Drew just let the come-on drop flat. He refocused his attention on the morning's paper which was turned to his article:

"Conrad's Brigade: Our Nation's Cry for Help." His eyes dropped to one statement he made in the second paragraph.

He read it aloud: "As attempted suicide is often a disturbed person's cry for help when their life careens out of control, so the Armageddon Brigade of E.J. Conrad is our nation's way of crying for help. Our national psyche has been pierced to the core by the evils of abortion, relativistic values, and disregard of our sacred traditions. And yet just as suicide is no answer, and mutes the voice of the one trying to cry out, so Conrad's Brigade is no answer for us as a people. Its extremism is a kind of national suicide, and that they say they are acting in the name of conservatism actually mutes the voice of the true conservative, a voice that must be heard in our land today."

There it was: Far too weak a condemnation for Shawna Forester, he knew, but maybe too strong of a one for many of his readers. Still, he felt it to be the truth, and he would stand by it.

"You did some good research for me in preparation for this article, Ashley. I wanted to tell you that I appreciate it."

"Certainly," she said quietly. "And this daughter of George Marshal -- Shawna I think you said her name was – what was she like?"

Drew just shook his head for a few seconds before speaking.

"Well...let's just say pretty much what you and I believe, she believes the opposite. But, still, sincere and earnest in her own way."

"I hate that. There's nothing worse than a sincere liberal. They are like a driver who is hopelessly lost on a desert back road, but still convinced that they know where they are going. They won't admit that they are wrong until they are out of gas, and everyone in their car is dying under a cactus somewhere. I suppose she's pretty."

"What makes you suppose that?"

"Because...you had that look in your eye when you came back from seeing her."

Drew's door suddenly swung open, and Harold Carmichael stood there, breathing heavily, with his face as white as a sheet.

"Oh, my God, Drew. Did you hear? They did it. The crazy jackasses went and did it!"

Drew and Ashley exchanged confused glances.

"Did what?" Drew asked, suspecting that he didn't really want to know the answer.

"San Francisco. They blew up the whole frickin' town! It was nuclear...the President was there."

"It was nuclear?"

"A nuclear bomb! They must have planted it in the city and set it off."

"While the President was there? Oh, my God!"

"Turn on your television. Go ahead, turn it on. Who knows? Maybe I'm just losing my mind. I sat there watching mine by myself and couldn't believe it."

Drew's legs didn't want to move at first, but he finally overcame their inertia and stumbled over to the large screen television set that took up the southeast corner of his office, and turned it on. Peter Jennings looked like a man with a bad case of the flu.

"Okay, what we are about to show you," the anchor said, speaking in an extremely deliberate manner, "is the last feed we received from our San Francisco affiliate. Let me warn you, most people will find what you will see to be highly disturbing."

The scene switched to a smiling Sally Chan with San Francisco's downtown Marriott in the background.

"Burt, President Albert Packard just finished the kind of stirring speech he is known for, one calling for increased aid to cities, and a new resolve to help the poor and struggling to get on their feet through job programs. His words met an excited, supportive audience. Right now he is greeting some of those supporters, previous to his going inside for a meeting with mayors from across the country."

The camera panned a lively crowd, full of men, women and children of all ages. Toward the front Packard could be seen vigorously shaking every hand offered to him, as he made his way toward the door.

"As you see, the high security here is not keeping Packard from interacting with the crowd..."

A bright flash of light washed out the image for a split second, but the audio feed was maintained.

"Oh, my God, what was...Oh, my God!..."

A sudden violent wind hit the crowd and then the video turned to white fuzz, and the audio feed cut out.

The station switched back to Peter Jennings who was staring soberly down at his notes. He neither spoke nor lifted his head for several seconds. When he finally began speaking his voice shook.

"At present, there is no confirmation of exactly what happened to the President or to any of the other high-level officials in his party. We do...uh, I almost have to say, 'unfortunately,' have another video feed to show you. It is from our Sacramento affiliate, which is as you may know, a little over a hundred miles to the Northeast of San Francisco. It is video only. We are told that there was no one there able to narrate what you will see. However, I'm afraid it speaks for itself."

The unmistakable dark form of a mushroom cloud rose in the distance beyond the Sacramento skyline. It was laced through with lightning and a variety of glowing colors, giving it a beauty that mesmerized those who watched. Everything about it seemed so discordant – something beautiful, which at the same time was full of the ugliest kind of death, rising gracefully above the horizon – something that previously had only been part of tests, war on foreign soil, black comedy and nightmares, now actually spiraling above an American city – something that most people had convinced themselves would never happen now on national news.

The cameras focused again on Peter Jennings.

"Vice President Sam Arlington has been recalled to Washington D.C., and an emergency session of Congress has also been called.

"On the international scene, world leaders are expressing shock and dismay. Prime Minister Robert Bradley of Great Britain has called his nation to be in concerted prayer for the American people and the world. Privately, many are concerned about what these events will mean for the balance of power in many sensitive areas of the world, where US power has played a part. Already there are reports of troop movements toward the borders of India and Pakistan, North and South Korea, as well as in the Middle East.

"Senate Majority Leader Alvin Martin has called on the American people to not panic, but rather to have faith in the American political system, and constitutional processes for the succession of power. He also has asked that all Americans pray for him and the other leaders of the nation in this most urgent time of crisis."

Drew turned off the television set. He sat still for what seemed an incredibly long time, with his eyes shut and his hand over his mouth.

Ashley wept. "I can't believe this! I have friends in San Francisco. I have family in San Francisco. My uncle. My cousins."

Harold Carmichael sat uncharacteristically quiet and immobile.

Drew reached over and turned on his stereo to 750 am, a talk radio station. The now familiar voice of E.J. Conrad rang out:

"'Fallen, fallen is Babylon the Great! For all nations have drunk of the wine of the wrath of her fornication, and the kings of the earth have committed fornication with her, and the merchants of the earth are waxed rich through the abundance of her delicacies.'

"Again I earnestly call all Americans who would honor God to, 'Come out of her, my people, that ye be not partakers of her sins, and that ye receive not of her plagues.' San Francisco, that Sodom of America, has fallen to the mighty wrath of God. Remember Lot's wife and do not look back in regret. This is but the beginning of the judgments that God will visit upon the people of this world. Flee the cities of this world! God has many weapons in store of which this world has not even dreamed. 'Then let them which be in Judea flee into the mountains: Let him which is on the housetop not come down to take any thing out of his house: Neither let him which is in the field return back to take his clothes.'"

Drew turned off the broadcast.

"Okay, our job isn't watching the news, and it isn't listening to it; it's writing it. Right, Harold?"

"Right. Oh, God. Okay. We'll need to beef up our crew covering the White House beat. We'll have to turn that place upside down to learn all that is happening in this interim, the transference of power...if necessary, of course...and plans for retaliation and defense. Then we have to get the human stories in San Francisco. We need someone to get as close as possible to what is left of the city, and write about what they find and see."

"I can do that."

"I appreciate your willingness, Drew, but there's another task for which I think I need you. Unfortunately, it may be even more dangerous."

"What?"

"Somehow, some way, I need you to get an interview with E.J. Conrad."

Chapter Six

"Come on, move!"

Brian bristled at the command, which was reinforced by a rifle barrel poking him behind his right ear.

"I'm moving, I'm moving! Give me a break, I'm still recovering from a head injury!"

"Yeah, so you say."

Brian's head was indeed starting to throb as he made his way up the steep incline, which he assumed would lead to Conrad's headquarters. His gaze drifted to the right and the magnificence of Mount Saint Helens. He knew about the mountain. That is what had guided him to find where Conrad was. Looking up at it, he could imagine the power that had decapitated it now over twenty years ago.

His distraction caused him to stumble, and once again he felt the barrel-shaped prod behind his ear.

"Come on, watch where you're going!"

What especially irritated Brian about the situation he was in was that he had helped train the recruit who was now bullying him. The guy hadn't known the difference between an automatic rifle and a pellet gun before he had schooled him. He had seemed to look up to Brian then.

The trail they were on now started winding it's way up a mountainside, and Brian could see the ultimate destination high overhead – a small cave entrance where some familiar looking faces looked down on him as he ascended. Word of his arrival had no doubt reached them, and Brian could envision them debating his trustworthiness.

He was now high enough to survey the valley. Brian was both impressed and startled at the number of anti-aircraft guns he saw around him, and he knew he wasn't seeing them all. Others were no doubt hidden in camouflage, and pulled back inside some of the many caves that honeycombed this valley. And where had they hidden the surface-to-air missiles? He was sure they had them. Brian could also sense the high level of alertness of those who manned the guns, and those who were now running back and forth between positions. Many eyes, both aided by binoculars and unaided, searched the skies.

When Brian reached the cave entrance, a young soldier came out and began patting him down, searching every pocket and cuff.

"We did a full strip search when we picked him up," said the soldier who had led him up the mountain. "Didn't find a thing."

"Yeah, well, my orders are to do it again, so don't get all huffy."

Apparently satisfied that he was unarmed, the guard waved the two of them on in. They wound their way down a corridor, past a room with a high ceiling, and which appeared to be set up as a planning room; and then down another corridor, and into an inner sanctum, lit only by battery-powered lanterns. E.J. Conrad stood there, with his eyes on a map on the opposite wall.

The soldier cleared his throat, but Conrad didn't react.

"Sir, I have escorted the prisoner to you as you ordered, Sir."

Conrad turned and looked at them. His eyes were in shadows, but it was clear that the face showed no friendliness.

"What's his story, soldier?"

"He claims to have been injured in the operation, Sir, and not able to return until this moment."

Conrad took a few steps toward Brian and his eyes came out of the shadows. They were somber eyes that seemed to be examining Brian's soul. Then quietly and without passion he spoke.

"Shoot him."

Brian felt his heart spasm and his throat tighten over his Adam's Apple, but he did not move or speak.

"Yes, Sir!" barked the soldier from behind, and then Brian felt a rough hand grab him behind his right shoulder.

Just then a smile broke across Conrad's face. "No, no. I'm kidding! I trust this young man as if he were my own son. Leave us, soldier. I'll take it from here."

Brian felt himself shudder. Then he quickly reminded himself that he must assert control over his body. Conrad had sharp eyes and they seemed to notice everything. Those eyes slowly moved closer to Brian, and Brian gave what he trusted to be his most natural looking smile.

"It's good to see you again, Sir."

Conrad reached out with his arms and gave Brian a warm embrace. Then he pulled back and looked right into Brian's eyes.

"I was worried about you, Son. When that good-for-nothing Wiley Cody came back without you, I was worried for a while that he might have done you in."

"No, no. Not that he wouldn't have if it were to his advantage. But I just got knocked around by the panicky crowd, I guess. I...uh, need to plan my escapes better, probably. I looked around for Cody, but I guess he does a better job at getting away than I do. Anyway, I woke up the next morning in the hospital."

"Yes, well, I wouldn't be too impressed with Cody's ability to escape if I were you."

"Sir?"

"Never mind. How did they treat you in that hospital? Did they suspect you? Did they bring in the authorities?"

"No, no. They figured I was just another victim. The FBI was around, of course, and they did ask me a few questions. But they were asking everyone. I checked. Once I was well enough to walk around, they let me go."

"Be careful with those FBI guys, Brian. They'll mess with your mind. They really will."

"Yes, Sir. I'll be careful."

"I fear for you sometimes, Brian. You're an innocent, pure kind of guy – just the kind of guy that God loves the most. But the danger is that you don't always know where the evil is. You've got to know where the evil is, Brian."

"Yes, Sir."

"Jesus said, 'Behold I send you forth as sheep in the midst of wolves: be ye therefore wise as serpents; and harmless as doves.' He was talking to men like you with those words, Brian. You have the innocence. But you have to learn that wisdom of the serpent."

"Yes, Sir. I don't know about the innocence, Sir, but you're right about the wisdom. There's a lot I just can't figure out sometimes. And I don't always know where the evil is."

"Keep listening to me, and I'll show you, Son."

Brian looked into the old man's eyes and saw a love that made his heart break all over again.

"Yes, Sir. I will, Sir."

Suddenly the ground shook with a force that almost knocked Brian off his feet.

"They're here," said Conrad. "The time has come. I must meet with some of my generals. I'm clearing you for action. Stay here and a soldier will come for you to show you how to get down below. We need you with the ground troops on the periphery."

Conrad promptly rushed off in the direction of the large room Brian had passed through earlier. But true to his word, the soldier who had searched him at the cave entrance was back within seconds.

"Corporal Marshal, I am Corporal Evans. My orders are to escort you along the lower escape route from the cave, and to supply you with a weapon and ammunition, which you will use to help us defend the Eastern periphery. Follow me."

Without further word, Corporal Evans turned and ran down one of the tunnels, and it was all Brian could do to keep up with him. The ground was shaking at regular intervals, throwing Brian against the cave walls as he ran. Fortunately Corporal Evans now hit a narrow area of the corridor, where he was having to squeeze through and which slowed him down enough to allow Brian to catch up. Brian shielded his still-tender head as he slipped through after him. Just as they made it through to a wider area, an explosion rocked the ground and knocked out a side of the cave about fifty feet ahead of them. Both Brian and Corporal Evans were thrown to the ground. The soldier got up immediately and Brian followed his lead, as he headed past the gap in the cave wall.

Brian, however, paused briefly to scan the action on the outside. Planes darted across the sky, dodging puffs of smoke. One exploded in a ball of flame. Down below, fires scattered throughout the forest indicated where bombs had hit. Brian could hear shouting from down below, shouting which seemed urgent, but not desperate. He could not tell on which side the advantage lay, but both sides were definitely making their power felt.

"Come on, come on!"

Brian looked down the tunnel in front of him and saw Corporal Evans waving him on. He followed him past a couple of more narrow areas to a steeply descending path, and then down a pole that reminded Brian of a fire station pole. At the bottom of the pole was a stash of ammunition, guarded by four of Conrad's men. Corporal Evans grabbed an automatic rifle and tossed it in Brian's direction. Then he tossed him an ammunition belt and a helmet. Brian quickly strapped them on, and followed Corporal Evans down still one more corridor, which suddenly opened into an outdoor forested area.

As Brian ran, he wondered what he would do if he suddenly came face-to-face with the enemy. Should he think of them as the enemy? Could he think of them as anything other than the enemy? It would be kill-or-be-killed. What was he supposed to do – fight half-heartedly? Anything less then full effort would garner suspicion – or leave him dead.

Bombs falling disturbingly close rocked the ground and pulled Brian's thoughts to the immediate task of survival. They raced down a path dodging tree branches and thorn bushes on either side. Still, Brian was glad they were there because he knew this growth at least partially hid their flight from the view of the planes overhead.

They reached a clearing on the other side of which Brian could see a bunker. Corporal Evans now dropped down and started running closer to the ground. Brian followed his lead, and he was glad he did because he immediately heard bullets singing past his head. Brian and the corporal simultaneously hit the ground and now started crawling through the thick meadow grasses. Brian had done this in drills many times before, and he had to keep reminding himself this was definitely not a drill, and that the pops and zings he heard all around him were the sounds of live ammunition.

Peeking up just above the level of the grasses, Brian saw a bright flash of light ahead of him, and he instantaneously buried his face into the dirt. A second later a weight landed on Brian's back and he could feel warm liquid spurting onto his neck. As Brian pulled himself out from under the weight, he verified what he had suspected – it was the bloodied, spasming body of Corporal Evans. The shell had apparently landed just feet ahead of the soldier, close enough to blow off his right shoulder and part of his skull and flip him over onto Brian. He quickly looked away, and with a greater sense of desperation clambered toward the bunker, now a little over a hundred yards away.

Brian determined to hear nothing, see nothing and think of nothing but reaching that bunker, and with that focus it seemed like only seconds until he felt a firm hand pulling him by the shoulder down into the shelter.

"Who was it who got it?"

"Corporal Evans."

"Damn! A good man." The speaker now took a second look at the face of the one he had pulled in. "Hey, aren't you Brian Marshal?"

Brian nodded.

"I heard you didn't come back after the New York operation."

"Yeah, I was injured. It took me a while to get away."

"Hey, no need to explain to me. You trained me, remember? I'm Joey Harlow."

Joey held out his right hand and Brian shook it, if for nothing else, to thank him for pulling him into the bunker.

"Some of the guys said you went AWOL, but I didn't believe 'em. Good to have you on board because we are in a real fight here – a real fight, that's all there is to it."

"We'll be fine," interjected a soldier from the other side of the bunker. "God is fighting on our side – just like he did with

Gideon, and Samson and David. These guys coming after us don't know what they're up against."

"Yeah, I guess so," responded Joey. "Still, it doesn't hurt to have another good man on our side."

The words immediately wedged themselves like a tiny splinter into Brian's soul. *Another good man.* Really? *On our side.* If he only knew.

Drew Covington opened his briefcase, dropped in a file and a mini-recorder, then carefully closed it again.

"So, why do you have to be the one?"

The question had come from Shawna who stood with her arms folded on the other side of Drew's desk.

"I mean, it seems to me that there are a lot of reporters on the staff of *The Oregonian*, and a lot of them are more expendable than you are. What about that Ashley, or whatever her name is?"

Drew shook his head. "She's on her way to Washington, D.C. Besides, getting in to see E.J. Conrad is not going to be an easy task. Reporters and writers from across the country are going to want to do it, and Conrad isn't going to trust just anybody. I'm the one on staff with a national reputation, a conservative reputation. He'll let me in. He's got to. He couldn't forgo the opportunity to project a positive image through someone who he thinks might agree with at least some of what he stands for."

"Yes, but you wrote that article against him! At least it was kind of against him. I mean, the allusion to national suicide was a good one, but would it have killed you to cut out the ranting against abortion and sexual minorities for just one article? He might have taken that for a veiled kind of support."

"I write what I believe! So let's not argue about that again right now."

Drew walked over to the fax machine to check and see if any faxes had come in that he wasn't aware of. Shawna moved to the picture window, and stood there with her arms quietly folded.

Drew picked up a fax from a friend in Seattle and tossed it on top of his desk, and then he eased over next to Shawna.

"I oppose what Conrad is doing. You know that. There's no way I would write something I thought might help him."

Shawna closed her eyes for a moment. When she opened them again, she looked at Drew's hand, turned upward on the window ledge. She slowly slid her own hand next to his, and reached out with a slender index finger to stroke his finger tips. Then as she edged over closer to him her hair brushed against Drew's cheek and she gently lay her head on his shoulder. Drew was afraid that if he would move it would break the spell, and the dream would vanish; but the sweet smell of her hair and her soft contours against his shoulder drew him irresistibly, and he began kissing first her forehead, then down her cheeks to the corner of her mouth. The warmth of her breath against his own cheek sent chills down his spine, and he brushed his lips against hers. He took a breath and then returned to those lips, which parted, and to Drew it was as if they shared one breath. Her arms wrapped around him and she dug her long fingernails into his back, as if she wanted to penetrate into him at the same time she pulled him into herself.

When she pulled away there were tears streaming down her cheeks. She turned and looked away towards Mount Saint Helens.

"They're fighting over there, Drew. It scares me. I can't get close to you and have you die. Not now."

"What? Later, I can die?"

"You know what I mean. Not after my father. And that's where my brother is. That's bad enough."

"I'm not going to die."

"How do you know that?"

Drew took her hand in his.

"Okay, I really don't know. These are dangerous times, Shawna. But what you've just given me is a reason to be careful. I haven't had anyone I've really cared about...well... in a really long time."

As Shawna gazed into his eyes, Drew could see the sadness.

"Me neither," she confessed. "And God, you're such a jerk. How could it have happened?"

Drew laughed. "I thought this was the kind of time we were supposed to be whispering 'sweet nothings' to each other. I feel short-changed!"

"Yeah, well, live with it."

Shawna curled her arms around Drew's neck and brought his lips down to hers again. As she did he pulled her closer, feeling the softness of her curves against his body.

Reluctantly, he pulled away from her. "I really do need to get going, Shawna. Time is an issue here."

Shawna shut her eyes and leaned her forehead against his chest. "So what is going to be your approach with this...this self-appointed savior of the world?"

Drew turned away and finished putting what he needed in his briefcase. "I'm going to remind him of what he already knows. I have an audience that agrees with a lot of the things he would like to accomplish, and if he wants to convince them of what he is doing, he has to try to convince me."

Shawna's eyes opened wide and her body stiffened. "I don't want you to do that! I don't want you to make him think you're anything like him!"

"I need to get the interview, Shawna, and this is what I need to do to get it."

"Anything to get an interview – is that it?"

"Not anything! I'm just using what I have. I really do have some things in common with him. I mean, I don't really want to get into this right now, but..."

"So, what is it? Your opposition to a woman's right to make her own moral choices and control her own body, somehow joins you together in some kind of bond of brotherhood?"

"Shawna, don't!"

"Listen, Drew, if we're going to have some kind of romance or...whatever...what? – you think we should just base it on never talking about anything we might argue about?"

"I didn't say that..."

"But that's what you're trying to get us to do! That's no relationship. My beliefs – both religious and political – are important to me, Drew! And I guess yours are important to you. I don't want to just ignore them. I believe in a woman's right to choose. I believe in being ecologically responsible. I believe that gay people have a right to happiness, and that God loves them as much as God loves straight people. If all that is going to cause problems for you, then now is the time I should know it."

"Oh, God, Shawna, why now?"

Shawna folded her arms and glared into his eyes. "Because we're here together, now; and the issue has come up, now."

"Okay, if we must get into it now, everything you just said irritated me. A 'woman's right to choose'? What about the fetus' rights? I know, I know, they don't have status before the law, but I don't give a crap about that. They have a right before God to live. If God gives life, then only God should take it away; and if God doesn't give life, then we or whoever does give it, is God, and we're all even worse off than we thought!"

"Oh, come on..."

Drew wasn't about to give her an opening, "And...and, this stuff about ecological responsibility – what makes you think I don't believe in caring for the ecology? A person would have to be totally ignorant to feel that way. I just don't believe that Greenpeace or the Sierra Club, or any of those other 'self-appointed saviors of the world,' as you say, has a right to force their view on us as to what is ecologically responsible, and to destroy our business in the process...."

"Oh, I see," interrupted Shawna, "We're not God, and the Sierra Club isn't God, but don't get in the way of Almighty Big Business, may his name be praised!" Shawna threw her arms up above her head in a mock act of worship. "If they deplete the ozone layer, if they poison our drinking water, if they strip the planet of our oxygen-giving forests, then they must know what they are doing, and let us all bow down!"

"And," Drew continued as if she had not spoken a word, "what right do you have to imply that I think God doesn't love gays? God loves everyone, but their behavior is a different matter."

"They just want the right to live and love, Drew! God, how arrogant of them! They want to live and love."

Drew's whole body was shaking as he stared down into Shawna's now steely glare. Neither spoke for what seemed to Drew an interminable period of time. Finally, he turned away.

"Hey, man, was that fun! Why did we wait so long? We must do that again soon!"

"If we are together again, we WILL do it again."

Shawna's response sent a shiver through Drew. He wanted to turn and look into her eyes to get a better idea of what she meant, but he was afraid. He picked up his briefcase, and rearranged some things on his desk, as if their position mattered to him at all. Finally, he did turn toward Shawna, but he still avoided looking directly into her eyes.

"I've got to go now."

He took several steps toward the door, and then stopped and just stared for a moment at the floor.

"I'm a conservative, a man, and a believer in God, Shawna, and not necessarily in that order. I'm not a heartless beast."

"Okay." Shawna's voice was now much gentler. "I like that. And I'm not a 'baby-killer.' I'm just a woman. I'm a woman who's seen too many other women suffer with unwanted children, children whose fathers have skipped off into irresponsibility. But...I know you are not that way. And, to tell the truth, I don't think if it ever came down to it I could have an abortion myself. I just want...wait, that's all too long. Yours was short."

Drew felt the smile return to his face, and he looked over at Shawna now. "That's okay. I'll owe you."

Shawna returned his smile.

He now darted toward the door.

"Be careful." The words came in a soft, trembling voice from behind him.

With no energy to turn again, he just nodded and sprinted toward the elevator.

∎∎

E. J. Conrad looked out the mouth of the cave that was his headquarters, and surveyed the valley below. The damage was extensive. Fires were still burning various places, including where planes flown by federal forces had crashed. They had lost several anti-aircraft guns, a variety of tanks that were helping defend the periphery, and over a hundred men. Still, they had held their ground, and federal forces had been forced to withdraw, largely because they had lost a number of planes. One that had been shot down crashed in a small nearby town, killing twenty to thirty residents.

Conrad looked up in the direction of Mount Saint Helens. Only the lower two-thirds of the mountain was showing. The top was veiled by the clouds that so often seemed to define life in the Northwest.

He pulled back inside the cave. As he entered the Generals' Strategy Chamber, he was met by one of his aides.

"Begging your pardon, Sir, but Drew Covington is still waiting for the interview that you promised he could have. Do you wish me to have him escorted out of our province, or do you still want to see him?"

"I'll see him, Lieutenant, but not just yet. First I want you to send word to all the men, as well as all the women in support services, that we are going to gather outside the mess tent for a service of worship and praise, thanking God for the mighty victory he has given us. It will be at 0900 hours, and only those manning radar and peripheral sentries will be excused from attending. Drew Covington will be our guest at the celebration."

"Yes, Sir."

As his aide went to spread this word, Conrad withdrew to the section of the cave that served as his private chamber. He just needed the moment away from people observing him. It was where he could look for a few precious moments at the photo of Emily next to his bed. He still had difficulty believing she was really gone. He had for some time known that God would be using him in a great way to make his will known in the world, but he had always thought that when it happened she would be there by his side. She always had been before. Now it sometimes just didn't seem fair that she couldn't be by his side for this.

He sat the picture down on the crude bedside table, and then he knelt on the cave floor next to his bed.

"Oh, God..." As he said the words, he realized that he didn't really know what he was praying for, what the petition was that he was wanting to bring to God. All he knew was that everything was looking so big, and at that moment, a rare moment for Edward James Conrad, he was feeling so small.

"Oh, God...help me."

That was enough. That was all the prayer he could think of, and all the prayer he needed.

By the time Conrad reached the mess tent, some twenty minutes later, the area was already standing room only. A portable pulpit had been set up for his use, and three of the soldiers had brought up guitars and drums, and were leading those present in some praise songs. Conrad was more familiar with traditional hymns, but he knew that the young men who formed the core of his forces related to these more current tunes. They were just finishing one that was called "Awesome God."

Conrad looked over to Lieutenant Marshal who gave him a hand signal that all was set up and ready for him. The two soldiers with guitars led in one more song. To Conrad's delight it was an old standard, although it sounded a little different than he was used to with the different instrumentation:

"Onward Christian soldiers, marching as to war
    With the cross of Jesus, going on before.
Christ the royal Master, leads against the foe;
        Forward into battle, See His banners go!"

As much as Conrad liked that verse, he enjoyed the next one even more:

"At the sign of triumph Satan's host doth flee;
    On, then, Christian soldiers, on to victory!
Hell's foundations quiver at the shout of praise;
    Christians, lift your voices, loud your anthems raise!"

At the end of the song, Brian nodded to him, and with the vigor of a much younger man Conrad leaped upon the makeshift stage and strode to the microphone.

93

"Hell's foundations quiver – indeed! Can I hear a 'Praise God!' for that?"

Throughout the valley resounded the shout of ten thousand soldiers and support personnel, and Conrad was sure it penetrated far into heaven:

"Praise God!"

Conrad surveyed the faces of those nearest the stage. Off to the left he could see Drew Covington, flanked by two of Conrad's Generals. Toward the right were his son, daughter-in-law, and six-year-old Emily, his granddaughter. He smiled deliberately in her direction before raising his arms in the direction of heaven and continuing.

"'We have heard with our ears, O God, our fathers have told us, what work thou didst in their days, in the times of old. How thou didst drive out the heathen with thy hand, and plantedst them; how thou didst afflict the people, and cast them out. For they got not the land in possession by their own sword, neither did their own arm save them: but thy right hand, and thine arm, and the light of thy countenance, because thou hadst a favor unto them. Through thee will we push down our enemies; through thy name will we tread them under that rise up against us. For I will not trust in my bow, neither shall my sword save me. But thou hast saved us from our enemies, and hast put them to shame that hated us.'"

With these last words, the crowd erupted in frenzied cheers.

"The words I have spoken are the very words of our God, revealed in Psalm 44, and they are as true today as they were then. I hope none of you present here today want to claim for yourselves the victory we have had. I hope none of you present here today want to credit our fine Generals with the victory we have had. I hope none of you present here today want to credit me with the victory we have had here in these last days. I am only the servant of the Lord. Whom then shall we credit?"

The huge crowd shouted as one: "The Lord!"

"The Lord! Yes, the Lord! 'But THOU hast saved us from our enemies, and hast put them to shame that hated us.' I feel sorry for those who are in the federal forces. Now, you notice, don't you that I don't say 'United States forces' or 'American forces.' You and I are as American as any one of them! I still have my 'Proud to be an American' sign in all of my vehicles, and I trust you all do too!"

All throughout the crowd people screamed and cheered at the top of their lungs.

"But we're fighting for something bigger than America here, and it's the eternal kingdom of God."

"Amen!" came a voice from the front of the crowd, "God bless you, Doctor Conrad!"

Throughout the crowd echoed more voices, "God bless you, Doctor Conrad!"

"But I do feel sorry for those in the federal forces, as I was saying. They have been taught to trust in the arm of man. They have been taught to trust only in their modern weaponry. Well, we also have modern weaponry. But we have something more – we have the power of God on our side! It is that power which we trust!"

This time the cheering exploded from the crowd with such intensity that Conrad could not even attempt continuing for several minutes. Soldiers were hoisting up other soldiers on their shoulders and dancing. Air horns were being sounded and confetti thrown in the air. Conrad motioned for quiet, and the noise level abated to below that of the PA capability.

"Yesterday those who depend upon the arm of man came, and they thought they would get rid of us like a surgeon removing a pesky little growth. But they met something they hadn't counted on – they met the very arm of God! They depended on their radar and electronic targeting, but our firepower was directed by the Almighty! They depended on their fancy stunt flying, but God saw their moves before they even entered their little pea brains! They depended on their name as US Air Force and US Army, and we depended on the name that is above every name, the name of our Lord and Savior Jesus Christ!"

Soldiers near the front began a chant that reverberated through the valley. "Praise his name! Praise his name! Praise his name!"

"Yes! Praise his name!" continued Conrad, "Praise his name, because he has brought us the victory! They probably thought we would cower and be afraid. But whom shall we fear?"

"Nobody!" one solider yelled at the top of his lungs.

"No, the Lord!" Conrad said, correcting him. "He alone shall we fear. 'Let all the earth fear the Lord; let all the inhabitants of the world stand in awe of him.' If we fear and honor the Lord, we need not fear anyone else. 'Though an host should encamp against me, my heart shall not fear; though war should rise against me, in this will I be confident'!"

These words brought on another round of raucous cheers and dancing. By the time the worship celebration was over, Conrad's voice was starting to get raspy, and even the most vigorous young soldiers were showing the signs of diminishing energy. Conrad said a quick silent prayer that no attack would come for a while. Even though the worship celebration was necessary to retain God's favor and spiritually invigorate their forces, physically they now needed rest. Conrad did too. But an important task still awaited him back at his headquarters. An interview with Drew Covington could win those who were sensitive to the presence of God to their movement and bring new recruits to their forces.

■■■

One young soldier led Drew Covington down the cave corridor, even as another soldier followed behind him with what Drew imagined to be a readiness to bring his weapon into play should Drew make what the soldier considered to be an unwarranted move. There should have been no concern about that. Drew wasn't about to do anything that would jeopardize either his own life or the successful completion of this, perhaps the most important interview of his life.

They reached a dimly-lit room that seemed to be the terminus of that particular section of tunnels, and on the opposite end of the room stood a man who Drew instantly recognized as Edward James Conrad. Conrad gave him an instantaneous smile.

"Drew Covington! So glad to finally meet you face-to-face. Corporal Stevens, Corporal Collins, thank you for escorting Mister Covington. You are dismissed."

After the soldiers left, Conrad returned his attention to his guest.

"So what do you think of what you have seen so far?"

"Was that production for my benefit?"

"No," replied Conrad, bristling somewhat at the suggestion. "That was to praise God for what he has done. You were brought in to observe, but it wasn't for your benefit. You see, Drew, we here are what this country has professed to be, but has never quite attained – one nation under God. We wouldn't think of having anything good happen to us without gathering to praise God together. Even some of my own military leaders don't quite understand that yet. They think that worship celebrations like the one you just witnessed invite the enemy to sneak attack while we have our guard down. But what they sometimes forget, and what the United States has forgotten almost entirely, is that the victory belongs to the Lord. It is the people that acknowledge him who God blesses with victory. Throughout Scripture the people of God have lost only when they have forgotten that."

"Well, I must admit that certainly is a more refreshing perspective than Democrats and Republicans fighting over who gets credit for anything that happens to turn out right."

"Exactly. This country has numbed itself to the voice of God, and instead looks to human agents to credit for their victories. But that is passing away. Drew, we are in the end of time. The signs have been pointing to this for a long time."

"But, Doctor Conrad, you are an educated man, and surely you realize that people have proclaimed that many times before – Jan Mathys and the Muenster Revolution of the Sixteenth Century, Oliver Cromwell in the Seventeenth Century, William Miller and the Adventist Movement of the Nineteenth Century. Cromwell in particular thought that if he could just set up godly rule, even if by violent means, Christ would come."

"Your grasp of history is commendable, Mr. Covington. But the instances which you cite were simply unfortunate misreading of history and Scripture. How could they think the time had come when Israel had not even returned to the Holy Land by then? It was still being trodden down under the Gentiles. Paul wrote to Timothy that in the last days, people will be 'Ever learning, and never able to come to the knowledge of the truth.' Never has that been more true than today. Knowledge grows exponentially, but still people don't know what life is about. You see, Drew, many of the things you write about are symptoms, signs if you will, of the end of time. People desecrate the image of Christ and the government subsidizes it through the NEA. That is the spirit of antichrist! The despising of life through abortion, the disregard of family values shown by so-called gay liberation – it is all part of this great deception."

Conrad now moved right in front of Drew's face, as if afraid that any more distance than that might endanger the delivery of the truth of what he was about to say. "Drew, even what you just said was prophesied in Second Peter: "...there shall come in the last days scoffers, walking after their own lusts, and saying, Where is the promise of his coming? For since the fathers fell asleep, all things continue as they were from the beginning of the creation."

"I agree with you," interjected Drew, "in so far as what you are saying about the moral deterioration of society, and the lack of true knowledge. But let me play devil's advocate with you for a while. An opponent might say that there is at least a degree of contradiction in the fact that, in order to fulfill all this Scripture against evil, you have killed hundreds of thousands of innocent people through a nuclear detonation in a densely populated city."

"But there are no innocent people, Drew – or at least no innocent adults. That is the problem with abortion – it kills the only true innocents, children. Whether actively or passively, every adult in our society has conspired together to make this society what it has become. Jesus said, 'He that is not with me is against me: and he that gathereth not with me scattereth.' If you are not working to establish God's kingdom, if you are sitting apathetically by while your society erodes, then you are responsible. Before we detonated the bomb we called out of that city all who would hear the voice of God. The rest...the rest perished in their hard-heartedness."

Conrad turned and walked away towards a massive desk, which was apparently his. He picked up the front page of that morning's *Oregonian*.

"Don't take any of that to mean that I am without feelings for those who died. I feel for them deeply. But I have a calling that cannot be turned aside even by my own soft-heartedness. Besides, now more than ever, death is just a temporary reality. It's all passing away."

Drew was trembling from head to foot, and his body's reaction angered him. He was a professional, and he couldn't let his personal reactions interfere with such an important story. But the trembling angered him also because it wasn't clear to him what it meant. What was he feeling right now? What was he supposed to say to ideas that while objectively crazy, were delivered as if they were completely rational? If in fact he was right about God having sent him, didn't a lot of what Conrad was saying logically follow? At the very least Drew was seeing firsthand how Conrad had garnered his following.

"As much as I...uh...disagreed with Albert Packard, he was the President, fairly elected. He was the President of a country to which we have all pledged allegiance."

"We have a higher allegiance, Drew! Surely you can see that! And killing Albert Packard was the least of my regrets. The man was the antichrist, Drew. Of that I am sure. Three days after he was sworn into office – three days! – he was already holding seances in the West Wing."

"You know that for sure?"

"I know that for sure. My sources are impeccable."

"But I know my Bible well enough to know that if he truly was the antichrist, he would have wreaked a lot more havoc than he did before he died. He wasn't in office long enough..."

"You know your Bible do you? Then perhaps you have heard this passage: 'And the beast which I saw was like unto a leopard, and his feet were as the feet of a bear, and his mouth as the mouth of a lion: and the dragon gave him his power, and his seat, and great authority. And I saw one of his heads as it were wounded to death; and his deadly wound was healed..."

Conrad paused dramatically with those words, and then he went on: "...and all the world wondered after the beast. And they worshipped the dragon which gave power unto the beast: and they worshipped the beast, saying, Who is like unto the beast? Who is able to make war with him?"

Drew found himself backing away from Conrad, but he wasn't sure if he was seeking to flee the man or the man's words.

"Okay. Okay. The dragon gave power to the beast. The dragon is Satan. And the one with the deadly wound that was healed was..."

"The antichrist. Albert Packard himself."

Conrad walked up again to Drew and now his face was poised and rigid within inches of Drew's own.

"I don't think the man is going to stay dead, Drew. And when he doesn't, then you will know."

It was one of the few times in his life that Drew Covington simply could not speak. E.J. Conrad quietly turned and left the room, leaving Drew sweating and trembling. When the soldier came to escort him out, Drew could not leave quickly enough.

Chapter Seven

Ashley Cambridge had found her seat in the briefing room quickly, but she soon realized that she might be in for quite a wait. It was now a half-hour after the scheduled press briefing, and there was no sign that it would begin soon. The more experienced reporters evidenced very little surprise at this turn of events, but this was Ashley's first such event, and it caught her a little off-guard.

She had covered part of the Presidential campaign, and she assumed that the quality of her work in that capacity, along with what Drew had described as her stellar work on the background of his article on the Armageddon Brigade, had won her the prestigious, though temporary assignment. Even with irritations such as this delay, it was her dream come true.

While she was waiting, she looked around at the faces of the many other reporters gathered in the room. There were, of course, those men whom she caught stealing glances at her. Ashley was used to that. Being beautiful was part of the basic reality of her life, and persistent male attention was as much one of her assumptions as it was that she would have food to eat that day. The men who grabbed her attention were not those who looked at her, but rather those who were looking at something bigger – the world-shakers who were too busy making things happen to watch others. When she found such a man, it was her special challenge to get his attention. That had been her challenge with Drew Covington, in particular.

And so Ashley surveyed those reporters, male and female, who weren't looking at her. Reporters often had a rather blase look on their face. Most of them who had any experience had seen it all, and very little shocked them. But the faces of these reporters, to the last one, evidenced the signs of tension and anxiety that were part of the moment. Some were ignoring the "no smoking" signs, and were seemingly getting away with it for now. Many were exhibiting nervous mannerisms, like rocking themselves back and forth, pacing, or constantly shifting their weight. Several female reporters were sitting with their legs crossed, and swinging the top leg rapidly up and down, as if they were keeping time to some hard-driving rock beat. Ashley looked down at her own leg and realized she was doing the same thing.

An hour after the news briefing was scheduled to start, a young woman in a dark blue business suit entered and strode quickly to the podium.

"Good afternoon, ladies and gentlemen of the press, we are sorry for the delay, but if you will all take your seats we will begin."

Those still standing shuffled to their seats, and people quickly quieted down.

"For those of you who don't know me, I am Kari McDonald, Assistant to Press Secretary John Harnish. As most of you know, John was with President Packard in San Francisco. I want to update you on what is currently happening to assure the most efficient functioning of our government in this time of crisis, and afterwards I will take questions. But please realize that in a crisis such as this, much less is known than we would like to know, and even some of that cannot be presently shared for reasons of national security."

"First of all, Vice President Sam Arlington is functioning as President. We want it to be clear that the reason he has not been permanently sworn in as a new President, is we are not at all sure that President Packard is dead. We are proceeding in the same manner at present as if he were incapacitated. Of course, many assume that he and his entire entourage, including John Harnish..."

Kari McDonald had been speaking in a professionally controlled manner, but at this moment her voice broke, she put her hand to her mouth, her face contorted, and tears started to trickle down her cheeks. She very quickly wiped them away with her hand, and she returned to her script.

"Uh...many assume that his entire entourage...has perished. But we do not know that for sure as yet. When it has been determined beyond reasonable doubt that President Packard is dead, Vice President Arlington will be permanently sworn in. In the meantime, he still holds the full power of the Presidency. All surviving cabinet members retain their positions, and leadership at the Pentagon has been unaffected. All top civilian and military leaders are being shuffled between D.C. and various undisclosed locations.

"Vice-President Arlington has declared the area within a one hundred mile radius of San Francisco a federal disaster area, and personnel from FEMA are on the scene, as well as people from private organizations such as the Red Cross."

"The nuclear detonation in San Francisco has been determined by the FBI to be the work of the Armageddon Brigade, headed by Edward James Conrad. His forces are heavily armed, due in large part to defections from some of our own high-level and mid-level military personnel. They have concentrated their forces in a mountainous area near Mount Saint Helens, as well as in the mountains of Northern Idaho. Groups sympathetic to Conrad have sprung up across the country, but they don't seem to be as well organized."

"The Pentagon is already directing counter-strikes against the Brigade, and National Security Advisor Karen Steele has pledged that their main forces will be eradicated within the month. Nevertheless, I am obligated to say once again that this group is heavily armed, and more devastating attacks may occur before this is all over."

Kari McDonald lifted her eyes from her script, and breathed deeply. "I will now take your questions."

A reporter from the New York Times was recognized.

"In saying that this group is heavily-armed, are you saying that they could detonate another nuclear device?"

"We cannot say if further nuclear attacks are possible. We are certainly working to prevent any such recurrence, but we have no intelligence information at present that indicates that further attacks are imminent."

The reporter followed up, "But did you have any advance intelligence information of the first attack?"

"Certainly not. President Packard would not have been allowed to go to San Francisco had there been any reports of a possible nuclear attack."

Ashley's own hand shot up, but a reporter from the Associated Press was called upon for the next question.

"What military leaders specifically have defected to the Brigade, and are further defections anticipated?"

"We have put together a list of these traitors, which we will make available to you. The most prominent defection was General George Dawson, a much-decorated and highly revered leader with service in both Persian Gulf conflicts, as well as Afghanistan. I'm afraid that he took a lot of weaponry with him, as well as a number of his closest advisors. We knew that General Dawson was unhappy with Albert Packard winning the Presidency, but we thought that he was more loyal to the country than this."

"As far as other defections are concerned, we are thinking that those prone to defection have already done so."

Ashley got her hand up quickly, and Kari McDonald pointed in her direction.

"Ashley Cambridge of *The Oregonian*. How could things in this country have disintegrated so quickly? After September 11th, we had a united country. Now, after the election of a liberal Democrat, we have defections in the military, and our own citizens detonating nuclear bombs in our cities. What happened?"

Kari McDonald's jaw visibly clenched, and she gave Ashley an icy glare.

"Ashley, is it? Ashley, you must be aware that the divisions in this country have roots that extend far deeper than the beginning of this administration. Yes, these divisions were rightly put aside when the country was brazenly attacked from the outside. But obviously for some people 'United We Stand' only holds for when their side is in power."

Kari picked up her papers. Hands were going up all over the room, but she ignored them.

"Ladies and Gentlemen, I'm afraid that's all the time we have for questions right now. There will, however, be another briefing tomorrow. Good afternoon."

Ashley immediately went to work on her laptop, and put together an article on what she had heard. The lead would be that the administration could not promise further nuclear attacks would not occur. That would get a headline and grab the readers' attention. It would also get them asking her question that she would then answer: how did this all happen? Kari McDonald's answer would be given, but that was obviously inadequate. It put all the blame on the people with conservative perspectives. The fact was that this administration had been unable to articulate a vision that would keep the nation moving forward together. For that failure they would have to be held accountable.

As Ashley was finishing up her article, she began to sense someone watching her. It didn't take long to find out whom. Looking to her right she saw a short, balding, middle-aged reporter coming her way. As he got closer, Ashley noticed the kind of know-it-all smile a man has on his face when he takes it upon himself to "instruct" a woman he sees as less-knowledgeable.

"Oh, God!" she said under her breath, focusing as she did on her laptop, and hoping that focus might dissuade the invader. No such luck.

"You're new on this beat, aren't you?"

"Afraid so."

"I thought so. I was sure I would have noticed such a beautiful woman had you been here before."

"Probably. And had you noticed me before, you would have probably already come up to me with a lame line like that one, and I probably would have already said, 'Get lost, Asshole!' which would have made this time totally unnecessary."

Ashley immediately returned her attention to her computer, which didn't have any stronger effect on the man than it had the first time.

"All right. But I've got to tell you that to make it in this town, you've got to know how to get to the real information. You don't think you get it in this room, do you?"

Ashley looked up from her keyboard.

"Bernard Meredith is the name – twenty years on the D.C. beat. Stick close to me and you'll be where you need to be, when you need to be there. You'll find out the things that 'Miss Stick-up-her Ass' there will never tell you, and the fact that you know what you know will frustrate the hell out of her – or whoever becomes the permanent mouthpiece for this administration."

"Okay, Bernard," Ashley said in an only slightly more polite tone, "you've got my attention. Now what can you tell me to convince me that you can deliver on your bravado?"

"Well, for one thing I can tell you where Ms. McDonald up there was either lying or badly misinformed by her people." Bernard pulled up a chair and sat on it backwards, with his legs spread and his chin resting on the back of the chair. "Take that question about more nukes. The administration knows they are missing more warheads, and they are missing from the same place where the first one came from. I've talked to people who have seen the inventories. The administration doesn't want to have any more panic than they've already got, and they think they can root this group out before they are used. And that thing about no more defections? – Please! I know two generals myself who are ready to bolt, and the only reason they haven't is that they are being watched like a teenage Goth in a shopping mall."

"And President Packard, what about that?," asked Ashley, unable to hide her interest. "It seems they should have a pretty good idea by now whether the man is dead or not."

"Oh, they know, they know," replied Bernard, knowingly. "My sources tell me that he is in a highly secret room at Sinai Hospital in Baltimore, and that while he had some bad radiation burns, he'll be ready to walk out of there in a matter of days. All that has to be decided is *when* the administration wants it to be known that he is alive. They are wanting to balance the need to reassure the public with their desire to keep him from being a target again before it is absolutely necessary.

"Now," continued Bernard, "you have to admit that is an awful lot of information, given freely to this point because I am such a nice guy, and wanting to help you out. But if you still think I'm an asshole..."

Ashley folded up her laptop, stood up and took Bernard by the arm.

"I'm afraid I mistook you for another asshole. To make up for it, I will let you buy me dinner."

■■■

Shawna Forester looked out over the conference room at the faces of those gathered there. It was a small but impressive group. She recognized prominent politicians, entertainers and business leaders, and it all made her wonder what she was doing in such company. Of course, she actually did know in her mind. Her place had been paid for with the price of those bullets that had riddled her father's body, an act of violence that at the same time seemed like it happened yesterday and in a dream world long, long ago. With that act she had taken on a new resolution to work harder for the principles for which her father had spoken. The attack on the national headquarters of the ACLU gave this resolve a focus: she would work toward a new national organization that would speak for liberal values of freedom and tolerance. She had found others wanting to work for the same thing, and this informal gathering was the result.   Senator Karen Emory from Oregon, who had helped her make many valuable contacts, was now calling the meeting together. After everyone found a seat, the Senator stepped up to the microphone.

"First of all, I want to thank all of you for coming together on such short notice. But you know the gravity of the present situation in our country, and so you know how important it is that we are here in the nation's capitol. Our country is at a crossroads. We must decide whether or not the principles of freedom upon which our country was founded will prevail, or whether we will toss them aside as inconvenient. Those who struck at the ACLU believed that our freedoms are secondary to their own vision of what America and the world should be. Even while our country fights them, we will lose to them if we become like them. That is what we cannot allow to happen."

The Senator's words were interrupted by applause throughout the room. She signaled for quiet.

"It has been said that all that is necessary for evil to win is for good people to do nothing. We are here today to say to the world that we will not sit by and do nothing."

Again the room erupted in applause.

"The initiative for this fight has not come from a politician or a wealthy business leader. It has not come from a big-name entertainer or someone with the power of a formal organization behind her. It has come from a public school teacher, Shawna Forester. But Shawna is not just any public school teacher. She is one who herself was a victim of the violence in which we are now all embroiled. She is the daughter of George Marshal, a former university professor and state legislator, who was brutally murdered because of the stand he had taken for our freedoms. You have read his story, I am sure. But Shawna is here to make sure that his story does not end with his death. Ladies and Gentlemen, I present to you Shawna Forester."

There were only about eighty people in the room, but they all rose almost as one to give Shawna an ovation. The reaction surprised, and even frightened her a little. She wasn't normally very comfortable when expectations of her rose too high. But she knew now that she would have to get past that. This project was far too important to be thwarted by her own insecurities. When the room quieted down she stepped up to the microphone.

"Okay. Umm...I'm not really much of a public speaker...or at least not when those listening are over twelve..."

There was scattered laughter throughout the audience, and it helped Shawna to relax just a little.

"Which reminds me, I am told that there are rest rooms down the hall, if you need them during my presentation. Of course, if you need to go, just remember to raise your hand with one finger or two..."

This brought more laughter, and Shawna took a deep breath.

"There are a lot of people who could do a better job than I talking to you about the technical aspects of the law and the constitution and such, so I'm not going to do that. I thought instead that I would tell you a little of my own personal story of why I'm here, and why I think this is so important. The Senator has already reminded you about my father. I've got to say that was the most traumatic experience of my life to that point, when my father was murdered. The bombing of San Francisco, which touched us all, has actually surpassed it since.

"My father loved this country and what it stood for. I still remember the time when I was seven years old and he and my mother took us to New York City for the first time. I remember my father standing on Ellis Island, looking up at the Statue of Liberty, with tears in his eyes..."

Shawna stopped and held her hand up to her mouth. It didn't entirely keep her own tears from coming, but it seemed to help her maintain some semblance of control. She trusted that her audience would be patient, and they were.

"Okay, I won't apologize for the emotion, because the deep feelings I have are why I am here. Anyway, I think the reason why my father loved this country was not just the kind of loyalty one has to the country of one's birth, but it was more. He loved that the Statue of Liberty was there shining a light of welcome to the poor masses, the masses coming to us after being under the heel of the oppressive governments of the world. He loved that everyone has a right to speak their mind in this country, no matter how unpopular their opinion. He loved that the vote of a poor person on welfare is counted the same as that of a rich industrialist. In short, I think what he loved wasn't that our country was 'our side,' but what our country gave to the world, to humanity. He was a deeply religious man, and he loved that our country, more than perhaps any other seemed to live out the idea that all people are equal in God's eyes.

"Now, he knew that we needed to do more. But he was glad that our country had the historic principles of freedom and equality to guide us and give us something to reach for. And so when he worked to preserve the rights of gay and lesbian people, he was

109

working to help us as a country better realize our historic principles. And when he worked for what he called welfare reform, which was much different than what other people call welfare reform, he was working to help the poor regain the right to have dreams and reach for them. He wasn't wanting to cut taxes so the rich could be richer. He was wanting the way we help the poor to really help them toward a future of hope. He always believed enough in America to believe that we could be better. But he also believed that the way for us to be better was to more fully hold to our historic principles.

"Now our country is being threatened by those who want to destroy America's historic principles. Instead of freedom, people like E.J. Conrad want us all to submit to his idea of who God is and what God wants. Instead of equality, Conrad wants us to grant him special status above every one else to determine the fate of our country and our world. But I also want to say to you – and this is important – Conrad is not the only one who threatens who we are. Others, when they see the threats of violence, want to take away everyone's rights, thinking that doing so will help us buy our security. Others want to strip people who look different than we do of their rights. Others want to take away from women the right to make their own choices. Others want to dictate what is moral. We cannot allow them to do that. That is why I am proposing today the foundation of a new organization I am calling, The Foundation for American Principles."

Once again those gathered in the room gave her a standing ovation. This time it seemed to Shawna to last for three or four minutes, and when it ended Shawna could feel her heart reverberating in her chest, and she was starting to feel a little light-headed. But she knew there was more that needed to be said.

"I am starting this foundation with ten thousand dollars that was given as a memorial to my father. I know it isn't much for starting a national organization, but what I am hoping is that it will inspire people like you to give more to really get it going. As a teacher, I talk to children each day about what our country is about, and I always try to be honest with them. I want to continue to tell them that our country is one that strives toward freedom for all and a chance for the common person. I want that to be a civics lesson, and not a history lesson of what we used to be. I want the children I teach to be proud of where we have been as a nation and proud of where we are going. Won't you let me continue to teach them in this way? Thank you."

As the audience rose once more in applause, Senator Emory came over and gave Shawna a big hug. Then she whispered in Shawna's ear.

"You did it! You said the right things. It's going to happen!"

Shawna was glad that the Senator was holding on to her, because she was feeling even more light-headed. The persons who now came up to congratulate her and give her words of support seemed like they were in a dream sequence. Names were disappearing from her mind the moment after they were spoken. The Senator had an aide taking down names and pledges of support, and so Shawna didn't have to worry about that. Still, she worried that something important was going to be said that she would miss or forget.

After most had cleared out and just as Shawna was beginning to look forward to escaping to lying down in her hotel room, she saw off to one side the face of a young woman whose countenance somehow seemed different than the others. The expression was less exuberant and the eyes more probing. Next to her stood a balding middle-aged man. A supporter grabbed her attention momentarily away from the two, and when she looked back at them, they were coming her way.

"Shawna, you don't know me, but we have a mutual friend – Drew Covington."

"Oh, yes...of course."

"I'm Ashley Cambridge. That was quite a little speech you gave, especially for someone not experienced with public speaking. I can't say that I agreed with all of it, but it was certainly interesting. You know, I think Drew would find it interesting also. You wouldn't mind if I sent him a copy of the tape I made, would you?"

Shawna tried to quickly run through her mind what she had said, and how Drew might react. It probably wouldn't be good. Still, what could she say?

"No, not at all. By all means send him a copy, if you like."

"Okay, I will." Ashley turned to her companion. "Oh, Bernard...I'm afraid I left my purse back under my chair. Could you go back and get it for me?"

Bernard nodded and headed back toward where they were sitting. After he left, Ashley quickly turned her attention back to Shawna, bending in her direction and whispering.

"Oh!...and I hope that you will be discreet about mentioning Bernard if you see Drew again. He's just a guy who is helping me professionally. There is nothing personal in the relationship, but you know how jealous Drew gets. I'm afraid if you mention that you saw me with a man he could get all bent out of shape, and it would hurt...well, what we have together. You're a woman. You understand, I am sure."

Shawna felt like she was in an airliner that was in free fall. She had risen so high, but now the ground was looming before her.

"I...uh...sure."

Bernard returned with the purse, and he turned to Shawna.

"Hi, I'm Bernard Meredith, with *The Washington Post*. I'm going to write up what I heard today. I can't assure a front page or anything, but I think you will be pleased."

Shawna managed a smile. "Thank you."

Bernard continued. "I've got to say, you did a great job, Teach. With Senator Emory by your side, you could become a real player around here, and I pride myself in connecting with those who are players."

"Yeah, well, I will be going back to Portland in a week or so, but I do plan to come back fairly frequently to work on getting the foundation set up."

"Say, I was just thinking...I promised Ashley I'd take her with me to meet with a guy I know with some real inside information..."

Ashley stiffened up. "You promised me that I would be the only one..."

"Chill! Chill! She's not a reporter. Besides, I know this guy, and the more good-looking women there are around, the more he opens up to impress them. You want him to open up, don't you?"

"Of course, but...and please don't take offense at this, Shawna...but I want the information well before it gets leaked to everyone else."

Shawna was feeling the tension building in the back of her neck. "Uh...it's okay, Bernard. I admit, it sounds like it would be a fascinating experience, but I really need to lay down for a while, so..."

"Are you sure? Think of the stories you could tell your students about how D.C. operates!"

"No, no. I'll just have to tell them about the meeting I *almost* went to. It was nice to meet you, Bernard. Ashley, give my regards to Drew."

Shawna turned quickly and exited the room before Bernard had a chance to raise any further protest. She really would have been fascinated by the chance to be involved in some meeting with an official that she was sure would later be referred to as "a high-level official, under condition of anonymity," and had her need for rest been the only issue, she would have gutted it out. But she couldn't take much more of Ashley Cambridge. The reference to her relationship with Drew had ripped through Shawna like a knife. Were they really that close or was Ashley involved in wishful thinking? Sure Drew had some pretty backward ideas, but at least he seemed like a man of principle. He wouldn't have gotten that close to her had there been someone else. Of course, he was a man, and Shawna's experience with men would not let her rule the possibility out.

When she got back to her room, Shawna immediately kicked off her shoes, flopped on the bed and turned on the television with her remote. CNN was on. It was filled with many of the same shots she had seen before of refugees fleeing what was left of San Francisco. It was hard to watch. She remembered before seeing refugees from drought and war-stricken areas of Africa, and it had wrenched her heart then. But that this was people from her own country, from a city where she had visited many times seemed surreal.

Now, however, a new report came on. There were pictures of a highway jammed with traffic. It was in Chicago. Shawna turned up the volume.

"People are fleeing the city of Chicago today, as a report has come in that this mid-western metropolis might be the next target for a nuclear attack by the Armageddon Brigade. Although there seems to be no way of verifying the rumors, police and FBI officials are frantically searching apartments and public buildings where suspicious behavior has been reported. The citizenry are in a state of panic, many are moving out to be with family members in the smaller cities and rural areas of Illinois and Indiana. Others are leaving with no place to go. Accidents have clogged Interstates and over a hundred traffic fatalities have occurred. Mayor George Romano has called for calm thinking, but his words are falling on deaf ears, with a populace that has been inundated by images of what once was San Francisco."

Shawna switched off the television. She felt guilty about it, but she could take no more. She fell back on her pillow and stared up at the ceiling.

"God help us."

They were the only words she could think of. They were definitely not just a casual expression.

■■■

Ashley looked around the little greasy-spoon cafe. There was nobody there but the cook, who was hitting on the waitress.

"God, Bernard, if you have been leading me on, I will rip open your gut with one of their dirty forks."

"Don't worry, I'm a man of my word."

"Oh, yeah, like when you said I was the only one you were inviting to join you."

"Drop it, will you, Ashley? I told you it would have helped him open up better."

"Yes, well I'm not adverse to using my feminine wiles on a man, but I will be damned if I am going to be part of a harem!"

"Relax. I wasn't trying to put together a harem for anyone. I just know what helps this guy talk. Let's grab a table. He's just a little late. I know he'll be here any minute."

The two of them sat in chairs at a corner table that sat four. The waitress came over and without a word tossed some menus on the table and left again.

"Okay, lousy service and the ambiance of an inner-city bus station. I guess it must be for the cuisine that your guy had us come all the way to Baltimore."

"The lack of business is good. It gives us more privacy. Apart from that I don't know why he insisted on Baltimore in general or this place in particular. I didn't want to ask any questions."

A man with glasses and graying temples appeared at the door. He was heavy, close to three hundred pounds by Ashley's estimation, and probably in his forties. He looked in their direction and headed their way.

Bernard stood up. "Arnold, good to see you, my man. We were beginning to think you had gotten lost. Arnold, this is Ashley Cambridge, the young woman I told you about. Ashley, this is Arnold Culpepper, from Karen Steele's office."

Ashley held out her hand rather demurely. "In the office of the National Security Advisor, huh? I am impressed!"

Arnold gave her an anxious smile. "Uh...so am I, Miss Cambridge, so am I. But we don't really have a lot of time, so let's sit down and order, shall we?"

After giving their orders, Arnold got right down to business. "You two been staying in touch with the news today, or are you just concerned with what everyone else doesn't already know?"

"Hey, we're reporters," responded Bernard. "Of course, we have been following the news."

"Then you've heard about what's going on in Chicago?"

"Certainly. What a mess!"

"A frickin' mess for sure. The whole God-damned nation is tottering on the brink. Do you know, they actually had the report they were next on the list since yesterday noon, and they have been trying to keep a lid on it? They should have done a better job, because now the whole city is flying apart."

"Keep a lid on the threat of a nuclear bomb?" Ashley gasped. "Are you crazy? You want them to let a huge city sit still to be nuked?"

"What good does it do, really? They aren't going to evacuate a city of that size. People just panic and end up killing each other in the panic. Hell, if I were Conrad I would just plant a rumor in every big city in the country, and wait while they killed each other trying to get out. The Chicago scare is probably just that. It wasn't from FBI sources, just some anonymous telephone tip. Hell, the FBI says that Conrad only had three nukes, tops. They used one on San Francisco. They use the others right away, and they lose all their trump cards."

Bernard jumped in: "Okay, so did they know in advance about San Francisco?"

Arnold stared down at his glass of water, which he swirled around a couple of times. "I don't know."

"You don't know or you won't tell us?"

Just then the waitress came with their order. As she distributed the various dishes around the table she seemed to feel obligated to talk about everything from the weather to how the Orioles were doing. None of the three at the table talked, but still she lingered, giving her own theory as to why the Orioles could never quite make it to the Series. Ashley told her "Thank you" three different times, with a tone that she thought conveyed that they were done with her, but to no avail. Bernard was the one to finally put the pleasantries aside.

"Okay...what's your name again?"

"Barbara."

"Okay, Barbara, we're done with you, now. So get the hell away from our table so we can talk."

The waitress stiffened up and glared at him a moment, then she turned and stormed back toward the kitchen.

"She was just doing her job, Bernard," responded Ashley in an indignant tone.

"To hell with her job. She wasn't letting me do my job. So come on, Arnold, answer my question now."

"What, you think you can force answers out of me because you pay me a little money, buy me some second class food and bring along a hot female reporter?"

"I didn't say that."

"Well, it might surprise you, but I'm not here today for any of that, and I don't care how hot she is!" Arnold turned to Ashley. "Listen, no offense, you are beautiful and normally I would share with you my old grandma's most personal secrets, but there are other issues right now."

"Yes," responded Ashley, "I'm sure you're concerned like all of us about what is best for the nation. But as reporters we believe people have a right to know."

Arnold nodded. "I am concerned. I've got to tell you, I'm really concerned."

Arnold diverted his attention to his food, devouring his burger and fries like it were his last meal. All the time he was staring off into a corner of the room and periodically just shaking his head. Ashley and Bernard quietly started eating themselves, hoping that he would loosen up better with less pressure. Their patience was finally rewarded.

"I really don't know, you know."

"About San Francisco?" queried Bernard.

"Yes, about San Francisco. But there have been...rumors. Some people I know say the FBI knew but kept their mouths shut because they don't like Packard or his views. But I haven't seen any hard evidence to confirm that. What scares me most, though, is that it is just part of what I'm seeing. There are a lot of the military types who don't like Packard. Some of them defected. But others just seem to be screwing things up from the inside. Hell, you've got to believe something like that is going on, because otherwise they would have wiped Conrad out by now, nuked him at least."

"But he's on our own soil," objected Ashley, "not to mention he is surrounded by our own citizenry. The fallout, physical and political, would be everywhere!"

117

"He's a cancer, Ms. Cambridge! You burn him right out of there, even if you've got to take some healthy tissue with him, because if you don't he'll be everywhere, and you won't be able to stop him."

"I agree," chimed in Bernard. "God, it seems like we haven't learned a thing from September 11th and dealing with Bin Laden and Hussein and the others."

Arnold gave a cynical laugh. "Learned something? Are you kidding? People talk about the lesson of September 11th, but people haven't the foggiest idea of what it is. You remember that movie that was out a number of years ago, *Memento*?"

The other two both nodded.

"The guy thought he was learning something about who had killed his wife, but he hadn't learned anything. His problem was he couldn't remember anything more than a few minutes old, even when he wrote it down. God, it's like our whole nation is like that guy in *Memento*. Anything we think we have learned has been transmuted into something else by the time we need it for the next situation. Vietnam was that way. And now September 11th."

"So," interjected Ashley, "you say the Chicago authorities shouldn't have said anything about the bomb rumor. Does that mean that if they did know something about San Francisco, they were right in keeping it quiet?"

"Not in keeping it from the President."

"I mean keeping it from the people."

Arnold just sat there slowly shaking his head. Ashley couldn't tell for sure if he was shaking his head "no", or simply trying to shake off some troublesome thought.

"I don't know. I guess I think that Chicago is different. Chicago is probably just a rumor. Conrad has got bigger fish to fry."

"What do you mean?"

Arnold just looked at Ashley a moment. Then he glanced over at Bernard. "You haven't asked me why I changed our meeting from D.C. to here in Baltimore."

"Who the hell cares?" replied Bernard. "There are bigger issues..."

"Why did you change it?" asked Ashley, sensing a new fear behind the official's apparent change of subject.

Fear now seemed to seep into every corner of Arnold's face. His eyes opened wide in a horrified stare off into a completely empty corner of the cafe. He opened his mouth a couple of times before he could manage expelling the words.

"I didn't want our meeting to be interrupted by...by flashes...bright flashes...and heat...and wind..."

"By a nuclear bomb?"

"Yes..."

"By a nuclear bomb?"

"Yes!!"

"D.C. has also received a phone threat?" asked Bernard.

"No. The FBI placed an operative in Conrad's group. Someone he trusted. He got the word from Conrad's own mouth. The guy's a bit of a loose cannon, but I...I believe him."

Ashley suddenly became aware that she was sitting in her own sweat, but it didn't matter.

"When?" she asked. "When, Arnold?"

Arnold shook his head. "He wasn't able to get that information, but he thinks it's soon." Arnold was trembling now. "They've been rotating us in and out of D.C. But I'm scheduled to be there for another month. I'm not going back."

None of the three touched their meal from that point on. Nor did any of them speak. Bernard and Ashley paid the bill and then went out to Bernard's car. They just sat there quietly for several more minutes.

Ashley finally whispered: "The Baltimore airport."

Bernard nodded. "The Baltimore airport."

Ashley thought of Shawna. She wondered if she should say anything.

Chapter Eight

Drew Covington climbed to the top of the hill, and looked down at the city – or what was left of it. He couldn't believe what he was seeing. San Francisco, city of romance, elegance and trolley cars, was basically gone. In its place was a gaping hole, partially filled in by the waters of the bay. He had been to this city so many times. Here he had honeymooned with his wife. Obviously that was when they were still in love. That was when hanging around Fisherman's Wharf, feeding the seals and strolling along the boardwalk was a timeless heaven, a heaven that didn't bring with it the panic of unmet deadlines; but rather promised there would always be enough time, and that one could enjoy eternal moments where love was all that mattered. They had visited the city much later in their marriage, in an effort to recapture the old passions, but they weren't there anymore. In their place was a melancholy that lingered with the fog, as Drew had walked the streets alone, seeking to find direction.

The streets were gone now, and the fog was more of a menacing radioactive haze. Drew felt the zipper on the protective suit he had been issued, and he wondered how much protection it really offered. At best it was protection from the present moment. You could not look at the gap that had once been San Francisco, and believe that there was any real protection from the dangers of the morrow. Drew signaled to the photographer who had come with him and they trudged back down the hill. Then they loaded their gear in the rental car and drove back to the refugee camp set up in Pleasant Hill.

The refugee settlement in Pleasant Hill, like many of the others in the area, was set up on the grounds of a large new church building. The church had a gym and workout area, and with it the showers that the refugees needed. Volunteers from a variety of local congregations helped with meals, as well as with the care of children whose parents were either dead, or had not yet been located.

Drew had volunteered for this assignment after his interview of Conrad. After getting a better picture of how Conrad thought, he wanted to see this result of Conrad's thinking processes. It had been sobering. That morning he had had to watch a fifteen-year old girl die. She had burns over seventy percent of her body. She should have been on the telephone flirting with boys, shopping at the mall, or driving her parents crazy with loud music. Instead, she was lying in a make-shift hospital bed, trying not to think of the pain, and wondering where her parents and friends were. Drew was holding her hand, one of the few unburned parts of her body, as she died.

Drew now looked out over the streets between the church and the hospital. On one corner were a large number of demonstrators, holding up signs like, "The End is Near," and "Don't be Left Behind." Some of the demonstrators themselves showed marks of weathering the conflagration – body burns, singed hair and scarred spirits. Unlike what Drew was used to seeing with such religious demonstrations, this group was attracting a lot of attention. Some persons were kneeling in prayer. Others seemed to be involved in vehement arguments. Few persons simply passed by. Drew could hear the whirring of his associate's camera.

As Drew moved closer to this group, a middle-aged man ran up to him. His clothing was tattered and there were burns on his face and arms.

"Sir, did you know that Jesus is coming soon? We are entering a time of great tribulation after which Jesus will take his own to himself. Please tell me that you are ready to go with him!"

"Uh...I have some time. Why don't you tell me more about this?"

"He's coming soon. There is a lot I don't know – all the signs and all. Others in our group know it better, and I'm kind of new to this. I was a stockbroker in San Francisco, and not paying much attention to God. I was raised in a little Baptist church. I don't know why I turned away. I guess it was the money, and everything seemed so...so good. I had a big house and a nice family. They're all gone now. I didn't know what I had. But, let me tell you, this has woken me up! My wife, she was a Christian before. I'm going to see her when I go with Jesus!"

Tears were steaming down the man's face, and without even thinking about it Drew reached out with his hand and brushed some of them away. His own action startled him because he never before would have so gently touched another man's face. Still, the man seemed a little comforted.

"I don't know the Bible really well," said Drew, "but I do remember a verse that says, 'He will wipe every tear from their eyes.' I think that's what God would say to you right now."

The man broke down and reached out and hugged Drew with all that was left of his strength. This also was something that Drew had rarely done with a man, and yet now he could think of nothing more appropriate. He only wondered how painful it must be for a man with such burns. Drew eased away from the man and looked into his eyes.

"Thanks for worrying about me. I believe in a God of grace, and I will be all right. Go and care for others, and I will pray for you."

The man nodded and immediately began looking for others with whom to share his story. Drew watched him head off toward an older man who was coming out of his apartment. Then Drew turned and continued on his way toward the church.

Interestingly enough there was no proselytizing going on in the church itself. Perhaps it was because people were so busy running around caring for burns, fetching water for parched throats, and cleaning floors dirtied by those who's sensitive stomachs regurgitated their lunch. The senior pastor of the church was doing just that right now, down on his knees not before a cross, but before a bent-over old man. The man was apologizing profusely for the involuntary action, and a young woman was trying to convince him it was okay and that he should lie down on his side of one of the over-crowded beds.

Off to Drew's left there was an old man wearing a yarmulke, dress shoes, jeans and a corduroy shirt buttoned up to the top button. He kept trying to get the attention of the volunteers who passed by quickly.

"Excuse me!...Excuse me!"

Perhaps because he seemed like one of the healthiest persons there, no one was stopping. Drew walked over in his direction. The man saw him coming and his eyes lit up.

"Excuse me, sir. I am Jonathan Weisel. I was wondering if you could answer some questions for me?"

"If I can. But I gotta tell you, I'm as confused right now as the next guy."

"So we share our confusion. That can be good, too, right?"

"Sometimes it's the best you can do."

"Okay, now, you've been walking around this place, right – the church, the town?"

"Yes."

"Have you run across any other Jewish people?"

"Well, none who have identified themselves as such – or who were wearing the little hat."

"Yarmulke. Yes, well, I was afraid of that. I don't know what I'm going to do. The people of this church are very nice to care for us and all, but tonight the Sabbath begins and I have no one to celebrate it with."

"I imagine the pastor would be the best one to ask about that. He's pretty busy right now, but I'll see if I can help you get his attention."

"That would be most kind of you."

Jonathan looked at Drew for a moment with a more sober demeanor. Then he put his hand on Drew's shoulder.

"Tell me, my son, are you a Christian?"

The directness of the question took Drew off-guard. In a less direct, less open way he had been asking himself the same question of late. Could he call himself by the same name as those who had blown up this city? Was he of the same religious perspective of those who stood out on the street corner right now, warning people of the coming wrath of God? Then he thought of Christ himself. He thought of what Christ had taught. He thought of what Christ had promised and claimed.

"Yes...yes, I am."

Jonathan nodded. "And do you believe your Christ is coming back soon to take people to God?"

"I don't know. If he is, he certainly didn't mean to do it this way."

"No, I think not. Jesus – Jeshua – was at least a good Jew, I think. He would not have his people blow up a city. Do you remember the story of Jonah?"

"Sure – the whale and all."

"At the end of that book, God talks to Jonah, who wants him to blow up the city of Ninevah, because they are Israel's enemies. He wants to blow up a city of hundreds of thousands of people. God tells him, 'You have been concerned about this vine, although you did not tend it or make it grow. It sprang up overnight and died overnight. But Ninevah has more than a hundred and twenty-thousand people who cannot tell their right hand from their left, and many cattle as well. Should I not be concerned about that great city?'"

Jonathan looked directly in Drew's eyes. "Those who did not know their right hand from their left were the children. Jonah wanted to blow up children and innocent animals to vindicate himself and his people. Those were the ones your Christian friends blew up in San Francisco."

"They aren't my friends, Jonathan."

"Of course, of course! I know. You are a good man. I guess I have you here, so I'm telling you. I have to say, I'm a little bitter. Every time Christians talk about Jesus coming back, they talk about leaving the Jews behind. What? Do they think Jews don't want to go be with God? We practically invented him! When I was a child, my older sister always wanted my parents to leave me behind. 'He's in the car. Let's go quickly!' she would say. Fifty miles later my parents stop and I'm not there. So, I'm a little touchy about this 'left behind' business."

Drew smiled, then turned his attention to the more serious issues the man was addressing. "I guess I'm glad that I'm not the judge of that. But I do believe in Jesus, Jonathan. I guess that is different than you."

"Of course, of course. But it might surprise you to know that I know some things about Jesus. 'When you feed the hungry, clothe the naked or visit the sick, you do it to me' – not those words, but something like that. Maybe also, 'When you incinerate your neighbors, it burns me up.' Hey, that's pretty good! The Jonathan Weisel Version. So maybe we have little radiated molecules of Jesus falling on our heads. Do you think that is as good as baptism? Maybe God will take me after all!"

Drew laughed. "They should have you entertaining their guests here. 'Three shows daily. No waiting.'"

"No, I know me and I would demand my own trailer. They don't have the space."

Drew thought of how good it was to smile and wondered how long it had been since he had been able to do that.

"No, but it's pretty dark humor," Jonathan continued, "and I'm not sure how healthy that would be for a lot of people around here. Seriously, though, I look around here at the people, old people with burns, children sick from the radiation, and I think maybe I would like to talk to God. Not a long talk – I know he must be busy, but a talk. 'People...really? What were you thinking? The world would have been so much better with a few more varieties of talking birds. They are good company, really! And the good thing is that they don't blow each other up. Hand them a gun and they fall off their perch. Okay, so they bomb windshields and statues just a little, but you clean it off with a little Windex, and all is forgiven. And they make the children smile. Children...with little freckles across the bridge of their nose...big brown eyes...laughter that gurgles like a mountain stream...children who bounce into every room like they own it, and call to you, 'Grandpa...won't you play a game with me...?'"

Jonathan's lip was now trembling and tears were streaming down his face. Drew's own eyes moistened and his throat felt thick. It was several minutes before Drew was able to speak again.

"What was her name?"

"Renae. She was four." He held up five fingers before Drew's eyes. "Five in September."

Drew reached over and grabbed Jonathan's hand firmly. He squeezed the hand several times. He wanted to also say some words of reassurance, something about hope and the eternal survival of an innocent spirit. But there were no words. He made his living by words, but now that he really needed them, they deserted him. Not so with Jonathan.

"You know, normally I wouldn't say anything, but if they see us sitting here holding hands, they might bomb us."

Drew's smile returned, and he dropped Jonathan's hand back into his own lap as if it were a borrowed comb.

"Hey, I need to go see that pastor right now. Do you still want me to see about whether there are other Jews around?"

"Would you? That would be most helpful."

After assuring Jonathan of his assistance, Drew began looking around the packed facility for the senior pastor. When Drew found him he was signing for a delivery of food in the kitchen.

"Hello, Pastor Roberts. I'm Drew Covington of *The Oregonian*. I realize you are a very busy man, but you told me that you might have some time about now to do an interview with me for the paper. Is that still going to work for you?"

"Sure, I'll make it work. I need the break anyway."

Frank Roberts, Drew knew from advance information, was a man in his early fifties, and yet he retained the muscular build of a construction worker. He was about 6'2" and Drew estimated him at around 225 pounds. He was balding in the middle, but one still would describe him as having ruggedly handsome features. He moved with the brisk step of a man of action, and he spoke with the confidence of one who was used to being listened to.

Pastor Roberts ushered Drew into his office, and shut the door behind them. The office was not as large as Drew's own, but it featured a large mahogany desk, a couple of leather overstuffed chairs and a library that filled three of the walls with very few gaps. The pastor had to take a phone call and Drew took the opportunity to examine some of the volumes. He found everything from current best-sellers to hardbound classics by Augustine, John Calvin, and John Bunyan. Paintings of Mother Teresa and Martin Luther King Jr. hung near his desk.

The pastor hung up the phone and sat down at his desk. "Okay, what can I do for you?"

"Well, before we start I promised one of your residents that I would ask you, are there any synagogues or gatherings of Jewish people around here?"

"Oh, certainly, certainly. There is a small synagogue right down the street. Point the man out to me and I'll be glad to direct him."

"Great. I'll do that." Drew thought of all he had seen that day. "You're doing some pretty impressive work here, Pastor."

"We're helping where we can, but the job is much bigger than us."

"I think I told you that my editor wants me to write a series of articles about the impact of the bomb on the surrounding towns and the people who survived. I assume you help people with spiritual direction. What are some of the issues you are having to deal with?"

"That would take more than a series of articles in a newspaper. It would take volumes – three or four Michener-size novels, at least. I guess you start with the mourning of the dead. How do you do it? You look at a person and all of a sudden a spasm of pain comes to their face, and you know they just thought of one more person they'll never see again. It's hard enough to mourn a mother or a child or a spouse, but when there are also aunts and uncles and cousins, and best friends from college, how do you do it? And it's not just the refugees, either. I lost a brother and a number of former parishioners, and every volunteer in this church could tell a similar story. We just end up crying together. I guess that's all you can do."

"And how do you deal with the fact that the group responsible feels strongly that they're doing God's will, and that they are enacting God's judgment on evil at the end of time?"

"Before this happened, I remember seeing a bumper sticker that said, 'God protect me from your followers.' I was kind of irritated by it at the time, but now I just keep thinking about how appropriate it is. Jesus revealed a God of grace and mercy. But there are a lot of people around who cannot handle a God of grace and mercy, because for them the main function of God is to zap those they don't approve of. They want to strike out at the world, and the judgment of God gives them an excuse.

"I'm not saying that God never gets angry or judges anyone. E.J. Conrad, for one, will have to face God's judgment. But I just have this strong belief that God is a lot more gracious with us than we generally are with each other."

Drew found himself getting so wrapped up in the minister's answers that he almost forgot why he was asking the questions. He was glad that he had remembered to turn on his mini-recorder, because he was too preoccupied to remember to write things down.

"The grace of God – how do you help people who have gone through all of this experience anything like the grace of God?"

"John tells us in 1 John 4:12, 'No one has ever seen God; but if we love one another, God lives in us and his love is made complete in us.' That is what we try to do here – let God's love live in us. If these people can see God's love in us, they can find hope."

The pastor paused with his mouth slightly open, and looked off into an empty corner of the room, as if searching for one more thought that was eluding him. After a few seconds, his gaze returned to Drew.

"Also, a lot of these people feel such a strong need for...for vindication, for forgiveness. It's as if somehow they feel responsible for the fact that they survived while others were not so fortunate. Their brother was 'the good one' who should have lived. Their innocent child should have lived while their own cynical confusion should have perished. We all have this concept of what justice demands, and generally somewhere in our mind we say that justice demands that we die. I guess that may be what is behind the atoning death of Christ on the cross. Christ died to pay the penalty that we have convinced ourselves that we owe.

Meanwhile, we see nothing but innocence in our loved ones who have died.

"What we do for these people is listen to their guilt and reassure them once again of the basics of the Christian faith. We all are sinners. We are all forgiven by God's grace."

Drew leaned forward and peered into the clergyman's eyes. "Pastor, what about the Second Coming? Could it be that Christ is indeed coming again? We really have messed the world up. Don't you think he might want to come back soon to, you know, fix it all?"

Frank Roberts smiled. "I get the feeling that isn't just a professional 'for-the-article' question. I get the feeling that question comes out of your own personal struggle."

Drew nodded. "You see, I've interviewed E.J. Conrad, and yes he's gone off the deep end, and yes, he's rationalized his own acts of violence. But the man genuinely believes Jesus is coming and with him a better world. And, forgive me, but it seems that so many Christian ministers have given up on that. Everything is going to keep on like before, and all we can expect is a sweet little sandaled Jesus walking beside us while our children get abducted and raped, while AIDS and cancer ravage the innocent as well as the guilty, and while the power-hungry rule the world in their greed. Isn't it supposed to be better than that? When does justice get to really rule on this planet? Will the meek really inherit the earth or is that all bullshit? Er...excuse the language, but you know what I mean."

Reverend Roberts picked up Drew's mini-recorder and held it up nearer to Drew's mouth. "Keep going. This is going to be one heck of an article."

Drew laughed. "Okay, so I kind of reversed the process here a little."

"No, it's okay. I like what you were saying." The Pastor walked over to one section of his library to the left of his desk. "I have volumes and volumes on eschatology. I took a course on it in seminary, and I've read most all of the books by those popular authors who claim they understand it all, and you know what? I still don't know a damn thing. That's all, Drew. Put that in your article. I don't know a damn thing. Well, except maybe what Jesus said, 'I will come like a thief in the night.' And, oh yes, one more thing – that I'm called to pray, 'Thy kingdom come, thy will be done, on earth as it is in heaven.' That's all I know. But I pray that prayer every day, and all the more earnestly now that all of this has happened. Because, you know, there's one little scenario you left out of your passionate, insightful question: I don't like sitting around while a man who thinks he's God's messenger blows up a city I loved that was full of God's children."

One lone tear trickled down the pastor's cheek. He shut his eyes, and Drew wasn't certain whether it was to stop further tears from coming or the flow of memories that had brought on that tear. In either case they both sat silently while that lone drop meandered down the clergyman's cheek to his chin.

It took several more minutes in all before Drew was able to quietly brave his next question: "If Jesus comes...do you think you will be one of those going with him?"

Frank Roberts sighed deeply. "I suppose that depends on which Jesus comes."

"What do you mean?"

The pastor looked once again directly into Drew's eyes. "If it's the Jesus I see in the Bible, I would follow that man anywhere. That's why I'm in the profession I am in. But if it's the Jesus of E.J. Conrad, or the Jesus of those who are looking for even a God-initiated blood bath...well, I think even if he wants me, I'll say, 'No, thanks. Just leave me here to minister to the bleeding. And you know what? I think the Jesus of Scripture would say the same thing."

"But doesn't Revelation refer to a bloody tribulation initiated by God?"

Roberts shook his head. "Drew, Revelation was written for Christians who were getting the crap kicked out of them by Rome. The book was about the fall of Rome, the antichrist was the emperor Domitian, who they thought was Nero come back to life, and the apostate church they were worried about were the Christians who were buckling under the pressure. Revelation gave them hope because in its veiled language it spoke of the fall of

Rome and the triumph of the church over Rome's violence. That has all happened. Yes, it does have a general vision for the kind of world God will eventually bring, much like the prophet Isaiah gave, but he wasn't giving any blueprints for that. We don't get any blueprints. We do our part and trust God for the rest. That's the deal."

There was an urgent knocking at the door. The pastor gave the okay and the door swung open. An anxious elderly gentleman appeared.

"Pastor Roberts, they are rioting out front again. We've called for the police, but I think we need you."

The minister bolted toward the door, and Drew followed right behind. Near the church door a church layman handed the pastor a little sack, and then the minister ran outside. When they reached the streets, Drew could see that on the corner where the demonstrators had been, there was a much larger group that had erupted in violence. Fists were being thrown, and even a few rocks and bottles were flying through the air.

Pastor Roberts ran to a nearby bus bench, stood on it, pulled a gun from the sack and then fired it into the air. Those fighting let go of each other and looked around for the source of the gunfire. Frank Roberts fired again.

"Okay, that's enough! The police are on their way. Unless you want to be hauled off to jail, you've got to stop this, right now!"

Drew looked around for his photographer. He found him off to the right, doing his job, and so Drew's attention returned to the confrontation. A burly man in a torn shirt and with about a week's growth of hair on his face stepped out of the crowd toward the minister.

"Who the hell cares about going to some damn jail! We don't have homes any more. We don't have families any more! Don't you get it? And it's all the fault of religious fanatics like these guys, and like YOU, Preacher! You want to send us all to hell? Well, we're taking you with us!"

People throughout the crowd erupted in cries of approval.

"You got that right!"

"You tell 'em, Karl!"

"Kill 'em all!"

The pastor fired another shot into the air, and its effect was less than before, though enough to talk over the crowd. "You can't spread the violence like this! It's what Conrad wants, and it will only make things worse!"

The man who had been identified as Karl flung his fist into the air. "Worse for you, maybe! Pull him down!"

Another gunshot went totally unheeded as people in the crowd pulled Frank Roberts from the bench. As one more gunshot sounded Drew saw the face of the pastor wrench in pain, and then he fell beneath the level of the mob that now surrounded him.

Drew found himself running toward the mob and shouting. "Pastor's down! Pastor's down!"

Drew's words fell on deaf ears as people throughout the crowd were swinging fists at each other. Picket signs were now becoming weapons, sometimes in the hands of those who had originally carried them, and sometimes in the hands of persons who had confiscated them. Drew pushed past a couple of young men who were bloodying each other's face, and then someone jumped on his back and started beating on his head and shoulders. Drew fell to the ground and rolled over, dislodging his attacker. Drew hit him with a sharp blow to the face and the man's head recoiled back against the pavement, knocking him out. The crowd was now packed in around him so tightly that he could hardly breathe, but Drew struggled desperately to his feet. He was no longer sure where Frank Roberts had fallen, but somehow he must find the one who had given his life to rescue others.

Drew pushed and shoved his way past two groups of combatants when suddenly a post from a picket sign cut across the right side of his head and shoulder. He staggered as blood began streaming down his face past his right eye. Still, Drew was determined not to be stopped, and he careened past another group before being shoved and falling on a bench. It was the bench upon which the pastor had been standing before being shot. Drew dropped to his hands and knees and looked around at ground level.

He spied a body about fifteen feet to the left, and he sprung to his feet, tossing aside several demonstrators before reaching his target.

Frank Roberts' abdomen was covered in blood, his eyes were wide and he was gasping for breath. Upon seeing Drew he latched onto his arm with the little strength he had left.

"Okay, I think the gun...the gun was a bad idea."

"Oh, you think?!" responded Drew. "Don't talk!"

Drew wrapped his arms underneath the injured man's upper legs and lower back.

"Okay, this is going to be tough for us both, but we've got to get you out of here. You ready?"

"You can't carry me," gasped the Pastor. "You're hurt, and I'm too big!"

"Then pray, because we're going!"

Drew pushed off with his legs and lifted the man up in one smooth motion. Still, he winced as he felt something pull in his abdominal area. Frank Roberts cried out in agony, but he quickly stuffed his own fist in his mouth to stifle any further screams. Drew staggered past several combatants, but they let him pass apparently thinking that the two of them had been bloodied enough already. Between the blood and the sweat in his eyes, he could hardly see where he was going, but he just kept walking away from the loudest screams and cries of the melee. The muscles in his arms seemed on fire; his legs threatened to buckle, but he just kept telling himself to move a few more steps, and then a few more. Suddenly, there was someone trying to pull the injured man from his arms.

"No!" he cried, seeking to swing the pastor away from the invader. Then through the only area of his left eye which he could see through at all, he recognized a couple of the laymen of the church.

"Hey! We've got him! We've got him! It's okay. You can let go."

Drew relaxed his arms, and as he did, the world started to swirl around him, and the voices he heard merged into an indiscernible static, like a radio between stations.

The next thing Drew knew, he was lying in one of the beds inside the church. An older African-American woman, one of the volunteer nurses, was tending to a bandage on his head. Drew could manage but one short utterance.

"The pastor?"

"Yes, yes. We think Pastor Roberts will be okay. He lost a lot of blood, but thanks to you, he's going to make it. Man, were you in the Marines or somethin'? We couldn't believe how you pulled him out of that mess!"

Drew tried to shake his head "no", but it hurt too much.

"Now, now, no need to try to answer me! I ask questions all the time, but there's no need to answer. I can do the talkin' all by myself. You're a hero around here now. Everybody loves Pastor Roberts. Of course, several others tried to get to him, but they didn't make it. A couple of them were hurt pretty bad, too. It's a good thing the police came. With all they have to do these days, we weren't too sure. But they came, and threw some of those hotheads in jail. Man, this world is gettin' to be such a mess. I hope Jesus comes soon. That E.J. Conrad, he thinks Jesus is goin' to be pleased with him when he comes, but he's got another think comin'! Jesus said, 'Who then is a faithful and wise servant, whom his lord hath made ruler over his household, to give them meat in due season? Blessed is that servant, whom his lord when he cometh shall find so doing.' And THEN he talked about the EVIL servant who begins to smite his fellow servants, and the lord would come and 'cut him asunder.' That's what Jesus will do. I sure guess droppin' bombs on people qualifies as 'smitin' fellow servants,' wouldn't you? Now, don't you answer me! Yessir, droppin' bombs will get the judgment of the Almighty, for sure. Especially nuclear bombs. First San Francisco...and now D.C...."

"What?"

The nurse looked down into Drew's eyes. "Oh, that's right. I forgot, you have been out for a little while. It wasn't five minutes after we got all of those rioters out of here that we heard on the news that a nuclear bomb exploded in D.C. Apparently the news had reported that there were rumors they would be a target just hours before they were hit, but..."

Drew started thrashing in his bed, trying to get up. The nurse grabbed his arms and held him down.

"Hold on, Son! Where do you think you're goin'? You're an injured man! You may have acted like Superman out there pullin' Pastor Roberts out of the mob, but let me tell ya', you ain't him!"

"I got friends in D.C.! They're there now!"

"Yeah, and I had friends in San Francisco, but it's too late for them, and I hate to say it, but if your friends were still in D.C., it's probably too late for them too. You've gotta take care of you right now."

"No! It's not too late for them. It can't be too late! You've got to help me get on a plane."

Drew started pulling back the covers, but the nurse grabbed his arms again and called for help. A couple of male nurses came quickly and they helped hold Drew down while she administered a sedative. As it began to take effect, faces flashed into Drew's mind. The face of Ashley. The face of Shawna. The face of Ashley was as she was when he saw her last, lively and smiling because of the new opportunity given to her. The face of Shawna was sad and full of tears, but just inches from his own face, with parted lips. Only the sedative would be able to take that face out of his mind.

Chapter Nine

The first Drew knew that he had fallen asleep was when the "ding" of the "Fasten Seat Belts" sign startled him awake. The captain then came on, announcing that they were approaching the Baltimore Washington International airport, and by the time he had finished his spiel Drew was back in touch with his present reality. Looking down at the seat beside him probably helped in this process, as he saw there the focused, wide-awake face of a worried five-year old. Drew had flown from Sacramento to Portland simply with the intent to find Jeremy at the home of the neighbor who cared for him, give him some words of reassurance and then head off to see if he could find Jeremy's mother. Jeremy would have none of it. Drew had told him that it could be dangerous being in the area, and that it was no place for a little boy. He had also told him that his mother would want him to be safe at home, and that he could search more quickly if he didn't have to keep an eye on a little boy. Jeremy didn't wail and flail about as Drew had expected. He didn't scream angry, out-of-control words. He simply looked up at Drew's face with a haunted sadness, and a little tear streaming down his face, and whispered, "Please, Mr. Covington, please! I gotta help you find my mommy!" From that moment Drew knew that all resistance was futile.

"My ears feel funny."

Jeremy's words brought Drew back to the present, and he handed the boy a stick of gum. "Here, chew this for a while."

"Do you think my mommy will be at the airport?"

"I don't think so. We're probably going to have to look for a long time. I just don't know, Jeremy."

137

Jeremy took hold of Drew's hand and looked out the window as he chewed his gum. All of the sudden Drew didn't know if he was really ready to be landing yet. He didn't know if he was ready to handle his own inner turmoil, and a little child as well. But regardless of his mental state, the plane kept on descending.

As the plane banked to the left, Drew looked past Jeremy's head and out the window. There he could see in the distance a giant crater, partially filled with water, where Washington D.C., the nation's capital, used to be. A collective moan echoed throughout that whole side of the cabin, and Drew found himself contributing to the pained reaction. He could hear a woman in the seat behind him starting to cry, and that reaction also seemed to spread throughout those seated on that side of the 737.

After such a jarring approach the actual landing was remarkably smooth. No sooner did the jet finish taxiing to the terminal, than Jeremy had sprung up from his seat, pushed past Drew and started to make a mad dash down the aisle. Drew had to grab him quickly.

"Wait, Jeremy, wait! We have our things in the overhead. You don't want to leave without them, do you? Besides, we have to wait our turn."

"But I want to go find my mom!"

Drew lifted Jeremy into his lap.

"I want to find your mom, too, Jeremy. But you know it's going to be difficult. It's going to take time. We'll leave our things in the hotel, and we'll start right away. You have to promise me that you won't run ahead of me. You have to promise that you'll let me lead here. I know places to look. But this is a big city, and I don't want to lose you. Your mom would never forgive me if that happened. Will you promise me?"

Jeremy nodded and then threw his arms around Drew's neck, burying his head in his chest. Drew held him tightly. At the same time he wondered if maybe he shouldn't have just run down the aisle with Jeremy, leaving behind his luggage, his atypical deference to politeness and, more relevantly, his fears of what this search might bring. Maybe he should make "and a little child shall lead them" the order of the day. Would it matter that much in the long run?

Drew stood up, sat Jeremy down, and pulled their two small bags out of the overhead. They had packed lightly, avoiding having to check anything through, and for that foresight Drew was thankful, especially since in other ways he hadn't been thinking that clearly. He looked down the aisle at the assortment of persons that now filled it waiting their chance to exit. In the days to come there would be many more such persons whom they would have to find their way past in order to have any chance at all of accomplishing their mission. He would have to have the optimism and energy of the child standing next to him to get it done.

"Okay, Jeremy. You can go first. But hold onto my hand so you don't lose me."

When they reached the terminal, they found it so packed with people that they had to struggle for every step forward they took. Jeremy kept wanting to tunnel under groups of people, and Drew had to keep reminding him that he couldn't do that, especially while carrying their luggage. When they reached the main concourse, Drew picked up Jeremy and stood up on one of the seats in a lobby area, in order to get a clearer view of where to go for ground transportation. He saw the signs off to his left, and he was beginning to climb down when a face on the other side of the concourse caught his eye. At first people kept passing in front of her, so he couldn't be sure, but then she turned his direction, just as the crowd temporarily cleared. The face was familiar and unmistakable. It was Ashley Cambridge. Drew yelled and waved, but his efforts were useless. The din of the crowd drowned out his every effort. Drew jumped down from the chair, and still holding Jeremy he started to push his way through.

"Who's Ashley?" shouted Jeremy, picking up on the excitement. "Does she know my mom?"

"I don't think so. But she might know something that will help us look."

When they got close to the spot where Ashley had been, Drew started yelling out her name. No response. He pushed past people in the direction that he thought she might have been going and he yelled some more. Jeremy yelled out the name as well.

"Ashley! Ashley!"

Drew heard what sounded like it may have been a response coming from near some pay phones, so he started moving in that direction, and yelled some more. Suddenly he heard a distinct response in a familiar voice.

"Drew!"

Underneath the limited shelter of one of the phone booths stood Ashley Cambridge. He ran up to her, let Jeremy slip down to the floor and threw his arms around her.

"Oh, God, I can't believe it's you!" she exclaimed. "I haven't been able to get through to anyone since the bomb!"

"How did you get out?"

"Didn't Harold tell you? I had an interview here in Baltimore. The guy was high level in Karen Steele's office. He told me the FBI had a warning the bomb was coming. But it wasn't an hour after we started reporting it that the bomb was detonated! God, I've been feeling so scared and alone!"

Ashley sought to hold Drew even closer, but he pushed her to arm's length.

"You haven't been able to get through to anyone since the bomb?"

"No. It seems to have really messed up both cell phone usage and e-mail. Circuits on conventional phones are constantly overloaded."

Drew looked down at Jeremy's worried face.

"You gave people about an hour's warning, you say? Do you know if many people were able to get out?"

"Some, maybe. A lot of them probably thought it was just another rumor. Still, I hear the highways jammed up really fast."

"Ashley, you remember Shawna Forester. She was in D.C. for a meeting at the Hilton..."

"Yes, I saw her."

"You saw her!"

Ashley nodded.

"Did she come with you?"

"Uh...no...we invited her. But she was tired and wanted to go to her room to rest."

"Her room in downtown D.C.?"

Ashley nodded again. "I'm sorry...I mean, we tried..."

For the first time Ashley seemed to notice the boy who was with Drew.

"Is this...?"

"Her son..."

Ashley's face turned white and her mouth quivered. "I...uh..."

Drew was afraid of looking down at Jeremy himself, and thankfully the boy wasn't saying anything he would have to respond to. He felt light-headed, but he fought to retain his wits about him. Nothing was certain. There had to be hope. There had to be some possible way....

"What have you heard about refugees? People who got out by car...people who survived the blast and who came in this direction...?"

"Yeah, well...the hospitals, of course... I heard they're way overcrowded...Oh! and I heard that they have set up kind of a tent city over at Camden Yard."

"Camden Yard?"

"Yeah, where the Orioles play...normally."

"Yeah, I knew that. I just...okay, Jeremy, that's where we need to go."

Ashley was now breathing in short, rapid breaths, and Drew worried that she might hyperventilate. "Ashley, are you going to be okay?"

"Me, sure...uh, I'll go with you, okay? I might get some stories there, and, well, I don't want to be alone right now."

"Do you have a car?"

"No. I got here with a guy who left town on the first plane he could get on. I would have too, except Harold insisted I stay. I don't know why I listened. I'm not a selfless person, Drew, you know that. And a story just isn't worth all this."

"Okay, then, I guess it's the bus. There ought to be an express between here and Camden Yard, wouldn't you think?"

"I think so."

"Well, we'll drop our things off at the hotel, and take the next one in, then."

It took nearly an hour for them to squeeze their way out to the ground transportation area, get on the shuttle to their hotel, which was a little over a mile away, and then get to the hotel itself. By the time they reached their room, Drew was ready to collapse, but he knew they had to keep going, not only for Jeremy's sake, but for his own. Ashley's report of Shawna's disposition such a short time before the blast had stunned him, and yet it had also filled him with a new sense of urgency. Had she survived the blast, she would need them with her as soon as possible. If she had not survived...well, that was just not something to consider right now.

Drew learned that the express bus to Camden Yard stopped right in front of their hotel, and for that he was thankful. When they got to the stop, however, they found a crowd of people already waiting. The first bus filled to overflowing before they could get on and so they waited for the next. During their wait, Drew imagined scenarios whereby Shawna may have escaped the bomb's destruction. She changed her mind and sought to catch up with Ashley and her reporter friend. She got a burst of renewed energy and decided to go for a bus ride. She heard the rumors in time to escape. None of them seemed too likely.

Drew found himself looking at Ashley, and having new questions come to his mind. They were disturbing questions, but questions which he ultimately decided to voice.

"Ashley...?"

"Huh?"

"How long did you say it was between when you learned of the bomb from that guy, and the time it was actually detonated?"

"Well...I didn't exactly say. It was maybe an hour and a half."

"So...enough time to call the downtown Hilton, and let Shawna know..."

Ashley visibly tensed up. "I had to get the report in to Harold. That was my first priority. There were a lot of people who needed to know. As it was, we were only able to get the word out to the public about an hour before the blast. There were a lot of things to talk through, you know, not wanting to create any more of a public panic than was necessary and all. I had a lot of things on my mind..."

"You knew she was a friend..."

Ashley's jaw set firmly and she closed her eyes. "Drew, please, I did the best I could."

"You did?"

Just then the next bus pulled up, and Drew let it serve as an excuse for Ashley not answering his question. It was just as well. Drew knew that no sufficient answer probably existed anyway.

The bus was packed probably beyond the level of normal safety considerations. The three of them had to stand, and even then it was shoulder to shoulder. Drew picked up Jeremy so he wouldn't get crushed, and probably also for a little mutual reassurance. Drew noticed that Ashley kept looking at Jeremy, and then looking away.

When they got to the stadium at Camden Yard, quite a few people on the bus got off with them, apparently with a similar agenda to their own. Once Jeremy could see which way they were going, Drew could no longer restrain him, and he ran ahead. Drew and Ashley ran after him, not to stop him, but to avoid losing him.

When they reached the lower level of the spectator area, Jeremy stopped and the adults caught up with him. Drew picked him up and they looked out over what normally was the playing field. Tents were packed almost right up against each other. A large tent with a red cross on it was situated near the home team bullpen. Persons were also scattered throughout the seating area, some just sitting down as if they were watching a game, some asleep in awkward positions, and some lying down on the steps.

Jeremy threw his arms around Drew's neck and buried his face in his chest. "There are too many people! We'll never find her!"

Drew stroked the little boy's head and held him tightly. "No, no. Don't say that. It's good that there are a lot of people. These are all people who got away after the bomb went off. It's good that there are a lot of them. We'll just have to be patient that's all. We'll have to look really carefully."

Drew really was heartened by the number of people there. Perhaps it didn't make much sense, but somehow it said to him that the chances of Shawna having gotten out were a little better than he had feared. Still, because there were a lot of people, searching through all of them would take a lot of time, and Drew didn't feel any more patient about it than Jeremy. If there were just something that could speed the process up, where they could sift through all the people there quickly, or where if Shawna were there she could be assured of seeing them. That's when he saw it – just beyond the center field fence, the Sony JumboTron. He remembered years before when he went to a Seattle Mariners game with his little nephew, his nephew had been doing a little dance in the aisles between innings and they had put him on the JumboTron there. Relatives had seen him and commented on it later. The cameras were probably here. If he could get Jeremy's picture up on the JumboTron, and Shawna were anywhere in that park, she could see him! Other people in the stadium could do the same thing. But he was going to lay first claim. He would just have to find the right person to talk to. He would rely on any power recognition of his name could muster. And if that didn't work, well, as a reporter he did have a little experience breaking into places where people thought he didn't belong.

■■i

There are few experiences more disconcerting to an introverted person than to be under stress in a foreign place, surrounded by strange people, and having nowhere to turn to find some time to yourself. That is where Shawna Forester found herself. Tents were everywhere on the field. She looked up at the stands and there too people were everywhere...Wait!... everywhere except that patch of empty seats high up in the upper deck. It would take a while to get up there, but the one thing she had right now was time. She started to climb the stairs in the direction of her target.

What Shawna didn't have was anything that would help her get home. She had no ID, no checkbook, debit card, or credit cards. She had left her purse in the hotel. And now there was nothing left of it. It was all atomized – along with her driver's license, her lip gloss, the gum she had bought that morning, and her pictures of Jeremy. Why was she thinking of that right now? Hundreds of thousands of people were probably dead, and she was thinking of the contents of her purse.

She could have been there with her purse. She had thought that when she got home from the meeting, she was going to hit the bed and be out like a light. Had she done so she would have never woken up. What had kept that from happening? The disturbing reports on the news had been part of it, but as she thought back she knew that she was going to have trouble even before she turned the television on. That's why she had turned it on. She wanted to get her mind off of what Ashley Cambridge had said about Drew and "what they have together." That was surely the new definition of getting out of the frying pan and into the fire. To stop thinking of the man she had started to love and how he may have just been stringing her along, she turned on the television set to hear about people dying while they were running for their lives. Anyway the combination of those items of bad news was like mainlining four or five cups of Starbuck's – there was no way she was going to sleep, and she knew it.

That's why when Carla Enrico called to invite her to a party, she decided to go. Carla had heard her speech. She and some friends who were interested in supporting the Foundation for American Principles were throwing the party near where she taught at the University of Maryland at College Park. It was just outside of D.C.

Carla Enrico was one of those people with whom you never have to worry about keeping up your end of the conversation. Her mouth was in high gear from the moment she picked Shawna up in front of the Hilton, talking about everything from the situation in Chicago to the effect of the war on the price of gasoline. They had weaved their way through downtown traffic and made it onto I-295 before Shawna realized she had left her purse behind. It was okay, Carla had reassured her. She wouldn't need it at the party.

They never made it to the party. A bright light had flashed off the rearview mirror. The explosion had been like a huge frightening monster that had suddenly risen up in the back seat, roaring with all its might. Carla had lost control of the car. The next thing Shawna had known she had woken up in the crumpled wreckage of Carla's car alongside I-295.

The last she had heard, Carla was still alive. She had severe facial lacerations and a head injury so they were taking her to the nearest available hospital. Shawna's observable injuries were minor, so they decided to transport her to a hospital further away, in Baltimore, to save room in the nearby hospitals for those more severely injured and those who had been closer to D.C. When the hospital had released her they had transported her here. She wasn't even sure why.

By the time Shawna reached the highest row of the upper deck, she was breathing heavily. She had been working out three or four times a week, but still the combination of what she had been through and those long flights of steps had pretty much taken everything out of her. She collapsed in a chair that was thankfully twenty or thirty yards from the nearest person, and she looked out over the stadium.

A variety of images now flashed through Shawna's mind: her father's garden; playing with her brother as a grade-schooler in the sands of Cannon Beach; Carla's stunned expression as she lay in a pool of her own blood; Jeremy's face as she told him of the news of her father's death; Drew Covington's lips just before he kissed her. Such images started Shawna crying once again. First there was the trickle of a single tear down her cheek, and then a flood of tears and sobs that Shawna simply could not hold back. Her whole body was in spasms from all she had lost and all that would never be again. She had never felt more alone in all her life. She longed for the father who had always been there for her, and who had especially been so understanding after her divorce. She longed for the brother with whom she had once shared so much, but who now seemed like a stranger. She longed to touch the little hands of her son, to hold and comfort him, and in the process let him comfort her. It was like her life had become a vast, dark, empty pit opening up before her and calling her to jump in. Shawna fought off that image. There had to be a way she could get home to

Jeremy. If she could get home to Jeremy, things would suddenly look better.

Shawna wanted to pray, but she didn't know what to pray, or even if prayer wasn't a little audacious right now. Could she pray for protection or special help at a time when hundreds of thousands had died, when people still mourned the deaths of at least that many in San Francisco, and when the whole nation feared the next act of terror by a madman? Still, she hungered for her son, and who could she go to but God? At least God needed to know what she felt – *she* needed God to know that much. If she could tell God how she felt, she would not feel so much alone.

She closed her eyes and whispered, "My son! Please, Lord, I want my son! If I have to die the moment after, let me see my son!"

It was just then that Shawna opened her eyes and saw the image that caused her tear-swollen eyes to open even wider. It couldn't be! Surely her earnest desire had now given rise to hallucination -- but it was such a large, clear hallucination! There on the screen in center field was a video picture of Jeremy. His image seemed to fill the stadium. Shawna covered her mouth with her hands in order to hold back sobs that threatened to once more overwhelm her. She looked as carefully as she could at the screen. The image was still there! And what was that beside Jeremy? It was a dugout. He was standing beside one of the dugouts!

Shawna's whole body shook with the emotion of the moment, and it was all that she could do to get her feet to start moving down the aisle toward the lower deck. What made it especially difficult was that she wanted to keep her eyes fixed on the giant television screen as she descended those stairs, believing that doing so would reassure her that the whole experience was not an illusion. But then all at once the image disappeared and the image of another child took its place. Shawna stumbled and nearly fell. But now she focused on the steps and the task of getting down them as rapidly as she could. She had not had an abundance of miracles in her life recently. This was not one she was going to let get away.

Drew Covington scanned the stands and ball field for any signs of the one they were looking for. Then he looked down at Jeremy. Jeremy's face was still alive with a sense of expectation, but Drew wondered how long that would last if his mother failed to appear. The use of the JumboTron had been an inspiration and procuring the privilege had been easier than he had feared it might be, but the risk of it all was that it might reveal their desperate state more quickly than they were ready to handle. Drew wondered how he would be able to convince Jeremy to give up the search should that become necessary.

"You know, Drew," whispered Ashley, "there really isn't too much chance of this working. Her hotel was almost right at ground zero. Don't you think it would be easier on him if we just told him that and got him out of here right away?"

Drew shook his head. "I understand what you're saying, but I'm just not ready to do that right now. We have to exhaust every possibility. Then if we come up empty, well, I'll do whatever I have to do. I'm not sure what that is right now, but I guess I'll know it when I have to know it."

Drew looked up at the JumboTron and saw the face of a little girl who he knew was trying to find her own mother. He wondered how many times in that stadium alone a similar story could be repeated, and beyond that, how many times it could be repeated between Baltimore and the remains of Washington D.C. Could he really expect that they would be among the lucky ones? He thought of the pictures of abducted children on milk cartons. How many times had that strategy been successful and how many times had it failed?

Drew looked at Jeremy once again. His face was still alive with expectation. What had Jesus said? "The kingdom of God belongs to such as these." A kingdom of hope and expectation. A kingdom of wide eyes and innocent faith. The world could sure use that right now. As Drew was looking at that face of the kingdom, the boy's eyes seemed to suddenly get even wider and his face exploded into a vibrant smile.

"There she is!"

Drew quickly turned in the direction Jeremy had been looking, and there running with all her energy in their direction was Shawna. Jeremy jumped over the rail and ran out onto the field to meet her, and Drew followed close behind. Shawna crumpled in front of her son. They threw their arms around each other and rocked each other back and forth. Drew wanted to join in the embrace, but he felt attempting to do so would dilute the special quality of the moment for mother and child. As he watched them, he felt a hand curl around his arm and a body move close against his side. It was Ashley. He was still angry at her for her not trying to contact Shawna, but he also knew how scared and alone she had to feel at this moment. He curled his arm around her.

As Shawna became more aware of her surroundings, she looked up at Drew. Drew had hoped that she would leap up and come to him, but instead he only saw a sad smile as she stood and almost shyly offered him her hand.

'Uh...I want to thank you for bringing me my son. You obviously know how much this means to me, so I don't need to say anything more about that. I'm glad you two have found each other, and I want to wish you my best."

Drew just stared down at the outstretched hand. What had happened here? Drew couldn't understand it. Why this formality? It was as if after causing his spirit to soar to the heavens, the reunion he had not even dared to hope for, but suddenly thought he had been granted, had disappeared like a desert mirage, and sent his spirit crashing to the earth. And staring at Shawna's hand was like staring at the earth as it loomed ever closer.

Drew shifted his gaze to Shawna's eyes, searching there for an answer to the mystery, but she looked away, and lowered her hand.

"Look, I know you two want to be alone, so Jeremy and I..."

Finally it got through to him. He pushed away from Ashley, and turned and looked with anger into her eyes, but she quickly glanced away.

"What?" she cried out defensively.

"Don't you say 'What?' to me! I thought you wanted comfort, but you were sending a message, weren't you? -- A message that was yours, not mine!" Drew returned his gaze to Shawna. "Well, I'm not going to let this moment be stolen from me!"

Drew put his hands firmly on Shawna's shoulders and pulled her body up against his, even as he brought his lips against hers. Stunned, Shawna started to resist, but Drew could feel that resistance quickly beginning to wane as he covered her face and mouth with his kisses. The warmth of her breath was a shot of adrenaline to his system and he could feel his heart racing as he now pressed his lips ever more firmly against hers. She wrapped her arms around him, digging her fingernails into his back, even while every breath that Drew did not claim as his own, came forth in sobs. As these subsided she managed to speak.

"She told me..."

"How could you believe what she told you? How could you not believe instead how we were together?"

"I...I don't know, it's just..."

Shawna's lips had started to tremble, and Drew kissed them much more gently.

"We have a lot we're fighting against here, Shawna. In the midst of all that we believe, believing in each other has got to be front and center. That's the only way we're going to make it. Okay?"

Shawna nodded her head and whispered, "Okay."

Drew looked back where Ashley had been and she was gone. Jeremy had moved up against his mother and had his arms wrapped around one of her legs. Drew looked back into Shawna's eyes. For that moment in time, Drew's world had been reduced to three people. He knew at some level that it was an illusion, but it was an illusion he needed, an illusion that couples had bought into through the centuries, that the world could be just two people and a child who loved each other, and all else wouldn't have to matter. They had fought off all enemies, and they had won; they had won this precious moment to hold each other, they had won this time to soothe each other's spirits with their words and touch, they had won this little time to take and make into something eternal. Drew would not release it easily. He explored every inch of Shawna's face with his eyes, gently kissing each spot. Shawna, in turn, nuzzled against Drew's neck and massaged the throbbing of his carotid artery with her lips and tongue. Drew's whole body shivered.

A gentle breeze seemed to come from nowhere for them alone. It cooled Drew's warming face. It tossed Shawna's bangs back and forth, causing them to gently caress her forehead. It caused Drew to shut his eyes, and remember breezes from long ago -- breezes in the mountains that had brought the smell of pine, breezes in his back yard when he was a child that had escorted to his senses the delicious aroma of honeysuckle and lilac, breezes along the Oregon beaches that had carried the smells of life emanating from the ocean. He looked down into Shawna's open eyes and it was like he had just taken her with him to all those marvelous places. They shared a smile.

Jeremy tugged on his mother's arm. "I need to go to the bathroom!"

Shawna laughed and reached down and picked up her son. "Well, I guess that's one way to return to reality!"

After finding one of the many stadium restrooms and helping Jeremy with his needs, Drew had Shawna relate how she managed to escape the bomb's destruction.

"Did you know at first what had happened?" he asked.

"Not really. It was so weird. It was like everything was happening in slow motion, and not real at all. I kind of expected to wake up in my own bed at home and find it all a very bad dream."

"Well, we're going to get you home. The lack of ID will be the biggest problem, but I can't imagine but that there are a lot of other people in the same boat, and that they have set up ways to handle it."

"We can certainly hope so."

As they exited the stadium, Drew noticed a large demonstration in one area of the main parking lot. He thought of the events of San Francisco, and considered avoiding the area entirely, but the news reporter in him got the best of him, and he resolved to check it out. Leaving Shawna with Jeremy at a safe distance he ran in the direction of the disturbance. The large group was definitely divided into factions and both sides were shouting at each other.

"Traitors! Murderers!"

"Repent or God will judge you!"

"Repent yourselves, assholes!"

Police were present trying to keep order, but there was still a lot of pushing and shoving. As he got closer, Drew noticed one large sign that said, "Beware Albert Packard! Beware the antichrist!" Several similar signs were distributed throughout the crowd.

Drew walked up to one of the persons with an anti-Packard sign. "What's this about? Packard's dead."

The man turned toward him. "Don't you follow the news, Buddy? He ain't dead! The administration says that he survived the blast and they have been keeping it quiet until he was better, but we know different. He was dead and came back to life! It's all in your Bible, if you have one. 'And I saw one of his heads as it were wounded to death; and his deadly wound was healed; and all the world wondered after the beast.' But don't be deceived! He is the antichrist, and this is the time of the end!!"

The demonstrator shouted this last message with all his might, and he was attracting a lot of attention. Drew thought of what Conrad had told him some time before. He didn't feel comfortable with the two groups gravitating in their direction, but the news he had received was too incredible and he had to know more.

"How do you know he is alive?"

"He's having a news conference later this afternoon, and that's kind of hard to do if you're dead! He wants to spread more of his lies because he works for the Prince of Lies, but don't believe him!"

"Are you with Conrad?" questioned someone from the opposing group.

The man took on a more guarded demeanor. "Just because we're against Packard doesn't mean we're with Conrad."

"You're with Conrad and you know it! You're religious fanatics and murderers!"

Drew turned quickly and ran, just as the two groups started swinging fists and throwing bottles. He kept on running and didn't look back until he reached Shawna's side. The world had now fully crashed back in on their lives, and it was no longer possible to turn away, even for a while. He wanted to head straight back to Portland, but there was now one more thing he had to do. He had to get to that news conference. He had to get back to writing news instead of hearing about it second hand.

■■

Ashley Cambridge looked around the crowded room. People were everywhere: seated in chairs, seated on the floor in aisles, standing at the back and sides of the room. The announcement that the news conference would be in this particular conference room at the U.S. Naval Academy in Annapolis really came at the last minute, and Ashley was a little surprised that it had filled up so quickly; but then perhaps she shouldn't have been. It's a reporter's job to find such things out and move quickly.

She guessed that almost half of the room was occupied by foreign press. This conference had been opened up to them, and it stood to reason that they would be present in large numbers. The conflagration that had started in the United States had been spreading to all parts of the world, and the incredible news that Albert Packard was alive and would shortly address this group impacted everyone in the world.

Ashley saw faces of every hue, and heard voices speaking such a wide array of languages and dialects that should someone have tried to convince her that she had mistakenly wandered into a meeting of the United Nations, they might not have had very hard a task.

As she scanned the persons in the crowd, she came to one who was turned away from her, but who even from the back looked familiar. It was then that he turned in her direction and she saw the face of Drew Covington. She could tell that he saw her, but still he just stared dispassionately in her direction. She quickly looked away.

No moment in her life had been harder for her than seeing Drew and Shawna embrace so passionately just hours earlier. Drew was doing with Shawna what she had hungered for him to do with her, and it was as if she were not even there. It had not been hard getting away unnoticed. She had been grateful when she had heard about this news conference because it had given her something else upon which to focus, something on which to use her professional acumen and energy. And now Drew's presence was ruining that.

Kari McDonald, who had recently been appointed to permanently take the place of John Harnish as Press Secretary, now approached the podium, along with several other notables.

"Ladies and Gentlemen of the press, we are ready to begin. We realize that not all of you have places to sit, but if you will settle in as best you can, we will try to not make this any longer than it has to be. We want to especially welcome the members of the foreign press today. We know you are all eager to get to the matters at hand, so without any further delay, Ladies and Gentlemen, the President of the United States..."

As Albert Packard entered the room, a collective gasp could be heard throughout the room. Ashley was not sure if it was because people hadn't been sure that Packard really was alive, or because of the visible radiation burn scars on Packard's forehead and lower arms. In any case, this initial reaction was quickly followed by a standing ovation, as a Navy band played "Here Comes the Chief." Packard stood at the podium for several minutes, waving and soaking in the adulation of the crowd before signaling for quiet.

"On this occasion," Packard started, "I cannot resist quoting Mark Twain, 'The rumors of my death are greatly exaggerated!'"

The crowd erupted in another round of applause, and the sight of the President vigorously strutting across the stage seemed to fan the flames of their ardor. Ashley thought it was seriously overdone, but then again she had never liked Albert Packard. Personally, she had hoped he really was dead.

The President returned to the podium and those gathered quieted down again.

"I know many people wonder why it was kept so secret that I was alive. I'm sorry if that caused undue stress to the people of this country and our friends around the world, but it was necessary. It was necessary for me to fully recover out of the public limelight, and to best provide for my protection during that time. Please understand that my input into matters of state was heard as Vice-President Sam Arlington guided the country."

Vice-President Arlington stepped forward and those gathered gave him a round of applause.

"Vice-President Arlington and I, along with many others, are alive today because of the policy we initiated after San Francisco of moving our top level leaders from place to place to minimize vulnerability. We will maintain that policy now as well."

The President continued. "The tragic course of this war -- and make no bones about it we are in a state of war -- have necessitated that I return to the helm. Our nation is in a state of crisis today such as it has not been in since the time of Abraham Lincoln and the first American Civil War. Indeed the depth of tragedy in our nation today is unprecedented. And it is not our nation only. The instability brought about by the cowardly attacks of the Armageddon Brigade has encouraged warlike factions in other parts of the world. War has broken out between North and South Korea, between Israel and an Arab alliance and between India and Pakistan. Thankfully, although these hostilities have brought thousands of fatalities, none of them have resorted to what the Brigade has used against people of their own country – nuclear weaponry."

The President was now visibly overcome with emotion. He opened his mouth several times, as if he were ready to go on, but each time he could not. Kari McDonald came up beside him and whispered something in his ear, but he waved her off. Finally, he once again found his voice.

"The cowardice of using nuclear weaponry against one's own people, and doing so ostensibly in the name of God, is history's new definition of evil. We can now set aside the example of Adolph Hitler, as inhumane as he was. We can now set aside the example of the Khmer Rouge and the Killing Fields. We can set aside all of history's attempts at genocide. Because in our day one has arisen who is attempting more than genocide. In our day an evil one has arisen who is seeking to kill off human society itself, starting with his own people.

"There are those people who are claiming that I am the antichrist, and claiming all kinds of terrible things against me. The truth is that they claim such things because I stand in the way of their political agenda. But if there is one alive today who warrants the title 'antichrist,' it would be the one whose actions stand in sharp opposition to those of Jesus Christ when he was on this earth! Where Christ said, 'The one who lives by the sword dies by the sword,' these people are trying to force their political agenda by the worst acts of violence in human history. Where Christ said, 'Judge not, unless you be judged,' these people would have us bind up our gay and lesbian population with oppressive legislation, and let bigots physically assault them with impunity. Where Christ sought to bring humankind grace and forgiveness, these people seek to erect a Christ who will execute their own vindictiveness! In my book, that all adds up to anti-Christ, and that is E.J. Conrad and the Armageddon Brigade!"

Many of those gathered stood and applauded enthusiastically, but Ashley was not one of them. She was not about to let horror at what Conrad had done translate into support for Packard's left-wing agenda. She knew she was not alone. Some in the back could be heard shouting "Antichrist!" and "Prince of lies!" These were quickly escorted from the room. But Albert Packard and his supporters would not be able to escort every dissenting voice from his presence. Ashley was resolved to make her own voice heard when the opportunity arose. She looked back at where Drew Covington sat. He was not applauding, but Ashley judged this was because he was rather deep in meditation. Normally he would be among the first to object to Packard's references to 'oppressive legislation' and 'bigotry,' but Ashley didn't know to what degree all that had transpired had changed him.

"Some have wondered why we have not responded more forcefully to the Brigade. In retrospect I have to admit that I have made that same criticism of myself. But let me say some things about that in defense of the approach we have been taking to this point. When terrorists from abroad have assaulted our people, we have been able to target those countries known to shelter such terrorists. We have put restrictions on their ability to get into this country, and we have retaliated against their military forces. But how do you do that when the enemy is among your own people, when they have no distinguishing way that they look? How can you strike against the country that harbors the terrorists when the country is your own country? If a foreign enemy had dropped two nuclear bombs on our cities, we would have had to retaliate in kind, but how can we drop nuclear bombs on our own country, especially where loyal people reside nearby?

"Well, we can no longer afford any vacillation. We must strike back, and the truth is, some who are loyal may be victims of our retaliation. Some civilians will die from friendly fire. But the one thing we can no longer afford to do is to act with measured moderation while crazy people with nuclear weapons decimate our cities. We will eradicate this menace from our society, we will do it completely, and we will eliminate the main concentrations of their forces by thirty days from today!"

Now even Ashley applauded, although she wondered if Packard could be trusted to deliver on his long-overdue promise. Not since Kennedy had a liberal shown any kind of backbone, in her mind.

After Packard's speech, he opened the floor to questions, and Ashley's hand shot up, along with hundreds across the room. Packard recognized a hand toward the center of the front row.

"President Packard, first of all I just want to say how good it is to see you alive..."

People throughout the room stood and once more applauded. Ashley scowled at the obvious selection of a friendly voice for first question. But his actual question, when it came, did perk up her ears.

"Mr. President, should we take your comments to mean that you might now possibly order nuclear retaliation against the Brigade, even though they reside on U.S. soil?"

The President hesitated but a brief moment before responding. "Let me say that we will use whatever weaponry we deem necessary to deliver on the promise which I just made. I will not, however, confirm or deny which weapons will be involved in our next actions."

The response created a buzz throughout the room. The next question was given to a reporter from India.

"President Packard, may I ask respectfully, if you end up using nuclear weapons against your own people, how will you at the same time expect the leaders of India and Pakistan to refrain from using such weaponry against each other? Won't you totally forfeit any moral voice you might otherwise have in that conflict?"

The President sighed visibly. "We, of course, have not said that nuclear weaponry would be used: we have only refused to rule it out. In any case, what we have asked countries like India and Pakistan is to hold to a policy of no first use. First use has already occurred in our situation, and it has been by our enemy."

Ashley was granted the next question. "Mr. President, there are many conservatives in this country who have not gone over to Conrad, and yet in your remarks you have made divisive remarks denigrating issues on the conservative agenda. What can you say to assure us that you can be President of the whole country, and not just your own liberal backers?"

Ashley's question brought a combination of hostile murmurs and scattered applause. Albert Packard just smiled and nodded his head.

"I apologize if I have offended those of our citizens who are conservative. I know that most conservatives love this country, and stand by her in this crisis. I only wish to say that I will continue to say what I believe, and I will expect my conservative sisters and brothers to do the same. That is what America is about. We must agree to disagree, even as we stand side by side against the enemies of our nation."

The next questioner took Ashley's issue even further. "Mr. President, I have to ask in relation to your last response, what about those leaders in the military and in the federal government itself, who are secretly aligned with Conrad already, or who are considering defecting to him because of the liberal perspective of your government? Don't you think it would be wise to moderate your stands in order to hold their loyalty?"

Packard firmly shook his head. "I do not know if there are as many of such people as you are speculating, but I will tell you this: I will not sell off my principles in order to buy the loyalty of those who are not ready to give such loyalty to our country unequivocally and without barter!"

The room erupted in dissension and some shouted and cheered while others booed and even began throwing wadded press notes at the podium. President Packard tried unsuccessfully to quiet the group down, but then a figure standing on his chair in the middle front of the room gained people's attention. He was a person firmly aligned with the conservative cause. As an apparent act of desperation, Packard recognized Drew Covington.

"Mr. President, as you know I am a man of conservative principles. I fought with every fiber of my being to keep you from being elected – no offense." There were scattered snickers throughout the crowd. "But at this moment of time I want to speak up for just one principle that has been identified with conservatives for far longer than any of us here have been alive. That principle relates to that beautiful bit of cloth that is draped behind you."

Albert Packard turned to look at the flag hanging behind him on the wall.

"I know this is supposed to be a time to ask questions. But about this principle I have but one short statement to make and it is this..."

Drew paused, and his silence was effective in getting those gathered to attend to his next words. He placed his hand firmly over his heart.

"I pledge allegiance to the flag..."

Drew's voice broke for only a second, but as he started up, others across the room stood and joined in.

"...of the United States of America, one nation, under God, indivisible, with liberty and justice for all."

By the time the short statement was finished, even the foreign press were standing in respect, and after the last word was said, those in the room were silent, except for some scattered sounds of weeping.

Ashley noted that instead of leaving the room, as his aides were urging him to do, Albert Packard jumped off the stage, walked up to Drew and firmly and silently clasped his hand.

Chapter Ten

E.J. Conrad's Humvee swung up onto I-5 just north of Longview, Washington. There they joined a convoy of other military vehicles, weaving their way past semis and other civilian traffic. People stared out their windows as they passed by and Conrad just smiled and waved, as if he were out for a Sunday drive.

Audacity – that was the order of the day. They had shown it in moving out of their mountain camp when the federal forces had not expected it. They had shown it in taking the battle to those forces that had been stationed nearby to contain them. And now they were showing it by joining other mountain forces in heading boldly into Longview, Washington.

At first Conrad had wanted to stay in the mountains. However, his military advisors had convinced him that doing so would make him more vulnerable. Moving in and taking over a city where there were more civilians would make the federal forces hesitant to use nuclear weaponry, and it would even make attacking with conventional weaponry more problematic. Besides, Longview was still within view of Mount Saint Helens.

A traffic helicopter swung down to take a closer look. At Conrad's signal, anti-aircraft guns mounted on the vehicle in front of them swung around and upward, opening fire. The copter exploded in a ball of flame, and civilian vehicles began swerving and pulling off the side of the road. Just then a squadron of fighter jets which Conrad recognized as F/A 18 Hornets appeared coming in from the west. But sweeping down the Columbia River from the east was a squadron of the Brigade's own F-18's, recently procured from a defecting Naval officer, and the jets engaged each other almost directly overhead. Conrad directed some of the vehicles in his convoy to move to the shoulders, while remaining at top speed. With the rest of his convoy spreading out across all lanes, the remaining civilian vehicles in front were being herded straight ahead with no opportunity to pull over. Just beyond them Conrad could see a roadblock consisting of both Army and local law enforcement vehicles. He ordered his forces to open fire.

Explosions now leapt up across the highway ahead. But whatever vehicles were knocked out were quickly replaced by others from alongside the road. A jet spun out and hit the ground near a forested area to Conrad's left, and the ground rumbled. Conrad had no idea whose jet it was, but with his focus straight ahead, he had no desire to figure it out at this point. Seeing the roadblock and explosions ahead, some civilian vehicles tried to stop, but they were rammed from behind and the side. A minivan tried to speed up and pull off to the right, but one of Conrad's Humvee's clipped his tail end and sent him spinning down an embankment, rolling into a ball of flame. Conrad now saw the civilian vehicles ahead of him as blockers that would help open holes in the opposition's defensive line. He got on his phone and ordered his drivers to look for the holes and burst on through. An explosion from behind rocked the ground again. Conrad figured that a federal jet had broken free enough to drop a bomb. That wasn't a good sign, but he refused to let it deter him. The roadblock was now only a couple of hundred yards ahead. Some more cars now tried to stop and were rammed repeatedly, but most put their hope in finding a way through. The first car now reached the roadblock. Unable to decide what to do, the driver apparently froze and hit a parked police car head on, flipping end over end and landing on his roof. Others tried for the gap that was created, but they smashed against each other's sides and slid into other blockading vehicles. An SUV trying desperately to find a hole between two police cars clipped one of them and flipped over creating a big hole on the right side. Conrad's caissons and trucks immediately began plowing through. Civilian cars heading for the same gap were fired upon. As Conrad's own Humvee sped through the gap, he pulled out an automatic rifle himself and fired on soldiers and police alongside the road. Turning and looking back he saw that another large gap had opened on the left side and his vehicles were streaming through there as well.

Up ahead was the exit for Longview. Conrad's convoy stormed down the exit, and were now careening down the streets of the neighboring town of Kelso, heading toward the Longview city center. They passed a middle school, where school children out in front eyed them with wonder. Conrad waved as they passed and several children waved back. Overhead Conrad saw his parachutists dropping from a transport escorted by more fighter jets. A local patrol car pulled up from a side road on the left, and the truck in front of Conrad immediately opened fire with a full barrage of automatic rifles and machine guns. The car burst into flame. They were soon joined by more of Conrad's forces coming in from Highway 4 Westbound, and they raced down Washington Way, a main thoroughfare of the city, at nearly sixty miles per hour toward their target destination of city hall and the police office. A couple of US Navy jets swung around and were now coming in low from straight ahead of them. Conrad's forces began firing and the jets returned fire, with bullets zinging against the grill of Conrad's Humvee and along the pavement next to him. Civilian vehicles were pulling up onto side roads and even onto the sidewalk to avoid the onrushing vehicles and the exchange of fire. The truck in front of Conrad's vehicle was hit and burst into flame, and Conrad's driver had to swerve quickly to avoid crashing into it. One of the U.S. jets, in turn, was hit, spun out of control and crashed into the commercial district to Conrad's left.

Brigade jets once again engaged the U.S. forces overhead, and Conrad could now see their target, the Longview City Hall, off to the left. As they reached that building, additional forces met them coming in from Highway 4 Eastbound, as well as from Highway 30 to the south. Conrad's driver slammed on the brakes, and he leaped out of the vehicle, carrying his M-16 with him. He followed a stream of soldiers into the front door of the modern brick building. Explosions from a couple of blocks away he knew to be from the assault on the nearby police headquarters. Soldiers broke off into each office, securing each area with little resistance as Conrad and an escort of about twenty soldiers broke on into the mayor's office. Conrad stepped up, placed the barrel of his weapon firmly between the mayor's eyes, and proclaimed with passion:

"In the name of God and his Armageddon Brigade, we are liberating this city! Don't think of resisting. By now our forces are throughout the city and are forming a barricade around the periphery. Do we have your cooperation or shall I shoot you now?"

The mayor's face went pale and he just stared at the intruder speechless.

"Do we have your cooperation," Conrad repeated, "or shall..."

"What...uh, what do you want from me?"

Conrad smiled. "We need you to call off the dogs."

■■

Brian Marshal stood at the door of the KLTV building in Longview, wondering what he was supposed to be doing. Oh, he knew what he was supposed to be doing from the Brigade's perspective -- helping to guard the building while Conrad was inside doing a television broadcast. But in a wider perspective he felt as if his soul were being torn apart by the conflict between promised loyalties.

He had tried to stop the disaster in D.C. He might have mitigated the number of casualties had the FBI believed him sooner. Why had they agreed to let him be with Conrad if they weren't going to believe him? And now this action had been decided on so quickly and so surreptitiously that he had no opportunity for warning. Would they still believe he was on their side?

Brian looked down in the direction of passing civilians. What was going through their minds as they looked up at him? They were essentially small town people, living here probably because they were born here or because they chose to live here instead of exposing themselves to the dangers and pressures of the larger cities. And now their sanctuary had been invaded. What would he do if several of them suddenly rushed at him and the other sentries in an effort to win back control of their homes? He wouldn't blame them. In fact, were he in their confidence, he probably would even advise it. Otherwise, they were about to be caught up in the center of a bloody conflagration, and their little city certainly would never be the same again.

The door to the television building opened and another soldier stepped out and informed Brian he could go inside and listen to the broadcast. He was being relieved in more than one sense of the word.

E.J. Conrad was broadcasting a message to the people of the Longview-Kelso area, as well as to anyone else who picked up the local station who cared to listen. Longview was a city of a little over 30,000 people, while Kelso, which was right up next to it, added an additional 12,000. Both cities were under control of the Brigade. Conrad was ready to begin. One of the television cameras focused in on his face.

"Citizens of Longview and Kelso, I am Edward James Conrad, servant of God in these Last Days. I am sure you are frightened and confused concerning what is happening in your city, but I want to assure you that although there will be some frightening things still ahead, this is just the beginning of the better world that is on the horizon for those who believe. We have liberated the cities of Longview and Kelso. Those cities are no longer in the hands of godless secular government. You might be interested in knowing that forces dedicated to the coming of God's kingdom have also liberated the city of Spokane and Fairchild Air Force Base. From now on, all laws, all behavior and all transactions in these cities and areas will be governed according to the Word of God. Scripture tells of a New Jerusalem that will come down out of heaven. This will be a city where finally, after all of these centuries, all will be done according to God's will and there will be no more mourning or pain. We cannot create that city: it will be a gift of God that will follow the coming of his Son. However, we can create model cities that will seek to mirror that city to come, and that is what we will be doing in the areas we have liberated. From now until Christ comes, Longview and Kelso will be together known as 'New Bethel.' Bethel was the place that Jacob encountered God and saw a stairway to heaven, and it means

165

'house of God.' You can be proud of this new name. Spokane in turn will be known as 'Zion's Gate,' both because of its status as a gateway through the northern Rockies, and because it's establishment will open a gateway to the coming of the New Jerusalem, the New Zion, on this planet.

"We are confident that all of you who live in these liberated cities will eventually be glad for what has happened, and your new roles in what God is doing. However, because in the short term some might not understand and might not catch the vision of what God is doing, we are putting a moratorium on all travel to places outside of these cities. Please understand that this, in part, is due to the fact that these cities are now surrounded by forces loyal to the old way of man, forces of the corrupt federal government that controls our beloved country. Partly it is also to give you the opportunity to know what wonderful things God will do with these cities in this interim until Christ comes. I believe that the Millenium of Jesus Christ will begin in these cities of refuge.

"Please take note of these changes in the legal system that will be immediately implemented: There will be no pornography allowed anywhere in either the city of New Bethel or Zion's Gate. Since there are those of the modern mind who may wonder what we deem as pornographic, it includes any magazines where women's breasts or genitals, or men's genitals are exposed or described, with the exception of medical manuals. It also includes any depiction of sexual activity or simulated sexual activity. All television and radio signals from outside of the city will be scrambled. Person's selling or attempting to buy pornography will be immediately jailed for a period of no less than six months. Public nudity, which includes the wearing of thongs or bikinis, as well as see-through or partially see-through clothing that exposes breasts or genitals, is hereby banned, and those violating the ban will be put in jail for a period of no less than six months.

"Child abusers and perverts had better immediately repent. Any person abusing a child, whether it be sexually or by violent physical assault, will upon being found guilty, be summarily executed. Zero tolerance! Those even attempting to abduct a child will be put in our jail, and we will be throwing away the key until the Lord comes. No exceptions! Parents, if you suspect anyone of threatening your children in any way, know that we are your allies and we will respond immediately!

"Drug dealers: Be warned that our soldiers and officers have the authority to execute you on the spot. Don't even *look like* you might be dealing drugs!"

Brian tried to think what his reaction might be had he not been through what he had been through, and had he been listening to Conrad for the first time. There was much that would have appealed to him. Even with all Conrad's strictness and violent methodology, some of the vision was tugging at his spirit even now. He knew that the vision would speak to at least a few others as well, but for many who would be repelled by this vision, he was also outlining the parameters of the nightmare they faced.

"Abortions are hereby outlawed anywhere in our city. Anyone performing or having an abortion in these cities will be tried as any other murderer, and if found guilty, will be executed. Young women, don't let yourself get into a position where this has to even be an issue!

"For those of you men or women who are homosexual perverts, be warned that in these cities you are no longer Hollywood's misunderstood darlings. Homosexual behavior will be punishable by death, and so-called cross-dressing will be deemed evidence of homosexuality. Be warned!

"Legitimate businesses may continue to operate as before, except for the fact that no businesses, apart from hospitals and similar emergency services, shall be open on Sunday.

"Criminals should be warned that while war carries with it many dangers, apart from that we are determined that the cities under our guard will be the safest cities in America. Those who endanger our citizens will pay!

"Some of you who are not living in the area of these cities may decide you want to be part of what we are doing. I am sorry, but with few exceptions we cannot admit you to the city. Letting others in at this point poses too many security problems. However, we need your support as the war will spread and we will be liberating other cities. Be there when we need you in your city!

"If you live in these cities and fail to see the wisdom of these laws, and you seek to escape, or you rebel against our authority, be warned that you will pay with your life. As Joshua told the people, 'choose you this day whom ye will serve'! But know that those who are faithless, those who betray our mission, those who choose against the Lord will most certainly perish!"

Brian felt a chill go up his spine. Was it just his imagination that Conrad seemed to be looking in his direction when he said those last words?

"As most of you know, I have always been a supporter of private ownership of guns. However, in this situation, we temporarily have to make special provisions. All of you who have weapons in your home, please understand that they are needed by the Brigade in order that we might achieve our goals. Please turn in the ones you own either at City Hall or the Police Department. Should a citizen even attempt to use a weapon at a representative of the Brigade, they will be shot on the spot, and we don't want to see that happen.

"We have released those persons in the jails and have taken them outside the perimeters of our city to be dealt with by the authorities whose laws they violated. However, that leaves us plenty of jail space, and if need be we will use every inch of it! Unlike the spineless authorities of the world, we have no scruples against so-called overcrowding of jails!

"We call upon all of the citizens of New Bethel and Zion's Gate to rejoice! If nothing else, we have brought to an end the time when the most exciting thing in your life was the next episode of your soap opera, or the local performance of some faggot rock star. Albert Packard, the great antichrist, is in the world, but he will be defeated. The Son of God is coming! Prepare your hearts!"

After his speech, Conrad went over to the station owners to make sure they knew what was required of them. Brian heard the instructions: it was to be broadcast by tape delay and without interruption or so-called expert commentary. Those watching should know that it is tape delay, in case hostile forces might decide to attack the studio on the assumption that Conrad was still inside. No rebuttals or opinions from those of the outside world would be permitted. Several of Conrad's officers would remain in the studio to make sure this was done.

As Conrad headed toward the exit he grabbed hold of Brian's arm and led him along beside him.

"We won some great victories yesterday, Brian, but I fear we still have some great challenges ahead of us. It's not the military challenges I fear so much. I really believe we can handle those. It's the challenge to win people's hearts that's going to be difficult."

They were now standing out in front of the studio, and Conrad turned and looked at Brian.

"You know, some people just look at the death and destruction that is happening, and that's all they see. They don't see that what is being destroyed is the old way of man, a society based on sin, materialism and the way of the flesh. They don't see that a better world is coming, and that for it to come, we have to raze the old world to the ground. We've got to help them see that, Brian. That's what you've got to help me do here in our city of New Bethel."

"What...what do you want me to do?"

"You've got to talk to the people. If we can convince the people here what this city can become, it can truly be a city of God, an example to the nation."

Brian felt the ground starting to sway back and forth, and both he and Conrad had to hold onto a rail to keep from falling over. In the distance, Mount Saint Helens emitted a large plume of smoke and ash. Even before it subsided Conrad had leaped into the street and began to dance.

"It's the voice of God! The very voice of God! He's telling us he's behind us! He's telling us that he's glad we are here! Beneath this marauding mountain a kingdom is being born, and its King is coming soon! Hallelujah!"

Brian marveled at the childlike way that Conrad danced as well as at the childlike way that he believed. For that one moment in time it did seem like the mountain was celebrating with him, and Brian was feeling like an uninvited child, outside of the celebration. It didn't help to know that he actually had been invited, but that his heart had declined the invitation. All Brian could think of was, here indeed was a man who was convinced of where God was taking this world, and what his own role was in that journey. As Conrad raised his hands toward heaven there was a sparkle in his eyes, a sparkle born of trust, a sparkle that was undimmed when to the rest of the world the sky seemed silent. He didn't need anyone else to hear the music to which he danced, and the spring in his own feet was the only testimony that he needed. Brian envied him.

At another level Brian was glad that Conrad's attention had been diverted. He felt that if he had been required to respond to the words of commissioning Conrad had been giving him, he might have betrayed the ambivalence of his heart. He couldn't convince the people of a dream that he himself had come to believe had run off course, and had indeed become the world's nightmare.

As Brian watched Conrad dance, his eyes were diverted to the eyes of a young woman out standing in the street just beyond him. Indeed, there were a number of people out in the street watching, some with an apparent sense of wonder, some with an apparent sense of horror. But the eyes that Brian watched seemed to show neither. They were watching calmly and analytically, like a scientist evaluating the behavior of a new species. Now he could tell that those eyes had shifted from the teacher to the presumed disciple: her eyes were looking at him. The eyes were a deep chocolate brown, and were quite beautiful. He could now see that they were also touched with sadness. Even though Brian stared back, those eyes didn't shift away or show embarrassment. She had short, dark brown hair and wore a white summer dress with little blue flowers on it. He wanted to drop everything right now and sit down in the middle of the sidewalk and talk to her, to get to know who she was, where she came from, and what she thought about all that was happening to her world, but he could not. Conrad would call them all away soon. And besides he didn't have the nerve.

A siren blared. Brian recognized it as the Brigade's own portable air-raid siren, but the people in the street only looked confused. While the other soldiers scattered he ran over to the girl in the white dress and those who were with her.

"Okay, you've got to get to your homes quickly. There's going to be fighting, and you're not safe here."

While the others scattered, the girl in the white dress just stood and looked into Brian's eyes.

"Do you think we are all afraid of you? Do you feel big because you can make people afraid?" The young woman had spoken in a thick accent that seemed to be Eastern European.

"No, no," replied Brian, more quietly. "I don't want you to be afraid of me at all. But please, jets will be here any second, and you really must find cover. I...I can talk to you more later if..."

Without any sign of fear or panic, the woman turned and ran down a side street, and then disappeared behind the back end of a little shop. Brian watched her leave and was deep in thought when the sound of jet engines overhead roused him to consciousness. He quickly scrambled down a side street himself, and started running as much as he could under the cover of the small buildings of the city of Longview. Brigade jets were engaging the encroaching fighters overhead, but he also felt and heard the impact of bombs seeking their downtown targets. Anti-aircraft artillery were already booming all across the downtown area. Brian reached his unit just in time to join them as they loaded into a truck that was heading over to reinforce the south side of the city. Conrad had that morning ordered the destruction of the Lewis and Clark Bridge, the only normal access to the town across the Columbia River, but amphibious assault vehicles were crossing the river and the forces on that side were calling for reinforcements.

A soldier named Carl ran in late from the direction of City Hall. He practically dove into the back end of the truck just as it was starting up.

"Man, they hit the City Hall! Did you guys know they hit City Hall?! Do you think they got Conrad?"

Captain John Conners just shook his head. "Conrad ain't in City Hall! What, do you think he's an idiot? He just made it look like he was moving into City Hall, and he set up an office for himself in some grade school. A local also gave him access to his old bomb shelter, built back in the 60s – the Cuban Missile Crisis and all. I'd bet that's where he is now. It's where I'd be if I were the Big Guy."

Brian sat silently for a moment. *Which grade school? What local and where did he live?* God, he felt like such a snitch! Still, the people he needed to talk to would want to know the answers to those questions.

"Is that shelter near-by? Maybe they wouldn't mind a little more company."

"Yeah, you wish," shouted Conners over the sound of artlillery. "But we have engraved invitations to join a party on the south side, and it wouldn't be polite to stand 'em up! Besides, all I know is that it isn't far from downtown."

A bomb exploded in the street a few hundred yards ahead, and the driver slammed on the brakes and took a sharp right through a residential area. Two blocks later he took a hard left and resumed the short trek toward the Columbia.

With the sights and sounds of the battle looming closer, Brian now found himself strangely calm. What frightened him the most these days was not the enemy without, but the enemy within, even though he wasn't really sure who either enemy was. At least he had a plan of action for the outward enemy. As long as he was on the battle lines he had to treat those on the other side shooting at him as the enemy. He had no other choice. What bothered him most was how easily he slipped into the role. Perhaps it was because there was a rage inside of him that was well-attuned to battle, so well-attuned, frighteningly enough, that all thoughts of who the enemy really was now faded into the background. Or perhaps it was the demons, whoever or whatever they were – demons that turned his eyes to fire, his heart to ice, and all his rationality to a wisp of cloud evaporating in the sun.

As Brian leapt out of the truck to join the Brigade forces, it seemed like all was happening in slow motion. Tracer bullets floated past him and over his head. Artillery from across and in the middle of the Columbia River flashed at him like sparkling stars, stars that calmed him even further. Still his feet moved him forward, while at the same time guiding him as he danced back and forth like a college scatback. Brian's M-16 seemed to knock out the beat to that dance, while it spread a pattern of escaping bullets at the soldiers emerging from assault vehicles.

Brian wasn't sure how long the exchange continued. Nor could he have told you if the bullets he fired at any specific soldiers found their mark. But after Federal forces began to withdraw, several other soldiers slapped him on the back; and when he returned to the truck, Captain Conners, smiled and tipped his helmet in Brian's direction. He had evidently made an impression. He just didn't know if it was the one he wanted to be making.

▪▪

E.J. Conrad looked out a window of the Saint Helens Elementary School in a residential section of what used to be called Longview, Washington. He could hear in the distance the sound of intermittent artillery fire, the remnants of a battle that had now wound down. They had successfully repelled the enemy attack. He had known that they would. Why would God have given him the sign of the volcano if he had not planned to fight by his side? Still, Conrad was beginning to feel a deep impatience. He looked outside at the school playground where his granddaughter Emily now played with several other children. As he looked at the peaceful scene he thought of several things. He first of all thought of how good of a job they had done at camouflaging his headquarters here. There were no soldiers or artillery visible on the outside. Of course, every school room had soldiers with automatic weapons peering out the windows, and several houses on each side were now also occupied by soldiers, but these could not be seen by overhead reconnaissance. The children out back also added to the impression that this was an innocuous place. Still, even with the logic of it all, he had mixed feelings about his granddaughter being there. He had longed so deeply to be able to watch her play in an area he knew was safe from all of the perverts and predators in the world. Finally he felt that could happen in this city. But now he had to worry about the dangers of this war, and what might happen if a bomb or missile meant for him might find her instead. He never worried about his own life. He felt he had divine protection.

173

But if something were to happen to her, he didn't know what he would do.

Something else bothered Conrad. Why hadn't Christ come yet? Conrad was doing what he had been called to do, and he was doing it more successfully than anyone other than himself had ever imagined. But he was ready now to reach the goal and share in the Glory of God. In spite of what some people thought, he really didn't like the killing.

Some Revelation scholars spoke of seven years here or three-and-a-half years there, but that was never the part that held Conrad's focus. He was a poet, not a mathematician, and it was the poetry of Revelation and its spiritual imagery and vision that drew him. What some people saw as literal time descriptions, he saw as poetic imagery. But now he wished that he had a better idea of how long this would all last. *Oh, well, God will tell me when I need to know.*

The voice of Conrad's aide came over the intercom: "There's a Mrs. Morrison here to see you, Sir. I told her to not bother you, but she is being rather insistent."

Conrad smiled and nodded to himself, "Yes, that would be Mrs. Carla Morrison. Send her in."

Carla Morrison was in her early thirties and was a single mother who lived in the community all of her life. Her case had come to Conrad's attention just the day after the beginning of the occupation. She burst through the door and then suddenly stopped, as if the audacity of her action had suddenly come to mind.

"Oh! I hope I'm not disturbing you, Mister Conrad. I just...well, the case of that man who...who did those things to my little daughter...I hadn't heard anything."

Conrad nodded. "Yes, yes. Well, you and your daughter don't have to worry about him anymore. We executed him this morning."

"Executed him? Already?"

"Yes, well, we heard your story. We heard his. We listened to what little Tonya had to say – sweet little girl. Girls like her shouldn't be subject to the sexual illness of animals like him. So we shot him. End of story."

"Really? No long court process? No worrying about him being released and coming back?"

"Oh, he's not coming back."

Carla Morrison just stood there for a moment while it all sunk in, and then a smile broke across her face. "Well...well, thank you!" She gave Conrad an impulsive hug. "Oh! Can you please tell me where you buried him? I just want to go there and dump dog shit all over his grave!"

Conrad shook his head. "I'm afraid you won't be able to do that. We don't have time or land to waste burying the likes of him, so we just tossed his body into one of our jets and dropped him, along with a load of bombs, on an encampment of Federal forces close by. I don't suppose there's much of him left."

"Oh! Oh! God, I know this is a terrible thing to say, but that's so cool! Thank you! Thank you again!"

Carla started to hug him once more, but Conrad held her back. "Don't thank me. Just thank God. And please remember to tell your neighbors, that's all I ask. They need to know that things are different now, and justice is real."

Carla Morrison promised that she would, and after shaking his hand and thanking him several more times, she left Conrad once again to his thoughts.

Conrad opened the window so he could hear more clearly the sound of Emily's laughter. She was remarkable. Not thirty minutes before there had been bombs going off throughout the city, but now she showed no signs of the anxiety everyone had been feeling at that time. She was overflowing with the joy of life. Now she was spreading out her arms and pretending she was a plane, and she was leading the other children around the playground, diving in on a plastic chicken that was part of the playground equipment. But there were no angry looks or fearful cries — only smiles and laughter. Conrad had been told that he wasn't to go outside except when necessary — for security reasons. But he couldn't resist. He ran out the school door and spread out his own arms, and his engines roared! He fell in line behind his granddaughter and two other rather surprised little girls and together they once more attacked the chicken. It didn't stand a chance.

Emily laughed. "The chicken is turning chicken!"

The other kids and Conrad picked it up as a chant: "The chicken is turning chicken! The chicken is turning chicken! The chicken is turning chicken!"

It was then that Conrad saw Corporal Brian Marshal. He dropped his arms and stopped abruptly.

"Brian..."

Corporal Marshal shuffled uneasily back and forth. "I...uh...beg your pardon, Sir."

"I didn't think you were one of those who knew where I was."

"I didn't" responded Brian. "But on the way back from the Southern perimeter I thought I saw your Humvee turn this way. I saw the sign for the grade school, and I knew you couldn't resist a grade school named after your favorite mountain. Any way, I was worried about how you fared in the bombardment, and I wanted to see how you were. Captain Conners had thought you were safe in some sort of shelter..."

"Thank you for your concern, Corporal. I had been in a shelter, but I was getting claustrophobic in that thing. Well built, though! Anyway, the bombing had abated and I wanted to get out."

"I know I wasn't cleared, and I hope it isn't a problem with you that I came by. I just..."

"Oh, Brian, you've been with me from the beginning. Of course, it's okay for you to come by. I trust you.."

As the young soldier looked at him, Conrad thought he saw in Brian's eyes a look of confusion, and he interpreted it as questioning the appropriateness of his playing children's games while the city was still imperiled.

"You know, soldier, playing with children does not make one any less of a soldier."

The look of confusion on Brian's face seemed to deepen for a moment, and then all of a sudden the tension in his face relaxed into a moment of recognition.

"Oh!...Yes, Sir. I certainly agree, Sir." I didn't mean to interrupt your time with your granddaughter, Sir. I was just wondering if I might have the privilege of sharing with you some questions I have been having. I mean, I realize I am just one of your soldiers, but..."

"It's okay, Brian. You have always been special to me. Go ahead and ask your questions."

"Thank you, Sir. I was wondering, Sir, how you think the war is going now, whether all is meeting your expectations?"

"My expectations are not important, soldier, only God's plans. But, yes, I believe God is showing by our successes that we are acting according to his plans. Those forces loyal to the antichrist, the so-called President of the United States Albert Packard, have found that we are not just another David Koresh, Saddam Hussein or even Osama Bin Laden, easily quashed. Not only have we held our positions here, but the city of Zion's Gate remains firmly in our grasp."

Conrad pointed toward the mountains to the East. "In addition to our troops in those cities, we have another 50,000 loyal to us in the mountains of the Northwest. They will soon move on the city of Boise and add that city to God's kingdom. Movements in sympathy to us have arisen throughout the nation, and indeed, throughout the world. Our actions have thrown Wall Street and markets around the world into a tailspin from which they will never recover. Revelation speaks of a time of extremely high inflation, and that time has come to this country and the world. It is all just a matter of time – and very little time at that."

Brian quietly nodded. Then he spoke almost in a whisper. "A lot of people have died, Sir."

Conrad nodded in return. "Yes, yes, and in the short run that is very lamentable. And many more will die before all of this is over. But it will not be long, Brian, before God will raise them all up, along with all of the dead of history, the good and the faithful to eternal life, and the evil and faithless to eternal damnation.

There will be no difference between those who have nodded off in their beds at ninety-seven and those who died in war at a tender age. All will be judged together, and for those who were faithful, their pains in this life will be quickly forgotten."

Conrad put his hands on Brian's shoulders and looked into his eyes. "The important thing is to be faithful, Brian. Under all of the toughness you show in battle, you have a tender heart, as I did at your age. I love that about you. But we cannot let that interfere with faithfulness."

Brian stared back into Conrad's eyes. "You think I have a tender heart?"

"I know you do, Son. I know you do."

Conrad thought he saw tears forming in the eyes of the young soldier, but Brian looked away from the older man, and that seemed to stem the flow.

"They're going to come after you, Sir – you particularly. What will happen if they..."

"They won't touch me, Son, so don't worry about that. Whatever they do, I am in God's hands. I rest assured in that promise."

"There are rumors," responded Brian, "rumors that they are going to nuke your cities."

"No, I don't think so. Packard doesn't have the guts. Besides, I have one of my people who will know if they make that kind of decision, and I will be out of here before they implement. Imagine them nuking their own city and not getting me! That may even make things easier for us."

Conrad saw the startled look in Brian's eyes. "Of course, I wouldn't want to lose any of my own men. But even if I do, none of that will matter when the Lord comes."

Brian nodded, almost imperceptibly. "Certainly. And you still have another nuke to get them back."

"Yeah, well, for the next few days anyway."

"The next few days?"

Conrad glanced over at the children who were still playing, oblivious to their conversation. Then he looked back into Brian's eyes.

"Yeah, I suppose I can talk to you about this. Brian, what has done more to undercut the good, solid Christian values which our country was built on than any other influence in our society?"

Brian shrugged. "The atheists, Sir?"

"No, no. Nobody listens to professed atheists. It's the commercial forces that just don't care about God one way or another that you have to watch out for, and the worst of these has been Hollywood."

"Oh yes, certainly, Sir."

"It's a city of the damned, Brian – literally. They do all they can to spread glitter over the ugliest, most evil acts in life, and they try to make all that is true a lie. Nothing but a bunch of perverts, skirt-chasers, and money-mongers, trying to make what they do look good and beautiful. Like Paul warned, they 'changed the truth of God into a lie.' Well, no more, Brian. No more. Fire and smoke will rise up from the heart of the great whore, and it will be no more."

"No more Hollywood," said Brian quietly.

"No more Hollywood!" affirmed Conrad with resolution.

Brian and Conrad stood there quietly for some time, lost in their thoughts. The only sound was the laughter of children and the whistling of the wind. The sounds of war were all gone for that moment in time, and it was as if the world knew nothing of what had been only a short time before, or what was coming in the weeks ahead. It was simply a moment of peace. The young soldier then focused again on his commander.

"Sir...you said something before the attack about wanting me to talk to people, to get them on our side?"

"Yes, soldier. I think you would be good at that."

"Well, then, if I have your leave to go, I will start that right away."

"Certainly, soldier, you have my leave."

Then, instead of saluting, Corporal Brian Marshal stepped forward and kissed his commander on the cheek. Before Conrad could grasp hold of a response, the young man had turned and left.

Chapter Eleven

Like a doe caught in an open field, the young woman stared at Brian and did not move. She was not wearing the same flowered dress as before, but Brian could never have forgotten that face, that tender, wounded expression. It seemed that at any moment she would bolt, and Brian almost felt he should approach her stealthily, with an open palm and a lump of sugar. Instead he spoke quietly.

"I am not your enemy."

The young woman's face turned slightly, and she looked at him now out of the corner of her eye. She took a couple of tentative steps in his direction.

"You overrun our city with your tanks and your troop trucks. You carry guns to keep us here and away from where you do not wish us to go. I have seen such actions before. I am not stupid. I will believe your actions rather than your words."

Brian looked around the streets of the city which Conrad called New Bethel, to see who might be watching. The only other civilians were about a hundred yards down the block, and were wrapped up in their own conversation. A smattering of soldiers posted on various street corners looked disinterested. Nevertheless, Brian took a couple of steps closer.

"Could we go somewhere private to talk? I have much to tell you, and I think you might like to hear what I have to say."

"No, but this is a fine place for two people who are strangers to talk. At very least we are strangers to one another, wouldn't you say? You are a man and you think I am pretty, so you want to talk to me. If I were not pretty, I could just as easily be getting the butt of your gun, and be told to stay out of your way."

"I'm not like that."

"Is that so?"

Brian took another couple of steps in her direction, and she held her ground, her jaw now firmly set and her eyes focused on him with a steely, penetrating glare. Brian knew that all she was saying made sense from her perspective, and had his own sister been in a similar circumstance, he would have advised her to take the exact same approach he found himself up against – outspoken and courageous, and yet firmly maintaining proper cautions. Still, from a personal perspective he hungered to get past those defenses, and touch this woman in emotional as well as physical ways. And there were now some urgent practical considerations which he needed her to help him with as well.

"What country are you from?" Brian asked.

"Romania."

"Is that where all that pain comes from which I see in your eyes?"

"Of course. Although I have since learned that this country is not without its sources of pain as well. I see you standing there with that rifle that could rip my body into pieces, and I think I have seen those like you many times in my own country. I was only eight years old when my family left, but I remember. The communists also thought they were there to give us a better world, you know. Nobody would be poor. The nationalism and religion that created wars would be eliminated, and we would all live at peace. But that's not what we got. Everywhere there were soldiers and secret police, and we all got to share equally in the poverty. I saw my older brother shot to death by such soldiers. I saw the look of fear in my parents' faces. The soldiers tried to make me afraid too, even though I was but a child. I vowed to never let them. One night we were all to be in our homes and I was outside. A soldier stuck the barrel of his gun in my face and he laughed in a mean and wicked way. But I just looked at him like I didn't care. Soon he went away."

Brian looked into the young woman's eyes and he could tell why that soldier had gone away. It was the look of a spirit that would not be beaten.

"You were very brave for such a young child."

"I did not think of it as being brave. I just did what I had to do."

"Of course," replied Brian, with as gentle of an inflection in his voice as he could manage. "How did your family escape?"

"Friends who were able to work their way into places of influence. Just a few months after they helped us get out, the government of dictator Nicolae Ceausescu was toppled. Communism in Romania was over. Neo-Stalinism was over. But the poverty of Romania remained, and the bad memories remained. My family never went back."

"You need to be brave again," advised Brian, "and you need to trust a friend again for deliverance. Listen...please, I don't even know your name. Could you trust me first of all with your name?"

"Why do you need to know my name? If you are planning to shoot me or rape me, my name would only remind you that I was a person."

"Yes!" Brian said in exasperation, "and it's exactly because I do not want to do such things that I desire your name."

The young woman cocked her head to the side again and looked at Brian out of the corner of her eye. After a moment of thought she shrugged her shoulders.

"I am Elena – Elena Enesco."

Brian smiled in relief, and held out his right hand. "I am Brian Marshal, Elena."

Elena cautiously took his hand, but rather than shaking it, Brian just held onto it gently.

"Elena, I want you to trust me to be the one to deliver you from this just like your friends in Romania did." Brian now spoke in a whisper. "I am no longer in sympathy with what is going on here. I'm helping the government to...to end it. But I need your help. Can you trust me enough to give me that help?"

Brian felt a slight trembling in Elena's hand, but her eyes held firm.

"What kind of help?"

"I could talk about that more easily in private."

"Nobody is close by. What kind of help?"

Brian's continued whisper had the added benefit of encouraging Elena to move a little closer. "I have some information that I need to communicate to the FBI. They can help end this. But it's not safe for me to communicate on city computers or city phones. I know Conrad has had soldiers cut phone and modem lines throughout the city, and he's taken a lot of computers and cell phones, but he can't have gotten them all by now. Do you have access to something I can use?"

Elena stood there quietly studying his face, as if she were a chemist studying an intricate formula. She showed no embarrassment over the period of silence which this created, even though it was making Brian shuffle back and forth. Finally she spoke.

"I might be able to find something for you. I'm not sure. But perhaps now is a good time for that place of privacy you requested earlier. I own a gift shop down the street. My apartment is situated above it. We can go there if you like."

Brian nodded and Elena took hold of his arm and walked him down the street and into the alley, down which Brian had seen her run the day before.

"There are other soldiers around," Elena noted. "Will they be suspicious?"

'No, I don't think so. Conrad has asked me to serve as kind of a PR person with people in the community. I'll just say that's what I am doing. And those who don't believe that will just think that...uh..."

"That you are 'getting lucky'?"

"Yeah, I suppose."

Elena stopped by what appeared to be the back door of her shop, and pulled a key out of her purse.

"Is that what you also think?" The tone in Elena's voice was lighter as she said this, though not to the point of being playful or flirtatious.

"I...uh...I think that I have gotten lucky in the sense of finding someone to trust who is at the same time very beautiful. I presume nothing more than that."

Elena nodded. "I like that answer."

Elena opened the door to her shop and Brian followed her in. His eyes were immediately drawn to some elaborately painted Easter eggs on a display near the center of the shop. He walked over and picked one up.

"Please, those were hand-painted in Romania, and they are very delicate. 'You break it, you buy it.'" And then for the first time since he met her a slight smile came to Elena's lips. "I'm sorry, but that is the gift shop owner's motto. Their Union makes me say it."

Brian chuckled. "Well, they are very beautiful."

"Painting them is a form of folk art in my country. I sell a lot of them out of my shop here."

"I'd like to buy one."

"For you, the special occupation and terrorism discount of five thousand dollars."

Brian quickly looked up and saw a twinkle in her eye.

"Okay," she continued, "If you must bargain with me, then thirty-five dollars, but not a penny less."

Brian laughed again, and reached into his wallet. He put the required amount down on the counter.

"U.S. currency, huh?" she quipped. "I was hoping for gold or something that actually was worth something. But if that is all you have, then it will have to do."

"Do you want me to just leave it here on the counter?"

"Sure," responded Elena, "the good thing about this inflation is that it means nobody wants to steal it."

Elena unlocked another door, this one exposing a staircase leading to the upper floor where her apartment was. Brian fell in behind her, but she turned and looked at him.

"When my family came here, and before my parents died last year, we vowed to never allow weapons in our home. So far I have managed to hold true to that vow. You will need to leave yours down here."

Brian unstrapped his M-16 and leaned it against the wall, and then he unbuttoned his holster and dropped a sidearm on the counter.

"Is that all?"

"That's it!" replied Brian.

"Good. Then if you would be so kind as to open that drawer, pull out my revolver and hand it to me so that I can shoot you?"

Brian had already opened the drawer before she had finished her sentence. He now saw it contained only a Nerf gun, and Brian smiled and handed it to her.

"No good," she continued. "I forgot my nephew neglected to leave the bullets. Just my luck. Anyway, come along."

Elena's apartment was decorated in antiques, evidently all from Romania or Eastern Europe. If it weren't for the flowers and the lively beauty of the owner, Brian would have felt like he were walking into a set for one of those old vampire movies set in Transylvania.

"This is very elegant," he said. "I thought your family was poor in Romania."

"Not always. We owned a vineyard at one time. Our home was in the foothills around the Carpathia Mountains, but our property was seized by the Communists and most of the profits sent off to pay the national debt. We were left with virtually nothing to live off of, but we were allowed to retain certain family heirlooms like the pictures and the old clock on the mantle, and many of what you call 'knick-knacks.' Our furniture we had to leave behind when we left the country, but I have purchased what is here at great expense, and had it shipped from Romania to replicate how I remember it being when I was a child. My father always taught me that I should never let anyone rob me of my heritage. That is what all this represents to me."

"Your father seems to have meant a great deal to you."

"Yes, he did," replied Elena. "And my mother as well. How about your father?"

Brian wondered if Elena could sense his chilled reaction. He glanced in her direction and from what he saw, he guessed that she had.

"I...uh...I've only learned to appreciate how much he meant since he died."

"Oh," Elena said quietly. "Well, I think I have some more mementos in which you might be interested in this closet."

As Elena opened the closet and began digging through things there, Brian walked over to the mantle and picked up a framed photograph. It showed a father, a mother, on older boy, perhaps in his middle teens, and a brown-eyed little girl who was held in her father's arms. The girl was no more than three or four and had an impish look in her eyes. Brian turned his focus to the older boy. There he saw the same look of pain he had recently seen in the boy's now adult sister.

"Is this the brother who was killed?"

The noises in the closet suddenly stopped, and Elena glanced at him past the opened door.

"Yes."

"And so now he knew he had inflicted some pain of memory on her like she had even less intentionally inflicted on him just moments earlier. He hoped she saw the sorrow in his eyes. She went back to digging in the closet, and a few seconds later came out with a familiar looking black case.

"Well, I guess I didn't really have any mementos to show you from the closet, only this much newer laptop computer. I do actually use it quite a bit, but I keep it out of sight since it clashes with the spirit of my decor. I guess that's why your friends missed it when they came earlier."

"All right!" Brian exclaimed, almost leaping toward Elena. "Let's power that baby up!"

By the time Brian was ready to type in the right e-mail address his hands were trembling.

"Can you type with your hands that way?"

"Hell, I can't type all that well normally," replied Brian, "but I'll get it done if it takes all night."

"Who said you could stay all night?"

Brian just smiled.

"I don't suppose I could help," continued Elena. "Too confidential?"

Brian thought for a moment. "No. It's not a matter of lack of trust. I figure you're trusting me, so I should trust you. You can watch if you want. But, I don't know, I've just got to do this myself."

Elena stepped over behind him, leaned down and looked over his shoulder. Brian could feel the warmth of her breath on his cheek, her perfume filled his nostrils, and he began to wonder if he should have taken Elena's offer. His fingers became even more erratic, and he mistyped his confidential code number three times. However, as he got into the body of the message, the words started to flow more easily, and as the words came Brian could feel Elena's hand tightening on his shoulder.

"Another bomb? Oh, God! He told you that?"

Brian nodded and kept on typing. Elena seemed to react with each word.

"Boise? I have a friend in Boise!"

"Yeah, but you can't tell her anything right now. We've got to let the government handle this."

"Yes, of course. That's always worked for me."

Brian noted the sarcasm but kept on typing.

"He's got some of his people among Packard's advisors? And this is the government you want me to trust to handle this?"

"We have no other choice, Elena!"

Now Brian's fingers suddenly froze in position above the keys.

"Are you finished?"

Brian shook his head almost imperceptibly. The sweat beaded on his forehead and began trailing down his cheeks.

"Brian?"

Brian leaned back in his chair and let his hands drop to his sides. "I have something else which I need to tell him, but I'm not sure that I can do it."

"Something harder than what you've written already?"

Brian nodded. The face of E.J. Conrad flashed in his mind. He thought of that time years ago when Conrad's eloquence had first caught his imagination. He had seen it as a vision of justice, order and righteousness. He thought of the relationship they had developed over the years. He thought of the last time Brian had seen him, playing with children.

"What is it, Brian?"

Brian's whole body was now trembling, and he felt his pulse pounding in his temples. "I've got information that could kill him."

"Well, that's good, isn't it?"

Brian buried his face in his hands. "You don't understand. You don't know what I've been through with this man."

Elena pulled up a chair next to him, and she gently turned Brian's face toward her.

"No, I don't know. So tell me. Tell me like I told you what I've been through."

As Brian looked into Elena's eyes, he realized that the pain he saw there now was a reflection of the pain she sensed to be his own. *How could she care in such a way when she had so much pain of her own?*

"You asked about my father. I was not close to him. It was my fault – I see now that he tried. But something just kept turning me away from him. We saw life far differently. When I met E.J. Conrad, I thought he was everything I was looking for in a father. My own father never challenged me; he never gave me a vision of something bigger I could be part of. He had his own vision, but I could never see it as my own. When E. J. Conrad spoke of God's kingdom, here on earth, it stirred my heart. I could see it. I could feel it. It made me want to give my all in order to be part of it. You can't understand what is happening now unless you understand that."

Elena nodded tentatively. Brian knew that she was trying to understand, but what she had seen herself was no doubt raising many questions for her.

"And even with all of the violence that he has been responsible for since, he has always been far different with me. His personal gentleness and his vision made it seem like the violence had a purpose, a necessary purpose."

"But Brian," Elena interjected, "surely you see now the pain and destruction he has caused."

Brian buried his head in his hands again, and nodded as he did. "But I'm having trouble putting the pictures together – the pictures of violence with the picture of the man who...who plays

189

with children and sees a better world for them. The picture of the man who lifted me up and helped me believe in myself, and the picture of the man who led me to the acts that now keep me up at night and cause me to hate myself."

Elena was starting to squirm. "You...you have been part of his violence?"

Brian could only bear to glance at Elena's eyes before turning away. Then he nodded his head.

"...in ways that I cannot bear to admit to myself, much less to you."

"You can only heal the wound that you expose to the air of another's acceptance."

"But what if it is of such a nature that there can be no acceptance?"

Elena was quiet for what seemed to Brian an interminably long time. Finally she spoke. "Then at least you would have taken the chance you needed to be whole."

It was the middle of summer and yet Brian felt a chill. He felt like he was stepping to the edge of a cliff to dive into dark, stormy waters far below. He took a breath and leapt.

"I was part of the assault on the ACLU. I didn't do the detonation, but I was there. It was after that that I was recruited by the FBI. Of course, I have had to fight in some battles since then, but that doesn't bother me because it's necessary to maintain my cover. There was...there was one other incident that does bother me a great deal, though."

Brian started to breathe more heavily, and his stomach was getting queasy.

Elena leaned slightly forward. "Yes?"

"Conrad felt...he felt my father was a dangerous voice, a dangerous voice who was leading our society along an immoral path. He...I guess to kind of test me...he sent me out with some other soldiers..."

Brian could feel his eyes becoming moist. He had always been an emotional man, and it frequently embarrassed him. But right now that tendency paled next to his greatest shame.

"He sent me out with some other soldiers and...and they...they killed him." Brian paused just a count. "We...we killed him."

Brian's whole body started to spasm and he felt like he would choke on his tears. He didn't have the strength to lift his head even if he had wanted to do so, and he frankly wondered why he hadn't collapsed into a heap on the floor. The silence that followed his pronouncement was heavy and seemed to last forever. He had no visual cues as to what Elena was thinking because he could still not bear to look in her direction. *But what else could she be thinking?* He had become everything that had destroyed her childhood. The land in which that had occurred was geographically far away, but he had brought it emotionally far closer than Elena would have ever wanted.

Brian now thought he heard the sound of Elena's crying over his own. He wasn't really sure. But of the next experience he was startlingly sure. A soft tissue in an almost equally soft hand was dabbing the tears from his cheek. When the first one became saturated, an equally soft fresh one picked up the task. And now Elena's other hand gently lifted his chin until he could see through the blur the contours of her face. As she dabbed the tears from his eyes, the beautiful details of that face became more clear. She had been crying. No one had dabbed those tears from her face. But shining through those tears was gentleness, not bitterness or anger.

Finally, she spoke with her words. "Brian, do you see that painting on the opposite wall?"

Brian nodded. "It's...it's great."

"It's of Saint Peter, Brian. It is my most prized possession...kind of my personal icon, if you will. Are you a Christian, Brian?"

Brian nodded again.

"Then you know his history. When he denied his Lord, the most precious blood of history spattered on his hands. But Jesus wiped them clean with his forgiveness, and Peter had a second chance. He didn't waste it, Brian. He gave his life in testimony to the Lord he had denied. That was his healing. Brian, you must become a Peter."

A shot of adrenaline could not have revived Brian's heart more quickly than had Elena's words. He felt like someone had just, for the first time, given him permission to breathe. Still, there was something that remained.

"But what do I do about Conrad?"

Elena brushed back the moistened locks of hair from Brian's brow, and with an expression that was at the same time gentle and firm, she looked into his eyes.

"That man is not your father, Brian; he is your demon. I think you know what you must do to exorcise him."

Brian's eyes fell back to the computer screen and its patiently-blinking cursor. His hands spread out across the keys. Those hands were poised for but a moment, and then they slowly began to peck out their message, which Elena read as it appeared:

"Conrad has a shelter, but his primary command post is at Saint Helens Elementary School. I found him there right after the last assault. A well-placed missile could take him out."

Brian read over the last sentence several times, and then before he could think about it any further, he clicked "send."

"God, I hope he keeps his granddaughter away from there!"

Elena, who again stood behind him, bent down and gently leaned her head on his shoulder. "You must not think that part is in your hands."

Brian nodded. Then almost instinctively, as a flower turns its face to the sun, he turned and found the softness of Elena's lips. He met no resistance.

■■■

E.J. Conrad slammed his fist down on his desk so hard that a piece broke off of the corner.

"How the hell did they find it?"

General George Dawson, peering out the window of Conrad's office at the Mount Saint Helens Elementary School, just shook his head.

"I don't think they could have, Sir, unless..."

"Unless what?"

"Unless we have a leak, Sir. That's a pretty disturbing thought – the location of that bomb was high-level information. I mean, I can see them knowing enough through surveillance to be prepared for Boise, but not the bomb. We've got a leak. There's no other explanation."

"All in one day! All in one day!" Conrad kicked a table, and a lamp crashed to the floor. "A lot of good boys died in that Boise assault. Who could have betrayed them?"

The General turned from the window and walked toward his Commander-in-Chief. "Was anyone outside of the command team and 'the delivery boy' told of the bomb's placement?"

"No! I..." Conrad suddenly froze. *It couldn't be Brian! He couldn't do such a thing! Could he?* Conrad went over that last conversation in his mind. He had told him of the bomb's general placement – nothing specific, but perhaps enough for it to be found, when paired with other intelligence information. He had also told him of Boise. But of all the young men he knew... *If it were Brian, what else might he have disclosed?*

"Sir?"

Conrad looked over at the general, whose face revealed his anxiety over Conrad's demeanor. It would be embarrassing to Conrad to reveal his suspicion. To the general it would appear excessively careless. But what else could he do?

"There is...one possibility." He called for his aide in the next room. "Get me Corporal Brian Marshal."

"A corporal?" The general's query came out almost like he was spitting out the words. "You told a frickin' corporal?"

"A friend!" Conrad cried out in response. "I'm sure he's not the one, but I just want to check him out."

The general threw up his arms in disgust. "With all due respect, what the hell were you thinking? What possible reason could you have had for putting these operations at risk by revealing confidential information?"

Conrad glared at his chief military advisor. "Nobody else could have done what I have done! You know that! So, show some real respect, and keep your criticisms to yourself. I am perfectly capable of recognizing my mistakes on my own."

General Dawson visibly bristled at the rebuke, but he quickly regained his composure.

"Yes, Sir."

"I made a mistake," Conrad continued. "He found me here with my granddaughter, and my defenses were down..."

The General stiffened again. "Begging your pardon, Sir. Here?"

"Yes, here..." As Conrad said the words, their import struck home to him. "Okay, let's get out of here!"

Conrad set off an alarm to warn others in the building, and then set off for the door. As the two leaders burst through the outer door of the school, Conrad quickly spotted the white trail streaking through the sky from the North. Soldiers from the school were scattering in all directions. Conrad looked for the Humvee, but it was gone. His aide had taken it to get Brian Marshal. *Merciful God, Marshal has done this too! Well, he was messing with the wrong man!* Just then, in what Conrad saw as an act of God, a woman who was a neighbor of the school pulled up in her pickup. Conrad, with the vigor of a much younger man, ran up to the passenger side and leapt in. General Dawson was but a few steps behind, and he high-jumped into the truck bed. Without any time to spare, Conrad pulled out his automatic pistol and put it to the driver's head.

"Turn this vehicle around, and get the hell out of here, NOW!!"

The woman paused but a second before she started twirling the steering wheel and redirecting the vehicle. Then she hit the accelerator and her rear tires squealed. Conrad estimated they had traveled for about five seconds before the missile hit the school. Fire and smoke shot up over their heads as the impact knocked the truck sideways into a parked mini-van. It then careened across the street and slammed into a tree.

The next thing Conrad knew he was sitting in the front seat of the truck with blood streaming down his face. The driver was semi-conscious, moaning, with her head resting on the steering wheel. Conrad pushed his door open and stumbled into the grass of someone's yard. He pulled himself up to look into the truck bed. General Dawson was not there. Conrad wiped the blood from his eyes with his shirt and looked around. He spotted the body near the minivan they had sideswiped. Conrad staggered across the road, knelt next to him and felt his neck. No pulse. Blood was pooling under the General's head.

Just then Conrad's Humvee, driven by his aide, pulled up next to them.

"God! What the...?" The aide interrupted himself, thinking better of the language he was about to use. "Begging your pardon, Sir. Are you okay, Sir?"

Conrad ignored the question and focused exclusively on the one sitting in the passenger seat. Brian Marshal could not so much as look in his direction.

Conrad stormed up to him, slapped off Marshal's helmet, grabbed him by the hair, and pulled his head back so he could look into the soldier's eyes. Brian's mouth said nothing, but his eyes said all that the older man needed to know.

"It WAS you! Merciful God, I can't believe it! It was you!"

Conrad pulled the corporal out of the car and slammed him down on the pavement. Then he began kicking the soldier in the side and the gut. Any thoughts the soldier may have had of fighting back were quelled by the fact that Conrad's aide now pulled out his M-16 and had it aimed point-blank at Brian's head.

"How the hell could you do this to me?" Conrad continued screaming. "I treated you like my son...better than my son. I taught you everything that God revealed to me. You've not just rejected me; you've rejected him!"

Brian spit blood from his mouth, and pulled himself up enough to finally look his assailant in the eye. "That's right, Professor Conrad, I have rejected him! I have rejected your god because of what he did to you, what he has done to the world through you, what he did to ME!...what he turned me into! I reject him. I reject him for the God of my father."

Conrad glared with incredulity at his former disciple. "There is but one Holy God! He will judge you like he judged your faithless father and found him wanting. He will judge you in such a way that you will in that day long for my own tenderness and mercy!"

Conrad gave the soldier one last kick in the groin, and then turned to his aide. "Lock Corporal Marshal up with the other perverts of the town, until we can give sufficient attention to his execution."

Three trucks full of soldiers came screeching to a halt nearby. The ranking officer of each ran over to their Commander-in-Chief's side. Conrad pointed in the direction of General Dawson's lifeless form.

"The General has made the ultimate sacrifice for the cause. Have some of your men properly care for his remains. If the Federal forces think they may have gotten me, they're going to go all-out to capture the city, and I don't want him still lying here when they do! I am putting all units on highest alert."

A medic jumped out of one of the trucks and ran over to attend to their leader. Conrad tried to wave the man off, but he was persistent, and Conrad finally gave in. Still, he just desperately wanted to be left alone, to let his heart bleed where no one could see it but his God alone. Unfortunately, his bleeding had become a very public matter.

Chapter Twelve

As a political conservative, Drew had complained for years about the Washington bureaucracy. Now it had taken him a while to realize that there no longer was one. While the top government officials had been rotated in an out of Washington D.C., and hence many of them had been saved from the nuclear assault, most lower-level and middle-level bureaucrats had simply been kept in place, and now they no longer were. They had been vaporized, along with their computers, their files, their palm pilots, the places they had met to plan over lunch, their athletic clubs, and for the most part, their previously-neglected families. In their place was a gaping hole, a gaping hole in the geography south of College Park, and a gaping hole in leadership of the nation.

The nation still had a President and Vice-President, and there remained some of the military leadership, although many of those were suspect. How many who survived did so because of inside-track information from E.J. Conrad on the destruction of the city? The economy and self-confidence of the nation had also received some critical blows. Trading on Wall Street was suspended indefinitely.

In the midst of this crisis, Drew more than ever, had a job to do. He had to report the news of what was happening, certainly. But more than this Drew was a commentator, a columnist who was to bring some kind of meaning to all that was happening, and as Drew was more and more beginning to believe, to point the nation to whatever sources of hope and direction that could be found. To do that meant he had to do some searching himself, searching through his own heart and the hearts of the people who had escaped the devastation of what had once been Washington, D.C. It was to that task he was now devoting himself.

Drew set up an interview station in a place that had already grabbed hold of an important place in his own memory – the visitor's dugout in Oriole Park at Camden Yard. An *Oregonian* photographer was there with him, and Shawna served as his assistant, lining up interviewees. Refugees wanting to be interviewed, and those just interested in listening and observing, lined up nine or ten rows deep.

The first person Shawna had lined up was a construction worker who had fled the DC suburbs with his family.

"You want to know what I think should be done? I think they should nuke those assholes in Longview and Spokane, and be done with it! How can we let them keep on doing what they are doing to our country? We were the greatest nation on earth, and now look at us!"

"But what about the civilians still living in those cities," responded Drew, "people who have nothing to do with what Conrad is doing? And what about the nuclear fallout that would result?"

"Did they consider that with us? I'm sorry about the innocent ones, but sometimes lives have to be sacrificed to save the nation. That's just the way it is!"

"It's obvious that last fellow has no family members living in those cities," opined a woman who had fled from College Park. "I have a sister and several nephews and nieces in Spokane. I've already lost a son and a lot of really great friends in what happened here. I'm not ready to lose anyone else! We have to be patient in going after these thugs. Otherwise, we will destroy everything!"

"What's left to destroy?" asked the next woman, who had been on a sales trip when the bomb hit. "I have no family left. Many here have no family left. Our nation is in shambles. People talk of recovery. What is there to recover, and where do I have to go to recover it? My life is over, and I say let's take those mother-fuckers with us!"

Many in the crowd around the dugout cheered these words. The next man in line was one of those who cheered.

"Hey, I don't think we should stop with Conrad's group. I say we take every one of those God-damned Christians out talkin' about Revelation and the end of the world, and we drop 'em off where the White House used to be, and let 'em live there in tents until their children are born with third eyes, and until they're all pukin' all over each other. They want to send us all to hell? Let 'em know what hell is!!"

The next man had obviously been crying, and he could barely talk. "Okay, we're all in bad shape...really bad shape. I...I really can't say what I've left to live for either. I had children. I had a home. But I think that's why I just can't say, you know, 'To hell with it, kill 'em all!' I don't want to do that to anyone else. I..."

The man decided that he could say no more. As Drew looked around at those gathered, he saw tears in the eyes of many more like him – hurting people, stunned by violence and left virtually without words.

Drew talked to thirty different people before he decided to cut off the interviews. It had been one of the most physically and emotionally exhausting things he had ever done. And ending it wasn't easy either. Many more people wanted to talk and give their opinion, and some didn't want to take "no" for an answer. Drew, Shawna and the photographer finally had to arrange to leave through the visiting team's clubhouse.

Writing his column on the experience was only slightly easier. Harold decided to put in the comments of the various interviewees almost unedited. Only the crude language and an occasional libelous comment were expunged. But from these comments Drew had to write something that would help make some sense of it all, and if possible, bring an element of hope. It wasn't going to be easy. He sat at his computer just staring at the screen for fifteen to twenty minutes before he could even type a word. But then as he got going, the words started to flow, and by the time he was finished an hour and a half later, he felt he had come up with something that was, if not inspired, at least a notch above what he had seen written on the subject to that point. He read over one part in particular:

"As Americans we have crashed head long into our own vulnerability. Before, we knew of it in our minds, but we dismissed it from our experience. We convinced ourselves that the only death we might face was that death that rumor had it came after many, many years of sitting in hot tubs, eating expensive dinners, and shopping for an infinite number of items we had been convinced we needed. War was something that was always held in someone else's country, and if our young people died, they died far away from the view of all but our news services. The destruction of whole cities was something that was only possible in movies we could leave and books which we could put down. The terrorist attack by Bin Laden against the World Trade Center warned us that something was not quite right with this vision of the world, but we chose to deal with that as an aberration from which tougher security measures against foreigners might deliver us.

"Now we have all found ourselves waking up in what seems like a foreign world. In just a blink of the eye, death has taken up residence on this side of the horizon, and we cannot find a place to look away. We are stunned. We are angry. And certainly there is much with which to be angry. E.J. Conrad and those who have been foolish enough to follow him have stabbed this nation in the heart. One who has spoken with many of us against abortion is now seeking to abort a whole society. Anger that seeks to bring him down from his perch and call him into account for the damage he has done is anger of the most appropriate kind.

"What we cannot do, however, is to let Conrad have what many are surrendering all too readily – our belief in the goodness and sanctity of life. We surrender that whenever we think that there is nothing left worth living for. We surrender it whenever we think only of what is gone, and not of what remains. We surrender that whenever we let him make us like him --willing to kill indiscriminately en masse, willing to vent our anger against the innocent.

"What we must do as a country is to, perhaps for the first time, find our commonality with the rest of humanity. We can no longer be the nation that simply rises above the tragedy and pain that besets the rest of the world. We must look to Cambodians who have been through the Killing Fields and learn from them what lies on the other side. We must look to the Holocaust that killed six million Jews, not in guilty regret, but to learn the clues and sign posts on the road to survival. We must look to Palestinians – not those involved in terror, but rather those just seeking to make their way through it all – and find our way to a home that cannot be taken away.

"What we must do most of all, however, and I say this without apology – atheists, you can stop reading now – what we must do is to let God lead us to the kingdom. There is something better than what we as people have discovered and created. To find it, we must get back to the source of life itself."

When Drew finished reading, Shawna was looking over his shoulder. She bent down and kissed him on the cheek.

"You really are a good writer," she whispered.

"You doubted?"

Shawna slapped him on the top of his head.

"Your editor called while you were working. I told him you would get back to him."

Drew nodded. "Probably getting impatient to get this material. God, I think that man was born impatient! I am sure he said his first words when he was fresh from the womb: 'It's about time!'"

"So, are you going to call him?"

"Wonderful! Two impatient people. I'll call him! I'll call him!"

When Drew got around to calling Harold Carmichael, the voice on the other end of the phone did not seem at all impatient. Rather it seemed uncharacteristically quiet and reflective. Still, Drew held tightly to his assumptions.

"Look, Harold, I know you're needing my reflections on those interviews, and they are coming. I just have a little fine-tuning that I want to do..."

"That's not what I called you about, Drew. Get it in as soon as you can. It will be okay."

"Then, what...?"

"I've got another assignment for you. I...how are things going between you and that Shawna woman?"

"Great. We haven't killed each other. Now, stop beating around the bush. What is this assignment you don't want to tell me about?"

"Well, we have word that Shawna's brother was the one who supplied the information to the FBI that helped them find the bomb in Hollywood and thwarted the attack on Boise."

"That's what I figured."

"But, now the word is that it got him arrested by the Brigade. Conrad is madder than hell."

Drew glanced over at Shawna, whose concern was showing in her eyes. He was trying not to make her anxiety worse, but he could think of no words to say.

"I...uh...that is a problem."

"Drew, I know this is asking a lot, but I need you to go there."

Drew felt his heart skip a beat. "To Longview?"

"Yes. You're the only one who can do it, Drew. I think you can get in there."

"Well, maybe," he said in a whisper, hoping Shawna wouldn't hear, "but in case you haven't heard they are thinking of nuking the place, and you know my skin, I burn easily!"

"I don't think they're going to do that..."

"'Don't think...'?"

"Okay, it's a risk, but we've got to know what is going on in there. You're a professional, Drew, you know the importance of this. Besides, they have her brother and they're probably going to kill him. Don't you think you should try to do something about that?"

Drew shook his head and let out a deep sigh. "Yeah, well, okay, but what makes you think I could really get in there? Conrad could easily have me killed before I have a chance to do anything."

"Even if he catches you, he won't do that Drew. He still wants to get you on his side, so he's at least going to keep you alive."

Drew looked over at Shawna again. He remembered her pain when she learned of Brian's role in the Brigade's violence. He remembered her tears when Brian went to Longview. Then he thought of his own words, ready now in his computer to be sent out to a world needing direction.

"Okay. Okay. I'll head out tomorrow morning. If I don't come back, plant a tree in your yard for me, and don't let your dog piss on it."

"You got it. But I can't promise about the dog."

As Drew hung up, Shawna came over and sat next to him.

"He wants you to go to Longview?"

Drew nodded.

"Okay, now," Shawna said. "Tell me the rest."

Drew looked questioningly at the woman he had come to love.

"There's something else that he told you that you're not telling me," Shawna continued. "I want it all."

Drew shook his head. "Oh, man, we've got to break this thing off. You're getting to know me too damn well."

"The rest, please."

Drew looked into her eyes. "It's your brother, Hon. Conrad knows what he's been doing and they've arrested him."

Shawna quietly nodded her head. "Okay. When are we going?"

"No! You're not going! They could nuke that city any day..."

"When are we going, Drew?"

"Shawna, I could get in and out of there much easier if you aren't with me, and..."

"Drew!"

"Man, this just isn't working. We're done, okay! I don't know what made us think..."

"Hey! The dog can piss on you along with the damned tree! I'm going to help my brother. Now, when are we going?"

"And Jeremy? What about him?"

Shawna's eyes were moistening and she looked away from him and up at a corner of the ceiling. "Drew, you know me, too. You know I can't just sit around passively waiting while two people I care the world about are in danger. You know I have friends who will look after Jeremy. If something happens to me...well, the world is a hard place these days, but he'll be okay. Now, please, don't make me keep fighting about this. When are we going?"

Drew threw his hands up in the air. "Tomorrow, okay? Tomorrow!"

Shawna nodded, and then walked slowly over to Drew and laid her head gently on his shoulder. "Okay. Then I take back what I said about the dog."

Drew smiled and curled his arm around her. He didn't know how he had come to love such a hard-headed woman, but he hoped that if the need came, her hard-headedness would be just as influential with E.J. Conrad.

■■■

E.J. Conrad leapt out of his Humvee and looked out over the crowd. Right in the middle of the intersection and spreading down both side streets were gathered about three hundred people, holding up picket signs, and singing songs. They were sitting down, linking arms and obstructing the traffic flow in front of the police station. Signs were being waved back and forth which said, "Stand up for your rights!," "Resist the Rebels!," and "He who lives by the sword, dies by the sword!" One woman in a summer dress with blue flowers held a sign calling for the release of Brian Marshal. Conrad took special note of her. The apparent leader, however, was a minister who was seated near the center of the intersection, and who was singing out the loudest of them all. Across the way was a small counter-demonstration. Conrad could see in their midst Carla Morrison and a few others who had appreciated his efforts to eradicate crime.

Lieutenant Tom Jenson stepped to his side. "Should we arrest them all, Sir?"

"Are you kidding, Lieutenant?" responded Conrad. "We don't have enough jail space for all of these people. Set up the portable PA and get me a microphone. Also, find out for me who all the leaders of this thing are, and divert traffic away from here."

Conrad sat down on the hood of his vehicle and waited for his instructions to be carried out. As he did, he watched the people in the crowd. There was obvious tension between those in the middle of the street and people who were part of the counter-demonstration. A number of people in both crowds were looking frequently in his direction, seeking to determine what course of action he might take.

When the PA had been set up, he was set up with a lapel microphone. He picked up his Bible from the Humvee, and called for the PA volume to be turned up as loud as it could be without distortion. After doing a little voice test, he stood on top of the hood of his vehicle.

"Ladies and Gentlemen, I know you have all been waiting for me," began Conrad. "I want to thank the members of the local clergy who have organized this gathering, because while waiting here it occurred to me that most of you have not had the opportunity to be part of one of my Bible classes. And since you all seem to have a lot of time on your hands, and since we now have all traffic routed around this area, I thought I might take advantage of this moment to correct that situation. So, starting with the first chapter of Revelation..."

The crowd stirred and people started murmuring back and forth.

"'The Revelation of Jesus Christ, which God gave unto him, to shew unto his servants things which must shortly come to pass...' Now I would call your attention to several important words here. First of all, it is a revelation that comes from GOD, and second that the things he will be writing about MUST come to pass..."

As Conrad continued to speak, going through Revelation verse by verse, several leaders tried to get the crowd singing even louder, but there seemed to be confusion about what song they were singing, with some singing "We Shall Overcome," some singing "Give peace a chance," and still others were trying to sing songs that Conrad didn't recognize. Still, he patiently moved on with his exposition.

"'Blessed is he that readeth, and they that hear the words of this prophecy, and keep those things which are written therein: for the time is at hand...' Now here we see that Revelation is not ultimately a book of horrors, but a book of blessing, at least for those who react with obedience. And you must ask yourself in what is happening today, are you reacting with obedience to the teaching of this book?..."

The battle of competing voices continued on for well over an hour, which suited Conrad just fine, because there was nothing he liked doing more than teaching about Revelation to a large audience. However, as Conrad also suspected, after a while the size of the group began falling off with each succeeding passage that Conrad spoke about.

After about an hour and a half there were a little over a hundred people left, and Conrad's voice was beginning to get a little raspy. He gave his notes to Lieutenant Jenson, and he read them for about fifteen minutes while Conrad refreshed his voice, and then Conrad came back for another forty-five minutes. The crowd had dropped to around seventy-five. The counter-demonstrators had all left at Conrad's bidding.

The old professor was now speaking about Revelation 6:8: "'And I looked, and behold a pale horse: and his name that sat on him was Death, and Hell followed with him. And power was given unto them over the fourth part of the earth, to kill with the sword, and with hunger, and with death, and with the beasts of the earth.' Now, what all of you here need to know is that this isn't the Walt Disney version of the Bible! And it's being fulfilled here and now."

Conrad looked out over those who remained. Then he jumped down from the hood of his car and called to Lieutenant Jenson.

"Okay, I don't think we're going to weed out many more by this method. I want you to cut out the leaders and put them in jail. Take your clubs and anyone who resists, break their arms. We have more beds in the hospital than we do in the jail."

Jenson lined up twenty of their burliest soldiers and they started plowing through the crowd. As they did the songs at first intensified, but in a matter of minutes the singing turned to wailing as clubs flew through the air. Ambulance sirens soon added to the cacophony. When they ran out of ambulance space, they threw victims in the back of army trucks and hauled them off to the hospital. Within forty-five minutes the intersection was clear.

The door to the jail cell slid open and soldiers started tossing men in like they were tossing bales of hay into a loft. The men offered little resistance and Brian noticed that two of them were wearing clerical collars. A heavy-set woman wearing a clerical collar was taken to another cell a little further down the hall and just as unceremoniously dumped in it.

One of the men thrown into Brian's cell first, a black man, crawled over to the edge of the cell and pulled himself up to a sitting position.

"Oh, man! I told you brothers that we needed some songs with a little more soul, but I didn't think they were *that* bad. They could have just politely asked us to sing something else!"

An older white man who could barely push himself up from a prone position on the floor, responded. "No, that ain't it, Amos. They were actually being nice. They figured that anyone who didn't have the brains to walk out on Conrad's little Bible class, probably needed some assistance."

"You got that right!" the man called Amos said with a combination of something between a laugh and a cry of pain. "If my old professors at Crozier Seminary had heard his exegesis they would have had a hissy fit."

"Yeah, well your liberal old seminary professors didn't know what they were talking about either, Amos," added a younger man who had made his way up to sitting on a bunk. "But any number of profs at Fuller Seminary could have set him straight about the difference between Armageddon and the Tribulation! -- not to mention where the Millenium fits into..."

"Oh, boys, boys!," the voice was coming from the woman down the hall. "Don't you know we get along so much better when we don't talk theology? Besides, had any of you been to Princeton you would have known what a real seminary was."

"Hello?"

Everyone now looked over at Brian, the source of the confused greeting.

"Okay, now this just isn't right," complained Amos. "We HAD a reservation!"

Brian stood up and walked over to the others, holding out his hand to Amos.

"The name's Brian Marshal. What did they bring you in for?"

"Amos Baldwin, Senior Pastor of the First AME Church." He looked over at the others. "And what DID they bring us in for?"

The older man now stepped up to shake Brian's hand. "Carl Tollefson of Trinity Episcopal Church. I wasn't exactly read my rights, but I think the charge was 'attempted sanity.'"

"It wasn't a serious attempt," interjected Amos, "only a cry for help."

"You aren't going to get much serious information from those two," said the younger man as he came over to shake hands. "I'm John Savage, Pastor of the New Hope Community Church. Conrad arrested us for demonstrating against his little regime here. We felt that the spiritual leaders of the community had to take a strong stand against his violence and demagoguery."

"Not me," quipped Amos, "I just said, 'More porridge, please!'"

"How about you?" asked Savage.

"Well, I'm pretty sure 'attempted sanity' wouldn't be a fit description. I'm not sure I know what sanity is anymore. Any way, I turned against Conrad and passed on some information to the FBI. Right now I think he's just trying to think of a painful enough way to kill me."

"Yeah, I think I saw them hauling you into jail that day," said Carl Tollefson. "Rumor was that you were the one who thwarted the assault on Boise and the third bomb attempt."

"Yeah, that was basically it – along with bringing down the missile on the St. Helens school where Conrad had set up his headquarters."

"I salute you," said Carl.

"We all do." The words came from down the hall. "I'm Maggie Morris, by the way. "The old boys club over there may not want to admit it but I was part of that demonstration too. In fact, it was my idea."

"True enough," said Carl. "Maggie is Senior Pastor at First Presbyterian, but she has this idea that we are predestined not to like her, which isn't true."

"Not at all," added Amos. "Our not liking her is totally a matter of free choice."

"Come on, now, guys, none of that is true," said John Savage. "You're giving Brian the wrong idea. The amazing thing is that with all of our differences here, we really do all genuinely like each other."

"Were there a lot of people out for the demonstration?" asked Brian.

"Not as many as there should have been," responded Amos. "The whole damn town should have been out there."

"That's the truth," said Savage. "I have to admit I was pretty disillusioned with some of my congregational members."

"Oh, come on, Savage," quipped Amos. "Your congregation wouldn't demonstrate unless they bombed all the Espresso stands and confiscated their Beamers."

"Cut the crap, Amos. My people are hurting from this just like everyone else."

"Okay, you're right. That comment was inappropriate."

"To answer your question," interjected Carl Tollefson, "I think there were from three to four hundred people out there at one point. Oh, and now that I think of it, there was one young woman out there with a sign that had your name on it – 'Free Brian Marshal!' So you aren't forgotten in here."

Brian felt a shudder go through his body. *Elena. Why did he have to find someone who cared just as he himself was facing his own almost certain death?*

"Yeah...that's uh...good to know."

"So, how come they put me in this cell within sight of you guys?" asked Maggie. "I'm not going to have any kind of privacy here!"

"We'll still respect you in the morning, Maggie." The comment had come from Amos. "Besides, you know you'd miss us."

As the others found places to lie down, Carl Tollefson came over and sat down by Brian on his bunk.

"So, you must have been pretty well trusted by Conrad to be able to get your hands on that kind of information..."

"Yeah, I suppose. But that's been my life – turn on the ones who trust you."

"You don't seem like that sort."

"Really? I'm afraid I'm not always sure what sort I am."

"What other trusting person have you turned on?"

"My father. I helped Conrad kill him."

The old pastor seemed stunned by Brian's admission for a moment, and he just sat there in silence. Then he looked over again at the younger man.

"You must have been a very confused young man."

Brian just looked down at the cement floor. "'Confused,' huh? Are you sure you don't want to use a word like 'wicked' or 'sinful' or 'evil'? Those have always been good clergy words, and to tell the truth, they all might apply."

"I think I'll stick with 'confused.' Why did you do it?"

"Do what? Kill my father or betray E.J. Conrad?"

"Well, both. Let's start with your father."

"That I'm not entirely clear on. I've always been kind of angry, I guess. Then along came Conrad. I guess me with E.J. Conrad is like a lot of guys when they're on alcohol or drugs – it was a bad combination."

"But you broke free of him – free enough to turn on him."

"Yeah, I did."

"People who break free of alcohol and drugs most often need some kind of recovery program."

"Well, I had people who helped. But...they're not in here."

The old clergyman nodded his head. "Well, there was a time in my life when I had to break free from alcohol. And what I found was that, while friends were very important, the best resources I could have were ones I could always take with me – they were internal. Inner peace. Self-acceptance. God inside of me, if you will."

Brian looked into his eyes. They were eyes that showed no sign of pretense, no intent to look away or deceive.

"Yeah, I need that, except, I don't know..."

"If you'll let me, I'll show you. The best resource you have in here is time and the opportunity to focus within yourself. Your life may not be long. None of us may live long. But each moment can be rich. You can live each moment intensely, and use each moment to look close up at life and yourself. God will help you in that. He will come to you in your silence and aloneness."

Brian felt a lump in his throat. "That's what my father was into...toward the end of his life. You kind of sound a little like him."

Carl nodded his head again. "Brian, I have two truths for you." He held his right hand, palm open, to his right side. "On the one hand, you have to be yourself. You cannot follow blindly in the steps of another and ever expect to get where God is calling you to go." Now Carl held out his left hand, also palm open, to his left side. "On the other hand, Brian -- and you need to think hard on this -- it's never too late to listen to your father."

The minister brought both hands together and held them, with open palms face up, in front of Brian. "If you really look into yourself, you will find that you don't have to choose between these."

Brian's eyes were a blur as he looked at the two hands before him. He took his right hand and gently covered them both. Then he looked into the minister's eyes again.

"Show me how."

Chapter Thirteen

Shawna Forester could feel her heart racing as she stared down the barrel of some kind of automatic rifle. Drew had warned her repeatedly of the dangers, but for some reason it had never really broken through to her mind until now that in an instant she actually could die. She looked over at Drew who was facing a couple of rifle barrels of his own. The soldier holding one of those rifles now lowered his barrel a few inches to get a clearer look at Drew's face.

"Hot damn! You really are Drew Covington! My old man got me reading your column and I remember your face up in the corner. Man, you write some good stuff! Dudes, this is Drew Covington. We can't shoot him!"

"Doesn't matter," said the soldier with his sights trained on Shawna. "Our instructions are to let no one into the city, and to kill anyone who tries. Seems to me these two are tryin' pretty hard."

"Guys! Guys! You've got to know I'm on your side! The things you're trying to do in this city are what I've written about all my career – clamping down on crime and porn, outlawing abortion, expecting the population to live up to a high moral standard – you've got to let me see it all in action. You've got to let me tell the world about it."

"The world don't give a damn," said the same soldier, not lowering his gun barrel even a centimeter. "That's why the world is seeing the wrath of God, and we're God's messengers."

The soldier's trigger finger seemed to tighten ever so slightly, and Shawna shivered.

"Yes!" exclaimed Drew. "But I've got to tell you, if you let them know the truth, you might save some more of them. Sad to say, they aren't getting the truth about what's happening here. Some people are even saying that you've turned the city into one giant sex commune, and that Conrad is satisfying his lust with all the best-looking young women."

"The HELL YOU SAY!!" the soldier shouted, finally lowering his gun barrel just a little. "Man, the Father of Lies is alive and well! Why God doesn't immediately strike people dead who tell such lies about a godly man like E.J. Conrad, I'll never know."

"They need a respected voice to tell them the truth. That's why I'm here."

The belligerent soldier looked over at Drew and then back at Shawna. He poked at her nose with the barrel, causing it to sting and bleed.

"What about the bitch? She agree with all you're saying, or is she just along for the ride?"

"Yes! Yes!" replied Drew. "She heard what you all were doing here, and I couldn't hold her back."

Shawna felt blood from her nose trickle past her mouth and down her chin.

"That's right. He couldn't hold me back."

The third soldier, who had previously been silent, now spoke. "How'd you get this far? The other side, they don't want people gettin' in here any more than we do. How come they didn't stop you or shoot you or somethin'?"

"Hey, it's all a mystery to me," responded Drew. "I thought we would be stopped, but we just slipped right past them. All I can say is God must have wanted us here because he cleared the way."

"Man, Drew Covington writing for our side!" exclaimed the first soldier. "That could change some minds for sure! I can see why God would..."

"Not so fast, Gomer!" said the soldier, whose rifle had dropped only to Shawna's chest. "We still have our orders from Conrad. I'm not letting anyone in here without getting his expressed permission."

"Name's not Gomer."

"Whatever." The soldier, who seemed to be in charge, looked back and forth at their two captives. "Okay, here's what we'll do. You two – face down on the ground..."

Drew and Shawna glanced at each other.

"Now!"

The two dropped quickly to the ground.

"Now Andy, you go back and check with Conrad. If he says let 'em through, you come back and give us the thumbs up. Then I'll escort 'em personally into the city. But if he says no, you come back and give us the thumbs down. Now, I mean to tell the two of you that if he does that, well, you better enjoy eating that dirt, because it will be your last meal. You'll hear a little pop, and then your heads will explode all over the ground, okay? Oh, and by the way, I wouldn't be lookin' at each other when that happens, if I were you! Understood?"

Shawna felt so tense she could barely move, but she nodded nonetheless.

"Great! Now get going, Andy."

Andy was apparently the third soldier. He wheeled around and ran back to where a Jeep was parked, he started it up and turned toward the town.

Shawna dug her fingernails into the dirt and waited. *This is the way your life might end. This is the way your child might lose his mother.* Had she answered too quickly back when Drew had warned her and brought up the question of Jeremy's fate? Wouldn't a really good mother have played it safe? Then another thought came to her mind: *Is there any such thing as playing it safe in a world that has E.J. Conrad?* She never had been one to bury her head in the sand while trouble overtook her. Would she have felt any less stressed or any less guilty had she gone home to play with Jeremy while her brother was executed and Conrad plotted to take over some other city, perhaps Portland itself? Probably not. Still, the face of Jeremy kept coming to her mind. She couldn't help visualizing the hurt and fear that would be on that face when someone would come to him and tell him that...

Afraid to look up, Shawna felt her stomach knotting up with the sound of every car engine, every car sound that could mark the return of the message that would determine their fate. When a vehicle finally came down the road and stopped nearby, she feared she would throw up on the ground on which she lay. She fought these emotions with all that was within her. She sought to relax her muscles. And she prayed.

Shawna listened as the footsteps from the soldier known as Andy approached and then stopped a short distance away.

"Well?" It was the voice of the soldier in charge.

There was what seemed to be an interminable silence. Then Shawna heard the "pop," and her whole body went into spasms.

"Hey, no need to get all bent out of shape – it was just a squirrel! You two can get up."

Shawna fought the urge to jump up and tear at the soldier's eyes. Instead, she rose slowly and looked over at Drew. His face was as white as hers felt. She tried to control her trembling, but it was no use. Drew noticed and bolted to her side, throwing his arms around her and holding her close. She collapsed in his arms and started sobbing. She didn't want to. She hated to show such vulnerability around these men. But Drew's arms just seemed to release all of the feeling that was inside of her.

"Hey! I didn't say you could do that!"

"Yeah, but you didn't say I couldn't, either. Besides, Conrad said I could come in and write, correct?"

The soldier nodded begrudgingly.

"Well, she was getting ready to pass out, and I really need her help."

"Yeah, well, let's get a move on. I'm needed back here, and I'm not overly fond of this little babysitting expedition. Andy, you come with us too. We'll need a driver."

On her way to the Jeep, as Shawna walked past the soldier who had tormented them, she couldn't resist looking into his eyes. They were dark eyes peering out at her through narrow slits. They neither softened nor hardened upon meeting hers, but simply observed, as if watching people passing by on a city street; and even then not a street in his own city, where he might recognize someone, but a city far away where everyone passing by was only in view for a few seconds of his life. The coldness Shawna saw in

those eyes made her quickly turn away. She had always advocated openness and understanding toward every human being. But now she wondered at what point people stopped being human beings.
■■

Drew Covington looked out the window of the downtown office that had been set up for his interviews. Outside was a line that extended across the street and around the corner. All of the people there Drew was sure were handpicked by Conrad and his cronies to tell the stories which they wanted to be told. Still, much of what he had heard so far seemed sincere.

The next person now entered the office and sat in the chair opposite the desk which for the moment was Drew's. Off to the side Shawna sat at a smaller desk, taking notes of her own, in case Drew missed something. Outside the office door stood Mike Clancy, the soldier who had escorted them to town after wanting to snuff out their lives like mosquitoes on his arm. Keeping him out of the interview room itself had taken Drew's most persuasive communication skills.

Drew sat down at his desk, turned his recorder back on, and picked up his pen. He had brought his laptop for this, but Clancy had confiscated it. Nothing was leaving this town, even electronically, that didn't have Conrad's stamp on it.

"Let's see, you're Mrs. Reba Martin, is that correct?"

"That's right, Mr. Covington, and can I say what a thrill it is to be interviewed by you? I read your column all the time! I never thought my name might end up in it!"

"Well, of course, individual names may or may not end up in what I write, but thank you for your words of affirmation. Now, what can you tell me about what life has been like for you here under the regime of E.J. Conrad and the Armageddon Brigade?"

"Well, you know, I was frightened at first, but they're kind of winning me over."

"Really?"

"Yeah. You know that before they came around a porn shop set up business just down the block from us. Now, I'm not proud of this, but my husband, he just couldn't leave it alone. I would

217

find pornography hidden away in the garage, and I would come home, and he would turn off the TV real fast, you know? It would turn out he had been watching pornographic videos. I would plead with him to stop, and he would try for a while. But then I would find it again. When the Brigade came in, they didn't worry about 'freedom of expression,' they didn't worry about people who say you can't define what is pornographic – they just shut 'em down! When the guy running that filth hole complained, they threw him into jail! I've gotta tell ya', that move may have saved my marriage."

"But what about the violence, the bombs?"

"Well, I'm just talking about what they're doing here. The other, well, they say we're fighting a war. When there is a war, there are people who die. All I can say is, when it's all over, if the whole country, the whole world, is run like they're running things here – well, I wouldn't object at all."

After Reba Martin left the room, Shawna could restrain herself no longer.

"I can't believe that woman! Because Conrad made her husband give up his girlie magazines and videos, she's ready to turn her back on his brutal slaughter and gross violation of human rights!"

Drew let out a deep sigh and shook his head. "Here we go again! I'm not defending Conrad's violence. He's a dangerous man. But on the other hand, you've got to understand how important family is to people. The government hasn't been defending family, and people are tired of it. Sickos can publish all kinds of filth that tears the family apart and, like she said, the government calls it freedom of expression."

"It IS freedom of expression, Drew! You fight it by publishing a better way. You fight it by couples talking honestly with each other about sex and love. You don't fight it by playing 'Big Brother' and policing everyone else's morals."

"That's fine for strong, healthy people, but what about those who are weak? Like the woman's husband, didn't you hear? He wanted to break free, but couldn't. These people are predators, preying upon the weak. Is it so terrible to want to rescue weak people from something they want to resist, but can't?"

"Yes, actually it is. Because that's how you open the way for demagogues who always think they know what is best for everyone else. I..."

"Okay, Shawna," interrupted Drew, "let's just cut this off right here. We aren't going to agree, and we've got other people to interview."

Shawna's jaw clamped shut, and Drew could see the fire in her eyes. He knew she had more to say, and so he wasn't about to call in the next interviewee yet. After about thirty seconds she spoke again.

"I want to know, Drew, that if I am going to be helping you write about what's happening here, that my opinions are going to be heard. Damn it all! This is far too important for me to just give in to you because of our relationship."

Drew could feel his stomach churning. "Shawna, you may have noticed that my column is not called 'Point – Counterpoint' or 'Crossfire.' The byline under it has one name: Drew Covington."

"I'm not trying to take over your stupid-ass column! I just want your word that my opinion will be heard!"

Drew shut his eyes and rubbed his temples. Had his headache started before Shawna's words, and he just now noticed it? Or had her words that wedged into his brain like spikes, set off this throbbing?

"Shawna, your opinion will be heard because it makes a difference to me and, whether you believe it or not, it influences me. But the thing that irritates me is that you still seem to have this fear that because I agree with some of what Conrad is doing, I'm going to let him off the hook or justify his actions, or even go over to his side. I'm not! Trust my character enough to believe that."

Shawna seemed to calm a bit with Drew's words, and she nodded her head.

"Not that I'm sure what I plan to write matters," he continued. "Conrad probably won't let us out of this city."

Shawna looked over at him. "You don't think so?"

Drew saw the worry in her eyes, and he just looked away. It hurt too much to see her pain when he couldn't do anything about it.

"Who knows? Let's just call in the next person. We'll take it one step at a time."

The next person was a young man in his early twenties named Jason Cooper.

"Okay, Jason, could you tell us what life is like for you now under the Brigade?"

"The kingdom of God is upon us, man. I just know it. This town is becoming so righteous. That Conrad dude really knows his Bible."

"What makes you so positive?"

"Man, my life's been a mess. I was all strung out on drugs an' all. But they've really cleaned up this city. I mean, the regular police used to do raids an' all, but I always had my sources. These guys have rooted 'em all out. One place where there used to be a crack house, they killed all the dealers, leveled the house to the ground, and said nobody could rebuild it – ever. Some kind of purification thing from the Old Testament. And, man, if you walk around here with pot on your breath, you better expect to be hauled off to the slammer! It's helped me clean up. Plus, some of the soldiers, they talked to me about Jesus, and he's really changed me. He's helped me put all those drugs behind me an' all. The kingdom's comin' soon, man. Conrad's just preparin' the way."

"Are you sure the people they are arresting and killing are all guilty?" asked Shawna. "Isn't that pretty extreme action for no real court process?"

"Hell, I don't know about that," answered Cooper. "Uhh...excuse the 'hell' part. All I know is, it's cleaned up the town."

After a couple more interviews, Lieutenant Clancy entered the room.

"Okay, Conrad has decided you've had enough interviews. He wants to see you both in his office right now."

"I really need to organize my notes a little first," responded Drew. "In order to write..."

"Organize your notes later. When Conrad says 'now," he means NOW!"

Clancy swung his M-16 in Drew's direction to emphasize his point, and Drew and Shawna quickly threw their papers into one satchel, and headed out the door.

Clancy had both of his charges blindfolded and cuffed. Drew actually found that a little reassuring. It was doubtlessly done to keep them from being able to reveal the location of Conrad's headquarters, and that meant that, at least at this point in time, the possibility of their release was being considered. However, when the car stopped and they were escorted into the building in which Conrad's headquarters apparently were, it became apparent to Drew that their strategy was not entirely well thought out. As they were escorted down the halls, Drew picked up on the distinctive smells of a hospital.

When his blindfold was removed, Drew found himself in a conference room that had been turned into an office. There was a large walnut desk upon which was an apparently functional PC. Next to it, lying on the desk was a laptop that Drew recognized as his own. In the chair behind the PC sat E. J. Conrad. He punched a few more keys and then looked over at his two guests.

"Well, well, this is a pleasure indeed – Drew Covington and his disgustingly liberal girlfriend, Shawna Forester. Shawna, we haven't met, but it is a special pleasure to have you here. I hope it wasn't too distressful to you when our little bomb disrupted your plans to start – what were you going to call it? – 'The Foundation for American Principles'?"

Shawna's eyes flared in a manner with which Drew was now only too familiar.

"A slight delay, that's all. All worthwhile projects have them."

Conrad walked up and stood with his face just inches from Shawna's, like a drill Sargent getting ready to blast a new recruit. Shawna held her ground, refusing to even let her eyes escape to the right or to the left.

"Not just a delay, Ms. Forester. God has plans of his own, and they don't include your little PC, candy-ass, rights-to-perverts organization."

"I see. The plans of your god only include killing millions of innocent people in a senseless war."

Conrad scowled. "I didn't choose this war. I abhor war. People like you chose it. You chose it when you took away our world of children pledging allegiance and saying their prayers, our world of women who were put on a pedestal, where their bodies were a revered mystery, our world of safe streets and respect for authority – you took it all away, and gave us back a world where children curse and even kill their parents, a world where everything vile and foul is laid out on every street corner, so a righteous man can't even find a place where he can look away."

Drew could see the fear creeping into Shawna's eyes, but he knew she wouldn't back down.

"A righteous person can always choose to look where righteousness is, Mr. Conrad. A world of choice – that's what I, and my father, have worked for."

Drew could see the smoldering, fiery anger in Conrad's eyes, and he fully expected him to strike her, in which case Drew knew both of their lives would be over. He could not do other than strike back in her defense. Miraculously, Conrad restrained himself from such an action. Instead, he turned and focused on Drew.

"Your girlfriend is right about one thing, Drew. Choices do have to be made. I think you know at least something about the Bible, Drew. As such, you probably know what the prophet Elijah said to Israel on Mount Carmel: 'How long halt ye between two opinions? If the Lord be God, follow him: but if Baal, follow him.' Drew, you've got to decide something here. If what we are doing is blessed of God, then it's going to happen with or without you, but you should decide to get on board and be part of it. If it isn't, then turn away, but you can't straddle between. I need you to write for us. I need you to tell these stories of the people you have talked to, people who have seen the benefit of what we are doing. Will you do that or will you not?"

Drew opened his mouth, but he could not respond.

"Scripture says that Israel answered Elijah not a word. Don't be like them, Drew. I want to make you an offer that may help you with your decision. If you write for us, and tell the story that we believe needs to be told, we will release both Shawna and her treacherous brother and they can leave the city. If not, both of you will get to experience our jails, and Brian Marshal will die a traitor's death. Drew, 'choose you this day whom ye will serve.'"

"Don't do it, Drew!" shouted Shawna, grabbing his arm. "You can't let him buy you like that!"

"But, it's your lives, Shawna..."

"I don't care! If you do this, you'll be part of his hate and destruction! You may even be letting him turn you into another one of him! I..."

"Lieutenant!" shouted Conrad as he opened the door. "Have someone escort this woman to our jail right now!"

"Mr. Conrad," Drew protested, "if you harm her, there is no way..."

"We won't harm her, at least not yet," Conrad affirmed angrily. "But I want her out of here before you make a decision. I want it to be your decision, not hers! I swear, I don't know what a person of your sensibilities sees in someone so corrupt in her thinking, but I'm not going to bother with that right now. You must decide, and she must go!"

A soldier who had come in, grabbed Shawna's arm, and Shawna struggled to break free, while she locked her eyes on Drew's. "You've got to listen to me, Drew! Tell him no! Tell him you won't prostitute yourself! You promised..."

The soldier pulled Shawna through the doorway, pulling her hands from the doorframe, and then slamming the door. Still, Drew heard her voice for a moment longer.

"Drew! We can find another way to fight this! You can't give up..."

Conrad looked somberly into Drew's eyes. "Drew, I told you some time ago that Albert Packard wasn't going to stay dead. They say that he was alive all along, but they're lying. He came back to life, just like Revelation says the antichrist would. I am not fighting this war against flesh and blood, but against spirits and the principalities of the air. Do you know that Packard is now considering making people show a 'mark of loyalty' to the federal government?"

"I know he is concerned that he cannot tell his supporters from..."

"It's the mark of the Beast, Drew! Can't you see that? This is a much bigger issue than pleasing a girlfriend who is too naive to see the signs of the times. When I offer you the freedom of Brian and Shawna in exchange for your writing, I'm not trying to force you to do something wrong -- I'm trying to give you an extra motivation to do what is right. You've got to believe me, Drew. God can do this without your help. But doing it with your help would make things so much easier."

Drew once again looked into the eyes of the old professor. He saw nothing but sincerity and determination. Just then a rumbling from Mount Saint Helens shook the ground.

■■

Brian Marshal couldn't remember if his spirit had ever felt so free. Perhaps when he was a child, but those times were hard to remember now. And to think such freedom would come to him at a time when he was in jail. He looked around him at that jail. The other men in his cell had quieted down. Amos was being as quiet as a man who had never recovered from a hyperactive childhood could be. He was wadding up bathroom tissue and trying to toss it into a plastic waste can. John Savage was lying on his bunk reading his Bible, and Carl Tollefson was in the corner of the cell, deep in meditation.

It had been a combination of the latter two activities that had brought Brian the sense of freedom he had found. He looked down at the Bible that had been given to him. Carl was having him look at just four verses, repeating them over and over to himself:

"He will not always accuse,
    nor will he keep his anger forever.
He does not deal with us according to our sins,
    nor repay us according to our iniquities.
For as the heavens are high above the earth,
    so great is his steadfast love toward those who fear him:
As far as the east is from the west,
    so far he removes our transgressions from us."

As long as Brian could remember, his transgressions, his ugly thoughts and actions, had been there accusing him. Had it been God accusing him? Had it been his father, unhappy with the angry son he had seen before him? Or had he simply been his own accuser, playing his own Satan to his own Job? Whichever had been the case, these phrases now reverberated within him: *"He will not always accuse...He will not always accuse...He will not always accuse...he removes our transgressions from us."* No jail the Brigade could put him in could ever imprison him more than he had been imprisoned by his own spirit of self-accusation. No jail the Brigade could ever put him in could keep him from being free if God were setting him free.

Brian became aware of his body now. His breathing would have been barely discernible to someone right beside him. His muscles were relaxed beyond what he could ever remember them being while awake.

"He will not always accuse...he removes our transgressions from us."

Suddenly he became aware of someone outside his cell, and he looked up. There he saw the face of his sister, the face of Shawna. He wondered if his reverie had produced hallucination, or if God were giving him some kind of vision for comfort. But then he saw the cuffs on her hands, and he realized that what he was visualizing was real.

"Brian! Are you okay?"

Brian jumped up, ran over and reached out through the bars to touch her on the arm. "I'm fine! I'm fine! How did you get here, and why are they bringing you in here?"

"Oh God, Brian! Conrad's trying to get Drew to write for him! He said that if Drew helped him, he would set us free. I'm afraid he might be considering it."

"He's a good man, Shawna. Trust him!"

"Come on!" shouted the soldier who was bringing Shawna in, "I hate to interrupt this 'touching moment,' but this is a jail, not a damned social club!"

225

The soldier led her back to the cell where Maggie Morris was, un-cuffed her and shoved her in. After the soldier left, Brian shouted down to her.

"You didn't tell me what you are doing in Longview in the first place."

"Drew's editor wanted him to write about what was happening inside the city," responded Shawna. "And, well, you've met Drew, he couldn't say no."

"But, what about you? You didn't have to come."

Shawna leaned her head against the bars and, as she looked over at him, tears came to her eyes. "I heard my baby brother had been arrested. What else could I do?"

Brian's throat tightened up and he couldn't say a word.

"Are you okay?" she asked.

Brian nodded.

"Have they said what they plan...?"

Brian shook his head.

"Yeah, well, I guess I also came to keep an eye on that right-wing boyfriend of mine. I'm not sure if I was more worried about him getting himself killed or being lured into some right-winger's Nirvana. He's such a Neanderthal! But I guess you're right, I really should trust him."

Brian introduced the others to Shawna.

"You get to talk to any of the residents about what's been happening here?" asked Amos.

"Well, yes, but I'm not sure they were too representative. Conrad had us interview some people who were all thinking that this town was the next things there could be to heaven."

"That's just pure BS," said Maggie. "My parishioners are afraid to leave their homes for fear of an air raid. They're afraid to confess anything to other church members or even me for fear they will be turned in as immoral. And they're scared to death their teenagers are going to be hauled into jail for some little offense, real or imagined. This whole town is in jail. We're just the only ones who get to eat the jail slop."

"And we're even going to get less of that, with the federal forces' embargo," said Carl. "I heard they may be cutting us down to one meal a day."

"Where are the other people they have been putting in jail?" asked Shawna.

"They put them all on another floor," said Amos. "They're afraid that all the pot smokers, drug dealers and porn sellers might get corrupted by us political types."

"So, who'd you say this right-wing boyfriend of yours was?" asked Maggie.

Shawna shook her head and sighed. She looked over at Brian as if asking whether she should answer or not. Brian just shrugged.

"Drew Covington," she finally answered.

Maggie almost seemed to jump away. "Drew Covington?! He's the one Brian said you should trust? I'm sorry but I've never been able to read that man's column without ending up positively nauseous!"

"Come on now, Maggie," interjected John Savage. "We've been friends for some time and you know that I read Drew Covington's column every week."

"Yes, but you have an excuse. You're certifiable! This woman seems like a sane person." Maggie turned to Shawna. "I've got to say that from what I read, I'm almost surprised that they had to bribe him at all to get him to write for Conrad."

Brian could see Shawna's countenance fall even from their cell down the corridor. Maggie obviously regretted her deflating words.

"Of course, I really don't know the man at all. You and Brian do. You know better."

Maggie made a clumsy effort to put her arm around Shawna to comfort her. Shawna smiled at her, but moved away.

"I want to go home to my son, but I don't want to be released this way. God, I don't even know what to hope right now."

Shawna walked over to one of the cots and lay down with her face buried in the pillow. Just as she did, the door to the jail opened. In walked Drew Covington, cuffed, with a soldier right behind him. Hearing the noise, Shawna looked back at the door. Seeing the face of the one who was there, she jumped up.

"Drew!"

Drew broke from his escort and ran down to Shawna's cell, pressing his face against the bars. Shawna met him there, pressing her lips against his. Brian saw the tears flowing unabated down her face, and he had a bittersweet feeling. Her sister deserved love as much or more than any person he knew. She deserved this affirmation of her judgment. She had not deserved the treatment that she had been subjected to in her previous marriage, nor had she deserved the years of loneliness she had experienced since. But the love he saw in that one moment was something that he knew he would probably never experience himself, and that also touched his heart with sadness. Suddenly, however, he became aware that the rest of those in their cells had broken out in applause, and as he thought of how relieved his sister had to be at that moment, he joined them.

The soldier who had escorted Drew there did not applaud. He trudged down to where Drew was and slapped him to the floor with the butt of his gun. Then he aimed the barrel at his prisoner.

"What?! You think I brought you here for a god-damned conjugal visit? Get over to your cell before I open up your skull and show your girlfriend what's inside!"

Blood was trickling down the side of Drew's head, but he responded immediately to the order. Still as he headed to his cell he turned and called back to Shawna.

"You see, that's why I didn't want you to come! Your safety was the only thing that made me hesitate..."

"I'm responsible for my safety, Drew!" Shawna shot back. "You're responsible for your integrity!"

"Oh, man, that is so PC!" Drew's response came just before the soldier threw him into the cell and slammed the door shut.

"Yeah, well that is who I am, Drew Covington, so you might as well just get used to it!" Then she added after a short pause, "And one more thing you should know -- I am so glad that you are here!"

Shawna reached out through the bars toward Drew as if she could span the hopelessly long distance between cells, and Drew threw her a kiss.

"Man, this is better than one of those morning soaps," said Maggie. "I think I might cry."

"Come on now, Maggie," quipped Amos, "you haven't cried since your church voted to start using guitars and a synthesizer instead of an organ for the eleven o'clock worship!"

"That was a travesty," she replied, "but you really don't know how much I cry, Amos Baldwin! Do you think every time I start to cry I say, 'Oh, I'm getting ready to cry: I better invite Amos over so he can see it!?'"

"Children, behave!" said Carl, with no little irritation. "Drew, what do you know about what's going on out there? We're starved for information."

"Well, not as much as either of us would like, I'm sure," replied Drew. "There are definitely some people who support the Brigade being here, there's no doubt about that. But I hear through the grapevine that the government really has a tight hold on food and other essentials getting into the town. Certainly Shawna and I know from experience that getting in is no easy task. I can't help but think that as food supplies get tighter, the people will grow more restless and harder to control. Americans aren't used to doing without."

"Any more demonstrations going on?"

"Well. Carl, I'm not really sure about that. There was some kind of commotion near the civic center, but I didn't get close enough to see what it was about. I certainly didn't hear of anything that was widespread enough to be effective."

"What do you know about what the government is considering to get these guys out of here?" asked John. "I mean, I would have thought the most powerful country in the world would have thought of a way to defeat this guy by now."

"Well, a lot of people have been saying that," admitted Drew, "but it's not as simple as it may seem. Conrad has sympathizers among the military leadership. There are outbreaks of rebellion all across the country, and nobody wants to kill any more innocent US citizens than is absolutely necessary. I mean, one suggestion has been to..."

Drew looked around him at the somber faces of those now gathered around him, and didn't finish his thought.

Carl finished it for him: "...to nuke us."

Drew nodded.

Both jail cells were completely quiet for a minute or two as people sought to absorb the truth of this previously unspoken possibility.

"Well," John Savage finally responded, "we've just got to trust God that they'll find another way."

Amos Baldwin just shook his head. The tension in his voice ran counter to his attempt at humor as he spoke. "'Atomized Black Preacher Dude.' Sounds like the next great miracle product, doesn't it? Spray him on and you too can lift a congregation to the gates of heaven."

"If we get nuked," said Drew, "we'll be blown to the gates of heaven, we won't need any help."

"Yeah, well, somehow that just isn't the same thing," responded Amos.

"Scary thing is," interjected John, "if I were them, that's what I think I would do."

Brian slowly nodded his head. He thought of how that would be, having to make a decision to drop a nuclear bomb on people to stop an even greater destruction. He was glad that he wasn't the President.

As Brian reflected on those things, somewhere in the back of his mind he heard the door to the jail open one more time. Then he heard Carl speak.

"Hey, that's the girl who was picketing for you, Brian!"

Brian looked up quickly and saw the flawlessly beautiful face of Elena Enesco. Behind her was a member of the Brigade's Woman's Auxiliary. Conrad didn't allow women to serve in his fighting forces. He thought of that as part of the corruption of the modern world. However, they did have a woman's auxiliary, and this woman was part of that, and was apparently eligible to escort female prisoners. Elena was wearing a full-length coat and no shoes.

"Elena!"

"No talking!" This woman was apparently even less tolerant of divergence from procedure than had been the soldier who had escorted in Drew. Elena was only defiant enough to give Brian a gentle smile as she passed.

The woman took Elena down to the same cell with Maggie and Shawna. After she shut the jail door and left, Brian turned his attention to the women's cell.

"Elena! What did they bring you in for, and why are you wearing that hot coat in the middle of summer?"

Elena shrugged. "I wanted to see you, Brian, and they wouldn't let me visit because you are a political prisoner..."

"Really?"

"Yes. And so I tried to get them to arrest me. That is not as easy as I thought it might be, not as easy as it would have been in Romania. I thought of leading another protest, but I am not a very good leader of such things, and the people, they are very scared after the previous arrests and beatings."

"Okay..."

"And I thought of smoking some marijuana, but to tell the truth I do not like that stuff. I only tried it once before, and it makes me sick. I don't know why it is so popular with American young people!"

"Uh...so you did what?..."

Elena gave Brian a little shy smile and threw open her coat. Under it she was wearing only a hot pink bikini with a thong. John Savage fell out of his bunk.

"I thought this might scandalize them enough to get them to arrest me. I borrowed it from a friend, but I don't really like it. It is rather uncomfortable and rides up on my bottom. Elena turned around enough to illustrate the problem, revealing as she did her near perfect, soft contours.

"Holy!..."

The expletive had come from Amos who now stood to Brian's right, slack-jawed. The stunned faces of Carl and John were right behind him.

"Hey!" shouted Brian. "What's the matter with you guys? You're ministers! Turn around! Don't you have some praying to do or something?"

"Not me," said Amos in a mesmerized whisper, "my prayers are answered."

"Back off!"

Drew put his hands on Amos' shoulders. "Come on guys, he's right, turning around is the right thing to do."

"Sorry about that," said Carl as he turned, "but we don't get to see that very often."

"Beats the hell out of watching Maggie, that's for sure," opined Amos as he also turned away.

Brian returned his attention to Elena. As he did, Elena suddenly became self-conscious, blushed and closed her coat.

"Elena, why did you do that?"

"I would have walked through the streets totally naked if it would have taken that to get in to see you."

"But...before the other day, you didn't even know me."

"I've been around people all of my life who I didn't get to know as well as I got to know you on that one night, Brian Marshal. You let me see your soul. Letting someone see your body is easy next to that. Your kisses were healing to me. After they arrested you I felt lonelier than I have ever felt in my life, and I realized that it was because I found someone who I had been looking for all of my life, and that he was gone."

Brian reached out his hand in Elena's direction. "Me too! Me too!" he whispered. "But I may not live long. Before you came down, I think I was at peace with that. But now..."

Brian could see that his last words had brought pain to Elena's face. Neither could say one word more, but rather they just gazed in each other's direction. For several minutes everyone in both cells respected the silence. Outside they began to hear the rumblings of bombs falling, and the staccato chatter of machine guns. Another air raid.

Finally, Maggie got up, walked over next to Elena and looked down at the other cell. "Amos. Those gates of heaven you spoke of. I think we all need you to take us there."

Amos looked uncertain.

"You're the one who can do it, Amos. I know you can. Do it for us."

Amos looked around at the others, and then quietly walked to the edge of the cell. He stood there for a moment, absorbed in thought. Then he turned back toward the women's cell.

"Well...I really can't take us there," Amos said, and he paused and just shook his head. "But...I think I know someone who might. The Holy Spirit...yes, Sir! He might just take us there if..if we let him, you know? I know he's done it before. Did it for Jacob one time, yes, he did! He was heading back to his family's home in Haran. Truth be known, he was actually running away at the time, running away from his brother whom he had cheated out of his inheritance. I guess we're all runnin' away from somethin', aren't we?"

People throughout both cells quietly nodded their heads.

"Brian, he's runnin' from having killed his father, maybe like that Greek Oedipus of old. Maggie, she's runnin' from strict old parents who beat her down and never said a kind word to her in her life. Don't you deny it, Maggie Morris, I know it's true – you told me yourself!"

Maggie nodded in acknowledgement.

"And me, me I'm runnin' from a childhood where if you didn't laugh, you'd just start cryin' and cryin' and never be able to stop. Children you played with shot dead in the street before you. Tryin' to fall asleep while adults on the other side of paper thin walls were yellin' and cussin' at each other, and the rats were crawlin' across your feet. Yes, Sir! I guess we're all runnin' from somethin.'

"Well, Jacob, he was a runnin' too. But like all of us who run, there came a time where he got T-I-R-E-D of runnin'!"

Amos drawled out the "tired" in the tradition of the great black preachers, and he was beginning to find a cadence.

"Yes, sir! He got T-I-R-E-D of runnin' and he had to lay himself down. He had to lay himself down with nothin' more than a rock for a pillow. Now that's getting pretty tired when you have to use a rock for a pillow, but that's what the Bible says, and I know it's true!"

The ministers gave a quick clap and said, "That's right!" They had been to the First African Methodist Episcopal Church, and they knew their role.

"He lay himself down on that rock and he had a DREAM!"

"Yes, sir!"

"It wasn't a dream like Martin Luther King's dream."

"Uh-uh."

"It wasn't the good ol' AMERICAN dream."

"No, Sir!"

"But it was a dream from God. Let me hear ya' say, 'a dream from God!'"

" A dream from God!"

"It was a dream from God, and in that dream Jacob saw a ladder."

Amos was now prancing through the cell, dancing like a rock star.

"It wasn't no paintin' ladder and it wasn't no little attic ladder!"

"Uh, uh."

"It wasn't even a big ol' shiny fireman's ladder."

"No!" Even Brian and Drew were now getting the rhythm of it.

"It was a ladder to heaven itself!"

"Yes, Lord!"

"It was a ladder reachin' to heaven, and the angels of God were ascending and descending upon it, and at the top was none other than the L-O-R-D himself, saying, 'I am the L-O-R-D, the God of your father Abraham and the God of Isaac.'"

"Praise him!"

"And while at the top of that ladder, God had a message for Jacob."

"Preach it!"

"He told Jacob, 'I am with you and will watch over you wherever you go'!"

"That's right."

"I am with you when those RATS are crawlin' across your toes!"

"Yes, Sir!"

"I am with you when those soldiers are beatin' on your head and tryin' to break your arms!"

"That's right!"

"I am with you when bad memories of childhood STAB you in the heart and make you feel ALONE in this world. But you're not alone! Hear me, brothers and sisters, you are not alone!"

"No, sir, not alone!" Brian stood and shouted the words with the others. He had never felt so much a part of other people than at this moment.

"I am with you in this jail cell with the bombs fallin' all around you, with the soldiers treatin' you like you are VERMIN, with the very threat of droppin' a nuclear bomb to INCINERATE you!" Amos was now shaking as he spoke, "I will be with you wherever you go, and in HOWEVER many pieces you go there! 'I will not leave you until I have done what I have promised you!"

Everyone in both cells, stood and started applauding, but Amos was not done.

"And when Jacob heard this message from his God, when Jacob took this message into his very soul, what does the Bible say happened then? What does it say, brothers and sisters? Well, I don't have my own Bible with me right now, but that doesn't MATTER to me, because I have hid his WORD away in my heart. It says, 'When Jacob awoke from his sleep, he thought, "Surely the Lord is IN THIS PLACE, and I was not aware of it!"

"That's right!"

"In this place, brothers and sisters! These are jail cells. People lost to drugs are brought to these cells. Prostitutes who SELL themselves because they don't know their value to God are brought to these cells. People who murder their brothers and sisters, and even their own children are brought to these cells. Nobody wants to be here. Nobody wants to come here. But I'm tellin' you all now, that the very LORD of heaven is in THIS place, and where the Lord is I will not fear to go."

"Yes! Yes!" Once again all stood and clapped together.

"And then the Word of God tells us that Jacob said something else, something so important that no one should ever forget it. He said, 'How awesome is this place! This is none other than the house of God; this is THE GATE OF HEAVEN'! This is the gate of heaven, brothers and sisters. Right here is the gate of heaven. You don't have to go into the sky to find it!"

"No, sir!"

"You don't have to die to find it!"

"That's right!"

"You don't have to be E.J. Conrad, blowing up cities and actin' like you're God to find it!"

"No!"

"It's here! Right here in this jail. Wherever we love in his name, God opens those gates to us. Whenever we believe when it's hard to believe, God opens those gates to us. Whenever we look at people with the very eyes of Jesus and see our brother and sister, the very Gates of Heaven will open up to us. Can I have a witness?"

"That's right!"

"And when those gates open, they open to eternity!"

"Yes, Sir!"

"JESUS stands at those gates and he invites us in!"

"That's right."

"He says, 'Come unto me all you who labor and are heavy-burdened and I will give you rest for your souls.'"

"Uh-huh.

"He says come in these gates, Elena, you modern LADY GODIVA, because like ol' King David when he brought in the ark of the covenant, you were naked to the glory of the LORD."

There was now laughing and cheering.

"He says come in these gates, Drew Covington, because even though Amos there don't like your politics, I am the LORD and I like your heart!"

"Yes, Sir!"

"He says come in these gates, Maggie Morris, because your Mama and your Daddy may have wanted to PUSH YOU DOWN, but I the Lord am here to LIFT YOU UP!" Amos leaped up on one of the cots and stretched out his arms toward Maggie. He was quivering with emotion. "He says, 'I HAD to make you a large woman to house that large heart!'"

The word "Yes!" resounded through the applause.

"He says, 'Don't let nobody in your way, Sweetheart, because there ain't NOBODY who loves the Lord like you, and I have a special room prepared for you!"

"That's right!" The words came from everyone except Maggie, who was now sobbing and holding on to the bars with all her might to keep her from falling to the floor. Brian knew the tears were tears of ecstacy.

Amos now leaped down right next to Brian, took a firm hold on his shoulders, while his eyes seemed to glow with light.

"He says come in these gates, Brian Marshal, because I don't see that sin in your heart anymore. I don't see it in my memory anymore. I don't see it in the archives of HEAVEN anymore. I asked your father, who is with me in GLORY, and what's more, he don't see it either, Child! It ain't there, son! It's gone. Must be covered with the blood of Jesus, son, but I don't see it. It's gone! Can I hear you say that, child?!"

"It's gone!" Brian's words came in a near whisper, as he fell into a trembling mass at Amos' feet. "It's gone!"

"It's gone! So you come on IN these gates, son, and don't bring in nothin' but that pure HEART of yours, cuz that's all I see!"

Amos now jumped back in the center of the cell and lifted his hands toward heaven.

"And the Lord of Heaven says, come in these GATES, Amos Baldwin, because even though I know the CORRUPTION of your thoughts, and even though I KNOW you aren't worthy, still the women of your church they PRAY for you, and those prayers they are MIGHTY!..."

Amos had now fallen to his knees and tears were streaming down his face as he lifted his hands to heaven.

"Those prayers they are mighty, and they have opened these gates to you! Come in, Amos Baldwin, for I am a God of grace, and you are my healed...forgiven...child."

The last words had almost come as a whisper, but all knew that was okay, because God was meant as the primary listener.

As Brian regained enough strength to look around, he saw a peaceful afterglow on every face. Maggie, the child of staunch Presbyterians, still had her hands lifted toward heaven. Carl stood over the collapsed Amos, gently stroking his head. John Savage was smiling at everyone like he had just announced the birth of a child. Drew Covington had found some bits of paper on which to write some thoughts that pressed forth from his always-active mind, and Shawna and Elena were locked in celebrative embrace. Brian's only regret was that he couldn't join them.

Brian now sensed another presence in the room, and instinctively he turned toward the jail door. There stood one of the guards, come in perhaps to check on the commotion, and now standing as a child stands when left outside the party. Brian had once known the feeling.

Chapter Fourteen

Ashley Cambridge had never known she could run so fast. An outdoor rock concert just outside of Baltimore had erupted into violence. She had been attending a press conference not far away, and so she had been called on to report at the scene. What she had expected was pushing and shoving and people hitting each other with beer bottles, but what she had found when she stepped out of her car was far more frightening. She hadn't gone five steps from her car when she had heard the pops – sniper fire from a nearby building. It had been answered by the staccato sound of an automatic rifle, fired from the top of a hill. Ashley had turned back toward her car when a bullet zinged past her ear and shattered the glass of her front windshield. It was then that she had started running.

Ashley was not sure where she was running to, and as she glanced around, she initially received no help. Right in front of her was the field where the concert had been held. Bodies were strewn across the field. Young men were running around, throwing speakers and sound equipment, and ripping apart the stage. The majority of the shots being fired seemed to be coming from off to her left, and so she looked to the right and saw a row of portable concession stands. Shots dug into the ground around her as she dove behind one stand that advertised huge burritos. Two men had already found refuge there, along with two young women who had apparently been working there.

"What the hell is going on here?" Ashley asked, once she had found her breath.

"Who knows?" screamed one man who was huddled behind a small grill. "Damn crazy world! I was here to help with crowd control, but ain't no way I'm controlling this! Probably those Armageddon fanatics."

"What kind of concert was it?"

"Heavy metal. A group called 'Satan's Pimps' – they draw a lot of Goth types. I think the Brigade must have infiltrated the group, because all of the sudden during a lull, people started yelling, 'Death to Satanists!' and then the bullets started flying. Man, it's hard to know what to feel at a time like this. First the music was turning my stomach, and then the people getting shot at who were listening to the music. It's just all sick! – sick and scary!"

"So what are you doing here?" The question had come from one of the girls who worked at the burrito stand.

"I'm a reporter. But my editor is going to get an earful for assigning me to this! First of all, I don't get paid enough to be shot at. Second of all, there was supposed to be a damned photographer to meet me here, and I haven't seen a sign of him. I am used to interviewing 'movers and shakers,' not pimply high school girls, working at a damned burrito stand."

The other persons went silent, and Ashley sensed some irritation.

"What?"

The others looked back and forth at each other, and then the girl spoke again.

"So...you want me to go out and ask them to stop shooting so you can go interview someone more important?"

Ashley rolled her eyes, and reached for her cell phone. Just then a couple of shots ripped through the wood frame of the stand like rocks thrown through crystal. The men made a break from the burrito stand toward the shelter of a large stone sign, while the girls scrambled off toward a row of cars nearby. Suddenly one of them, the girl who had spoken, crumpled as a bullet pierced the calf of her left leg. She screamed in agony. As she hit the ground, she reached out toward the fleeing girl, crying for help. The other girl looked back in horror, hesitated but a second, and then came back, pulled her to a standing position on the good leg, and then started dragging her as quickly as possible towards the cars.

Ashley took advantage of the diversion to take off toward what appeared to be a machine shed with its door ajar. Shots crackled from behind her, and another scream rang out. Ashley looked back. A shot had hit one of the two struggling girls. She couldn't tell which one, but neither did she want to look long enough to find out. She focused on the little slit of an opening in the machine shed door, and when she reached it she slid it open, rushed through and slid it closed again in a continuous, fluid motion. Some bullets were zinging off the roof of the sheet metal building, while some seemed to be penetrating even that shield.

Ashley spotted a tractor and, determining that it would give her the best cover, scampered to get behind its blade. Just then three dark figures shifted in the shadows to her left. Ashley felt a chill that seemed to penetrate to her soul. Out of the shadows and into the light shed by a small window rose a figure, but even in that limited light Ashley could see that the figure did not appear human. Fiery red eyes shown out from dark markings around the eye. Projections that seemed like horns rose from the forehead. The creature was naked from the waist up, and its skin appeared to have the texture more of a crocodile. Ashley fell backwards and tried to scream, but at first her lungs wouldn't give her enough breath. Like in a bad nightmare, she had lost her voice when she had most needed it. But finally it came forth and her shriek reverberated throughout the building.

"God, Lady! Are you fuckin' crazy? Shut the hell up!"

"You speak English!"

"What the hell are you talkin' about? Of course I speak English! And I fuckin' sing in English too. I'm the lead singer of the fuckin' band! Now shut the hell up, before they come in here and find us!"

Ashley couldn't say for certain whether she was now shivering with fear, anger or simply generalized hysteria, but she had definitely found her full voice.

"God, what a time to run into refugees from a damned Halloween party! You scared the shit out of me! If you're going to dress – or, or UN-dress -- like that, at least have the courtesy to warn a girl!"

"You weren't fuckin' invited, okay! Now keep your voice down!"

"Is she a virgin?" asked one of the others. "We should sacrifice a virgin."

"Satan would like a virgin." These words had come from the third figure in the shadows.

"A virgin?" gasped Ashley, unsure of how serious these creatures were, "Are you kidding me? I haven't been a virgin since I was fourteen!"

"We won't need a fuckin' virgin if everybody shuts the hell up!" the leader of the band said in his loudest whisper. "Those guys out there are some seriously violent dudes, and they're out to fuckin' sacrifice US!"

"Are we sure she's not lying?" asked the second shadow. "Maybe we should check."

"Check WHAT? You touch my body, and I'll make a screaming noise they can hear all the way to Conrad's headquarters!"

"We aren't going to sacrifice you, so shut the hell up!"

"Satan will protect his own," said one of the shadows. "We have to go to him and call for his protection."

The one who had spoken, now lit a candle. It was a black candle. He also lit a red candle and then he took a magic marker and drew a pentagram, an inverted, circumscribed five-pointed star, on the cement floor. In the candlelight Ashley could now see the hideousness of all three faces. She had never been a fan of the likes of Ozzy Osbourne or KISS or Alice Cooper, but she had at least become a little adapted to their bizarre appearance. This band, however, had obviously committed themselves to step far beyond these predecessors. The horns that sprung from their foreheads appeared to be the genuine article, and although Ashley knew that their red eyes, with slits like reptiles, came from contact lenses, the rest of their facial make-up made these also look like they had been formed there by the decree of some sinister seed long ago. Ashley knew that if she were somehow forced to touch the scales that made up their skin, her own skin would turn stone cold.

The creatures now began a chant, a chant directed not to heaven but seemingly to the shadows around them, a chant that was uttered in a tongue which Ashley had never heard before and which she hoped she would never have to hear again. Red liquid oozed from the corner of one of the creature's mouths, and although Ashley suspected it was one of those little packets made for the purpose, the effect was still as ghastly as the Prince of Demons himself could have hoped.

Just then the meow of a stray cat came from the corner of the building. The eyes of the creatures danced with delight.

"Satan doth provide!"

The band-leader got up and brought the cat to their circle, while one of the others produced a long, gleaming hunting knife. The band-leader tied the cat's paws together with twine, and the one with the knife, still chanting, raised it high above the hissing feline.

Ashley's scream pierced the night. The creatures all looked at her with their faces full of fury. The one with the knife stood and started in Ashley's direction. Just then the door to the shed slid open and there stood approximately fifteen young men in army fatigues holding automatic rifles. Ashley screamed again. Then for what seemed to her like an eternity the creatures and soldiers just stared at each other. The band-leader spoke in a trembling voice.

"My mother is a Baptist...down in Oklahoma..."

A wicked gleam came to the eye of the soldier toward the center of those at the door.

"I know all the words to *Amazing Grace!*"

The soldier just shrugged at the band-leader's words and raised his weapon.

"Gentlemen, we have hit the mother-lode!"

All at once the weapons began firing and the three figures jerked and spasmed as the bullets ripped through the facade and found the genuine redness of their blood. Round after round was fired into their bodies while some of the soldiers began laughing, as if they were involved in a child's game. But these playmates were not going to get up and ask for their turn to be the soldiers. By the time the bullets stopped firing, their forms were recognizable neither as human nor demonic.

One of the soldiers turned his weapon toward Ashley. Trembling violently, she still managed to pull out her press credentials.

"I'm not with them! I'm press! I'm press!"

The man just aimed his weapon. "We don't need any press coverage, thank you!"

The soldier toward the middle, whose actions initiated the carnage, pushed the other soldier's weapon away.

"No, wait a minute, Corporal Burns. Perhaps we do."

"What do you mean? I thought this was a Joshua operation."

"Yes, but I happen to know that Conrad is looking for some good press people."

"I write for *The Oregonian.* I've worked with Drew Covington!"

The soldier raised his brows. "Drew Covington, huh? Well, maybe we should take her along and have Samuels contact Conrad. If he doesn't want her...well, we can take care of her later."

"If you say so, Captain."

The man who had been identified as Corporal Burns walked over and helped Ashley to her feet.

"Your lucky day, I guess. You escaped those creatures, and Conrad needs press people. You must be doin' somethin' right."

"Lucky – yeah, I guess."

Corporal Burns escorted Ashley out into the now night air. She could still hear the occasional sounds of gun fire and grenades throughout the area, and out of the corner of her eye she saw what appeared to be bodies lying in the grass as well as in the street; but her psyche had been too traumatized already and she chose not to look any more closely.

Corporal Burns had apparently decided, or been convinced, to treat her gently, and Ashley was surprised now by the quiet tone with which he addressed her. He was going to have to cuff and blindfold her, but she shouldn't be too distressed – it was a necessary precaution to keep her from knowing things that she shouldn't know and which might otherwise get her killed. They would take her by Jeep over to see their commanding officer, General Alexander Samuels, in charge of guerilla action for the whole East Coast. He felt quite sure that Samuels would treat her well. She nodded her head in understanding, and the corporal started working on the cuffs. Whether his gentler behavior was due to the revelation that Conrad might have a use for her, or because he had now taken time to notice her, and like most men Ashley had ever known, now wanted her favor, Ashley really didn't know. But it was certainly what her raw nerves needed.

Corporal Burns eased her into the back seat of the Jeep, and then sat down beside her. He told her that the ride would be about two hours, and she should try to relax. Would she like some gum? Ashley declined. Two other soldiers jumped into the front seat and the Jeep pulled away.

"Excuse me," Corporal Burns now said, "but I need my book."

The corporal leaned across her body to get the book in question, and he lingered there long enough to give Ashley the distinct impression that the whole thing was a ruse to let him brush up against her breasts.

"Uh...you got it yet? Because you're kind of crushing me..."

"Oh...Yes! Of course, of course. It's just an old novel I've been reading. Helps pass the time. You read much?"

"A little. Mostly on planes or late at night before I go to bed."

"Read any Tom Clancy? This is Tom Clancy."

"Not really."

"It's about Jack Ryan. He really loves this country. We do too, you know. That's why we're doing what we're doing."

"I see. You blow it up because you love it."

"No. Because we love it, we attack what is destroying it – like those demonic goons back there."

"...and like me, before you learned Conrad might have a use for me."

"Uh...sorry about that. Most all of our operations are what we call Joshua operations, named after Joshua in the Bible -- you know, the guy who fought the battle of Jericho? Anyway, the Bible says that God told him to go into Jericho and all of the other cities and wipe them out completely, to kill everyone they found there. He told them that because the cities had to be purified from all of the moral pollution in them before Israel could occupy the land. That's what God wants to be done to this world, especially the United States – to purify it of all of the moral pollution that has been destroying it for so long. Once we are called to make something a Joshua operation, well, we can't look on the people we find as people. We can only look on them as targets to be destroyed."

"Yeah, well, I can sure see the need to wipe out the likes of those guys back there. I honestly didn't know if they were just dressing a part or if...if..."

"If they were truly demons? Hey, it looked to me that what was on the outside pretty well fit what was on the inside. And the scary thing is that these were just the ones who were showing their true colors. There's a lot more around like them who wear business suits – or even Abercrombie and Fitch -- on the outside, but inside they're no different. You have to understand that there has been a battle going on long before we came around – it's a battle between the forces of darkness and the forces of light. The forces of darkness have been trying to destroy the forces of light for a long time – you know, through political maneuvering and telling lies in the press about good, conservative people. It's just that now we're fighting back."

"Yeah, conservatives have taken their lumps in the press. That's why I got into the business. That's why I like working with Drew Covington..."

Ashley thought of the last time she had seen Drew, in the arms of Shawna Forester.

"...or at least I used to."

"Drew Covington is a good writer."

As their conversation hit an interlude of silence, Ashley's mind went back to the events of just a few minutes before. Even now it seemed so unreal. Did people who acted in such a way really exist? Was there really a being called Satan who...?

Ashley shuddered.

"Need a coat?"

Ashley shook her head. "No. No, I'm okay."

Equally unreal was her memory that the man now sitting beside her, touching her, and speaking soothingly to her, only a little while ago was aiming a gun at her, fully intending to use it to end her life. Why was she being so friendly and polite to him? Was it just fear that kept her from telling him to drop dead?

The emotional strain of the day's events, as well as this process of mentally revisiting them, had made Ashley really tired. She was afraid to fall asleep, and yet several times she found herself nodding off and then jerking back awake again. Each time she did she hoped that she would find that all that happened had been a bad dream, but the hum of the car engine, the sweaty smell of the soldier sitting next to her, and the reality of her hand cuffs and blindfold, kept telling her otherwise.

When the car pulled to a stop some time later, Ashley was not sure how long they had been traveling. Nor could she remember if there had been turns, and if so how many. The blindfold had had the desired effect – she had no idea of where she had been taken.

Corporal Burns led her out of the car and into some building, then down a corridor, down some steps and then into a room. Once in the room he took off the blindfold. Ashley squinted while her eyes adjusted to the light.

"I'm afraid the cuffs will have to stay on for a little while," said Corporal Burns. "After you talk to General Samuels, he will decide whether they can come off or not."

The corporal gave Ashley an awkward smile, but Ashley just looked away.

"Looked like you got a little sleep on the way over," he continued, undeterred. "You must have been kind of tired."

"I guess."

The room in which they were was like a small waiting room. There was a sofa and a couple of chairs on one end and nearby was a small television set.

"Uh...would it be okay for me to watch the television while I wait?"

The corporal shrugged. "I don't see why not. It's all trash, but suit yourself."

Ashley found the remote, and punched the power button. She switched through the channels until she found CNN. Corporal Burns joined her, and for a moment she thought he might prohibit news stations, but he just scowled and sat down next to her on the sofa. Ashley thought the female news reporter looked weary as she spoke.

"Last night a brutal assault on a rock concert outside of Baltimore left thousands dead and many more injured. Law enforcement officials say that the attack was the work of a guerilla group aligned with E.J. Conrad's Armageddon Brigade. The featured group was 'Satan's Pimps,' a heavy metal band whom detractors have accused of being heavily into Satanic worship. Music industry officials have said that it was all performance, but privately even some of them have expressed concern over the group's antics as shown here in some file footage. Please be warned that these visuals may not be suited to children, and those easily disturbed by violence may want to turn away. "

"Only a performance, hell!" interjected Corporal Burns. "They should have seen what we saw, right? And look at what they were doing up there on that stage!"

Corporal Burns pointed toward the television screen, which was displaying group members slinging dead, bloody animals and rubbing the blood on their faces. Ashley did in fact opt to turn away.

"The bodies of three members of the band, including lead singer Faustus, were found riddled with bullets in a machine shed near the concert site. Faustus, named after the character who sold his soul to the Devil, was born Billy Ray Carlson in Enid, Oklahoma."

"What do you think of your bargain with the Devil now, Asshole?" taunted the corporal. "Was it worth the price?"

"On the economic front," continued the reporter, "the price of gold and silver continued to skyrocket, with gold once again breaking all records at nearly a thousand dollars an ounce, and silver at just over a hundred dollars an ounce. Wall Street remains closed as industry leaders huddle with government economists on stock trading restrictions during this time of national emergency. One high government official, speaking under conditions of anonymity, predicted tight restrictions that would include automatic closure when the Dow suffers more than a two percent drop in one day."

Ashley thought of her own stock portfolio, now virtually worthless. Of course, she was young, and could rebuild. Her parents, however, had planned to retire soon, and now could not. She wondered if they were ever going to be able to retire.

"President Albert Packard, showing increasing frustration over fighting a powerful domestic enemy, called on loyal Americans to display a new sign of their loyalty. Since even Brigade supporters have displayed the US flag, Packard has had an insignia designed which features an eagle flying high above the globe, carrying an olive branch in its beak and a US flag in its talons. The insignia draws on traditional symbols, while combining the power of the eagle with the desire for peaceful solutions symbolized by the olive branch. Senator Robert Carlson of Texas, one of Packard's most vocal opponents and a rumored associate of EJ Conrad, has called for Americans of all persuasions to avoid the insignia. He claims that the number '666' is hidden in the design, and that Packard's efforts to distribute it confirm that he is indeed the antichrist predicted in Scripture."

"That's the truth, man, I've seen it!" exclaimed Corporal Burns. "And they're going to have people put it on their caps, which will mean that the number of the antichrist will be on their FOREHEADS, just like the Bible talks about!"

"I really don't know about all that Revelation and the antichrist stuff," responded Ashley. "I just want America to get back to the way it was when my Grandma was my age – old-fashioned values, that sort of thing."

"Hey, that's what Conrad is for...really!"

The door now opened and in stepped a distinguished looking man in army green with four stars on his sleeve. His temples were silver and his eyes a fiery blue. Ashley could tell from his demeanor that he was a man who expected respect and got it. Corporal Burns immediately stood at attention and saluted.

"You are dismissed, Corporal. Turn off that television and shut the door on your way out."

Corporal Burns did as he was instructed, and the General came over by Ashley.

"I am General Alexander Samuels, Ms. Cambridge. Have my men been treating you well?"

"Uh...yes. Well, except for wanting to shoot me when they first met me, if you count that sort of thing."

General Samuels sat down in a chair near the sofa. "Yes, I'm afraid that is war. I am sure it was a frightening thing for you, and I am sorry you had to go through it. I understand also that you had what must have been a terrifying encounter with those so-called band members."

"Yes. They looked so real. I've never been one to think much about the demonic, but when I saw them...well, I was convinced that I was about to be swallowed up by hell itself. Of course, later I understood that they were only costumes."

"Only costumes, Ms. Cambridge? Well, you're right, of course, in saying that they would have looked human under the outer clothing. But what really reflected their inner nature? Was it how they would have looked without what we call costumes? Or did they choose the costumes themselves in order to reflect who they really were inside – a demonic costume for a demonic spirit?"

General Samuels leaned in toward Ashley and peered into her eyes. "We are not doing battle with flesh and blood, Ms. Cambridge. We are doing battle with the one who incarnates evil itself."

Ashley just shook her head. "I...uh...I don't really know much about all of that. I never have been very religious."

"Yes, I suppose you're like most. You want to avoid the religious questions and just talk about the practicalities of who runs the country and how they run it. But you cannot avoid the religious issues, Ms. Cambridge. Sooner or later you must face them. When this country was like it's supposed to be, it was run according to Christian values. Back in the 50's and even into the early 60's people went to church and they prayed to God, and our country was strong. We didn't have the high divorce rates we have today. We didn't have the legalized abortion. We didn't have the disrespect of young people toward their parents and teachers. But we've changed since then, and you know it. I've read your writing, you know. You're quite good."

Ashley blushed.

"Thank you." It took a compliment of her writing to make Ashley blush. Talking about her appearance wouldn't do it. She took that for granted. Saying something to try to embarrass her wouldn't either. She was pretty much unflappable in that regard. But her writing was something of which she was still a little unsure.

"The country has changed because we have turned away from God," continued the general. "The events of September 11th, 2001 were God's shot across our bow as a country. It was God's call to get our attention and turn us back from whence we came. For a while it seemed to work. People started attending church again. They were praying and talking about God in the media. But that didn't last, did it? Attendance at church dropped back to what it was before. People still waved their flags, but they stopped talking about God. Just months after the event the courts were back trying to take 'under God' out of the Pledge of Allegiance. It's all tied together, Ms. Cambridge. If you want our country to return to solid conservative values, a return to God has to be part of it."

Ashley thought for a moment. She was beginning to feel that the general might be right, but somehow it all seemed so strange. Sitting there, she felt like she had been talking to a minister, and not to one who had ordered assaults on people of his own country.

"Okay, maybe there's something to what you are saying, but why do you have to start a war to make things right again? Don't you think we could find a more peaceful way?"

"No. Once people go their own way, they get enslaved to the pleasures of their own depravity. They won't freely give them up. They *can't* freely give them up. They are addicted to them. That's why people will never vote to give up pornography. That's why people will never vote to give up abortion, which is their ticket to be able to live sexually promiscuous lives. That's why people will never vote to rein in drug abuse, because they cannot let go of the pleasure of it, no matter how much destruction it brings. They are out of control, and they need someone to come in and take control for them."

The general stood up and walked over to a coffee pot that had been placed in a corner of the room.

"Want a cup?"

Ashley nodded.

The general poured two cups, brought them over and sat down again.

"E J Conrad believes this is Armageddon, the war of God against Satan at the end of time. I believe he is right. But even if he isn't right about that – and this is very important – I believe this war is right if only for the fact that it is necessary to re-direct this country down a path of righteousness. Democratic means have served us well in many ways in the past. But they aren't sufficient to correct what ails the country now. Every time we take a step in the right direction by democratic means, another administration comes along and takes us a step – or two – backward. Surely you can see, Ms. Cambridge, that we cannot abide that any longer."

Ashley's mind was spinning. The United States had led the world into democracy. And yet it did seem true to her that it was democracy that now had the country mired in a muddy pit, from which it was nearly impossible to move forward.

"What do you want from me?"

"Well, I do need to talk to E J Conrad. But I know that he has been looking for a good writer for our cause. I've got to say, he tried your Drew Covington, and was disappointed. It would seem that he does not have the courage to fully follow his ideas through to their logical conclusion."

Her Drew Covington. She had hoped that was how it would be, but that mush-minded liberal Shawna had taken him away. She was the one who was keeping Drew from truly seeing how things were, how they could be. Maybe this one time she needed to show *him* the way.

The general stood up, walked to the door and looked back. "You know, Ms. Cambridge, it may have been fortunate that you were there to see those so-called musicians. What you saw may well be where the country is going, unless we stop it."

And then the general left her alone to her thoughts.

Chapter Fifteen

Drew Covington leaned back against the concrete wall of the jail cell, and looked around him. Everyone seemed to be trying to get some rest, which was not an easy fete, since they were experiencing another air raid, and bombs could be heard falling throughout the city. It seemed to Drew that the bombs were falling closer now than they had been. Previously the bombs seemed to have been targeting the peripheral area of the city where the majority of Conrad's forces were stationed. Now they would occasionally fall near by, and the whole building would shake. Drew wondered how many civilians had been killed so far.

What a different world it was now. Here he was, a reporter in an American jail cell, arrested because of the stand he had taken in a political dispute, with bombs falling all around, bombs that were being dropped by US Government planes! Such probably hadn't happened since the last American Civil War, nearly a hundred and fifty years before. Is this what American history had been reduced to? This was a country that pretty much had changing the world in its charter. It had taken the radical ideas of a few French theorists and turned them into a reality where the common person actually mattered, actually had a chance at happiness in this world. This was a country that went into World War I, declaring it to be 'a war to end all wars.' In the sixties the country had declared war on poverty, and under Martin Luther King Jr. had a dream from a mountaintop of a country where racism did not exist. More recently the country spoke of a vision where no child would be left behind. But in the midst of it all, what had really changed? There was still poverty, war and racism. And Drew wondered how many of the young men wielding guns for EJ Conrad had once been children left behind.

Would the world never be better than it was? Were visions like those shared by King and Gandhi and even Jesus himself, nothing more than pipe dreams? -- nothing more than fantasies with which to anesthetize the spirit whenever the world ran over a person?

Drew looked over at the others again. They were starting to stir. Drew nudged Carl Tollefson.

"I've got a theological question for you, Carl."

"Yeah? A big one or a little one?"

"Not too big."

"Shoot."

"What's the meaning of history, in twenty-five words or less?"

Carl Tollefson looked at Drew over the top of his reading glasses, which he had just put on. "And what would be a BIG theological question to you?"

"One with a lot of big theological words."

"Yeah, well, I'll give you a big word – eschatology. It means study of the last things. Now your question has a big word, so we can call it a big question, and I can tell you, I JUST WOKE UP!!"

"You don't want to ask him anyway," said Amos. "He doesn't know squat about those things. I'm your man. Fire away!"

"I've forgotten more about eschatology than you'll ever know, Baldwin!"

"You've forgotten more about eschatology than YOU know, Carl Tollefson!" The comment had come from Maggie Morris. "I can field your questions from over here, Drew."

John Savage stepped over and sat beside Drew. "While they try to outdo each other in bravado, the two of us can talk, and I'll actually give you some answers. Eschatology..."

Drew just shook his head. "Why do I feel like I just drove a clunker onto a used car lot? If you grand philosophers can cooperate, maybe we can all just discuss this topic together. What do you say?"

The others all mumbled their approval.

"Maybe we should be clear about what you're asking first, Drew," said John Savage.

"Fair enough. E J Conrad believes he is God's instrument to bring history to a close through a climactic war against the forces of evil. Now we here have all dismissed him, but what would we put forward instead? Is it all just going around in circles? Is history all just a meaningless series of events where whatever we do, we still just wind up where we started? Or is there something better up ahead of us, something we ought to be helping to happen?"

"Yeah, well, I told you it was a big question," mumbled Carl Tollefson.

"Well, the truth is that EJ Conrad isn't entirely wrong," said John Savage. "I think we are near the end of time and Jesus will return soon. When he does, this world will be judged, and there will be a battle of Armageddon, where many will die. But his understanding of the signs and the sequence is entirely wrong. Revelation predicts that there will be a seven year time of tribulation where many will die from war, pestilence and famine, followed by a thousand year period called the Millenium when Jesus will reign; and only then, as a last ditch effort, will Satan's forces fight the forces of God in the battle of Armageddon. And when that happens, Jesus himself will lead the battle – not some human substitute. This war..."

"Wait a minute, Savage," Amos said, interrupting. "I realize that what you're saying is a common perception among Christians. Lord knows that most of my people would be nodding their heads and saying amen to all of that. But I've got to say this is the part I have some real problems with. Are you telling me that the only thing wrong with Conrad's thinking is his understanding of the timing and agency of the bloodshed?"

"Well, those are pretty big differences."

"No, no, I'm sorry!" said Amos, jumping to his feet. "I don't see much difference at all. Would it really make a difference if the one dropping the bombs that kill hundreds of thousands of people, adults and children, good and bad, as well as innumerable cats and dogs and pet gerbils and hamsters and...whatever...would it make a difference if the one who ordered it was one we call God?"

"Well, it's his right to judge..."

"No! I'm sorry. I don't think so." Amos was now pacing. Apparently for him doing anything close to talking about God was impossible while sitting still. "I was raised with violence. I went through my childhood with blood getting spattered on the walls all the time. But I came out of that time in my life with the understanding that that's the way *people* settle their disputes – and sick people at that. But I found hope in the fact that there was a God, the God of Jesus, who did things differently than the violence-sickened people around me. He took the violence and turned it into love. Now you want to tell me that he's no different after all? When all is said and done in this world, God is going to be just another gang leader blowing the other side to hell. Well, I'm sorry, but I find that thought a little unsettling."

"Come on, Amos, it's in the Bible. You know that!"

"Yes, well that just makes it all the more unsettling."

"I've got to say, I agree with Amos," said Maggie. "I'm not sure how Revelation even made it into the scriptural canon. It's a vindictive book that's hardly even Christian."

"That's a pretty convenient luxury," responded John, "to be able to decide what we will and what we won't accept as part of scripture. Besides, are the two of you telling me you don't want a God who will vindicate you against your enemies? It seems to me that with a guy out there who in God's name has nuked two American cities, a little righteous vindication might be in order. Scripture talks of God as a Great Harvester. Saving the grain and burning the chaff. The old Civil War song spoke of it in an only slightly different image: 'He is trampling out the vintage where the grapes of wrath are stored.' When there is evil around, God is a God of wrath."

Drew held up his hand like a stop sign. "Yeah, well, you're talking a lot about God, but you aren't totally answering my question. Where is history going? At least John is saying something better is ahead. Jesus is coming back and will fix what is wrong in this world. What do the rest of you have to offer that is any better than that? Or do you just want to take John to task for being traditional?"

"Revelation does talk about a time when there will be a new heaven and a new earth," replied Amos. "'There will be no more death or mourning or crying or pain, for the old order has passed away.' That sounds pretty righteous to me. I believe in that."

"Yeah, well, pick and choose, Amos."

"Everyone picks and chooses, John. Even the most conservative biblical scholar finds a way to reject what he or she doesn't like – by putting it into a different 'dispensation', or by calling radical demands 'hyperbole' or by making it symbolic. Jesus says, 'Go and sell everything you have and give it to the poor and come follow me,' and all the conservative, rich white American Christians rush to say, 'He didn't really mean it!' Yeah, tell me about 'pick and choose.'"

"You know, we are getting tied up with some things on which we don't agree," interjected Carl, "and I don't think that's helpful, especially since I think there are some things we can agree on. God is a God of hope. God is a good God who will renew Creation and make it right again. God will not remain content to let evil win. Can't we agree on those things?"

The ministers all nodded.

"You all don't have to turn into wooses, " said Shawna, speaking for the first time. "I was enjoying the argument."

"Enjoying an argument," said Drew. "Well, surprise, surprise!"

The laughter swept through the jail like a breeze.

"While I do believe there is something better ahead of us," continued Carl, "I also would say that faith isn't believing that Jesus is coming back; faith is the eyes through which you look at the world and see that he is already here."

"Ooooh!" crooned Maggie. "That is so profound, O Great One! Too bad you can't come over to our cell so that I could kiss the hem of your garment."

"I kind of like it," said Brian.

"Me also," chimed in Elena, now fully dressed in clothes that had been brought in for her.

"Okay, it wasn't bad," admitted Maggie. "But we do need a hope that something better is coming. That's why Amos' sermon the other day was so uplifting. It brought us some hope."

"Yeah, well you gotta know," said Amos, "that the Spirit knew about your short little white attention spans, so he brought you the abbreviated version the other day. If the Spirit had been movin' me to preach to the grandmas of my church, I'd still be preachin'!"

Another wave of laughter refreshed the inmates. It had died down only slightly when the door to the jail opened and in walked EJ Conrad. Beside him was the jail guard who had witnessed the end of Amos' sermon the day before. He was looking down at the ground, while the gaze of Conrad was riveted on Drew Covington.

"Laughter in my jail cells – well. It's not that I don't want my guests to be happy, but I find it a bit peculiar, considering the gravity of the times, and the fact that my own soldiers don't have enough to eat. Corporal Madison, make a note to cut back the level of rations for our jail guests – provided of course, it doesn't make them absolutely giddy."

Conrad walked down the corridor to a spot opposite of where Drew stood, and he looked somberly at him past the jail bars.

"Comfy, Mr. Covington?"

Drew didn't answer.

"Mr. Covington, I'm going to assume that the reason why I haven't heard anything from you since I had you brought here is that you might not understand that my offer still stands. I want to make that absolutely clear. If you choose to write for us, and make the true story of what we are doing known to the people of the world, I will not only release you from jail and put you up in some fine accommodations here in the city; but I will also release Shawna and her brother to the reprobates on the outside. I should also probably make sure that you know that this offer is for, as they say, 'a limited time only.' We have discovered that you are not the only writer we might choose."

Conrad turned and walked slowly back toward the door of the compound. Then he stopped suddenly and turned around.

"Oh, yes. I almost forgot. Should Mr. Covington decide not to cooperate, Brian, this will be your last day to live. We have your execution scheduled for tomorrow at sunrise. Have a pleasant evening, everyone."

The slamming of the door left both cells in absolute silence. Drew could however still hear the bombs and artillery fire in the distance. He walked over and sat on the cot next to Brian, and put his arm around the younger man's shoulder. The other men in the cell also came and quietly sat on the floor nearby.

Shawna was the first to break the silence. "Maybe tonight will be the night the US forces will liberate the city. They have been bombing more, and..."

No one picked up on the thought, and Shawna herself seemed to have abandoned it even before she halted her sentence.

"Perhaps I can write for them," offered Drew, "but do it in a code, you know, so that a different message comes through....like when someone is abducted by terrorists, and forced to give a statement of support for their cause. Actually...I guess it's exactly like that."

"It might work," opined Carl. "It worked for John on Patmos, when he wrote Revelation. The stupid Romans didn't have a clue he was writing about *them*."

"Except John wasn't being forced to write that he supported Rome or Domitian," said Amos. "Had he been expected to do that...well, I don't know..."

"I don't want you to do that."

Everyone looked over at Brian, from whom the words had come.

"Brian, they will kill you," said Drew. "We have to do something or..."

"No. I don't want you to do it. I feel partly responsible for all the deaths that have come about because of this war. I don't want to be responsible for anything more. I don't want to be responsible for your writing and gaining support for this war, and making it one day longer than it will already be. If people are going to have to continue to die because of what I helped start...well, then, it's appropriate that one of those people be me."

"Brian, you don't have to..."

"Yes, I think I do."

"NO!" The scream had come from the women's cell and echoed down the corridor. Elena had literally climbed up the bars of her cell, and was now rattling them with all her might. "No! No! No!"

Brian stood up and reached through the cell bars in her direction. "Elena, I..."

"No! No! No! You made me care, and now you will let them take you away? You cannot do that!"

Shawna and Maggie tried to pull her down in order to console her, but she would have none of it, and clung all the more tightly to the cell bars.

"No! They took my brother. They killed my brother. One is enough! They will not kill you! I will fight them this time! I will fight them with my bare hands! I will not be quiet! I will not let them kill one I love ever again!"

Instead of trying to pull her off the bars, Shawna and Maggie were now simply hugging her legs, which were at head level, and they were crying.

"I didn't fight before. I didn't know how to fight before. I was little. So little." Elena began sobbing, but that didn't stop her from one last outburst. "I am STRONG now! Let them come and I will show them how strong I am! They think I am still a little girl, but I am not. I am a woman now, and I am strong!"

Drew stood immobilized by the passionate words of this feisty young woman. On the one hand he wanted to quiet her down because of the dangers. But on the other hand, Elena's spirit spoke for him and touched him.

Just then the door to the jail compound swung open and in stepped Corporal Madison. He pointed his M-16 in the direction of the women's cell, but he was trembling.

Brian flung himself against the jail bars closest to the door. "Madison, listen to me! You aren't going to shoot her! We both know that. You won't because you don't believe any more! I can see it in your eyes. Believe me, I have seen that same look in the eyes of my mirror when I was in the Brigade, and I know what the look means! It means that you are in so deeply that you don't know how to get out. It means that everything you thought you had gotten in for, suddenly doesn't mean anything any more. You're tired of the blood. You're tired of fearing and being feared. Well, do something about it! You can, you know. You can let us out. You can let us escape."

Corporal Madison's M-16 remained trained on the women's cell, but Brian could tell that his words had hit their mark. Madison was trembling even more now, and Brian was sure that at the very least he could not hit the one he was targeting. Then the soldier lowered his weapon. As he did, he exposed even more his eyes that were full of terror and sadness.

"Okay. Okay. I am tired. You are right. I don't believe any more. Not in Conrad anyway. Not in the Brigade and the...the so-called Armageddon war."

The soldier heaved a heavy sigh. "But I'm afraid that it would do no good to let you go. This jail is surrounded, and we are in the center of the city. I would just be letting you out to let them kill you. And then they would kill me."

Brian leaned his head up against the bars and shut his eyes. Then he pulled way and nodded his head.

"He's right."

"I might be able to build an underground network of other disenchanted soldiers who could eventually get you out," continued the soldier. "But...that would take several weeks minimum." He looked at Brian. "It certainly could not be done by tomorrow morning."

Brian nodded his head again. "Well, it was worth a try. I'm at peace with that. Start on that underground network, though. That may be the best hope for the others."

"We cannot give up so quickly!" shouted Elena.

Brian looked over at Corporal Madison. "Either way, this could be my last night of life. You could help by letting the women come into our cell. We really need to be together right now."

"Should Conrad find out, it would endanger my position," responded Corporal Madison, "and I might not be able to help in the future."

"We will risk that," responded Drew. "And we need you to risk it with us."

Corporal Madison agreed and walked quickly toward the women's cell. "I will wake you extra early tomorrow morning, however, so that you can get back in your own cell by the time Conrad gets here."

The women moved briskly over to the door of the men's cell, and no sooner had the corporal opened it than Elena shot through the opening and leapt into Brian's arms. She began covering his face with her kisses. Shawna wasn't far behind her. When Shawna slid into Drew's arms he felt as if he had been ushered into a banquet room after a long fast. Indeed they had been given very little to eat, and yet his thoughts had not been on the food he had missed: they had been on memories of Shawna's tender touch. Now as her lips gently massaged his own and she dug her fingernails passionately into his back, his body felt an ecstasy that rivaled any orgasm he had ever had. When his awareness finally returned to the room around him, he was holding Shawna in his arms and looking past her into the eyes of Amos Baldwin. Amos was smiling, but his eyes also had a touch of melancholy.

"Okay, well, this idea of bringing over the women definitely has benefited some of us more than others."

After Amos' words, Maggie suddenly grabbed him and placed a firm kiss squarely on his lips.

Okay, Amos," she said, "join the party!"

Amos just stared at her for a second, stunned. And then he started laughing. It started as a chuckle and then evolved into a belly laugh that sent him crashing in hysterics on the floor.

Maggie wiped her lips and said, "Well, partner. It looks like my work here is done!" "Oh, yeah?" said Amos in between his laughter, "Well, don't think that means they're going to let you leave!"

Then both laughed some more, and the others joined in. After several minutes, Amos seemed to recover, and he looked around.

"God, what are we laughing about?"

It was a rhetorical question, but Brian's answer came promptly nevertheless. "Because those idiots out there think that I am the only one with a death sentence."

Everyone looked over at Brian and, noting his smile, they shared in it for a quiet moment.

"Hey, it's true you know. We're all going to die, and I don't just mean the people in this cell. It's going to happen to all of us, and the only tragedy is allowing yourself to not be ready."

"It doesn't have to happen to you now, Brian," said Elena as she clung more closely to him. "I'm not ready for it to happen, and I do not want you to give up."

Tears came to Brian's eyes, but he quickly wiped them away. "Elena is what makes this hard. I have to say that I have never had anyone like her." Brian squeezed Elena a little closer to him and kissed her on the forehead.

"In some respects I guess it would be easier if I did not have her now, because I could let go more easily. But in other respects, she, along with the others of you, are what makes this all easier. I truly believe that the moments I have lived since meeting Elena, and the moments we have had together in this cell are the only moments that I have really lived in my life. All before that was a fog, a haze, a nothing time that I had consented to call life. I don't remember who said it, but I once remember hearing someone say that the greatest tragedy was not dying, but rather to have never truly lived. At the time I heard it, I was one who had never truly lived. Now, thanks to all of you, I have. And so I am ready to face death, if that is what has to happen."

"But maybe it doesn't have to happen!" cried Elena. "I told you, I am not ready..."

"Do you have a realistic alternative? – one that doesn't risk having everyone else here killed along with me?"

Elena just shrugged and buried her head in Brian's shoulder.

"Elena, you once told me that because of what I had done, I might have to become a Peter, remember? You said he gave his life in testimony to the Lord he had denied. I remember that. Well, tomorrow morning when the cock crows I will be paying back a debt to the humanity I had denied."

Elena kept her head buried in Brian's shoulder, but her muffled voice came through nonetheless. "You must never listen to me! I don't know what I'm saying."

The group of friends sat quietly huddled together. The eyes of each one seemed to be focused within, searching -- searching for choices, searching for consolations, searching for a way to make sense of what their world had become. Drew looked around at each face and saw reflections of the turmoil within himself. He thought back over what had been his short history with Brian Marshal. Had he been honest with himself on that first day, when he heard what Brian had done, and when he watched Shawna express her anger at her brother, he would have said that sending him to a quick death would be both the just and merciful thing to do. Now it only seemed like one more senseless death, the loss of someone whose personal depth, though admittedly full of dark shadows, he had come to love and admire. Like Elena, he was not ready for this.

"Brian, you know that whatever happens tomorrow, we will be with you and our prayers will surround you and hold you up." The words of reassurance had come from Carl. "You will not be alone."

Brian nodded his head.

"...and our prayers will be with you throughout the night," added John Savage.

"I don't expect to be praying through the night," confessed Elena. Then she looked up into Brian's eyes. "I expect to be making a lot of...noise. I hope the rest of you are not light sleepers."

Elena then snuggled up to Brian more closely and kissed him lightly on the neck. The others looked back and forth at each other. Amos spoke first.

"Uh...if I'm hearing you correctly, might I speak for those of us here who are SLAVISHLY BOUND to tradition, and just MENTION the fact that you have an excess of clergy here at your beckon call..."

"No waiting," added John Savage, "...and we won't even make you get a license."

Brian looked down into Elena's eyes. "Yeah...I think I would like that."

Elena nodded. "Me, too." Then she looked over at Carl. "But make it quick."

"Quick...," said Carl. "Okay..."

He grabbed both of their right hands and brought them together, putting his own right hand over theirs. John, Maggie and Amos did the same.

"Do you?"

Brian nodded. "I do."

"...and you?"

Elena smiled a beautiful smile. "I do, too."

Carl looked over at Amos, who looked upward for a second, and then at the couple.

"God says, 'Yes!'"

"You're all witnesses?" John asked to no one in particular and everyone in general.

"I'm not sure I believe what I'm seeing," said Shawna, "but yes."

"Me, too," said Drew.

"Then it's done. And what God has joined together, let no one put asunder. Kiss your little hearts out."

After Brian and Elena kissed, Amos, who had torn up several squares of toilet paper, now threw them in the air.

"Wheee! That will be five thousand dollars, please."

"Put it on our room bill," said Brian before kissing Elena again.

After this prolonged kiss, Maggie stepped up beside them. "Okay, now you guys. I'm sorry, but I just have to do a little, more serious part." She put her hands on their shoulders and closed her eyes. "Creator God, you see these two precious people. You know we love them, and we know you do. Bless them now. Turn their night into an eternity. Even as they always know your presence, let them always feel each other's presence – together or apart. Amen."

Amens were whispered throughout the cell.

"Now that was the most beautiful ceremony I have been a part of," said Amos.

Drew chuckled at first, but then after a little consideration decided that Amos may have been right.

Amos now stood up and headed toward his cot. "Okay, you two, you've got to promise to give us all at least a half hour before you start making those 'noises' you were talkin' about, ya' hear? Because some of us haven't been part of those 'noises' for a while, and I don't want Maggie gettin' all inspired and comin' over and jumpin' MY bones. You know what I'm talkin' about?"

"For heaven's sake, Amos!" cried Maggie. "I think we all most certainly know all too well what you are talking about!"

"Good!" replied Amos. "Because I could BE more specific... I just don't want to embarrass John, that's all..."

"Go to bed, Amos," said John, interrupting. "I'm no more embarrassed by you now than I have been ever since I met you."

"What does that mean? I..."

"Let's ALL go to bed!" said Maggie. "Let's get to sleep and allow these two to enjoy at least some semi-private time."

The lights went out, and each person retreated into a different corner of the cell, with the exception of Brian and Elena, and also Drew and Shawna. Drew curled up on his cot and pulled Shawna down beside him. She nestled in with her backsides conforming to the contours of Drew's lap, in a spoons position. The softness of her bottom pressing against him, combined with the scent of her hair, ignited Drew's passion and he pressed even closer. Shawna turned her face toward him and kissed him lightly on the corner of his mouth.

"Drew," she whispered. "This is Brian and Elena's time. Let's wait for our time, okay?"

Drew didn't answer. He wanted her so badly right now – not only for the physical reasons, but because he wanted all that such a union brought to the spirit: a oneness with one whom he had come to see as completing him; a flowing of energy that revealed the perception that they were two separate people as the lie which it was; and a physical touching that massaged the soul and brought the spirit peace. Still he heard her words of caution with ears that were prepared for them because he knew their wisdom.

"I do want you, Drew. You know that."

Drew nodded his head.

"The first time together is very special to a woman. I want it to be right. I want it to be a time for us alone. I want it to be a time where we can celebrate not only our love, but the future we have together. Brian and Elena...well, they have only today..."

Brian could feel the warmth of her tears, some of which transferred themselves to his cheeks. He tenderly kissed those tears that remained on her side of the connection.

"Maggie's prayer – an eternity in one night. That is what they will have."

Shawna nodded. "So, you're okay with this?"

Drew gave a little laugh. "Well, I'm not sure I'll ever actually go to sleep like this – my body is wide awake and shouting at me – but I'll be fine. In fact, better than fine. Even with the frustration I feel, I would rather be in this jail cell in this bed with you, than with anyone else, anywhere."

Even in the darkness, Drew could see Shawna's smile light up. "Me, too," she whispered.

Drew was right about not going to sleep. It wasn't fifteen minutes later that he heard the light snoring that signaled that Shawna had fallen asleep, and it wasn't long after that when Drew heard the sounds of passion from where Brian and Elena lay together. Those sounds ebbed and flowed through the long night. Drew tried not to think about what would happen in the morning, and for the most part he succeeded, because he knew that thinking of morning would only take away from the sanctity of that night. And besides, morning was thousands of breaths away.

∎∎∎

"Everybody up!"

The harsh message had come from the mouth of Corporal Madison as he stepped inside the jail door. Right behind him was E.J. Conrad and a half a dozen heavily-armed soldiers.

Shawna looked down the corridor from the women's cell to which she and the other women had been returned not a half-hour before. She felt her stomach immediately tighten into a knot. Conrad walked over to near where Drew was now standing.

"I was hoping that we would have heard from you by now, that you would tell me that you had decided to do the right thing and support us."

"Yeah, well, that's the problem. I AM doing the right thing. I am not going to support you."

Conrad just stood there for a moment, staring at Drew with steely eyes.

"Too bad," he said in a voice barely audible to Shawna.

Conrad stepped back away from the cell bars and motioned toward one of the soldiers. Then as the soldier opened the cell door, he looked over at Brian.

"You're perfidy now comes to its just end, Mr. Marshal. In a sense, you are fortunate. Judas had to do this all for himself. See how caring we are that we are volunteering to do it for you!"

Brian said nothing. He simply held out his hands to receive the cuffs.

"For the rest of you," continued Conrad, "we have reserved the best seats in the house. It would be a shame to execute someone and not provide those who need the lesson of that execution the most a chance to fully experience and learn from it."

"Yes, but what will YOU learn from it, you beast from hell?" The words had come from Elena, as she stood now next to Shawna, clinging to the bars. "When will you learn that if you fight with violence and hate, the kingdom you establish will not be God's?!"

Conrad sent Elena an icy stare. "You have a feisty spirit, Ms. Enesco. But your words show that you know little of God and his Word, and unfortunately I don't have time to teach you right now."

Conrad motioned toward one of his soldiers. "Take them all out to the firing range."

As Conrad turned toward the door, Elena cried one more time, but her words came in a stressed voice that was almost inaudible. Shawna heard her, but she was quite sure that Conrad did not.

"I am no longer...Ms. Enesco. I am Elena Enesco-Marshal!"

Elena slumped to the floor and Shawna helped her to her feet. They held each other tightly as both began to sob.

The two women had steeled themselves slightly by the time they had reached the place of execution, a parking lot with a large stone wall butted up against one end. The wall already showed pit marks and some spattering of blood. A small group of citizens were standing around waiting to watch the execution, but it was unclear whether they were there of their own volition, or whether the other troops standing nearby had an influence on their presence.

Brian was brought out last, and he was allowed to walk slowly past those who had spent his last days with him in jail. Carl Tollefson, Maggie Moore, John Savage, Drew – each one gave him a hug and whispered some encouragement that Shawna couldn't hear. Amos Baldwin was closer and when Brian came past him, Amos gave him a "thumbs up" and said but five quick words.

"The Gates of Heaven, Bro!"

Brian's smile seemed to explode across his face.

"The Gates of Heaven."

When Brian came to stand in front of Shawna, she felt the tears well up in her eyes once more and her throat tightened. The previous night she had thought of the words that she would say, but now suddenly those words were gone without a trace. All she could do at first was look into his eyes. As she did so she saw love there, love which was gentle, unforced and unconflicted, love which she had hungered to see in his eyes for longer than she had cared to remember. She wanted to memorize that look so that she could call it to her memory whenever she wanted, but the soldier who was escorting Brian was prodding him to move along. And then it came to her that the words she needed to say were nothing more or less than words that had already been said, but which could have fresh meaning coming from her own lips.

"The Gates of Heaven...Bro!"

Brian's own eyes moistened. "The Gates of Heaven, Sis!"

Shawna hugged him as tightly as she could, kissed him on his cheek. Then she pulled back and turned her eyes away. It was too painful to try to hold on. Still, she watched out of the corner of her eye as Brian came to Elena. Their embrace seemed so natural that it seemed to Shawna that they must have been born for each other's arms. The awkwardness that comes from holding one of recent acquaintance was long gone, and in its place was a gentleness that one more often sees in mature love. Shawna was now drawn to look at them more fully. In Brian's eyes was none of the regret one would expect to see. Rather the love there, if it were shaded with any other hue at all, it was shaded with peace and confidence. Brian whispered some words that were inaudible even at this distance of less than five feet, but Elena heard him. She heard what was on his lips. She heard what was in his eyes. And when she pulled away from him, the peace in Brian's eyes had penetrated into her demeanor.

Brian refused the hood they offered him. Shawna was not sure why at first, but after they tied him up against the wall, she was ready to hazard a guess. His eyes were drawn upward toward the sky, the sky which he had not seen in some time, the sky whose light blue hue and wispy clouds seemed immune to the turbulence below, the sky which seemed to dwarf even the nearby hills and mountains. Brian had refused a hood that would have blocked the sky. As the soldiers who had tied him moved away and others lifted their weapons, Brian's body seemed to be lifted toward the sky upon which his eyes were fixed. Shawna saw no tension in his limbs, no fear in his mouth and no wariness in his eyes. She now understood what the ancients had seen when they spoke of saints.

As the pops and cracks pierced the air, the little red pocks seemed to explode from within Brian's body, and his body quivered before being released to sag toward the earth. Shawna just looked upward toward the sky. As she did her spirit grew calm. She fell to her knees, not in weakness but in peaceful submission. She lifted her arms toward that sky so high above, and for a moment it seemed that she would lift from the ground and soar above all that was around her. But the same soldiers who had released Brian, called her back to earthbound existence. They tugged and pulled until she looked into their demanding eyes, and agreed to start moving back to her cell.

Shawna looked around her and smiled. Elena, Amos, Drew – all of them – all of them had also fallen to their knees and had lifted their eyes and arms to the sky -- and yet none seemed to know of the actions of the others. Shawna found much peace in that. The gates had indeed opened wide.

Chapter Sixteen

Drew Covington's head began to swim. *Oh, man, that's what I get for getting up too quickly!* He braced himself against the bars of the cell. As he did he looked down at the dirty plate which was all that remained of his meal for that day. There had not been that much more on it when the guard brought it in. Maybe that and not how he had gotten up was the true reason behind his vertigo.

Amos Baldwin, who was lying on his cot, put one finger up in the air, as if he were about to say something profound.

"Okay...a plate of Applebee's barbecue pork ribs, with the corn on the cob, and those baked beans and cornbread."

"What?"

"My last meal. That's what I would ask for if they decided to kill me and gave me a last meal."

"Hell, Baldwin!" called Maggie from down the hall. "They didn't give Brian a last meal. What makes you think they would give you one?"

"I'd ask. Brian didn't ask, did he? No, Sir! He was too much in the Spirit. He didn't need any last meal. Me, I'm feeling very much in the flesh and I'd ask. I'd ask for barbecue ribs."

"Oh, man, Baldwin! Shut up!" protested John Savage. "Or maybe we'll convince them to shoot you...and we'll steal your last meal!"

"I agree," said Drew. "I don't want to hear any talk about ribs that I can't have."

"Steak fajitas."

Everyone in the men's cell looked over at Carl, the source of the new not-on-the-menu suggestion.

"Come on, Carl, don't go there," objected John. "Just because Amos..."

"No, really, steak fajitas – with lots of guacamole and sour cream, some pico de gallo."

"So, have you guys never actually BEEN to a nice restaurant?" The question had come from Shawna. "I mean, come on, Applebees? I'm a teacher and even I know there's better food in the world. Newport Bay Restaurant in Portland -- The sautéed seafood medley is to die for."

"You guys!" John threw up his arms in exasperation. "At least you could talk about good old American food. I mean, no one has even mentioned steak yet – like the thick, juicy Sirloins at Ruth's Chris steakhouse from Seattle."

"Oh, man, you can cut those with a fork!" added Carl.

"*Et tu*, Reverend Savage?" moaned Drew.

"People are dying out there!"

Everyone looked over at Elena.

"People are dying out there," she repeated, "and you are all obsessed with food? We are alive and we have something to eat. That is enough. Out in the world there are those who have barely survived nuclear bombs. Their skin is burned and they are afraid to even consider what their future will be. Do you think they are obsessed with thinking about fancy food? What other terrible things have people experienced at the hands of that mad man out there? We don't know. We know we had a friend who was shot to death. That much we know...."

As Elena's voice trailed off there was relative silence in both cells. Shawna and Maggie walked over to Elena and put their arms around her as she quietly wept. With the silence Drew became more aware of the distant sounds of bombs and artillery on the outside. He wondered what those bombs were landing on, and what was left of the town and the area around it. He wondered if any progress was being made in the effort to defeat Conrad. He wondered if anyone anywhere was still living a peaceful life.

Amos stood up and looked out through the cell bars in the direction of the women's cell. "Elena, we have even less control over what is happening out there than we do over the food.

Sometimes you just need to pretend that you have a choice somewhere."

"I know that!" screamed Elena. "I know that!"

"We all loved Brian," Carl said quietly.

"I know that too," responded Elena through her tears.

Just then the jail door opened and in walked Conrad, followed by Corporal Madison. The old professor walked directly over to where Drew stood near his cell bars.

"Ah, Mr. Covington! Are you losing weight? A new diet perhaps? I must say that your face is looking a little sallow. Your former readers wouldn't even recognize you as the same one in that little picture in the corner of your column. Of course, they are your *former* readers, so maybe it's not important. They have other writers to read now."

"Getting bored with incinerating children, Conrad?" asked Amos. "I guess it would be more interesting doing your violence face-to-face. Of course, you do want to make sure there are either bars or guns between us, you chicken-shit little bastard!"

"Ah, yes. Trash talk. Your people are so good at that, Mr. Baldwin. I suppose you expect me to say, 'Reverend Baldwin', but you have no such status in God's eyes. Corporal Madison, train your weapon on Mr. Baldwin's head, and if he says one more disrespectful word, you have my permission to waste one bullet."

Carl and John immediately moved to Amos' side and urged him to keep quiet. Conrad turned his attention back to Drew.

"Anyway, I really have come on a friendly mission here. I have come across an old friend of yours, Drew, and I knew that the two of you would want to see each other."

Conrad looked back toward the door where another soldier now stood.

"Private Harrington, please call in our mystery guest."

The private went back through the door and in a few seconds returned with a woman. As she turned toward him, Drew recognized the face of Ashley Cambridge.

"Ah! You do recognize the face of your attractive former colleague! Ashley come on over here so you can get reacquainted."

Ashley walked over and stood next to Conrad.

"I have to say that Ashley has been doing such an excellent job filling in for you that I doubt that they even miss you at all there at *The Oregonian*. Oh! And I should probably also say that we really don't need you to write for us anymore because..."

"Ashley!" said Drew, interrupting, "You're going to write for Conrad?!"

"Don't act so shocked," responded Ashley. "You've sold out, Drew. You've abandoned the reader base that once used to respect you so much. They needed your guidance and you sold them out! It's time now for conservatives to be saying 'We're tired of you gutless liberals destroying our country, and we're not going to take it any more!' But what have you said? 'Oh, ask politely for the good old values, but for heaven's sake, don't do anything at all forceful!' Well, that isn't going to do anymore, and E J Conrad understands that. I'm truly sorry that you don't."

As Drew looked into Ashley's defiant eyes, he couldn't help but feel like he was looking back into some previous life. In that other life the issues of conservative and liberal were much more clear cut. In that other life the people closest to him were the people who most thought like he did – people like Ashley who cringed at the same time he cringed and who loved to sit and agree together over morning lattes or evening glasses of wine. He thought of those around him in those two cells. The only one he would have associated with much before was John Savage. *Have I sold out?* He couldn't think of one issue that he had changed his mind about, except for perhaps the situations in which violence should be used. He could think of very few of those any more. He couldn't think of much that he had written that he would now repudiate. But he had been touched by different people, people from whom he would never turn away.

"I'm not selling out, Ashley. But even if I were, that's better than selling out on humanity. That is what you are doing by siding with him."

"It won't be long before you will regret not having done the same, Drew," warned Conrad. "I feel sorry that you didn't see fit to work with us, not so much for our sake, but for yours. God provides. And God has provided us with Ashley. She will do at least as well, and probably even better than you could have. But I am sorry for you because you have turned God away, and in so doing you have turned away from the kingdom God will soon bring to this earth. When that happens you may wish that we would have done to you what we did to your young friend, Brian. At least for him his end was quick."

"Any kingdom you usher in, I want no part of. Rather I would be privileged to be with Brian wherever he is now."

"Soon enough, Drew. Soon enough."

Conrad took Ashley's arm and turned to leave, but Ashley held back and looked down at the women's cell.

"This is what you did to him, bitch! He'll die because of you. I hope you're happy!"

Shawna smiled. "Yeah, for the most part."

Ashley scowled and headed out the door with Conrad. Corporal Madison was the last one out, and he smiled and sent a secretive "thumbs up" in Drew's direction before slamming the door behind him.

■■■

"What should I tell the men, Sir?"

E.J. Conrad looked over at the young captain. "About what, Conners?"

"The food, Sir. As I was saying, Sir, they are complaining because they're having to eat the same things over and over again. The cooks are running out of everything due to the embargo. Is there anything...uh...positive I can say to them?"

Conrad let out a deep sigh. "Positive, huh?"

"Yes, Sir."

Conrad walked over to his desk, reached in the top drawer and pulled out his Bible. He quickly leafed through it until he came to the passage for which he was searching.

"'And the whole congregation of the children of Israel murmured against Moses and Aaron in the wilderness:

"'And the children of Israel said unto them, Would to God we had died by the hand of the Lord in the land of Egypt, when we sat by the flesh pots, and when we did eat bread to the full; for ye have brought us forth into this wilderness, to kill this whole assembly with hunger.

"'Then said the Lord unto Moses, Behold, I will rain bread from heaven for you; and the people shall go out and gather a certain rate every day, that I may prove them, whether they will walk in my law, or no.'"

Conrad closed his Bible and walked over to Captain Conners, looking at him eye-to-eye. "Do you know what that bread was called, Captain?"

"Yes, Sir. 'Manna,' Sir."

"Yes, 'manna.' Do you know for how long they ended up eating that manna, Captain?"

"Uh...no, Sir."

"Forty years, Captain. For forty years they ate manna – that and quail meat. That's all they had. Do you suppose they ever got tired of it over that forty years?"

"Uh...shi...uh, gosh...I would think so, Sir."

Now Conrad moved so close to the captain that their noses almost touched.

"Yes, they did, because they were faithless ingrates!" he barked. "That's why they all died in the wilderness and didn't get to see the Promised Land. Do you want the same for us soldier?"

"No, Sir!"

"Then I suggest you talk to your men about this biblical story, and let them know what it teaches us, soldier!"

"Yes, Sir!"

"And what does it teach us?"

"To look for manna, Sir?"

"To trust God's provision, and to be grateful for what you get!"

"Yes, Sir!"

"Dismissed!"

As Captain Conners shut the door behind him, Conrad walked over to a spot in his office that had become his personal worship center. A cross carved out of mahogany stood on a small table. On either side were candles that were kept burning twenty-four hours a day. He got down on his knees, hesitated just a moment and then leaned forward, putting his face on the floor and his hands out in front of him. He would probably not have admitted it to anyone, but the humility of this prayer position, so typical of Islam, was something he admired in people of that faith. They were infidels and he knew Christ would judge them, but they knew how to pray in a humble manner.

"Oh, God Almighty, look upon your humble servant and hear his prayer. My people are a stubborn people and hard of heart, but do not hold this sin against them. They are fighting hard for you and for your kingdom. They live in a land of unclean lips and yet they try very much to keep their words pure and pleasing in your sight. Do not vent your wrath upon them. Rather, hear their cry and send us your provision, as you sent the manna of old. Give us your victory, and we will give you the praise. We pray in the name of your Son, our Savior."

The old professor remained in his prayer posture for several minutes, quietly searching for any word of direction that he might receive from his God. All he heard was the sound of his own breathing, and the muffled noises of passers-by outside the hospital where his office now had been situated. Shortly there came another sound – a knock on the door. Conrad said his "Amen" and rose to see who it was.

Upon opening the door, Conrad found Ashley Cambridge on the other side. While Ashley knew enough of Conrad's moral sensibilities to dress conservatively, nothing short of a straight jacket could hide the curves she had been graced with. The old professor felt the urge to survey her form from head to foot, but fortunately he found her green eyes so riveting that they were able to hold his attention and keep his eyes from wandering any further.

"Oh, Ashley. Won't you come in?"

As Ashley brushed past him and walked into the room, Conrad could no longer maintain his discipline and his eyes dropped to below her waist and a perfectly formed bottom. Conrad came to realize how little time he had spent with women since his wife had died four and a half years earlier. Of the ones he had dealt with, most were the spouses of his military officers, and none looked like Ashley Cambridge. Conrad closed the door behind her and lifted his eyes before hers turned to face him.

"I finished the article I promised to do for you. I e-mailed a copy to you, but I thought you might also like a hard copy."

Ashley held out the copy and smiled at him once more. Conrad took it and motioned for her to be seated. He put the copy on his desk, but then sat in the chair next to Ashley.

"I'll look at it later. I prefer to do such things when I am alone."

"I'm afraid a lot of the newspapers that normally take Drew's column have made it known that they will not accept this," Ashley continued. "I think we will end up in only around a third of them. The others are afraid of looking subversive. But from what I have seen, once the other papers start running what I write, it will be hot news and the other papers will not be able to leave it alone. They may only print excerpts, but they will print something."

"I perfectly agree – I knew you had a good head on your shoulders."

Ashley blushed. "Well, I just want to do a good job for you. I believe you are the most important man of the Twenty-first Century. I want to serve you well."

Now it was Conrad's turn to blush. "Well...that's very kind of you."

"You are spending your time and focus on your mission, I know," said Ashley in her most velvety-smooth voice. "While you are doing that, who takes care of you and what you need?"

E J Conrad's heart sputtered and then raced into high gear. In his younger years he never had any trouble attracting women, but now he was well into his sixties, and this woman was young and beautiful. He thought back to a couple of illicit unions he had had before his marriage to Emily. He always looked back at them with shame, and sometimes when things weren't going well, he thought they might be the reason why. God was punishing him for his old indiscretions. Was she talking about something like that?

"I...uh...I get taken care of fine. My wife has been dead for over four years now. She used to spoil me. She took care of every need I had, and every need I even thought of having. I'm not taken care of that well now, of course."

"Is there a woman in your life?"

"Uh...no."

Conrad had suddenly felt that he had lost control and that was making him extremely uncomfortable. He stood up, walked over to his desk and picked up the article Ashley had brought in.

"We need to talk of other things right now. I want you to put out a column like this every week. And as part of your preparation I want you to make sure that you attend my daily Bible studies where I discuss how our activities relate to Scripture. Do you have any problem with that?"

"No, not at all. I would like that."

"And your language – it may sound trivial to you, but I noticed that you used some inappropriate language when you talked to that Shawna woman in the jail the other day. While I understand the sentiments you expressed, you must avoid such language in the future."

"Certainly. I am sorry – the heat of the moment, you know."

After an uncomfortable pause, Ashley spoke again. "Uh...Mister Conrad, you suddenly seem unhappy with me. Did I do something...?"

"No, no. Not at all. It's just that we all need to be wary, Ms. Cambridge. The devil knows that a war has been mounted against him, and he will use every tool in his arsenal to keep God from victory, even a beautiful woman like yourself. You must not allow that to happen. You must study the Word. You must understand the importance of being pure and fully devoted to God. We can't allow anything to stop us now, or it may all come crashing down. You understand that, don't you Ms. Cambridge?"

"Uh...yes, Sir. I think so, Sir."

"Revelation speaks of a Great Harlot that will come in the Last Days and lead people away from the truth. I don't believe it is referring to a literal woman, but nonetheless it reminds us of how the beauty of a woman can lure people away from something even more beautiful – the kingdom God has in store for us."

"I wouldn't..."

"Yes, yes, I'm sure you have no wrong intention here. It's just that one has to be careful, you know..."

There was a knock at the door and Conrad jumped. His thought for some reason shifted to when he was a teen and his parents had knocked on the door of his room, and his thoughts had been where he knew they should not have been. He knew that his parents could not see his thoughts and yet...

"Come in."

The door opened revealing a general, rather than a parent. General Robert James smiled, bowed slightly in Ashley's direction and then turned his attention to Conrad.

"Sorry to bother you, Sir, but there are some matters that demand your immediate attention." He glanced over at Ashley again. "Classified matters."

"Yes, of course," Conrad replied. He also looked over at Ashley. "Ms. Cambridge, once again, thank you for your work. I will be interested in hearing of the reaction to what you have written. Please shut the door on your way out."

As the young writer left the room, Conrad watched General James out of the corner of his eye to catch the direction of his focus. The general looked in the opposite direction of the retreating form of the attractive young writer. The man had good military discipline...and he knew whom he served.

"Sir, may I have your permission to voice some concerns?" The general's question came immediately after Ashley shut the door behind her.

"Certainly."

"This military campaign is losing its edge, Sir. Ever since the attempted use of our last nuclear device and the unfortunate demise of General Dawson, it seems we have just been standing pat. I realize we have needed a lot of resources to defend our position, but unless we take the offensive again soon, my judgment is that we will be neutralized, and the war will be lost."

Conrad bristled. "Do you think so little of God that you believe he might lose?"

The general also stiffened. "It's not God, it's us. I just don't want any victory to be delayed because we were not worthy vessels."

E.J. Conrad strode over, sat behind his desk, and pulled out his Bible. The general noticeably sighed.

"Sir, unless you are planning to bring this nation to its knees by blowing trumpets and marching around cities, I doubt if you are going to find any battle strategies there that..."

Conrad stood abruptly, pounded on his desk and held out his Bible as if it were a gun aimed right at the general's forehead.

"General, EVERYTHING that has gotten us to this point has been found in this book! Everything! Like Gideon took on the Midianites with only three hundred men, we have taken on the mightiest nation on earth and we ARE bringing her to her knees! That could not have been done without the God who is at the heart of this book. 'Some trust in chariots, and some in horses: but we will remember the name of the Lord our God.' The weapons may be different today, general. But the principles are the same! And if you are not ready to operate by what is in this book, then you better find another army!"

"I didn't mean to disparage the Word, Sir. I would never do that. But we need a specific plan to retake the offensive. That's all I'm saying."

Conrad sat back down at his desk and let his Bible open before him, as it would. His heart was racing and his breathing was rapid. Why was it so difficult for people to see his vision? Why had he talked so long and people still didn't understand? Even as the question came to his mind, a Scripture from Isaiah came also: "And he said, 'Go, and tell this people, Hear ye indeed, but understand not; and see ye indeed, but perceive not. Make the heart of this people fat, and make their ears heavy, and shut their eyes; lest they see with their eyes, and hear with their ears, and understand with their heart, and convert, and be healed.'" Those who spoke for God had long faced a people who were slow to understand.

Conrad began thumbing through the well-worn pages of the book of Revelation. As he did he glanced up at the face of his general.

"What is the status of our offensive in Idaho?"

"The mountain forces there believe they might soon mount another offensive against Boise. That is a high-tech city and it would help us to take it. But it is still just small potatoes compared to the rest of the country."

"How about our guerilla forces in the rest of the country?"

"General Samuels reports that all they have been able to do successfully is to launch disruptive attacks such as the one on that Baltimore rock concert. Attacks on militarily significant targets have failed. Attacks in the Midwest have disrupted the farm economy, which has led to high food prices. But again, no significant military targets..."

"Hunger and inflated prices are part of the plagues of Revelation."

"Yes, but it's not enough. We talked before of the possibility of an alliance with the Arab nations, and I really think..."

"There can be no alliance between God and Satan! God will not bless those who yoke themselves with unbelievers."

General James shut his eyes and clenched his fists. When he opened both again he looked over at Conrad. "Then what would you suggest, Sir? We need some fresh ideas here."

Conrad returned his attention to the Scripture, and as soon as he did, he found it. He saw words that he had seen many times before, but this time is was as if they jumped off of the page. He stood and lifted up the Bible as he read from it aloud to the general:

"'And I heard a great voice out of the temple saying to the seven angels, Go your ways, and pour out the vials of the wrath of God upon the earth.

"'And the first went, and poured out his vial upon the earth; and there fell a noisome and grievous sore upon the men which had the mark of the beast, and *upon* them which worshipped his image.

"'And the second angel poured out his vial upon the sea; and it became as the blood of a dead *man*: and every living soul died in the sea.

"'And the third angel poured out his vial upon the rivers and fountains of waters; and they became blood....'"

Conrad shut the book and looked over at his general. "What does all of that sound like to you?"

"Uh...I don't know, Sir."

"Come on, General, open your mind!" Conrad impassioned. "Grievous sores – that's a disease! It's a bloody disease. What's the bloodiest disease you know about?"

The general's face turned white. Conrad could see the answer present in the man's eyes long before it came from his lips, but it did finally come. "Uh...that would be Ebola, Sir."

E.J. Conrad sat back triumphantly in his chair and threw his feet upon his desk. His face beamed forth the biggest smile he had shown in months.

"Yes, indeed, General. That would be Ebola. We have our answer. And it came from the place from which I told you it would come."

Chapter Seventeen

"So...you think it can be done?"

E.J. Conrad looked down at the spectacled man sitting in front of his desk. The man squirmed and seemed to be avoiding Conrad's eyes. That was okay. Conrad was looking for expertise, not social confidence.

"Doctor Conrad, I have worked for ten years with the center for disease control and ten more with the CIA. But in all of that time, I have for the most part been trained to keep things like you speak of from happening. So, I'm sorry, I know you are a godly man and I don't mean to offend you, but are you certain that this is how God wants it to be? Are you certain this is part of the plan?"

"Doctor Henderson, I will trust your expertise in scientific matters, and you need to trust mine in scriptural matters. All of history has been leading to this point and we cannot back down now. Revelation speaks of plagues that will precede his coming. I am certain that this is one of the plagues he is calling forth to judge his people."

Doctor Henderson slowly nodded his head. "Okay...because this...this is a pretty ugly disease."

"Sometimes we cannot avoid the ugly if we want to make our way to the truly beautiful."

The diminutive scientist now stood and began pacing back and forth in Conrad's office. Finally he stopped and placed his hand gently on the cover of Conrad's Bible, which was lying on his desk. He just looked down at it and felt that cover for a minute or two. Then he finally looked up into Conrad's eyes.

"Ebola is a vicious disease – the red eyes are one of the first clues, but that could just be an allergy, couldn't it? Then comes the diarrhea, vomiting, joint and muscle aches, severe stomach pain – now you think you have the flu or food poisoning. Then comes the internal and external bleeding, and it starts to eat away at your liver and your kidneys. By then most of the time it's too late for you. The death rate is up to 90%. That's the disease you're talking about spreading, right?"

Conrad nodded his head.

"The bad news for you is that in its natural form it does not seem to be easily spread. There has never been an outbreak in the United States, and those which have started in Africa have been fairly quickly contained. The natural reservoir of the disease is unknown, but it is most commonly believed that it zoontic, which is to say that it is spread by contact with certain animals, principally infected cynomolgous monkeys."

"In this country, we obviously can't bring mass numbers of people in contact with monkeys."

"Certainly. Once a human has been infected, the disease is spread through direct contact with the blood and/or secretions of an infected person. That is why it is most commonly spread in healthcare settings or to family members who are caregivers. It can also be spread through infected needles that are reused. That is why it has spread in African locations where poor medical techniques were used. Normally, once proper care and isolation techniques are introduced, the spread of infection is contained."

"Normally?"

"Well, that is to say, with the naturally occurring strains that have been spread in the past. In order to effectively spread a disease such as this you really need something that can be spread by airborne particles. Some natural strains of Ebola have been found in a primate research facility to have been transmitted through the air, but transmission through airborne particles has never been documented among humans in a real-world setting. Since the disease's spread has been so quickly halted, it is unlikely that this occurs."

Conrad stood up quickly and pounded on his desk. "Get to the point, doctor! All that you have told me thus far doesn't help, if we can't effectively spread the disease! Can we do it or can we not do it?!"

Doctor Henderson turned, walked away and then sat down in a chair in a far corner of the room, with his face turned away from Conrad. When the doctor spoke again, Conrad could barely hear him.

"What I have...spoken of...is the disease in its naturally occurring form. There is a laboratory-produced strain."

"A laboratory-produced strain?"

"One that was intentionally-developed. Not in this country, but in Russia. It's a strain that the CIA was able to obtain when I worked there. I have preserved vials in my possession. The documentation refers to a case where it was accidentally released in one lab and nearly all of twenty workers were infected within a week. Seventeen died, in spite of the best care they could provide. They concluded that it was almost certainly spread by airborne particles."

"And you can get us this virus?"

"I can, under one condition."

"What condition is that?"

Henderson stood again and walked over to face Conrad. "My family is from the Twin Cities area of Minnesota. I don't want it released there."

"How would we release it? – mail it in envelopes? Pour it into the water supply?"

Henderson stared into Conrad's eyes with a blank expression. He then blinked a couple of times before going on. "I'm sorry, Sir. I guess I have not made myself clear. This disease cannot be initiated in the manner you suggest. Even if it could, after past actions of that kind, the authorities will be watching for such things, and we would most certainly fail. This disease must be spread through infected human agents. Sir, you must infect some of your own people, people who believe in your cause, people who will know that they will most likely die in the process."

It was Conrad's turn to be silent.

"Sir, it is the only way," continued Henderson. "Certainly if infidel Muslims can give up their lives to advance their cause,

Christians who worship the true Way can find it in themselves to do the same. We would inject them with infected blood. The effectiveness of this strategy, Sir, is based on the fact that while you can regulate the importation of monkeys, and you can watch for white powder in an envelop, how can you guard against people? – normal American people, looking like everyone else, wandering around in shopping malls, office buildings, libraries and even doctor's offices – coughing and sneezing?"

"How many would need to...?"

"That depends on how fast you want to spread it and how far you want to spread it. A couple of hundred I would say, left off in strategic locations throughout the country would make a national epidemic of apocalyptic dimensions."

Conrad felt a shiver. He wrapped his arms around himself as he began pacing across his office. A couple of times he looked over at the face of the biochemist, as if he thought he might see there some sign of perfidy, some sign that what the man had proposed was just a joke or a deception to turn aside the cause. But all he could see was a sincere, though troubled, man.

Now Conrad's mind turned from the outward presence of the man who had formulated this idea to the Presence within, the Presence that had been guiding him all along, the Presence that had led him to that Scripture. It came again to his mind: "And the first went, and poured out his vial upon the earth; and there fell a noisome and grievous sore upon the men which had the mark of the beast, and *upon* them which worshipped his image." It was the Word of God. How could he shrink away? And then suddenly, another passage from Revelation came to mind, a passage that Conrad was sure had come to him from the mind of God himself: "And I saw the woman drunken with the blood of the saints, and with the blood of the martyrs of Jesus..."

Conrad could feel his pulse, which had been racing, almost immediately begin to slow. His breathing also now became slowed, almost to an imperceptible level. Conrad looked over at the scientist with a new peace in his heart.

"The infected, tainted blood of Christian martyrs – it is what will bring this country down, and begin the reign of God. That is how it needs to be. That is what God wills. So be it."

■■■

It was the only remaining cable hook up in the city. As a newsperson Ashley had hungered for the news and so she convinced Conrad to let her have access to this one. She needed to know what was going on in the outside world if she were to write credibly for the outside world. This television was in a conference room near Conrad's office in the hospital. Ashley found the remote, sat down and turned it on. The news was on Portland's KGW TV, an NBC affiliate.

"Great," she said as she heard what the reporter was talking about, "we're in a civil war, and this reporter is wasting time talking about an outbreak of the flu!" She shouted at the screen, "It's flu season, airhead! What did you expect? Get a grip!"

Now the woman was turning to what Ashley wanted to hear more about.

"With continued guerilla action being reported throughout the country, and lack of any progress against the Brigade strongholds of Longview and Spokane, Washington, pressure is building in Congress to authorize nuclear strikes against those two cities..."

"Oh, shit!" Ashley whispered.

"Over a hundred thousand people marched on the provisional headquarters of Congress in Baltimore today, demanding that the two rebel strongholds be immediately destroyed – even if it means nuclear strikes. Supporters waved flags and many also wore the globe and eagle insignia that Albert Packard had designed to indicate loyal support to US government forces, an insignia that Conrad supporters vow is a symbol of the antichrist. Several demonstrators said they saw no conflict between their symbols of support for Packard and their demand for a nuclear strike."

The camera switched to an on-the-street interview with a middle-aged construction worker.

"We support the President. He's a good man, no matter what Conrad's religious fanatics might say. But we want him to know that it's time to take a firmer stand with these end-of-the-world whack-os. I'm sorry for the good people who live in those two cities and can't get out, but what can you do? You can't let them hold the country hostage for the sake of a few hundred thousand people."

A young woman was the next to speak for the camera.

"Hey, there comes a time when it's either them or us, you know what I mean? They want to send us all to hell, let's give them a little hell-fire of their own, you know? Turn E.J. Conrad into a little 'crispy critter'! They would do it to us – if they had another one."

The next woman to come seemed a little more nervous, but she wasted no time giving her thoughts.

"Let me tell you, I'm a Christian, too. But I don't like being lumped in with the likes of E.J. Conrad. And I'm not one of those pacifists either – those people who want us to turn the other cheek while these fanatics kill and destroy. Jesus wasn't afraid to crack the whip when he needed to, and that's what we need to do here."

The news reporter was back on the screen.

"A small counter-demonstration was also staged by those holding up peace signs, and calling for Packard to a face-to-face negotiation with Conrad. Demonstrators and counter-demonstrators got into several shoving matches, but no one was arrested.

"Administration officials said that while the ideas of negotiation with Conrad was Quixotic and against long-established policy, those advocating nuclear strikes should be patient with a more deliberate military policy. Privately, however, several officials speaking on the condition of anonymity, have said that the administration is closer to okaying a nuclear strike than they have ever been. Assessments are even being made of the probable collateral damage to civilian populations. "

The news anchor now gave an emotionally arresting summary: "And so it is that while not long ago the term 'collateral damage' was used for the deaths of civilians in far away places like Afghanistan or Iraq, now for the first time the concept is being applied to US citizens on US soil. It is a measure of national desperation that those willing to accept such civilian losses now are at least more vocal, if not more numerous, than those crying for restraint."

What the reporter said next never finished the trek from Ashley's ears to her consciousness. That venue had already been filled with visions of missiles streaking toward her heavily-laden with nuclear warheads, visions of a blinding light flashing around her and a searing heat. How much would she be conscious of, if that happened? Would she feel anything? Would she know far enough in advance for the horror of it all to hit her? Might she even survive, or at least survive in the sense of those "survivors" she had seen now on so many news specials about San Francisco and D.C.? – her beauty abruptly stripped from her like a soldier dishonorably discharged, her skin no longer soft, but hardened with scars and lesions?

Conrad would say that God would protect them from such things, that such horrors were reserved for the faithless, those who opposed the Brigade and what God would do through them. But how could she know? And wasn't she really one of the faithless? She went along with General Samuels because he seemed so sure and because what she had just experienced seemed to validate his words. And then Conrad seemed even more sure, and the way he could take anything and relate it to the Bible and the Will of God, was simply dazzling. But that was all their faith, not hers. Her faith was like a little plant growing in a window box on the side of her house where nobody ever saw it. It was young and fragile. She knew it was there, when she took time to think about it, but the only time she took to water it was when she noticed it withering away. And now it was what was supposed to keep her from having a nuclear bomb dropped on her. She would have to find a more substantial shield than that.

Of course, it was also true that she had agreed to write for Conrad to spite Drew and Shawna Forester. It had indeed been satisfying seeing them in jail while she walked free. It simply hadn't occurred to her that they were all in a prison of sorts, imprisoned by a battle between different people's fears and different people's certainties.

Her attention was drawn back to the newscast. The economy was still languishing. There was drought in the Midwest. School children in Alabama had reported they had seen Jesus in the clouds. It all seemed vital to the news anchor, but somehow Ashley could not get excited about any of it. All she could think of was what might drop out of the sky onto her head.

The question at this point, of course, was what should she do about all of this? She couldn't simply tell Conrad that she had changed her mind and wanted out, could she? Or maybe she could. What was she thinking of? She saw how Conrad had looked at her. Like with most other men, Drew Covington being one of the rare exceptions, she could tell him what she wanted and he would follow along. She just had to prepare the ground a little. She just had to use all the weapons at her disposal.

■■■

General Robert James studied the list. After a few minutes he looked in Conrad's direction.

"I think we need some more volunteers. This simply won't do the trick."

Conrad scowled. "You mean to tell me that while Muslims who have no concept of the true meaning of the sacrifice of Jesus Christ on the Cross, can recruit thousands of people to carry bombs on their bodies or fly planes into buildings or...or...whatever...we cannot find a few hundred people who believe enough in the Lord's promises to lay down their life for him? How many do we have?"

"Eighty-seven. That's a start, but it's a big country, and we need this to spread far and fast."

"How many men and how many women?"

"Seventy-two men and fifteen women."

"Then we especially need more women. Women can get closer to others, spread the disease faster..."

"We don't have as many women in our ranks, and a lot of them are caring for children."

Conrad felt the building tremble. Pictures on the far wall swayed back and forth. Ripples danced across the top of the water in a glass on Conrad's desk. He smiled.

"Feel that, General? That's the power of God. That's a tiny sampling of the power of God. He's letting us know he's here. He's letting us know he's with us, and that he can handle it."

"Are you sure he's not telling us to get the hell out of here before that mountain dumps on us? – sorry about that 'hell' part...But you know the scientists are saying that the next eruption of Mount Saint Helens may be worse than the last..."

"Don't be faithless, General! We have the blood of the Lamb on our door posts. Shall the angel of the Lord not pass over us? The armies of the enemy will feel the fullness of his wrath, and they will flee before us. They will know that the Lord fights on our side, and then the whole country will tremble. The ash from this mountain will fill the skies, and what Revelation speaks of will take place: 'and, lo, there was a great earthquake; and the sun became black as sackcloth of hair; and the moon became as blood...' These things *must* take place, General. It has been ordained from the beginning of time. We are but the instruments by which God's eternal Will will be effected."

The general shifted back and forth on his feet. "I guess I just need more faith, Sir."

"We all do, General. We all do."

"What about the martyr volunteers, Sir? What do you suggest for me to do?"

Conrad shook his head. "Yes, that is tough. We can't be too open in our appeal or word might get out and they will be ready for us. Have we heard from our East Coast guerilla forces?"

"Not yet. General Sampson is working on it, but his forces are more spread out, of course, and it's harder for him to get the word out in a way that won't compromise security."

"Make sure he knows this is highest priority. I want some names from him within forty-eight hours. The longer we wait, the more likely it is that the word will leak out."

"Will that be all, Sir?"

"Yes, and tell Ms. Cambridge to come on in. We've kept her waiting for nearly forty-five minutes."

As the general headed out the door of Conrad's office, the old professor walked over to his desk, ostensibly to once again review Ashley's last news column, but also because he knew that it was the only place he could go in his office to check himself in a mirror. He glanced at the reflective surface and saw a man who was so much older than he thought himself to be; a man whose blue eyes used to contrast with rich brown hair, but which now seemed to blend with the abundance of gray; a man whose face used to present firm lines, but which now sagged wearily. He could remember when his dad used to look that way. He looked away.

E.J. Conrad felt that the contrast between the face he had seen last and the one he next saw was so stark that it came as a jolt to his system. Ashley Cambridge entered the room, shut the door and turned in his direction. Her green eyes were the center-piece of a face that was flawless in every respect. Conrad knew that she had never had plastic surgery, because no plastic surgeon could ever do such a perfect job. Every curve of her face was perfectly-formed, with soft cheeks flowing gracefully down to full lips, slightly parted like a rose that had just opened.

"Thank you for agreeing to see me, Sir. I know you are preoccupied with many things. Did you read my column? What did you think?"

"Uh...great! It was great," Conrad said, looking away from that face in order to recover his discipline and focus. "And I was really pleased that it received such a wide exposure. You were right when you said that once some of the papers ran it, the others couldn't leave it alone. I noticed, however, that they ran a rather large picture of you with the column. I thought that was rather distracting."

Ashley gave Conrad a pout, and shrugged her shoulders. "I'm afraid all of my life, men have had a hard time getting past how I look to what I have to say. I guess some male editors just felt they had to have the picture."

"Yes, well, I think...I think you're probably right about that."

"I'm glad you liked what I wrote, though," Ashley said, moving a little closer to the old professor. "The last time I was here you seemed displeased a little, like you thought I might try to lure you away from your mission. I want you to know that I believe in what you are doing and I would never do that."

"Oh, of course, Ms. Cambridge. Of course." As Conrad said these words, he backed up toward his desk.

"I want to do the best job I possibly can for you. That's why I thought it so important to have access to the outside news, like we talked about before. I just want you to know that whatever you want me to do for you, I will do – and I'll do it well."

Ashley had moved even closer to Conrad, and now she reached out and put her hand gently on his arm.

The words, "Get thee behind me, Satan!" flashed to Conrad's mind, but they never found a path to his lips. Other words found their way instead.

"You mean...other things beside writing?"

"Certainly. You're a man of God, Mister Conrad, but a man nonetheless. As a man of God, you want to change the world and bravely face whatever challenge God gives to you. But as a man you need to be nurtured and cared for in order to do those tasks. That's why God created woman, don't you think? That's why God created...someone like me."

As Ashley said these last words, she undid the top button of her blouse, revealing a substantial enough portion of her breasts for Conrad to know not only that they were not restrained by any bra, but that if he loosened one more button...

"Certainly God created you for more than just writing, Ms. Cambridge..."

Ashley took Conrad's right hand and lifted it up to her left breast, and then she pressed her lips against his, slipping her warm tongue snake-like between those lips and into the inner sanctum of his mouth. With his hand he could feel the hardened contours of her nipple, and she gave a sigh as she moved her right thigh up between his legs.

It was as if this last act jolted Conrad awake, and he pushed quickly away from her, staggering backward and nearly falling to the floor as he did. He looked up into her eyes as if he could see there an explanation for a deep confusion, but there was no answer for him there, and so he quickly looked away.

"Professor Conrad, I..."

Conrad held up his hand in Ashley's direction and shook his head, but he did not look her way. He walked over to his desk and picked up the newspaper with Ashley's column in it, but the words on it were just a blur. His mind was grasping for a response, a plan of what to do next, a way to push this all away from him and get back to what God needed him to do. But the feel of Ashley's lips and her body against his was seared into his mind and left little room for anything else. He thought of just sending her to jail along with the others, but wouldn't he then have to send himself to jail as well? What she had done he had longed for her to do. Besides, he didn't want those men down there to have the pleasure of....

Okay, he was sure now that wasn't what he needed to do. Conrad closed his eyes. He could feel his breathing start to slow back to normal. His heart also was no longer racing as it had when they touched. In his mind a clearer vision began to form. Images came from humanity's distant past. He turned and looked into Ashley's eyes, pointing a finger in her direction as he did.

"Woman, thou gavest to me, but I did not eat. What happened at the beginning will not happen at the end...you are banished from the Garden."
■■■

Ashley Cambridge couldn't help but smile. She had thought that it would take a while of being in Conrad's good graces for her to convince him to let her leave the so-called New Bethel. But all she had to do was to push his shaky sense of sexual morality, and before she had even realized what was happening, he was ordering her to leave.

Conrad had contacted Federal forces and had sold the transfer to them as an act of compassion. Ashley was emotionally stressed by life in New Bethel, and she was having second thoughts about her loyalty to the cause. All that was true enough.

Conrad didn't want her there if she wasn't totally convinced of what he was doing. Would Federal forces cooperate in transferring her to them? After a series of calls to the President and other high-level officials, they had agreed.

She was now seated in a Humvee, traveling down I-5 toward Fort Lewis, where she would be held under house arrest for a short while, as they debriefed her and ostensibly sought to determine if charges should be made against her. But she had already been assured that in return for certain information, such charges would never be filed. She was free from the danger of an imminent nuclear attack, and it would not be long before she was totally free. It had not happened exactly according to her plan, but it couldn't have worked out better. Even Conrad had behaved rather sweetly in the end, after his initial angry, condemning outburst. He had personally made sure that she had all her belongings, and that she had been given a good meal before being released. He had even made sure that she was inoculated against the recent flu outbreak. That was great. She had gotten angry at the reporter for making such a big deal of the recent epidemic, but she really did hate getting the flu.

Chapter Eighteen

"You're certain of this?"

Drew had looked straight into the young guard's eyes as he had spoken. Corporal Madison glanced nervously back at the door, and then nodded.

"They're recruiting people to voluntarily receive the virus, and then they're going to release them into the outside world. Those who volunteer have instructions to walk around wherever they can find the most people gathered together – shopping malls, sporting events, even synagogues and mosques. They're supposed to avoid the churches. Anyway, they were having trouble recruiting people at first, but Conrad has really been laying it on thick with the inspirational speeches and all, and now they think they have the number they need. They're planning to send out those from New Bethel in the early morning hours before dawn tomorrow."

"How are they getting them past Federal lines?" The question had come from John Savage.

"They have a sympathizer in the local command on the other side, and he is going to arrange to slip them through."

Drew glanced back and forth at John, Amos and Carl, but all he saw in their faces was the anxiety they all shared – there were no answers forthcoming. He turned back to Corporal Madison.

"You said before that you might be able to put together an underground network of other disenchanted soldiers to help get us out of here. Have you been able to do that?"

"Well that's slow work – finding people you can trust and all. I've found a few, but I could use some more time..."

"We don't have more time!"

"When...?"

"We should go tonight. If they're focusing on getting those infected people through the lines, it might distract them just enough that we can get out. Besides if those people get though tomorrow morning, we won't have much time to get out a warning and limit the spread. It has to be tonight!"

There was a chorus of agreement from both cells.

"Okay," the corporal said hesitantly. "I'll set it up. Let's go for midnight."

"Midnight it is," agreed Drew.

"But there's just one condition to all of this." The corporal said these words with more resolve than he had previously shown, and Drew immediately gave him his full attention.

"Condition?"

"I have to go with you."

Drew gave a sigh of relief. "That's no problem. It would be good to have an armed soldier along. But you could be subject to arrest on the other side. Do you want to risk that?"

"You guys will speak for me, right?"

Drew nodded.

"Well, then I'll risk it. Besides, the talk is...well...that the President is considering nuclear strikes against us – I sure don't want to be around for that."

"Nuclear strikes?"

"Yeah. There's been talk about it all along, of course, but recently Conrad's sources in the Federal Government seem to indicate that the President is finally ready to move in that direction. People out there are getting tired of all this. I don't blame them, actually."

"What's Conrad doing about it?"

"He's staying put for now. His advisors want to smuggle him back up into the mountains, but so far Conrad is resisting. The only thing he is doing differently is that he moved his office to that bomb shelter someone gave him. He doesn't like it, but it's safer. Of course, part of that was because of that Cambridge bitch..."

"Cambridge? Ashley Cambridge?"

"Yes, that's the one. The one he brought down with him that day and gave you all such a hard time. Anyway, Conrad got pissed off at her. I don't blame him for that. She had her nose so far up in the air, the joke was that it made our planes alter their flight patterns. Anyway, Conrad got pissed at her, and sent her off. I don't know why he didn't just put her in jail with you guys, except that I'm glad because I sure wouldn't want her around. But at least it would have kept her from blabbing to US forces. That's why Conrad changed his headquarters from the hospital – he was afraid she would tell them where he was. Still, the rumor is that he really got back at her though. They say he gave her a shot infected with that Ebola virus."

"Ebola virus?" Shawna had spoken from her cell down the hall. "They infected Ashley with Ebola virus?"

"Well, that's the rumor, and it comes from some pretty good sources – some guys I know who work in the hospital."

"When did this happen?" asked Drew, speaking with a new urgency. "And why didn't you tell us about it before?"

"I...I didn't think it was important. She sure didn't seem like she was any friend to you. Is she?"

Drew just stared blankly into the young soldier's eyes. What was the answer to his question? Ashley Cambridge had tried to destroy what had become the most important relationship in his life. She had done nothing to help save Shawna when she knew that Shawna was endangered by the pending nuclear attack on D.C. She had even willingly come to write for a man who she knew had killed hundreds of thousands of people through acts of violence and war. But he and Ashley also had a history together. He couldn't just disregard that. Even if he could in his mind, his feelings wouldn't allow it. They had been colleagues, working together on vital stories, rushing together to meet deadlines, laughing together when things got particularly crazy, and even on occasion crying together. When he had gone through divorce he had turned to her, and they had shared in a physical intimacy which, while it never resulted in any truly relational or spiritual intimacy, as far as he was concerned, nevertheless was still etched in his consciousness.

Drew looked down the hall, through two sets of bars at the face of Shawna Forester. Her expression showed the same confusion of feeling that he felt within his own soul. He turned back to the corporal.

"Yeah, she's a friend. I guess you would call her an estranged friend. In any case, I don't want her to die..."

Drew's eyes filled with tears, and they began to flow down his cheeks. They were tears for Ashley to be sure, but he also knew that they were tears full of the sadness of a myriad of events that had piled on top of each other during these months of time that E.J. Conrad had hijacked from the world. There were tears for hurting souls he had interviewed, the Jonathan Weisels , mourning young granddaughters and desperately trying to hold on to their humor; the pastors like Frank Roberts, still seeking to save a world that was careening out of control; the angry ones whose wide, traumatized eyes looked back at incinerated homes and families, and cursed Christians for their violent vision – he had tears sufficient for them all. And his tears, he knew, were for Brian too – Brian, whose young adult angst was seeded with hatred at the wrong time, and whose life became scarred by the pain done to others. Still, Drew knew that Brian had found his way home. That could not be said of Ashley Cambridge. That in itself deserved at least a few of those tears. He didn't want her to die. He didn't want her to die without finding her way.

"Well, in any case, I had better get going," continued the corporal. "If we are going to be heading out of here tonight, there is a lot of preparation that needs to be done."

Drew nodded his head, even though the words had claimed but one small corner of his awareness. Ashley Cambridge had been contaminated with Ebola virus. Once he had been forced to acknowledge that, what room could be left in his consciousness for anything else? He glanced again in Shawna's direction. The corners of her mouth turned up in a slight, but sincere, sympathetic smile.

"We'll be out soon, Drew," she said soothingly, "and then we will see what we can do."

"Right. We'll see what we can do," he repeated. Even as the words left his mouth, an unwelcome thought shoved its way into his mind past all of the resistance his desire to be consoled could muster – lately, "what we can do" had not been nearly enough.

∎∎

"They know they cannot stop us!" Edward James Conrad thrust his fist into the air as he spoke to those gathered in the school auditorium. "They could not stop us from planting the bombs that fanned their fears into flame. They could not stop us from taking these cities that were destined to be cities of God. They could not stop us with the bombs and artillery they have aimed at our city."

Over eight hundred soldiers and citizen supporters stood and cheered.

"They KNOW they cannot stop us, but what they can't understand is why. Why can't what still is the most militarily powerful nation on earth stop a much smaller band of armed insurrectionists? Is it our overwhelming fire-power?"

"No!!" The answer came as a shout from every corner of the room.

"Is it the military brilliance of a former professor of literature?"

"No!!" Those gathered shouted with a certainty of those who had been through the drill before.

"Then, is it compassion for our embattled citizenry?"

"No!!"

"Then WHY? Why can't they stop us?!"

"The power of God!!"

"The what?"

"The power of God!!" The response now thundered throughout the auditorium.

"That's right, my people, the power of God! As David said before slaying Goliath, 'And all this assembly shall know that the Lord saveth not with sword and spear: for the battle is the Lord's, and he will give you into our hands.' And later that same David said in the Psalms, 'Some trust in chariots, and some in horses: but we will remember the name of the Lord our God. They are brought down and fallen: but we are risen, and stand upright.'"

All those gathered now stood and applauded and stomped, and the whole auditorium seemed to shake.

"They have not stopped us before," Conrad proclaimed as the applause ebbed just a little, "and they will not stop us now. They will not stop us from being used of God in the pale horse judgment, as pestilence is spread throughout the land. Those who have ears to hear will hear, and the hearts of some may soften and respond in repentance. This is the Lord's doing and it is marvelous in our eyes!"

Hands now lifted in praise to God and there were tears in the eyes of many. Conrad motioned those gathered to quiet down a little and he began to speak a little more quietly.

"And now I have to say to you that this will come with a cost. Those we send out will be martyred for the Lord. Some of you have bravely volunteered to be among this group. This is sad in that we will miss you. But it is not sad for those of you who will be on this mission -- in fact, I envy you. You will be joining those who have down through the ages made the supreme sacrifice in order to establish God's kingdom. They have been waiting for you! They have been waiting for your sacrifice to make effective their own! 'And when he opened the fifth seal, I saw under the altar the souls of them that were slain for the word of God, and for the testimony which they held: And they cried with a loud voice, saying, How long, O Lord, holy and true, dost thou not judge and avenge our blood on them that dwell on the earth? And white robes were given unto every one of them; and it was said unto them, that they should rest yet for a little season, until their fellowservants also and their brethren, that should be killed as they were , should be fulfilled.'"

"You are going now, my martyrs of the present age, you are going now to join these who have given their all since the time of Rome. You will join those thrown to lions, burned as torches in the gardens of Nero; those hung, burned, drawn and quartered for translating God's Word in the Middle Ages and Reformation; those executed for evangelistic activities in the old Soviet Union, in

China, and in countries where Islam holds sway today – you will join all of these, and in the white robes of moral purity and vindication you will stand and cheer at the end of time when the rest of us join you in triumph!"

Once again the auditorium erupted in applause. Conrad especially noticed those sitting in the front rows, the rows designated for the volunteer martyrs. They indeed seemed most jubilant of them all. A couple of young women were dancing in the aisle. One man stood up in his chair and was jumping up and down on it, throwing confetti into the air as he did. When the chair collapsed underneath him, he just laughed all the more as he lay sprawled out on the floor.

Conrad breathed in the jubilation all around him. This was the supreme moment to this point. This was a moment that pointed to the victorious culmination of human history that lay just ahead. Tears were now streaming down his cheeks. He couldn't speak. He could remember oh so few times that had happened. He simply couldn't speak. But then Conrad decided it was okay, because this was an experience that was speaking for itself. Words from him would have only cheapened it all. God was there. God was ready. God was going to act. And the world was trembling in anticipation.

▪▪▪

Drew Covington leaped up into the back of the troop transport truck, and Corporal Madison dropped the flap behind him. Immediately the truck started rumbling down the street, and Drew sat down on the bench seat to avoid losing his balance. He could hear the rain splattering on the canvas of the truck as well as on the streets outside, and he could tell by the periodic sloshing up under the truck that the rain had been heavy enough that it was pooling in the streets.

"Good plan – the rain," said Amos. "I want to commend you for your forethought on that one, Corporal Madison. It reduces visibility and deadens sound. Of course it just makes worse the shivering that started when I learned we were doing this, but what the hell?"

"Yeah," deadpanned the corporal. "Rain in the Northwest –
I must have had some pull for that one, huh?"

Madison began passing out battle fatigues, which everyone
was to put on over their other clothing. Drew noticed that these
still had a US Flag sewn on the sleeve. However, they also had a
stylized angel holding an M-1 rifle, the insignia of the Brigade, on
the front pocket.

"Do you think anyone saw us?" The question had come
from Maggie.

"Hard to tell, for sure. I was able to get sympathizers posted
on the closest downtown observation posts, but you can't control
everything. Someone could have been having a hard time sleeping
and looked out a window. Who knows? You pay your money
and you take your chances. Anyway, if someone did see us, they
wouldn't necessarily know that it wasn't an authorized transfer."

Drew heard the sound of artillery fire towards what he
guessed was the east. He was not always good with directions.

"We're concentrating our fire power on the south side
tonight," said Madison, correcting Drew's perception. "Conrad
wants to distract them from the Northeast, which is where the
martyrs are being released."

"And we're going...?"

"Straight east, through the former town of Kelso."

"So maybe we should go over the plan one more time,"
suggested Carl.

Madison nodded. "When we stop, everyone grab a box of
ammunition. There will be a canopy off to our right, and we will
pile them under that canopy, next to some boxes already there.
Captain Newell, who is a sympathizer, will send his gung-ho
Conrad loyalists back in this truck to get more ammo. Those left
in that area will all be sympathizers. We will strip off our
uniforms, except for me.

"There will be a dry creek bed ahead of us and we will move
down it with all of you in front and me bringing up the rear with
my M-1 rifle. This will be necessary because we will be going past
a couple of gun and tank positions, and the guys there are
definitely not sympathizers. They have been told that we are

taking you to the other side as part of a prisoner exchange, so I will have my weapon trained on you, and you will need to have your hands in the air.

"Down the bed, about two hundred yards past the last gun position we will reach their first gun position. The commander there has been told who you are and what the ruse is to get you out. They will have some of their men posing as prisoners going the other way. As soon as we get to the first gun position, we'll need to hit the ground, because these guys are going to scramble, and Brigade loyalists are going to realize what has happened, and the bullets will fly."

"Man, I am absolutely going to piss my pants," declared Maggie. "I am definitely not a brave person. What if I freeze up altogether? What if when we're supposed to hit the ground, I can't move?"

"I'll be right behind you, and I'll kick your butt!"

Maggie looked over at Amos, the source of the threat. "This had better be one time you are not just spewing hot air, Amos Baldwin, because I am going to be relying on you to be the fastest ass-kicker in the West, no kidding!"

Amos patted the bottom of his shoe. "I'll be armed and dangerous. Your butt is mine!"

"This will require some acting on our part," said Elena. "The soldiers at those gun positions are trained to be observant and to be suspicious of everything. A soldier on the front who does not have such qualities, dies quickly. If they see in our eyes any deceit, if they see in Corporal Madison anything but a disciplined soldier ready to kill us, that creek bed will flow with our blood. Believe me, I know soldiers. We must show in our eyes and in our demeanor that the situation is exactly what it has been said to be."

"Gee, thanks, Elena," gasped Maggie, in between what had become shallow, rapid breaths. "Now I know I'm toast! I wear my heart on my damned sleeve. People see through me like cellophane!"

"You can do this, Maggie," replied Elena calmly. "You can do it because you have to. We all can."

Drew could see in Elena's eyes a quiet, disciplined confidence, the confidence of one who had steeled her soul before and knew she could do it again; one who owed her very life to the curtains she could draw at will across the window of her tender spirit. He now watched as Maggie drew that confidence in through her own eyes like an ocular injection, and her breathing almost instantaneously began to slow. In another minute, Drew could hardly tell if she were breathing at all.

Maggie smiled. "Okay, I can do it."

"We all can," Shawna whispered, "We all can."

The peace of that moment was quickly challenged as less than a minute later the truck lurched to a stop. Drew and Shawna exchanged glances. Drew was conscious of the fact that he had been avoiding looking at her, not because of any irritation or anger, but because he didn't want to acknowledge that the danger he was now facing, she was facing too. It was okay that he might die. It was not okay that she might.

Shawna reached out and lightly touched the back of his hand.

"Showtime!" whispered Elena, and she immediately picked up a box of ammo and scurried out the back of the truck.

Drew continued to gaze down at Shawna's hand for a moment longer, and then he got up abruptly, turning away from her. "Let's just do it."

Drew picked up a box of ammo and Shawna and the others followed close behind. As Drew stepped out of the truck and headed toward the canopy, he made a determined effort not to look around him at the soldiers in the area. He knew that Elena was right about the acting, and that he had to be part of it. Inordinate interest in what the other soldiers were doing would surely tip some people off that something wasn't quite right about them. Still, out of the corner of his eye he noticed that some soldiers were watching them. He tried not to think of what they were looking for, what they might be suspecting. He just did his work. He stacked the box he was carrying and immediately went back for more.

When Drew brought out the last box, he noticed a tall, powerfully-built officer to his left with a ledger. The man was shaking his head in disgust.

"This isn't nearly enough. Damn! What were these assholes thinking? We get attacked tonight and within an hour we'll have to be throwin' fuckin' rocks at them!"

A corporal standing beside him flinched. "Begging your pardon, Sir, but the language...Doctor Conrad..."

"Do you see E.J. Conrad here, Asslick?" yelled the officer Drew guessed to be Captain Newell. "If you don't, do you mind if I concentrate on what it takes to win the fuckin' war?"

"No, Sir. Of course not, Sir."

"Good! Then Corporal Asslick, here is a list of men. I want you to take them with you in that truck, and I don't want you to come back until you have enough ammo to wipe out the whole fuckin' city of Portland! Do you hear me? And if you have to, hijack a couple of more trucks!"

"Yes, Sir. Right a way, Sir."

As the truck pulled away, Captain Newell walked over to Corporal Madison.

"Better get your people going, Corporal. As sure as a bear shits in the woods that ass-kisser is going to report my language to somebody who will report it to Conrad. Now he may be too busy with the release of those shit-for-brains martyrs to do anything about it right away, but then again he might not be. Sooner or later this place is going to be swarming with Conrad butt-lickers, all eager to haul my ass to jail. You don't want to still be on our side of the line when that happens."

"Begging your pardon, Sir," replied Corporal Madison, "but if you knew he would report you, why did you do it?"

The Captain just shook his head as he bit off a chew of tobacco. "Wrong question, Corporal, wrong question. The question you mean to ask is, why did I get into this pussy outfit in the first place? And that may be a bigger question than you have time to listen to right now. Let's just sum it up by saying I was raised in the South by a God-fearing military family. You weren't, because if you were that would be all the explanation you needed.

To be a boy raised that way is to be full of contradictions. You believe in God and church – you've got to. But you also have to screw everything in a skirt, and the ones you don't screw, you've got to talk as if you had screwed 'em. Language that would shock your church choir becomes almost second nature to you when you're away from the church people and with your military friends. Pretty soon you're like two people – one lovin' God, and one screwin' around tryin' to prove how much a man he is. The guilt just piles on, layer upon fuckin' layer. I thought following Conrad would take care of it all, fighting for God to erase the kind of fucked up world I had helped to build. But it ain't workin'. It's just piled on another layer of guilt – guilt over all of the American lives lost. There's no sign of Christ coming. And my old Army self can no longer restrain the language of the brotherhood into which I was initiated many years ago, the brotherhood of the military male. So what do I do? I'm just going to turn myself over to the grace of God and the wrath of E.J. Conrad."

"What do you think he will...?"

"Get going, Corporal! That's an order. I'm not taking these risks for you to pussy around and get all these people killed!"

Corporal Madison saluted, and then turned and motioned in the direction of the dried-up river bed that was to be their path to freedom. Drew's eyes caught those of Captain Newell, and although he had never been in the armed forces, he did his best to give the man a proper salute. The Captain just laughed at his awkward gesture, but then he returned the salute.

Drew was the last one to get in line as they headed down the river bed; that is, the last except for Corporal Madison who brought up the rear with his M-1 rifle trained on those ahead of him. Shawna and Elena were directly ahead of him. Carl and John were in the lead, with Maggie and Amos behind them.

As Drew walked down the path, he felt as though the forest had eyes, and that the rain was a one-way mirror through which those eyes could see without being seen. They were most certainly out there. Tired, hostile men, nerves wrought from being shot at, wondering who these prisoners were who were supposedly being exchanged with the other side, wondering if the exchange would bring any new dangers to them. Perhaps even right now one of them was feeling an impulse to pull a trigger. Perhaps even now one of them was receiving a call that it was all a fraud, and that they should be cut down like the timber had in the clear-cut through which they were now passing.

Drew looked at the back of Shawna's head as she marched ahead of him, hands held high. He wondered if shots began, would he have enough time to do anything at all to keep those projectiles from finding the tenderness of her flesh? Would he have time to think anything at all before they bore into his own brain?

Drew closed his eyes momentarily and sought to clear his mind. He must control what he could control. He had to just keep putting one foot in front of the other. He had to believe that should anything happen he would know what to do in the seconds that followed. God would show him. God would do what he couldn't. There just weren't other choices. It was what he had to believe.

Drew saw off to the left what appeared to be a crack in the ground, and out of that crack peered human eyes. They seemed to narrow as they noticed him looking in their direction.

"Eyes straight ahead!" barked Corporal Madison from behind. Drew felt the soldier's bayonet prod the small of his back.

Up ahead Drew could now see through the rain the blurred forms of several soldiers standing with their hands also held high. The position of those soldiers and the armed soldiers at their feet, also marked the goal for which he and the others were headed. If they could only get that far. Drew estimated that it was now about the distance from third base to home plate on a ball diamond, about ninety feet.

It was then that the voice cried out. It's harshness as it penetrated the gentle rain made Drew hesitate, it seemed so out of place, like a jackhammer in a wilderness.

"Unauthorized transfer. Waste them!"

Drew spun around in the direction of the voice, and as he did, searing heat burrowed into his left shoulder and he was thrown to the ground. The idiocy of that first move penetrated even more deeply than the bullet had. *Shawna! My first move should have been to protect her!* He now lifted his head out of the mud and looked ahead to find her, but she was nowhere to be seen. What Drew could see was blood-curdling. Amos Baldwin had indeed kicked Maggie Morris to the ground, but before he could join her, at least two bullets tore through him. Maggie screamed, and pulled his bloodied body down on top of her. John Savage and Carl Tollefson were still standing only by virtue of the fact that their bodies were being riddled with bullets from many directions.

"Get them down! Get them down!"

Drew now recognized the screaming voice as his own. He simultaneously recognized that the scream had come too late. There was a dull stare in the eyes of Carl Tollefson as he finally fell to the ground. John Savage limply fell just a moment later.

It would haunt Drew later that he would have no time to mourn the loss of these gentle men of God who had taught him so much, who had lived and laughed with him, who had lifted him at one of the lowest moments of his life.

"Shawna! Shawna!" The screams came from deep within his soul. But the only answer to them came from the woods in front and behind them as automatic weapons barked at each other, and their bullets whizzed past overhead. Drew tried to lift his head just the slightest bit to see where she might be, but the effort itself made his head swim. And then the sounds and sights around him faded from his consciousness.

■■■

Drew awoke to an awareness of bright light.

"Nappy-time is over!" Drew instantly recognized the voice and sure enough directly over where he lay now appeared the face of E.J. Conrad. "We all hope you had a pleasant sleep, Mister Covington. Unfortunately, some of your comrades who decided to go on this ill-conceived adventure with you will be sleeping a much longer period of time."

Drew looked around. He was in a hospital room. Two armed soldiers were standing near the door. He looked back up at Conrad.

"Which ones?"

"Which ones, what?"

"Which ones...are dead?"

"All of them..." said Conrad, observing as he did Drew's shocked expression before he added, "...eventually." Conrad had obviously decided to get his entertainment by provoking him. "Right now? Well, the bodies of Reverend Tollefson and Reverend Savage reminded me a little of Swiss cheese. We questioned them, but I'm afraid all we got out of them was blank stares. The insolence! And I'm afraid Corporal Madison won't be able to face any firing squad either."

"Did you bury them?"

"Bury them? They weren't worth the time. To avoid the stink, however, we tossed their bodies into the Columbia. I'm sorry you didn't get to say 'Bon Voyage.'"

Drew's jaw clamped down tightly as the anger welled up inside of him. It was all that he could do to open it to let his next words escape.

"...the others?"

Conrad pulled back the curtain. In the next bed Drew could see the heavily bandaged body of Amos Baldwin. Amos slowly turned his head Drew's way and waved.

"It was Maggie, Drew. She saved my butt."

"...and you saved hers?"

"Yeah, I guess."

"For now," added Conrad. "She's feeling a little lonely rattling around in a cell all by herself. I'm afraid she was a bit traumatized. Gee, I hope she doesn't do anything crazy before we have a chance to execute her...with some company."

Drew looked over again in Amos' direction.

"She was really out of it, Drew," Amos said. "I'm scared for her. She was seeing demons and everything."

"If you are just going to execute us," Drew continued, again looking at Conrad, "why did you go to all of this trouble? Why didn't you just have someone finish us off where we lay?"

"I didn't want to let you off that easily! I wanted you to think about it first. I wanted you to think about how stupid you were to oppose me, to oppose God!" Conrad eyes now flared as he spoke. "You could have helped us a lot, Drew, had you stood by those principles you used to write about. You could have been part of something beautiful, something God-given, the establishment of God's kingdom on earth! Now you'll die a criminal's death and rise again only to face the wrath of God. I pity you, Drew. Your life could have made a difference."

These latest words of Conrad didn't really faze Drew. They only served to show him how desperate his opponent had become to find a crevice in his soul into which he could drive a wedge.

"I did what I needed to do." It was all he could say. It was all he needed to say. Conrad's whole demeanor became visibly rigid. Several times it looked as if he were going to say more, but he did not. Finally, he just turned to leave.

"Conrad!" Drew's summoning of him stopped the old professor, who turned to look back in the direction of the injured man. Drew's recent assertiveness now wavered as he sought the words for the question he had feared asking. "Uh...Elena Enesco-Marshal and Shawna Forester...what about them?"

Conrad scowled. "You know we couldn't retrieve all of the bodies. It wasn't exactly a playground out there."

As Conrad left the room, Drew fell back against his pillow, trembling.

"Oh, God!...Oh, God!... Oh, God!" No further words would come. He had once been considered one of the most eloquent newspaper writers in America. But for this moment in time, there simply were no other words that could be said.

Chapter Nineteen

The late model limousine sped south on 1-5 toward Portland. To the front, back and side were police cars with lights flashing and sirens blaring, clearing the way as they quickly made their way through traffic.

Shawna Forester looked over at the young woman who sat in the seat beside her. There would be no way that she would have been there had it not been for Elena Enesco-Marshal. Shawna thought back over the events of the previous night. When the voice had come out of the darkness of night, even before one word had penetrated to her mind, she had found her body being hurled to the side of the path, and by the time she had comprehended the whole statement, Elena had pressed both of their bodies into a ditch surrounded by tall grass. It had been the most terrifying moment of her life, even more so than when the bomb went off in D.C. She could hear the screams. She could hear the initial screams of Carl and John before they suddenly fell silent. She could hear the continuing screams of Maggie and Amos. She could hear Drew as he desperately called out her name. Even as that had happened, Elena had thrown her hand over Shawna's mouth, and shook her head. She wanted to call back to him. She wanted desperately to go to Drew's side. But she also sensed the wisdom of Elena's actions. Just one word could have drawn fire to where they lay. Just rising up even five or six inches could have meant bullets finding her head. She knew that if she and Drew were to ever be together again, they would have to do what they needed to do to survive apart. She had made it. She had decided to believe that Drew had as well.

She and Elena could afford just one thing on their minds right now – stopping the spread of one of the most deadly diseases known to humankind.

■■

Drew Covington found himself back in familiar confines, but with a much more ominous feel. The jail cell in which he had spent so much time in recent months was hauntingly empty. Amos Baldwin, still bandaged and barely able to move, was lying on a lower bunk. Captain James Newell had been unceremoniously dumped in with them just that morning, but he had been moody and stand-offish. Gone was the spirit and the camaraderie. Spontaneous worship that had lifted them to the gates of heaven was just a memory that lingered in the shadows like a phantom.

What was down the hall felt even more empty. Maggie Morris was alone in her cell. Drew sometimes heard her talking to herself down there, and whenever he did it brought him to tears – tears for the fact that Maggie's passionate soul had been so severely scarred, tears for the ones missing from the cell, missing from his life.

Amos was stirring on his bunk.

"Drew?"

"Yeah, Amos."

"How is Maggie doing down there?"

"She's been quiet, Amos. She's sitting on the bunk, rocking herself."

Amos slowly swung his legs off of the bunk, and pulled himself up to a sitting position, wincing as he did.

"You're going to break those stitches and start bleeding again, if you're not careful, Amos. Where do you think you're going?"

"I'm getting up, thank you," he responded. "You took one in the shoulder, and I don't see you lying in bed."

Amos grabbed hold of the upper bunk, and pulled himself up to a standing position.

"You were hit twice in the abdomen and once in your leg, so it's not exactly..."

"Yeah, bite me." Amos shuffled over to the bars and looked down in the direction of what had been the women's cell. "Maggie! Maggie! We're here for ya', Babe!"

Maggie just kept rocking, and didn't even look their way. Amos began to sway on his feet, and so Drew rushed over, put his arm around him and led him back to the bunk.

"We can't let this happen to her, Drew!" Amos said, once he had recovered his orientation. "She...she might be the only other one of us left. She saved my life. I had been kind of...kind of mean to her sometimes. Sorry about the 'only one left' comment, it's just..."

"I know, I know. I was out there like you were, so I know the prospects. I just don't want to give up hope. Not yet." Drew put his hand softly on Amos' shoulder. "Anyway, you weren't mean to her, Amos. You just liked to provoke her. It was because you liked her. She knew that. Everyone knew that."

"Yeah, I liked her. I liked her a lot. I hope she knew. I hope she *knows*. I mean, it's the way I've always been, never able to say when I cared for a woman. It was always easier to joke. And besides, who would have thought? A black preacher dude and a queen-size white woman from Princeton! I just hope she knows."

As Amos finished his sentence, the building began to sway and the bars began to creak. Both Amos and Drew lost their balance and were thrown back onto the bunk. Then the swaying stopped.

"Whoa, that was the biggest one yet!" proclaimed Drew.

"Makes you wonder which one's going to get us first, doesn't it?" quipped Amos. "Conrad or the mountain. My money's still on Conrad."

Even as Amos finished speaking, the door opened and in stepped E.J. Conrad. Four armed soldiers came in after him, all with their weapons trained as if they were expecting insurrection.

"You felt it, didn't you?!" The face of Conrad was beaming. "But do you understand that that was a message from God himself? 'Tremble, thou earth, at the presence of the Lord, at the presence of the God of Jacob!' God himself is ready to enter the fray! The return of Christ is imminent, and then your little plots will be shown for what they are – rebellions against the Lord of the Universe."

"Boy, we are full of ourselves, aren't we?" said Amos, speaking with some effort. "Tell me, do they give you a magic decoder ring when you're Lord of the Universe?"

Conrad scowled. "I wasn't calling *myself* the Lord of the Universe, you impudent little snot. I know what God will do because God speaks to me, as he did to Moses long ago. But then again, I forgot. It must be terrible being a so-called man of God, such as yourself, and not having a clue what God wants or plans to do. I guess that makes me pity you most of all."

Amos opened his mouth, as if to speak, but no words came. Drew knew what Conrad also knew – that his words had touched a nerve. Amos Baldwin had a passionate faith, but he also had an unsatisfied hunger to hear the voice of his Master, to know the answers as well as he knew the questions, to have the certainty that Conrad professed to have.

"Conrad, you are one arrogant little prick!" These words had come from Captain Newell, who filled the void left by Amos' silence. "And boy, it felt good to say that to your face! That is, instead of behind your back like all of the other officers do!"

Conrad's eyes now burned with the fire of his anger. "I know better than to think that the other officers in my charge are like you, Mister Newell. Why do you think you were the only one turned in? Why do you think we are doing so well, if not for the blessings of God and the loyalty of my men to this godly cause? All except for you, Mister Newell. Well, I guess even Jesus had his Judas."

Conrad's visage now wrenched into a rigid parody of a smile. "But enough of such pleasantries, gentlemen. I have come to you with good news. We have decided not to execute you today. We are too busy celebrating the fact that our martyrs made it across enemy lines – unlike another less-competent attempt the same night. Anyway we don't want to mar the celebration. There will be time enough tomorrow. I would urge each of you to spend your time preparing to meet your God. Who knows, Jesus may even return this night, and we will be spared the trouble."

"He is coming! Beware!" The voice that had come from down the hall startled all of them. It had come as a voice none of them recognized, an old woman's voice, a hissing voice. What surprised them all the most was that it was a voice that came from Maggie Morris. As all stared in her direction the voice came again, reaffirming her message.

"He is coming! Beware!"

Conrad just shook his head. "Well, the crazy woman might not be so crazy after all. Even she warns you."

"No-o-o-o!" Maggie spoke the word like a howling dog. Then she changed to a haunting whisper. "Not them! Not them! You! You beware! He is coming. High-flying birds will scream through the air, trying to beat him here, trying to turn your ashes back to ashes, but the time will not yet be. And then he will come. And ashes indeed will be your end."

Conrad's face turned white. "Crazy woman! You know we will execute you too!"

Emotionally scarred as she was, Maggie was not intimidated. She belted the next words out as if hers were the very voice of God:

"'How you are fallen from heaven,
    O Day Star, son of Dawn!
  How you are cut down to the ground,
    You who laid the nations low!'"

"That is not about me!" cried Conrad. "How dare you...!"

"'Alas for you who desire the day of the Lord!
    Why do you want the day of the Lord?
    It is darkness, not light...'"

"It will not be darkness for me. You are a crazy woman! Crazy!"

Conrad fell as he backed up toward the doorway. The soldiers rushed to help him get up, but he pushed them away and stood up on his own.

"Tomorrow you will be dead, crazy woman! And for you it will certainly be an act of mercy."

Conrad turned and stormed out the door, and the soldiers, their weapons trained to the last moment on the incarcerated wounded, followed right behind.

Still stunned, Amos, Drew and James Newell stared down at other cell.

"Maggie?" asked Amos, "Are you okay?"

Maggie smiled weakly. "No. No. I'm not okay. I have to rest now." She shuffled over to her bunk and lay down in a fetal position.

"At least she is speaking," said Drew.

"She sure scared the hell out of ol' Conrad," noted Captain Newell.

"Yeah, I noticed that," responded Drew. "To tell the truth she kind of scared me. She spoke like she really knew something, like in her broken state she had been granted supernatural knowledge."

"Maybe so," said Amos, quietly, "but she is still not the Maggie we know. I want the old Maggie back."

Drew gently squeezed Amos' shoulder. "So do I, Amos. So do I."

■■

"Make sure you keep the mask and rubber gloves on. Even so, it would be best if you didn't touch anything in the room."

Shawna Forester nodded to the nurse, and pulled the mask up over her nose and mouth. She then edged past the two soldiers posted at the door and into the hospital room. Ashley Cambridge was sitting up in bed.

"Nurse! I told the others I don't belong here. I just have a little flu. Damn shot didn't take, I guess. I..."

Ashley now looked more intensely into the eyes of her visitor.

"Shawna?"

Shawna nodded.

"What are you doing here? You were..." Suddenly panic flashed through her eyes, and she began to pull away. "There are soldiers at the door. I'll scream..."

"I'm not here to hurt you, Ashley. I escaped from Longview. I promised Drew that I would come see you, that I would check on how you were doing."

"I'm fine. I have the flu. I don't know why..."

"It's Ebola, Ashley. I'm sure they told you..."

"No! No! My muscles ache. My eyes are getting a little red. I have a headache and some fever. It's the flu."

"Ashley, the shot they gave you wasn't a flu shot. It was live Ebola virus. They wanted you to spread it..."

"No! No! You're just angry. You're trying to scare me because of what I said down in the jail cell and...and...and because I didn't warn you about the bomb, and...I tried to take Drew."

Shawna saw the fear in Ashley's eyes. She slowly walked over to a chair beside Ashley's bed, and sat down. Then she reached out and gently touched the hand of her former rival. Ashley didn't withdraw it, but rather sat frozen in place. With tears now streaming down her face, Shawna spoke quietly.

"I'm not here to hurt you, Ashley. I've forgiven you. Drew has forgiven you. But I'm afraid that what I am telling you is the truth. We know it from inside sources with Conrad, and the medical authorities here tell me they have confirmed it. I was the one who told the authorities to find you and get you treatment. It's the truth, Ashley. I'm sorry."

Ashley's eyes were wide with horror and her body began to tremble. For several minutes she couldn't say anything. Then when the words came, they came in a barely audible whisper.

"I trusted him. I trusted him..."

"I know. I know."

"I don't want to die, Shawna." Ashley now spoke with more volume and energy. "I shouldn't have to die just because I made some mistakes!"

"Well, a person doesn't always die, I mean..."

"What chances...?"

"I...uh...I understand that it's about fifty to ninety percent fatal, but that means..."

"At best, I have a fifty-fifty chance!"

Shawna nodded. Tears were streaming from both of their eyes now. Shawna knew that every excretion from Ashley's body was a potential source of this devastating disease, and yet she still wanted to wipe the tears from Ashley's eyes, to somehow console her and make it all better for her. But she used all her restraint and contented herself to speak though her words, the holding of Ashley's hand and her own tears.

"I'm sorry, Ashley. I know it isn't fair. I wish there were something I could do."

"I only went to Conrad's side because they said it was what God wanted...and...and I saw the demons...and I thought that Conrad was right about God...but then I got scared there, and I didn't know what God wanted...and...and I STILL DON'T! I still don't, Shawna. I might die. I might have to meet God, and I haven't a clue!"

Ashley was sobbing now, and all Shawna could do was sit and cry with her. And hold her hand. The one thing Shawna refused to do was to let go of Ashley's hand. After several minutes, Ashley found her voice.

"You're a good person, Shawna. Tell me what God wants. You know, don't you? You've got to tell me."

Shawna felt her head spinning. She had never considered herself an expert on the questions that Ashley was raising, even though her own faith had become more and more central to her life. She searched her mind for at least one little morsel to offer this starving soul. And then it came to mind.

"'What does the Lord require of you but to do justice, and to love mercy, and to walk humbly with your God.' It's from the prophet Micah. I think that says it for me better than anything else. Those are things I guess Conrad never learned."

The tears continued to stream down Ashley's face. "I don't know, Shawna. You know me. 'Humble' never has suited me too well. I've never been too concerned with justice. And I don't think I really even understand what mercy is. What can a person like me do?"

"Just put yourself in God's hands, Ashley. He knows what mercy is. That's why God sent Jesus – to point us to the mercy. Receive his mercy, and then you can give his mercy."

The flow of Ashley's tears seemed to slow at least a little as she thought of what Shawna had said. Then she seemed to remember something.

"Drew – is he still in Longview?"

Shawna winced. She hadn't been wanting to think about that. "Yes. Conrad recaptured him. I think he was hurt."

Ashley just stared at Shawna for a moment. There was something about the look in her eyes that frightened Shawna. When Ashley spoke again, her eyes were looking down.

"Shawna, the reason I got scared in Longview, the reason I wanted to get away from there...it was because I heard they were getting more serious about...about nuclear retaliation." Ashley was trembling again now. "What I have heard since has just confirmed that. Shawna, I think they might strike Longview any day now."

Shawna felt a chill. She wrapped her arms around herself and shut her eyes. Then she nodded.

"Okay. Okay. Well, there's not a lot I can do about that right now. Thanks for telling me."

Shawna fought to keep the images out of her mind, images from her memory of the bombing of D.C., images of Drew's smile, images of Amos and Maggie. She sat for several minutes in silence as those images darted in and out of her brain. Then, as much is self-defense as anything else, she returned her attention to Ashley.

"Ashley, is there anything else I can do for you right now?"

Ashley shook her head.

"Then I've got to go. There are some people from the Department of Homeland Security I must talk to. I'll be back later to check on you. If you need someone to talk to, have someone give me a call."

Ashley nodded. Shawna gave her hand one more squeeze, and then turned and left the room. Outside the door she was led to an area where she stripped off her sterile robe, cap, gloves and mask, and washed in antiseptic soap. Afterwards the nurses led her to a doctor's conference room. Two men in dark suits were there waiting for her, along with a woman in a black dress with a red jacket. They all stood as she entered the room.

"Ms. Forester, I am Paul Erikkson from the Department of Homeland Security; this is Charlie Ng, also of the Department, and Charlotte Monroe of the Center for Disease Control. As we all know, this is a matter of utmost urgency, so if you would sit down here, we'll get started right away."

Shawna sat in a chair opposite the others, and Paul Erikkson wasted no time in getting to the point. "Ms. Forester, do you know how many people were infected with Ebola, and do you know any of their identities?"

"I'm afraid I don't know any of the names of the people infected. My understanding from the soldier who was helping us is that there are around two hundred. Only forty-five were from Longview, or 'New Bethel' as Conrad calls it. About seventy more were from their forces in Spokane, and the rest were recruited from among their guerilla forces, mostly on the East Coast."

"Ms. Forester, were you able to learn anything about where this strain of Ebola came from?" The question had come from Charlotte Monroe.

"Corporal Madison had heard that it was a laboratory-produced strain that had been made in Russia and obtained by the CIA. I don't know how or when."

Charlotte looked over at the two men. "That is consistent with what I have found. Vials of a strain of Ebola are missing from a CIA lab."

"How bad is this strain?"

"It's ugly. High probability of spread by airborne particles. Mortality rate on the high end – at least eighty to ninety percent."

"Is there a way to inoculate against it?"

"No. Not at present."

"Is there a way to treat it that lowers the mortality rate?"

Charlotte shook her head slowly and delicately, like she were trying to shake off a headache. "Patients receive supportive therapy consisting of balancing the patient's fluids and electrolytes, maintaining their oxygen status and blood pressure, and treating them for complicating infections. Maybe this lowers the morality rate a little. It certainly does not cure it."

"The bottom line?"

"We are going to have to act fast, or we are going to have an epidemic the likes of which this country has never seen. Whole cities will be crippled by the numbers of dying people. It will be equivalent to the Medieval Black Plague."

■■■

E.J. Conrad sat staring at his computer screen and rubbing his temples. He had read the message three times, and still he was having difficulty letting it register in his brain. "The voices of restraint have lost out. Nuclear retaliation is imminent. I advise immediate evacuation of you and other key personnel, from both the cities of New Bethel and Zion's Gate."

Conrad finally bolted upright from his seat, stomped over to the door and slung the door open.

"Miss Arnold! Did I or did I not say that I wanted to see General Robert James immediately?!"

His secretary's somewhat panicky voice responded, "Yes, Sir! You did, Sir! We are trying to locate him, and we will get him here as soon as possible!"

"You do that! And make sure he knows that I have neither the time nor the patience to be waiting on him!"

"Yes, Sir! I will, Sir!"

Conrad slammed the door again behind him. He began pacing back and forth in his office. After a minute or two he stopped, pointed his finger upward, looking heavenward, as if through the ceiling.

"Lord, I have done everything you have told me. I just don't understand this! You have told me that you want me here in this city near your mountain. But you are letting them send nuclear weapons our way." Conrad was now shouting, "You've got to show me what you want to me to do here! Whatever it is, show me! Show me!"

The strength of Conrad's last words had startled him. He needed to regain control. He needed to put things in perspective. Sure, Christ was taking longer than he had expected to return and join in the battle. Sure, nuclear weapons were a dire threat, but had God not led him past huge obstacles already? He just had to find God's way past this one. He just had to keep hold of his faith.

The door opened behind him and in stepped General Robert James.

"You sent for me, Sir?"

"Yes, I did. But I didn't interrupt you having lattes with your friends, did I? I couldn't forgive myself if I did something as crude as that!"

"Sir, I..."

"Spare me your excuses! We could be under nuclear attack as we speak!"

"Yes, Sir. As you know, I received that e-mail also, as well as a phone call confirming it. From what I understand we probably have just enough time to get you and our key personnel out of here. That is part of what I have been working on. You see..."

Conrad turned away from his general and took several steps toward his desk. The statement which the general made was one he had expected, and yet it hit him like a hammer. Leave the city which had become the embodiment of his dream, of his mission even? The mountain had spoken to him so many times. Why change his plan because of a human message?

"I'm not leaving."

"Excuse me, Sir?"

"I said I'm not leaving."

The general stood frozen in place, his mouth hanging slightly open. Conrad turned back toward him.

"General, I know this comes as a surprise to you. Actually, it's somewhat of a surprise even to me, but God has been working on my heart as I was waiting for you, and when I heard your words about preparing to evacuate me, the message came to me even as the words came out of my mouth: God doesn't want me to leave this place. I must have faith in what God has told me to do."

"But Doctor Conrad, you must understand that this is extremely dangerous. Our own inside sources have told us that an attack is imminent."

"We have Star Wars weaponry, have we not? We can knock a missile out of the air, can we not?"

"Sir, it is true we have in place such anti-missile weaponry, both defending New Bethel and Zion's Gate, but it is unreliable at best. They will probably send more than one missile toward each city, and decoys as well. You're talking a nuclear version of Russian Roulette, Sir."

"General James, how would you describe my demeanor over against when you came in?"

"You seem more calm now, Sir."

"And if you had seen me a few minutes before you came in, when I went out to yell at Miss Arnold because you were not here, you would be amazed at the transition. The reason for this change, general, is that God has given me a message. It is a message that I must trust."

"But, Sir..."

"General, leaving this city would be tantamount to saying that we no longer believe God protects us. It would be defeat. We cannot let our weakness of resolve lead to God's defeat. We must trust the weaponry that God has provided, that it will work. Make sure that we are prepared to intercept, and you and I and the command team will head for the shelter."

"That shelter won't withstand a direct hit, Sir, even from a small warhead..."

"Then it won't have to. God will provide."

The general who had fought in Vietnam, Afghanistan, and twice in the Persian Gulf was now visibly trembling. Still, he lifted his right hand to his brow in salute.

"As you say, Sir."

"And one more thing, General," added Conrad.

"Yes, Sir?"

"We need to show them we're not afraid of them. So let's be extra hospitable and even give them a target for their weapon. Put a bull's-eye in the intersection near the police station. And, oh! We need a greeting committee! Pull our 'guests' out of jail and stake them to the intersection."

Conrad went to the window in his office and looked up at the partially-cloudy sky. "Tell them to smile really big if they see some streaks heading our way."

Chapter Twenty

"All right! Everybody up!"

Something about the desperation in the eyes of the soldier who had made this pronouncement frightened Drew even more than it ordinarily would have.

"Conrad said he was planning to execute us tomorrow morning."

"Plans change! Come on now, we haven't got much time!"

Drew figured he had nothing to lose, so he decided to play the only card he had. He leaned back against the wall of the cell, making it clear that he had no intention of getting up.

Amos and the captain followed suit.

"Haven't got much time for what? I'm certainly in no hurry."

By this time there were eight armed soldiers in the cell block, and each of the prisoners quickly had two M-1s aimed at vital areas.

"Look," continued the soldier who had spoken first. "I'd just as soon shoot you here, but Conrad has a different plan, one we're not overly fond of having to carry out. We could shoot you here and say you made a break for it. We could yank your injured bodies out of here, slamming you against every wall, door, bench and light pole we can find. Or you can go out peacefully. It's your choice."

Drew's bluff had been called, but he still felt a strong aversion to yielding passively. "You still haven't told us what the big hurry is."

Two soldiers had already pulled Maggie out of her cell, and they now slammed her up against the bars of the men's cell, opening up a cut above her eye. Her scream brought all three men to their feet.

"All right! All right!" cried Amos, "God! Have you no humanity?"

"The time for humanity is over, scumbags. Now move!"

Amos, barely able to walk himself, threw his arm around Maggie, giving all the strength he had to help her avoid a painful fall. He whispered something in her ear that Drew assumed were reassurances. Captain Newell's words as they moved through the door opening to the outside world were definitely not reassurances.

"If these soldiers are in a hurry, then someone – or someTHING – is coming that they don't want to tell us about. Either a major offensive that they suspect might break through or..." The captain's voice trailed off as he looked out into the middle of the intersection in front of them. "...Or a nuclear strike is imminent. Looks like the latter."

"Stop chattering and move!"

Drew's legs suddenly seemed to go numb, and yet he knew they were working because he still moved forward toward the bull's eye that he now knew marked their final destination.

"Conrad moving the whole population of the city out to this bull's-eye, soldier?" Captain Newell demanded as if he were still one of those in charge. "He might as well, you know!"

One of the soldiers slammed the butt of his rifle up against the side of Newell's head, and he fell sprawling to the ground. He lay there dazed until two soldiers grabbed his arms and started dragging him toward the center of the intersection.

Drew thought of trying to escape but there were probably sixty heavily-armed soldiers within a hundred feet, and he knew it would be futile. When he reached the bull's-eye, two soldiers grabbed him, pulled him down to the ground and began binding his hands and feet with rope that Drew estimated was about a half-inch thick. Then they drove spikes in near his head and feet and tied the rope to the spikes. They did the same to the other prisoners.

Several women of the town, apparently members of Amos' congregation, began running toward him, but three soldiers with M-1s moved into their path.

"Stay back!" cried Amos. "Nuclear missiles are coming! Move away from the center of the city! Find shelter!"

The women were now sobbing, holding out their hands in the direction of their pastor.

"You must go!" he insisted, shouting with more energy than Drew imagined he could have after his injuries. "I'm in the hands of God. Don't cry for me; cry for the children of this world!"

The women continued to weep and hold out their hands toward him.

"The Lord bless you, Reverend!" one of the women cried. "The Lord bless you real good!"

Most of the other civilians in the crowd were quickly scattering, apparently heeding Amos' advice to move to the periphery of the city. Some of the soldiers also deserted their posts and scattered. Still the women remained. And now, led by one large black woman, they began to sing:

"I'm just a poor wayfarin' stranger,
    I'm travelin' through a world of woe,
But there's no sickness, toil or danger
    In that bright land to which I go.
I'm goin' there to see my mother..."

Drew could hear Amos' voice in a near whisper echo, "...to see my mother..."

"She said she'd meet me when I come,
    I'm only goin' over Jordan,
    I'm only goin' over home!"

Others, both black and white, joined in with the women. Some seemed to barely know the words, but the large black woman in front belted her words out with such strength and pathos, that more volume wasn't needed. Their hands were now all raised to heaven, and Drew felt like those hands were raised on his behalf.

"I know dark clouds are goin' to gather 'round me.

I know my way'll be rough and steep..."

The woman's voice had now built to a fevered passion, and Drew knew that the tears streaming down his face were not tears drawn out of him by fear, but the tears of a revived spirit, a spirit that had broken free from fear, even while his body lay bound.

"But beautiful fields lie just before me,
    Where God's redeemed their vigils keep.
I'm goin' there to see my loved ones,
    Gone on before me one by one,
I'm only goin' over Jordan,
    I'm only goin' over home!"

Drew looked over at Amos and saw the tears streaming down his face as well. The preacher was shaking his head in wonderment.

"They should be saving themselves. They should! But see how they care, Drew. They care for me! I never knew that they cared this much."

"Their pastor taught them well," Drew responded in a near whisper.

Just then four missiles shot into the air from various points in the city. Even as they climbed rapidly into the heavens, Drew spotted two vapor trails high in the sky, coming their way from the North, and two more coming from the East.

"Four birds coming!" cried a soldier, and suddenly they were all scrambling into the available trucks and Hummers. Tires squealed, and a couple of civilian women began screaming. But the women from Amos' church and the group of ten to twelve others who had gathered around them, continued to sing, repeating now that second verse:

"I know dark clouds are goin' to gather 'round me.
    I know my way'll be rough and steep..."

The words of the song had massaged Drew's soul, and yet they had not totally anesthetized him against transitioning to a future life. He had others in this life he preferred to see before any celestial homecoming.

"Newell!"

The captain responded to Drew's appeal with a grunt.

"Newell, what are the chances of those missiles being knocked out by that volley they just shot off?"

"Well, the good news is that two of those birds are probably decoys. The bad news is that we don't know which two. Hittin' any of them is a bit of a crapshoot. Hittin' the right ones will take a near miracle. But, hell! What else have we got?"

Newell glanced over in Amos' direction. "If you're prayin', Reverend, pray one for me, okay? I mean, I'm not necessarily lookin' for any miracles here, just a little consideration from the Good Lord, when those birds do their job. I've got a mother up there, too..."

"They won't touch us." The startling words of assurance had come from Maggie.

"They won't have to touch us, preacher lady," replied the captain.

"Their fire won't touch us. I saw it. I saw it all. Doilies in the sky."

"You saw that, Maggie?" queried Amos. "In what, a vision? Is that what you were saying to Conrad?"

Just then there was a bright flash in the sky, followed by another. Fire boiled in the heavens high above them, and after those boiling flashes of light cleared away, what was left appeared to Drew as...

"Doilies in the sky," whispered Maggie.

Two other vapor streams continued on, unimpeded.

"Newell, you better be right about two decoys, because here they come!"

The projectiles loomed larger rapidly and it was becoming evident that one would hit nearby.

"The jail! It's hitting the..."

There was a loud explosion and the brick and stone of the police headquarters flew into the air, scattering all around them. Miraculously no one was hit with more than some small pieces of debris.

"Decoys!" shouted Drew. "Both of them, decoys!"

A shout went up from both the prisoners and the women, and with the soldiers now gone, the women rushed to the prisoner's side and began working on untying the ropes.

"Quickly!" urged Captain Newell. "Those soldiers could come back any minute now!"

"They're too thick and too tight," cried one woman. "We can't pry them apart!"

"Break some glass!" cried Newell. "Cut the ropes with the shards!"

One woman ran over to the side of the road, picked up a rock and threw it through a drug store window. Right away the alarm began sounding, but the women ignored it as they ran over to pick up glass for cutting.

Just then Maggie's body became rigid and her eyes opened wide.

"He's coming!"

"Who, Conrad?" queried Newell.

"No!" responded Amos. "You said that when Conrad came down to the cell, didn't you, Maggie? Just like you spoke of 'high-flying birds.' The missiles! You were speaking of the missiles!"

"He's coming!"

The ground began to rumble, and in the sky overhead the clouds parted as ash shot up into the air.

"He's coming!" repeated Maggie.

"The mountain's blowing!" screamed Newell. "Cut these ropes, quickly!"

The women began quickly working on the ropes. Drew's eyes were fixated on the sky overhead, on the huge boiling cloud of gasses now stretching for miles above them into the heavens. Mount Saint Helen's was forty miles from Longview, but it felt like all the power of Creation itself was spewing from the ground right next to them. The last eruption had not wreaked its destruction this far to the West, but the size of this column of ash was far more foreboding.

Drew's body trembled, partly from the motion of the earth, and partly from the overwhelming sense of awe that he felt at the spectacle.

"He's coming!" cried Maggie again. "Prepare to meet Thy God!"

"Okay, you're free!" said one of the women, as she cut the last rope binding Newell's arms. "Now, let's get out of here!"

"Grab a sled from that drug store!" shouted Drew. "Amos won't make it on his own. We'll have to drag him on it."

One of the women did as instructed and they quickly used the ropes to tie Amos to the sled so he wouldn't fall off. Drew grabbed hold of the rope, and his hand was immediately replaced by another hand, a feminine hand, the hand of Maggie Morris.

"I pull. You lead the way."

■■

Shawna Forester was quickly ushered into the large, dark-paneled office that was the base of operation of National Security Advisor Karen Steele. She was sitting behind a large desk and at the same time talking on a cell phone and studying a stack of reports. She glanced in the direction of Shawna and the two men from the Department of Homeland Security who were escorting her, and she motioned for them to sit down in some leather chairs apparently set up for the purpose. It was less than a minute later when Steele came over and joined them.

"Ms. Forester, thank you for your help on this matter. I'm sure you understand how vital it is to national security to stop any attempt to spread such a deadly disease, if indeed it is occurring. I have read the reports of Mister Erikkson and Mister Ng, and I understand that you don't know the names of any of these alleged disease carriers. Is that correct?"

"Why do you say, 'alleged'? There *are* disease carriers. I just don't know their names."

"Did you see them get these shots? Can you verify from direct knowledge that Ebola virus was in the needles with which those shots were given?"

"Ms. Steele, just hours ago I visited Ashley Cambridge. She has this virus and she received a shot at the hands of E.J. Conrad!"

"That could be an isolated incident..."

"...And Charlotte Monroe from the Center for Disease Control has verified to us that vials of Ebola virus obtained from Russia by the CIA are missing. What more do you need to..."

"I'm not saying this isn't happening, Ms. Forester. I am just saying that until it is positively verified that Ebola is being spread by Conrad supporters, it is not in the national best interest to start a panic."

Shawna's jaw dropped. Suddenly her temples began to throb and her heart started racing.

"Not start a panic? Not start a panic! You let this disease get a good start by pussy-footing around, and you will see a panic! We may not know the names, but there is something we can do to prevent this if we act right away. We need to put out a national bulletin on all the media to warn people to stay home for at least the next week. They need to stay away from the shopping malls, away from all sports, concert and entertainment gatherings and away from any kind of religious or political gatherings. They should only leave their homes when absolutely necessary..."

"I would tend to agree with that approach," offered Charlie Ng. "The American public..."

"Ms. Forester, gentlemen, that is exactly the kind of action that would start a panic. And don't you realize that part of what has weakened this country is not just what has happened to it by direct military attack, but also what has happened to our economy? What you advise would only make that worse! Why, I wouldn't be surprised if Conrad might not deliberately try to start this kind of rumor, just to further cripple the national economy."

"Karen, I'm not sure that Homeland Security Chief Gonzales would agree with your analysis," said Paul Erikkson. "We have enough information to know that we must act with utmost urgency..."

"Carlos Gonzales was the one who asked me to be here at this meeting, since he has so much else to deal with right now. Now, I concur with several of your recommendations, including the testing of blood donors for Ebola, and possibly even issuing an alert to all medical treatment centers to be on the lookout for the disease, but this suggestion of what amounts to a national quarantine when no epidemic exists..."

Shawna sprung to her feet. "But an epidemic *will* exist if you don't..."

Just then Karen Steele's secretary burst into the room. "Begging your pardon Ms. Steele, but there is something coming on the news that you need to see."

The secretary darted over to the television set and flipped on the set. The words "News Bulletin" were just disappearing from the screen and a female news anchor appeared.

"Months of debate over firing nuclear weapons at US cities ended today with sobering results. The city known to most of us as Spokane, Washington, was just moments ago struck by at least two missiles with nuclear warheads..."

The screen now displayed a telltale mushroom cloud.

"Oh, my God..." whispered Shawna.

"The city, whose metropolitan area prior to its occupation was home to over 300,000 residents, had also recently been the base of operation for over 75,000 rebel troops of E.J. Conrad's Armageddon Brigade. Those troops, sometimes reinforced by rebels based in the mountains of Idaho, had repeatedly resisted more conventional efforts to root them out. Many in the Administration had been warning for some time that such an extreme action would be necessary to end the insurrection which has crippled the country.

The newscast now switched to another rising cloud, and Shawna screamed. This cloud was equally dark and rose at least as high as the mushroom cloud over Spokane.

"Federal forces at first thought they had also scored at least one hit on the city of Longview, Washington, as well, when this cloud arose over the city. But military officials quickly learned that missiles headed for that target had been shot down by a successful deployment of air defense missiles under the control of Brigade forces. The city's reprieve, however, was short-lived as Mount Saint Helen's, which is approximately forty miles away, blew its top just moments later. It was quickly evident that this eruption is even more violent than the one in 1980. All roads and highways out of the city were quickly jammed with vehicles of all kinds seeking to leave the city. Administration officials advise that this eruption presents an extreme threat to federal forces stationed there, as well as to citizens and rebels of the Brigade."

The video now showed the panicky attempts of the citizenry to exit the city, with the rising cloud in the background.

"In an even more frightening development, reports are coming in of nuclear explosions along the India –Pakistan border, as well as in Iran. One Administration official, speaking under condition of anonymity, said, 'All restraints seem to be off. This just might be Armageddon after all!' The President advised citizens not to panic."

"Oh, my God!" cried Karen Steele. "It's like he said! It's happening! I...I've got to go!"

The National Security Advisor rushed out through the open door.

"So do I," echoed Shawna. "I've got to get to the Longview area!"

Charlie Ng grabbed her by the arm. "You can't do that right now, Ms. Forester. It will be total chaos. Besides..." He looked over at Paul Erikkson, and apparently received the reassurance he was seeking. "We need you to get the word out on Ebola. We need you to do it right away."

"But Ms. Steele said..."

"Forget what Ms. Steele said. I know that Secretary Gonzales will support you, and together we will take the message to the President within the hour. Ms. Forester, because of your relationship with Drew Covington, you have the connections with the press and you must utilize them. If we have to face a massive epidemic of Ebola in addition to these other crises, this nation will come apart at the seams, and nothing the President or anyone else does will be able to stop it. I frankly don't know anything about this 'end of time' stuff. But I still think that United States is a great nation, and I don't want to see it end on our watch. Get your message out now, Ms. Forester, or it will be too late for all of us."

The shelter shook with a violence that startled E.J. Conrad, and he looked over at General James.

"Is it...?"

The general shook his head and picked up the phone. It took him just a few seconds to get the information he needed. "We shot down the missiles, but the mountain is blowing. Ash will clog up the shelter's ventilation system and suffocate us. We've got to get out of here!"

"The mountain? Mount Saint Helens!"

"Of course, Mount Saint Helens!"

"But that means God is finally acting! Why should we flee when our Lord is only announcing his presence?"

"Okay, I'm done, Conrad! You stay here and greet your God. Me, I want to live!"

General Roberts opened the hatch that led to the outside world, and he and several other military leaders who had been allotted space in the refuge began to climb out.

"You are deserting your God? You are fleeing in the hour of triumph?"

"We're staying with you, Grandpa." E.J. Conrad looked down into the eyes of his six-year old granddaughter, Emily. She was managing her best brave face. Then Conrad glanced over at her parents huddling in the corner.

"It's the time we've been waiting for. Let's go out to meet our Lord!"

When they reached the outside, the column of ash from the mountain loomed so far overhead that Conrad almost fell backwards trying to look to the top.

"'And the second angel sounded, and as it were a great mountain burning with fire was cast into the sea; and the third part of the sea became blood'!"

Cars were speeding past where Conrad stood, tires were squealing, as people sought their way out of the city. Still Conrad stood with his arms raised to heaven and his eyes alive with hope.

"'And I beheld when he had opened the sixth seal, and, lo, there was a great earthquake; and the sun became black as sackcloth of hair; and the moon became as blood'!"

"Dad! Come on, we should go now!"

Conrad ignored the appeal from his son. He was Moses and instead of the sea parting at the raising of his rod, this column of ash now stood massive and high above the earth at the command of his raised arms. The ground beneath him trembled, but that did not keep him from standing firm and tall. A few hundred yards to their left a large rock that had been shot in the air by the mountain fell with a crash through a roof.

"'And the same hour was there a great earthquake, and the tenth part of the city fell, and in the earthquake were slain of men seven thousand; and the remnant were affrighted, and gave glory to the God of heaven...'"

"Dad! The ash is starting to fall! The mountain seems to be coming apart! We can't stay here."

Emily broke free from her parents and began to do a dance around her grandfather.

"And the seventh angel sounded; and there was a great voice in heaven, saying, The kingdoms of this world are become *the kingdoms* of our Lord, and of his Christ, and he shall reign for ever and ever'!'"

"...for ever and ever!" echoed Emily.

There! There he is! No, for that moment he had thought he had seen in the fire and lightening of the mighty column of ash, the glowing face of Christ, but what he thought he had seen quickly faded, and suddenly the smoke and fire seemed to take on a more ominous face. It was then that E.J. Conrad thought he heard the sound of coughing. He looked down to see his granddaughter Emily on the ground, coughing and wheezing from the now falling ash. The sight of her there was like a mighty slap across the face. Ignoring that he himself was now inhaling the deadly ash, he began to move in her direction. Her parents beat him there. They placed a cold, wet cloth across her mouth, and then his son turned to him, and shouted through a cloth of his own.

"You want to die? Go ahead! But we will not let you sacrifice our daughter on the altar of your God! You can come if you want. But if you don't, you just pray to God that it's not too late for her!"

"You can't leave now!" cried Conrad. "This is the hour of his victory! I promise you! He will come now!"

Conrad's words didn't slow the retreat of his son and daughter-in-law, and he made no move to do so physically. The sight of Emily's suffering had weakened his resolve. He turned with his face back up to heaven.

"You have to come now, Lord! We can't wait for you any longer! We have waited two thousand years! – two thousand years of our evil rebellion, two thousand years of everyone going his own way, two thousand years of human lust and violence, and still you don't show your face?!"

Conrad coughed and sputtered and fell to his knees on the ground.

"I have believed, O Lord! I have done your bidding! Don't make me stand alone on the mountaintop, while denying me entrance!"

Now Conrad no longer saw any sky, just a descending darkness that threatened to swallow him, to enfold him in its dust. His breath nearly gone, he held his hands, now clenched in fists to heaven, and with all the strength he had within him, he screamed:

"'How long, Lord? Wilt thou hide thyself FOR EVER?!" Then he slumped back to the ground, and with his last breaths he muttered, "'...shall thy wrath burn like fire?'"

Conrad now thought he saw some light, swirling in the darkness, swirling in with other images of what was, what had been, and what might never ever be. He was no longer sure how much of it was real. All he knew was that now he had to sleep, sleep in the soft blanket that enfolded him.

■■■I

Drew Covington felt like his shoulder was on fire. He looked down at it, and saw that blood had soaked through the bandages as well as his jail clothing. The ash falling from the sky had mixed with the blood, forming a grayish-red paste. But it was the ash still falling from the sky that concerned him the most. He held a moistened cloth a little more tightly across his mouth and trudged on.

Maggie had not been able to pull Amos' sled for very long by herself, and so now Drew was sharing that task. That was aggravating the shoulder even more. The ash on the ground, however, was actually helping as it provided a slick surface over which the sled could glide. Captain Newell had offered to help, but the blow he had taken to the head from the butt of the soldier's rifle had made him woozy and disoriented, and Drew wondered if maybe he needed to be on a sled himself.

Drew looked around him at the streets they were passing. They were jammed with wrecked vehicles. Some had no doubt been wrecked as people tried to escape the incoming missiles, and some joined them when the mountain blew. In any case, street traffic was now impossible and the people who were moving were moving either by bike, motorcycle or on foot, as they were.

What drove Drew forward now was his desperate hunger for untainted air. He knew it was up there somewhere. The cloth he was using to cover his mouth was becoming caked-over with ash, and he was coughing and sputtering with nearly every step. The coughing and hacking he heard from the others also seemed to becoming more and more frequent. Maggie was wheezing, and Captain Newell seemed like he could keel over any minute. They were leaning on each other as they walked.

Drew's mind was being drawn to visions of Shawna. He had tried to just let himself believe that she were dead, but he could not. The face that was in his mind was alive and vibrant. It was pleading with him to keep moving forward, to keep fighting the urge that he felt to just lie down and die. He saw her face now as he saw it when he kissed her last, a face just inches away from his own, warm and alluring. The vision of that face fanned a hunger for her presence that rivaled even his hunger for oxygen.

Up ahead Drew could now see what appeared to be the edge of town, beyond which was the Columbia River. His hope was that they might find somewhere along that river's edge a boat that they could use to move more quickly down the river. What he actually saw as he crested a hill and saw the river was even better than he had hoped. All along the river's edge were boats of every kind, boats from people from the Oregon side, motor boats, row boats and even yachts, boats that were waiting to ferry Longview's refugees to freedom and safety. Boat owners were seeming even to compete with each other for the privilege of hosting each person that emerged from the chaos that had once been Longview.

A sturdy man of Asian descent threw his arm around Drew, while a young black man grabbed the sled that carried Amos.

"We've got a spot just for you!" the Asian man cried, "but we've got to hurry! We'll get you to a hospital down the river."

Drew wanted to yell out, "Thank you! Thank you! Thank you!" But it was then that he realized how little breath he had left. No words would come out of his mouth. Maggie, Captain Newell and Amos were all the same. He just hoped that the man could see the gratitude in his eyes.

They all were hoisted into small fishing boats that were going to transfer them to a yacht further out in the Columbia. Just being able to lie down and being close to the surface of the water seemed to make breathing easier. As the boat pulled away from the shore, Drew couldn't resist the temptation to look back. According to the biblical story, Lot's wife had been turned into a pillar of salt for doing that. But Drew didn't look back in regret or uncertainty; he looked back in wonder, wonder that he was alive considering that out of which he had come; he looked back in contemplation, feeling the need to mark the time when a city of God became a human hell; and he looked back in resolve, resolve that in the wandering journey of humankind, this treacherous side trail would not be forgotten.

Chapter Twenty One

Drew pulled the paper mask down over his face and glanced over at Shawna. He could see in her eyes the same hesitancy that he felt. Still, there were some obligations you didn't even discuss; you just did them. Shawna opened the door and both went in.

It was the first time that Drew had seen Ashley since she had contracted Ebola. As he came up beside her bed he was stunned at the degree that such great beauty could be robbed in such a short period of time. The main place Drew saw it was in the eyes. Gone was the beautiful green of her iris, and in its place was a dull gray, around which were corneas of red. Those eyes had become sunken into her face, as had her cheeks. Even under the covers Ashley's body appeared much more slight than before, and overall she appeared to have aged thirty or forty years. Next to her on the bed stand was an emesis basin still partially filled with blood. Drew sat on the left side of the bed and Shawna on the right.

Shawna spoke the first words. "Ashley, I told you I would be back and I brought Drew this time. He's out of Longview. Conrad is dead and the war seems to be over. Isn't that good news?!"

Ashley nodded her head, however slightly.

"You look like you've had a rough time," Shawna continued. "How are you holding up?"

Ashley moistened her lips a little and then spoke in a near whisper. "Better, actually...not as scared."

Drew reached down and gently took Ashley's hand. It was cold and bony. Ashley slowly rotated her head in his direction.

"Sorry...so sorry."

Drew just shook his head. "It's okay, Ashley. It was a hard time for us all. You made some bad decisions."

Ashley smiled. "Was a spoiled brat...only wanted what I couldn't have..."

Ashley hiccuped a couple of times, and screwed up her face like there was some kind of bad taste in her mouth. Shawna poured her a glass of water from the pitcher on the bed stand, and propped her head up a little to give her some. After taking just a few sips, however, she turned her head away.

"Other victims...?"

"Of Ebola?" asked Shawna.

Ashley nodded her head, and then hiccuped again.

"There have been a little over a thousand cases," reported Shawna. "Considering what could have been, that isn't bad at all."

"Shawna enlisted Harold Carmichael and together they got the word out," added Drew. "Otherwise it would have been much worse."

Drew and Shawna exchanged a quick, almost secretive smile, but Ashley noticed.

"Your love...for each other," she whispered in little gasps, "don't hide it...it's okay. It's good to know...there still is such a thing."

Drew reached over with his right hand and took Shawna's left hand. With each still using their other hand to hold Ashley's, they formed a triangular connection.

"Can't talk any more," said Ashley.

"Don't try, then," said Shawna.

Ashley began coughing, and as she did she looked over at the bed stand. Shawna read the signal and picked up the emesis basin and held it near her. Ashley coughed up around a third of a cup of what was mostly blood. Drew picked up a nearby towel and wiped her mouth. Ashley looked at him with dreary eyes, but no words were said.

Drew and Shawna took hold of Ashley's hands once more, and they simply remained with her in silence. After a few minutes Ashley's eyes closed. After a few minutes more Drew noticed that

Ashley's breathing had become labored and irregular. It was about thirty minutes before it stopped altogether.

Drew and Shawna left the room, stripped off their protective clothing, scrubbed with antiseptic soap, and made the trek down the stairs, through the lobby and out into the street without so much as saying a word to each other. When they reached that street they both, still without saying a word, looked up at the sky. It was what would pass in the months to come as a sunny day in Portland. The ash from the mountain and the debris from the nuclear detonations that destroyed Spokane lingered in the atmosphere, creating a haze over the city. And yet the sun was unmistakably there, and that wasn't always true in the Northwest.

Drew reached over and pulled Shawna close to him. He kissed her tenderly on the lips and stroked her hair.

"I've changed my mind, Shawna. Marry me right away. Marry me today, before anything else has a chance to change. Marry me before we age one more day or the ugly things of this world have a chance to sneak up on us."

Shawna shook her head. "No, Drew! Come on now, we agreed to this. A double ceremony with Amos and Maggie."

"Well! They can change their minds, too. Let's call them and make them change. Tell them that...that you're pregnant, and that my parents are making us."

Shawna smiled. "I'm not pregnant, and if I were, what thirty-year old cares what his parents think?"

"Shawna..."

"Drew, listen. Amos wants to wait because he's not fully recovered and because, well, he's not really sure that Maggie might have said 'yes' because she's still...you know...a little crazy."

"Of course she is! That's why he should act now, before she comes to her senses."

"Come on now, Drew. You know Amos is a great guy."

"Yes, I know -- just a little humor. I could hold him up for the whole ceremony..."

"Could you hold him up for the honeymoon?"

Drew screwed up his face. "Oh, please...!"

"Then it's settled. It's just a few months, and the time will go quickly."

As far as Drew was concerned, time couldn't go quickly enough. As much as he had to look forward to in the wedding, there was also much he wanted to put behind him. The country and the world wanted to put it behind them as well. The bombs set off in Spokane, Iran and Pakistan, rather than snowballing into a cataclysmic end, seemed to shock the world into what could only be described as a frightened self-awareness. Peace talks broke out everywhere. Protests were attended by some of the very people who had been involved in the destructive decisions. It was as if a line had been reached, a limit to the flow of blood that all recognized and respected. The blood had reached the horses' bridles and now it was time to stop, to think and to become human again.

There were practical decisions to be made and the nation made them. A national election was set up to choose a new capital for the country, and Philadelphia, the City of Brotherly Love, was selected. Monuments were set up at the edge of the blast zones where Washington, D.C., San Francisco, and Spokane once stood. Only a few generals, and some high-ranking government officials who had been feeding information to Conrad and secretively supporting his movement, were prosecuted. Included among these was Karen Steele. The others were allowed to quietly blend back into the society. It was a time for healing.

A symbol of the move toward national healing was a six-year old girl named Emily Conrad. For several days she struggled in a Seattle hospital seeking to recover from inhalation of volcanic ash. The nation prayed by her bedside. Her seventh birthday party, celebrated after her return home, was broadcast on every news program in the country.

While Shawna Forester looked to the future and planned a wedding, Drew Covington took some time to survey and reflect on the past. He joined with the volunteers who cleaned up the mess in Longview, and while there he took time to tour the wreckage of the jail that for months had been his home. Debris from the roof that had collapsed when the missile decoy had hit, now littered both cells, as did volcanic ash.   He thought he could still hear the voices there – voices of laughter, voices of wisdom and of fear. One voice came out especially clear, and it came from behind him. Drew turned and saw the face of Elena Enesco-Marshal.   She looked every bit the same as he had remembered, except for a slight swelling of her abdomen.   Elena ran up to him, threw her arms around him and kissed him on the cheek.   He held her close and for a few minutes they simply stood and rocked each other in their arms, while their tears blended on their cheeks.   Still, when Elena finally pulled away, there was a smile on her face.

"There are so few of us who really understand this place, Drew.   I am so glad that you have come here, and that I don't have to look at it alone."

"I wasn't feeling like I was alone.   Brian, Carl and John – they're still here, I feel them."

Elena quietly nodded and once more surveyed the ruins.

"So, when is the baby due?"

Elena gave him a little pout.   "You were not supposed to guess that!   You were supposed to think that I had gained weight from no longer eating jail food!"

"I know you better than that!   You are not one to gain weight from undisciplined eating."   He looked down into her smiling eyes. "You were the one who had strength and discipline when we really needed it.   I cannot thank you enough for having that discipline when Shawna needed it."

Elena nodded.   "I was not going to let them beat me again."

"Yes, well I am going to talk to this city about erecting a monument to you."

Elena shook her head.   "Only if it is to all of us!   Only if it is to all of us!"

Drew smiled again.   "To all of us."

"Anyway," continued Elena, "you should be able to compute the due date as well as I can.   You were within ear shot on the night of conception."

Drew did some quick computation in his head.   "That would make it around the first of May."

"Yes.   Spring will mean new life for me – and the world!"

"I am sure that Brian would have been so proud."

"If it is a boy, I will name him Brian. If it is a girl, I will name her Shawna. I'm sorry, you two will just have to think of other names when you get pregnant. First come, first served."

"Fair enough."

Looking ahead to a time when he and Shawna would have a child was difficult for Drew. Looking ahead to the marriage was as far into the future as he wanted to go. He had not yet been able to release a habit he had developed in jail of living one day at a time.

Longview was not the only place that Drew revisited. Camden Yard in Baltimore was no longer used for refugees and was being cleaned up and readied for a much-shortened baseball season. It would help with the national morale, people said. They were probably right.

The crater where the heart of Washington, D.C. once stood was no easier to look at now than it had been before. Maybe it was even harder. It spoke to Drew of something that had been robbed from the nation that might not ever be replaced. Something there made him think again of Lot's wife and he moved on.

The place he moved on to next was the place where San Francisco once stood. He found the church in Pleasant Hill, which had pretty much become an extension of the local hospital. The large gym was full of beds, all with patients suffering in some degree from the effects of radiation. Pastor Frank Roberts still hovered over them all like a mother hen.

"Water!" he yelled out to an aide. "This man needs more water. Hell, make it wine. This still is California, and we might as well let him enjoy himself while we're at it!"

"Can't you just ask for water, and turn it into wine?"

The pastor turned and faced his visitor. "Drew Covington! I might have known you would be the smart-ass!"

Drew walked over to him and they embraced.

"So, what makes you come back here?" Frank Roberts asked. "Doing a follow-up article?"

"I don't know," responded Drew. "Maybe. Mostly it's just personal. I'm just trying to put all this together somehow."

"Yeah, well, if you are able to do that, you've GOT to write about it. There are a lot of us around looking for some answers."

"Naw. You're too busy being part of the answer to be looking for it, Frank. These people are lucky to have you around."

"Well, I don't know that they would consider themselves to be lucky, but thanks."

Drew looked around at those sitting on and lying in the hundreds of beds gathered there.

"How are they doing, Frank – the people here?"

The minister shrugged. "It really varies from person to person. There are people here who are just going through the motions of living. There's nothing left for them. Their family is dead. Their homes have been incinerated. The only thing that keeps them from dying is the stubborn beat of their hearts. Others -- and some of them have been through the same thing – others just amaze you. They're encouraging the others around them. They're telling jokes. They're planning for the rest of their life. There's something that takes guts, don't you think?! To go through something like these people have been through, to lose all you have worked for all of your life, and to still be able to plan to raise a new life from scratch? I admire them. They remind me of how it was the first time St. Helens blew. The speed and manner with which life came back amazed all the scientists. The life God gives us is full of little resurrections."

Drew stood there for a while, trying to formulate something in his mind. Then he returned his focus to the clergyman.

"Do you think it was God? Do you think it was God who was behind the mountain blowing in that way at just that time?"

The pastor shrugged once more. "I don't know. I believe he was behind you being there at that point in time. That's about all I can say."

Frank Roberts was now getting more preoccupied with the needs of the patients he was assisting, and Drew felt it was time to leave. But then the clergyman turned to him one more time.

"Oh, I almost forgot, there's an old friend of yours over there in the northeast corner."

"A friend of mine?"

"That's right. Jonathan Weisel – the old Jewish man you had me help find a synagogue for."

"Of course! He's still here?"

"Well, more like here again. I'm afraid he is struggling with radiation sickness. But you know those two types of people I told you about?"

Drew nodded.

"He's the second."

Drew found the old man sitting up, leaning against a pillow propped against the wall. When his eyes met Drew's, there was an immediate smile.

"Ah, my old friend, Drew Covington! But I'm afraid there are no angry mobs to rescue people from today. Could you come back tomorrow? Maybe we could arrange something."

"The same old Jonathan, I can tell already."

"Well, actually, not quite the same. I have been around too much radiation, they tell me. It's making me throw up a lot. You should see some of my eruptions. Okay, I can't quite compete with what Mount Saint Helen's did, but I am a small man, and that used to be a big mountain. Pound for pound, I do myself quite proud."

"That doesn't sound too pleasant."

"What? It adds some suspense to an otherwise boring life. When will the next eruption come? Scientists from the U. S. Geological Survey have placed delicate instruments all around my bed, and monitor them daily. What is interesting, though is that they say that lower life forms when exposed to radiation sometimes grow extra appendages. That could be fun! My uncle had an extra toe on his right foot and he used it to start conversations with women. Me, I'm thinking a third eye would be nice. I was thinking of a second male organ, but at my age I don't know what to do with the one I've got, so why put yourself through that? Still, the women would be impressed, don't you think?"

Drew laughed. "Jonathan, you are scandalous!"

"What, scandalous? Both of them would be circumcised!"

Drew couldn't remember when he had laughed so hard.

"So," the little man continued, "why have you come to visit me on this fine day? Taking a post-apocalyptic inventory?"

"I guess. I'm not really sure. I think I'm just retracing some steps, like you do when you've lost something."

"Always a good idea. Retracing our steps sometimes helps us find our next steps."

"Yeah, I think that might be it."

"I know!" the old man declared, "You could be our Ezekiel!"

"Our what?"

"Our Ezekiel! Or don't you read what you call 'The Old Testament'? I swear, we share our part of the Bible with you Christians, and what do you do with it? You treat it like a thousand-page preface! If you want us to keep sharing it with you, start reading it, or we'll take it all back! Ezekiel the prophet!"

"Okay, Ezekiel the prophet. I know a little about him. I just didn't know..."

"Ezekiel the prophet one day went back to the scene of one of Israel's greatest defeats. Maybe like you he was retracing his steps, looking for what had been lost. Anyway, he came to an old battlefield that had become a valley full of old dry bones. And then he heard the voice of God. The voice said to him, 'Son of man, can these bones live?' And Ezekiel wisely answered, 'O Lord, you alone know.' You see most of us would have seen those old dry bones and simply said, 'No way!'

"All of us have to make a choice, Drew. Our choice is whether we're going to focus on the fact that we see dead bones, or that in the midst of all the deadness we can still hear the beautiful voice of God. Anyway, God said to Ezekiel, 'Son of man, these bones are the whole house of Israel. They say, "Our bones are dried up, and our hope is lost..."' Then you know what God did? He gave breath to those old bones, and they stood on their feet again as a mighty army."

Jonathan let what he had said sink in for a moment while he caught his own breath.

"You are a respected columnist, Drew. People listen to you. You need to be our Ezekiel. You need to tell the people the bones can live."

When Drew returned from his trip to his office in Portland, he stood by his window for a long time, looking at where Mount Saint Helens had once stood, and thinking of the bones. Mount Saint Helens, like Mount Mazama seven thousand years earlier, had totally destroyed itself. Nothing was left but a crater. Mount Mazama had become Crater Lake, one of Oregon's most beautiful tourist attractions. No doubt on some future day such a lake would thrive where the marauding mountain had once stood. Right now, though, it just seemed like a huge hole in the horizon.

Drew was finally ready to return to his writing. He once again felt like he had something to say. He told his readers about Jonathan Weisel and Ezekiel's dry bones. He told them about Mount Saint Helens, Mount Mazama and Crater Lake. But he told them something with even more personal significance – he told them that that he was regaining his own ability to dream of something better.

He wrote:

"Humanity thrives off its visions, and if this world is going to not only survive but really come to life once more, it must dare to recapture its dreams. It has been during our times of greatest national vigor that we have been most vocal in proclaiming such dreams and holding them close to our hearts as a people. Martin Luther King had a dream of former slaves and former slaveowners at a table of brotherhood. He had a dream of his children being judged by their character and not the color of their skin. His dream brought a people to life.

"Going even further back to our founding, we had our birth in a dream, based on the thoughts of radical rebels, that a nation which truly lived out the idea that all people are created equal could become great. This dream that we brought to the world gave new hope to the common person of every nationality and every country.

"Even older than these dreams is the dream of a kingdom of God. The prophet Isaiah spoke of it as a time when 'they shall beat their swords into plowshares, and their spears into pruning hooks; nation shall not lift up sword against nation, neither shall they learn war any more.' Can we still dream that dream, or has what E.J. Conrad done forever seared that part of the human spirit that hopes for a peaceable kingdom for all humankind?

"Conrad must have never read Isaiah. He seemed to filter everything through that most mystical and obscure of books, Revelation. Even there we hear of a God who will 'wipe away every tear from their eyes' and of a time when mourning, crying, pain and death would be no more.

"We must not surrender our dreams of something better. Rather we need to include in our dreams a clearer vision of what we are looking for and how we must get there. We might not all believe in God, but those of us who do should never dream of a God who is less than the best and most beautiful that we have seen in people. In a world where evil not only resides, but has sunk its talons deep into all that is, we will need to speak of divine judgment. But when all is said and done that judgment cannot end up as ugly as the evil that is judged. Retribution and hate has to be part of what we are putting behind us, not where we are going. I cannot earn my heaven through another person's hell.

"What we seek is a kingdom without crime and war and the fear all that entails; a kingdom where power is not used to oppress; a world where love wins out over manipulation, where life prevails over death, where each child has the twinkle of excitement and hope in his or her eyes. To believe in God is to believe that this can happen. It is to believe that if history does not have this as a direction, we should refuse to live one more moment of it. It is to believe that even if such a world were not eternal, to live one moment in it would be to justify all that has gone before."

Drew paused with the mouse pointer poised over the icon that would send these words to his editor. What he had written was in most respects more like a sermon than a news column. But what else could he do? What else could he write? After months of dealing with E.J. Conrad, this was where his heart had landed. He clicked "send."

∎∎∎ı

Shawna Forester stood in the church narthex and looked across to the other entry door. There, decked out in a dress of shimmering pearl, stood Maggie Morris. Shawna mouthed "Ready?" and Maggie nodded and smiled. Inside the sanctuary the sound of the wedding march bellowed forth and the doors to that sanctuary now opened.

Shawna wasn't really sure that she felt the floor she walked upon. She saw the smiles of those to either side of her aisle as she glided past, the smiles of people some of whom she knew and some of whom she had never met. But knowing them or not did not really matter all that much. Those smiles, along with the succulent perfume of the lilacs adorning the path, drew her forward toward a new life.

Maggie and Shawna reached the front of their respective aisles, precisely as planned, and then they turned to the center where Drew and Amos stood with the minister. Amos stood with the help of a cane, and he flashed a sheepish grin at the approach of his betrothed. Shawna could actually see Drew trembling! Harold Carmichael and a noticeably pregnant Elena Enesco-Marshal stood to the side of them, as did Shawna's son Jeremy, who waved to her excitedly as she approached.

Shawna gave her bouquet to Elena and took Drew by the hand. Touching his hand at such a moment sent shivers through her body. Looking into his appreciative eyes made her virtually orgasmic. The minister was saying words, and she knew that she should be listening, but the message of her beloved's eyes mesmerized her and shut out all other communications, all others, that is until those magic ones of "Do you take...?" Yes! She took him! She took him to argue with from then until eternity. She took him as the one on whom she would vent all her passions – the political ones, the emotionally expressive ones, as well as the erotic ones. She took him as the one to stand and lie beside her until that day when one or both took silently to the grave. Even then she knew in her heart they would still be one.

The rest of the service blended together as in a dream. The ring was slipped on her finger. Their lips touched in a kiss. What she had known for a long time was proclaimed to the world – they were one.

As she knelt together with her husband and the two friends who had also become her family, Shawna had the sense that this moment in time touched all of the world. The prayer that was sung seemed to echo throughout creation, and to confirm that sense. It was an immensely personal prayer. It was an ancient prayer.

"Thy kingdom come. Thy will be done. On earth as it is in heaven."

ABOUT THE AUTHOR:

Keith Madsen has written a variety of plays, as well as small group material for Serendipity House and Group Publishing. This is his first published novel. He has served as an American Baptist Pastor for thirty years. Keith lives in Portland, Oregon with his wife Cathy and two of his children, Brandon and Kayla.

For further information, contact our website at *anewsea.com*.